PRICE WAR

Cover design by Miblart

Edited by Dan Hook

Version 1.0, February 2023

richardholliday.co.uk

PROLOGUE

On any other day, at any other time of year, Acacia Close was quiet, anonymous, and tucked away. There were hundreds of Acacia Closes, or Crescents, or Drives; all identical in their bland conformity to the suburban dream. But this Acacia Close was to prove the flash point. Beyond the asphalt at the end of the road where it met Oak Crescent, Acacia Close ceased to be.

That day wasn't any other day. It was an anonymous summer day that would propel *this* Acacia Close into history, though none of the residents of the eighteen detached houses quite knew it when it happened.

As the trees moved in the breeze, the leaves making that *wssshhh* sound that leaves do when moving in unison, a diesel engine gurgled, getting louder and more definite with each passing moment. The rattle followed the vehicle as it rounded the corner from Oak Crescent into Acacia Close and dissipated as the van stopped outside number fourteen. Doors clunked at the back.

Swallowing hard, the driver trooped up the ten-foot driveway to the door. He pushed the ringer and, inside the house, muffled by the masonry, the bell rang with a two-tone *ding-dong*.

'Come on, love,' the driver said to the door. The door didn't reply, and neither did it open. He glanced over his shoulder, fidgeting. A buzzing sound had followed him that whole afternoon. *Hurry…*

With the buzzing came pinpricks of heat on the back of the driver's neck. It was two in the afternoon. Surely they'd all be at work instead of-

'Where the hell have you been?' the woman said, cracking the door open. She glanced past the delivery driver to his van. It was an anonymous blank van, milk-white, like her face had turned. She grasped for the cardboard box in the man's hand. 'Get that outta here, for Christ's sake!'

'You'll need to sign…' he began, but as fast as the parcel left his hand, the door swept closed.

The driver shook his head and turned around. The PDA in his palm croaked to life. He squiggled with his finger something that looked like a signature. They never checked. Plus, the old bag had her parcel now. He pulled out the keys to the van and opened the door. He stopped, his hand on the handle.

It was that mysterious buzzing sound again, like a swarm of little hornets driving lawnmowers.

'Crazy,' he said, clambering into the van. He put the key in the ignition and turned. The van vibrated, the engine rattling back out of its brief sleep. He reached over to grasp for the seatbelt, but didn't put it on. *It'd keep.*

This would prove a wise decision.

With a *clunk*, he put the van into reverse and clicked the handbrake off. Lifting off the clutch, the engine gripped, and it shuddered backwards a couple of feet.

The driver stamped on the brake after hearing three loud thumps on the side of the van. He turned his head. By the door was a man in a helmet. He pulled on the door handle. It clicked, and the door squealed.

'Out! Out!' a voice screamed from inside the helmet. The driver looked to the passenger side. A few old manifests littered the seat. The passenger door opened. It was another figure in black leathers, with hot pink piping along the seams. The driver felt himself being dragged out of the van and onto the patchy concrete surface.

'What do you want?! I ain't got no cash! Honest!' the driver yelped. The first figure loomed. Underneath the helmet were piercing petrol-blue eyes and a cloth covering across the rest of the rider's face.

'You know what this is?'

The driver glanced to the logo on the leathers, stitched with the pink piping. 'You're… you're them! What do you want from me? I ain't who you're looking for, I swear…'

'This is a yellow zone. You know that?'

'Yeah, but—'

'And you know what that means? You don't belong here.'

'I'm not from them!' the driver yelled, holding his hands up in terror. 'I'm just from the—'

'Shut it,' the rider said. 'It's a yellow zone. Doesn't matter. Your kind ain't welcome here. Your van might as well be blue as the fucking sea. And I don't like the sea.'

'Wh-what do you want?' The driver said, scrabbling until he was up against the tyre of his van. He glanced behind the van. There, a group of five identical mopeds with black-and-pink panniers parked in a semi-circle, blocking him in. He heard the doors opening and grunting with effort. 'Hey! Those packages ain't yours!'

'You gonna do anything, pig?' the lead rider laughed taking off his helmet. A shock of stark, blonde haired appeared. Then the driver yelped as the lead rider thrust his boot into his side. With a hiss, the driver fell over.

'Watch him,' the lead rider said to one of his companions. Then he looked in the back of the van, then to a pile of parcels dumped on the pavement. 'Nice. This one was worth following.

Now he's on our turf.'

'Hey, Iceblue,' another called. 'What should we do with this lot?'

'Set light to it. Outside her house,' he said, gesturing to number fourteen. The driver followed the lead rider's eyes. A curtain in the house twitched. 'She'll know better. And it'll be a warning to the others.'

The four other riders laughed, tossing the pile of parcels onto the astroturf lawn of number fourteen. One walked back to their scooter and pulled out a plastic bottle of clear liquid. The bottle had the scuffed remains of a sticky label, but the van driver had a good idea of the contents. Each rider took a bottle and threw the fluid over the pile of parcels. The sharp chemical stench of petrol permeated the air. Another rider flicked a flint lighter, and the parcels erupted with a dirty orange flame. Black smoke soared skyward.

In the houses on the opposite side of the street, curtains twitched. But not a single door opened. What was to happen would be left unimpeded. Nobody dared be a hero.

Quivering, the driver clenched his eyes shut as the lead rider - Iceblue - came over.

'Take him,' Iceblue said. The others shuffled, pulling the driver closer to the fire with a rough shove.

The wind heaved, pushing smoke from the fire across and around the van. Wispy threads enveloped the driver. The stench of the smoke from the fire went down into his lungs with each pitiful breath. 'Please, don't to this to me! I'm just doing a job! I didn't mean to cause trouble!'

'And I'm doing a job too,' Iceblue said, kneeling down. He got up and nudged one of his fellow riders with his elbow. 'Reckon he's had enough?'

The other rider snorted. 'Any more and he'll probably piss his pants, piece of shit that he is.'

'Oooh,' Iceblue said, balling a fist and theatrically pulling it back, as if he was drawing an invisible bow.

'Don't,' another rider said. The lead one gave a glance, and not a friendly one. 'We ain't got that right. If he ain't one of—'

'Fine!' Iceblue took a deep breath and lowered his hand. He knelt and slapped he van driver's face. 'Little bitch you are, you going to come back here ever again?'

'N-n-no,' the van driver whimpered. 'Never again, I promise you, I'll—'

'This is a yellow zone. Always has been, always will be. Now take your piece of shit van out of my sight before my good turn goes away,' he said, pushing the prone driver over.

The driver took a big snotty snort and picked himself up, throwing himself into the van. Gunning the engine into reverse, he spun the van around at the end of the close in a cloud of loose gravel. The driver glanced in the mirror once, watching his deliveries burn beside the riders. Then, with a squeal of tyres, the van vanished out of Acacia Close.

The news had talked about the battle in the board room, angst in the aisles, but what had happened in Acacia Close was something new.

The residents watched as, in a plume of grotty black smoke, the Price War turned hot like they'd all feared.

CHAPTER 1

'Danny!' Jane called up the stairs. Her voice reverberated off the walls and up the stairs of the big, empty house. 'Are you out of that pit?'

Danny wasn't. Beneath the crumpled ruins of the duvet, a mass of long brown hair covered his face. With a yawn, he brushed the duvet aside and sat up. He stretched. 'Yes nan, cheers!'

'Six months to the day you've been here, Danny, and still no job. Now get out of that bloody pit if yours!' Danny rolled his eyes. 'And none of that either!'

How could she tell?

The landing creaked outside. Danny took a breath, just as the door creaked open.

'Go away Nan.'

Ignoring him, she walked past the bed and toward the window. She pushed it open, and the hiss of the summer air outside streamed through the blinds.

'Now,' she said, 'that's not very nice. Look, let's not waste today.'

'Why? Nothing to get up for.'

'Sure there is. Just think,' she gestured to the window. 'Your mum and brother are watching you.'

'No they're not, Nan. I'm not six.'

'No, you're not. You're a man now. I'll make you some lunch

before I head to work. But don't waste the time you have left today. Please.' She cast an eye to his paper-laden desk. Job rejections. His P45 from those six weeks at Freshco's. Danny watched her pick that one up and saw the logo. He groaned. *That was a disaster.*

'Nan, please,' he said from beneath the duvet.

'This isn't going to make anything better,' she said. The duvet rustled, and daylight hit Danny's face as she tore it away. 'You're better than this, Danny.'

Danny sighed. His bedroom was in disarray. Boxes still lie in rough piles from moving in. Just under a hundred and seventy *tomorrows* and they'd not moved an inch. 'According to them,' he nodded at the pile of letters on his desk, 'I'm not. So why bother any more?'

She smiled. 'Just keep trying. I mean, look at me.'

'I'm trying not to,' he said.

Jane put her hands on her hips. She glanced down at the royal blue and grey polyester uniform. 'I don't wear this for fun, Danny Price.'

'Admit it, nan, you do a little bit!'

'Your lunch is in the fridge,' she said, turning to leave.

'Alright,' Danny said. 'Might go play some cricket with the guys later, anyway. What time are you doing?'

'That'll do you right. And don't you know my rota by now? Two until ten today. The graveyard shift.'

Danny smiled. 'Alright.'

'Oh, and Danny,' she said, nodding to a bag at the base of the door. 'Good thing I washed your kit at the weekend, wasn't it?'

The door closed. There was movement downstairs. Danny thought for a second then heaved out of the bed onto the lumpy bedroom floor that undulated with the age of the building.

With a glance at the clock, Danny sniggered. 11:47. Not much morning left today then.

'Bye, love,' Jane called, picking up her keys with a rattle and opening the door. 'There's post down here.' It closed a moment later with a definite clatter. Outside, the little engine of the Fiesta rattled and vanished.

He pulled on one of the creased grey T-shirts hanging out of the laundry basket and trod down the wooden stairs. They creaked, yawning with motion with every footstep. The carpet runner was pink and peach and just as faded by time. He paced into the kitchen, got a drink and went to the little table his nan had by the front door, next to the downstairs toilet. A pile of post was there. He took a sip of his drink, then exchanged the glass for the pile of glossy paper.

Most of it was indeed junk mail and quickly palmed through.

'What's this?' Danny asked, holding the final envelope. It was a glossy affair with his name printed directly onto the envelope, which itself was a pastel yellow colour. In the top left corner was a bold, golden logo of some stylised mountains. Yellowstone. 'What do they want?' Danny wondered, turning back into the living room and tearing the envelope open with his index finger. He stopped, pulling a glossy printed sheet out. After scanning the text, he let his hand fall and carried the letter to his side.

He took it upstairs to his messy desk and placed it next to his computer monitor.

But the logo in the corner caught the corner of his eye as he tried to dismiss it and get on the job boards. They never changed day to day. It didn't take long for Danny's search to end with him procrastinating his day away on Friendzone. Quizzes. Apps. Rubbish games. Updates from acquaintances and school friends that gathered like digital cruft in his virtual life.

His phone buzzed in his pocket. He glanced down, pulling it

out. It was his friend Henry Archer from university.

`You got this flyer as well?`

`Which one?`

`This one?`

A photo of the Yellowstone flyer appeared in Danny's inbox.

`Yeah, that one.`
`You going to apply?`

`Might do. Let's see. I don't`
`really want to be a delivery boy.`

`Do you have much choice?`

Danny left the invitation atop his pile of papers. Yellowstone were new to the area, indeed the country as a whole. Some of the adverts he'd seen on their TubeView channel showed off impressive facilities filled with gleaming steel and gliding robots, all looked after by chipper workers in casual attire and shiny white teeth. After a few non-starter jobs in the last six months, that culture appealed. Glancing out the window at the patchy lawn and empty houses all around, it seemed a million miles away from the decrepit lifestyle he found himself in.

'I don't know,' he said to himself as he lent back in his chair. He glanced again at his phone. Maybe this really was the ticket off the Basic he needed. Tossing the phone back to his desk, he repeated his thought aloud again: 'I really don't know.'

His phone trilled. Danny sat up, surprised. He had set his phone to vibrate. Picking it up, it still was.

'What's that?' he asked, again to nobody. Though since his

16

phone had decided it no longer wanted to be in vibrate mode, maybe it wasn't necessarily to nobody. There was a notice that took over the screen. At the top was the Yellowstone logo, just like the one on the invitation.

Daniel Price, you're just the sort of person who'd change the world at Yellowstone. Follow this link to complete your application. We're waiting just for you!

Another instantly followed it:

Cut the job searching and join us now. Or you'll be tearing envelopes open for the rest of your life. Just like how you tore our own open. Is that what you want, Daniel? We know that's been your life for the last few weeks. You wasted your time at Freshco. Now you're sitting on Basic.

They knew?! Danny glanced at his monitor. He turned the camera that perched atop away, then lent back in his chair. His eyes darted. It facing the wall wasn't enough. He reached under the desk and unplugged it from the computer tower, wrapping it up in its cord and throwing it onto his bed. The errant camera disappeared between the wall and the mattress.

Getting up, Danny glanced around his room. He pulled the duvet back over the bed in a cursory effort, but then let it go. Somehow, he had to get away from this room. His eyes glanced around the room. Maybe it wasn't just the phone. He pulled on a hoodie and jeans after closing the lid of his laptop. He picked up his kit bag. Within a couple of minutes, he was out into the arid summer air, hopefully away from any technology that could follow him.

He rounded the street corner and the lamp post embedded on the kerb, hands in pockets after pulling the hood over his head.

The fabric absorbed the fleeting whine from the top of the lamp post pole as the camera mounted to it swivelled in his direction.

That was the camera he should've been wary of.

***

The front door clattered closed later that day. Danny entered the living room, pulling down his hoodie. He threw his kit bag down with a clunk of polyester against parquet.

'Did cricket go on later than usual?' Jane asked, peeking in from the kitchen. 'A message would've been nice.'

'Yeah, sorry nan,' Danny said, pulling the hoodie off and throwing it loosely over a chair. He caught her glance. 'I'll take it upstairs in a minute.'

'Did something happen today?'

'It was… weird.'

Jane laughed. 'A lot of things are weird. We're losing another couple of stragglers at Kier Wood.'

'Anyone you know?'

'Old timers. Probably about time they went.'

'More work for you, though? Unless you're next?'

'Don't,' Jane laughed. 'Unless you want a job, of course.' Danny took a sharp intake of breath. 'Is this to do with a job, whatever this… weirdness is?'

'Sortof,' Danny started. 'Let me show you the letter.' He made for the stairs.

'Hoodie, Daniel!' Jane snapped. He stopped a couple of steps up and retrieved the hoodie and took it with him. He reappeared a moment later and showed her the Yellowstone invitation.

'Well there's no way you're applying, you know that, don't

you?'

'I thought it was junk—'

'Anything from *them* is junk, Daniel. I don't need to tell you twice, do I? I tell, you, after everything that's happened in the last few years—'

'—until I got this on my phone,' he finished, showing his nan the phone. The screen hadn't changed.

'Delete it,' Jane said.

'Really? You know, with all the false—'

'Danny, please, just delete it. Forget about it.'

'I've not had a job offer in ages, Nan. I kinda wanna—'

'No, Danny, you do not.'

His phone trilled again. Danny glanced.

We're still waiting for an answer. We won't forget you, Danny. Yellowstone needs you. And it needs you **now**.

'Danny, this is all wrong,' Jane said. She grasped his free hand. 'For me, don't do this. You can come work at Mertons. With me. They owe me some favours. I can get you an interview. Look,' she said, fishing around in her bag. 'I got you an application form. I know it's not what you wanted, but—'

'World's changing though, nan. The things I saw at uni… and I've seen their promo stuff, what Yellowstone are doing. It's exciting. It's the future.'

'They want to swallow up Mertons. Everything.' She squeezed his hand tighter. 'I won't have a pension. Or anything.'

'Nan, don't be melodramatic…'

Jane took a deep breath and finally let go of Danny's hand. 'I'm going to make you some dinner. Go and get yourself changed, freshen up. Sleep on the decision at least.'

Danny glanced to his phone. The two Yellowstone notifications glared at him. He dismissed them with a swipe. 'Alright. I'll think about it.'

'Thank you. Now can you at least go and shower before dinner, you're all nasty and sweaty!'

Danny laughed and trooped upstairs with the letter and his phone which both ended up lazily thrown onto his desk once more.

A little while later, he pushed through the door, specks of water still on his chest, with a towel wrapped around him. The sizzling of food and his nan's music reverberated up the stairs.

'Bring down your washing too in a bit, Danny, I'll put a load on!' Jane called.

Pulling on his clothes once again, Danny felt the *bzzt bzzt* of the phone on the laminate wooden desktop. He smiled almost sarcastically at the device, as if to say *finally you're working how I want you to!*

On the lock screen he saw a text message from Henry.

`Have you applied yet?`
`I just did, it was easy!`

Then another text:

`Just got confirmation! Come on, do it now,`
`we'll probably interview on the same date.`

Danny left the phone on his desk as he retrieved his socks. He stopped, one foot still naked.

'Sod it,' he thought, leaving the other sock on the floor and grabbed his phone and tapped a finger on the link on the Yellowstone alert.

By the time Jane called for dinner eight minutes later, Danny had applied and had been accepted, but kept it to himself.

***

'I'm very disappointed with you, you know that?' Jane said as Danny emerged in the hallway at the bottom of the stairs a couple of days later. He was in a casual suit, an open shirt and his hair freshly washed and his face smooth.

'Nan, please, relax. You said I needed a job, and well I think this might be the one. I've gotta get off Basic somehow.'

'I'd rather you stay on Basic. You know this is a Yellow zone!' Jane groaned. 'I didn't want you going anywhere near Yellowstone. They're bad news. You do look smart though. Your mum would be very proud, you know that.'

'Don't, Nan, was just a year or—'

'Doesn't matter.'

'I miss her,' Danny said. 'But thanks.'

'I'm not finished with you, young man,' Jane resumed. 'These aren't good people to be working for. Not good people *at all*.'

'So you said, but look,' Danny replied. He pulled a brochure out from his jacket pocket. It had come the next morning after his application had been approved, almost as if Yellowstone knew he'd apply and knew he'd be accepted. The glossy tome showed the same pictures as the website and the promo videos had. Happiness was Yellowstone. 'It's the future, and it's here! And remember the situation we're in. Companies like that… they're the future of this country.'

'Danny…' Jane murmured.

'And him, look,' he continued, flicking to a photo of the Yellowstone founder, Grayson Laurie, 'he's the man with the vision.'

'You finished?' Jane said, her hands on her hips. Her stony visage was not won over. 'Anyone'd think you've been bought, paid for and wrapped up already by that nutty *charlatan.*'

'He's not a charlatan! He's a visionary! You see what he did in the States!'

'Yeah, and he got chased over here by that congressional thing,' she snapped. 'You think your nan here's thick. When you get to my age, you can read people pretty—'

'Look, we had this conversation already,' Danny said, pushing toward the front door. 'I know you love working at Mertons. And you want me to work with at Mertons with you at Kier Wood... but if I go there, I'll be there for years. I want a challenge. I've earned a challenge.'

'Danny—'

Danny's phone buzzed in his pocket. 'That'll be Henry. He's picking me up so we can head up to London.' Jane shook her head. 'Please nan, be happy for me. I need this.'

After a few seconds of glancing at the floor, Jane looked at her grandson. Through her weathered face, a smile erupted like a canyon on her jaw. 'I know you do.'

Outside, a car pulled up, the silhouette coming through the net curtains in the bay window.

'Right, gotta go,' Danny said.

'Good luck,' Jane said, and the door clicked closed. 'I hope you're wrong,' she said to nobody, moving over to the sideboard. The second drawer was stiff, but that's why she'd chosen it. Pulling it open, she glanced at the pile of Yellowstone letters that she'd been ignoring. They were all addressed to Jane Greene and none of them were remotely friendly.

'I hope for your sake, Danny, you're right.'

.

CHAPTER 2

Danny stepped out of the house and into the summer sun. A gleaming, angular-shaped car was on the other side of the green. That was Henry alright. He always liked a flashy motor.

The front door closed behind Danny. He stepped out of the shadow of the house into the sunlight.

'Oh,' he said. Parked two doors down was a yellow and purple Yellowstone delivery van, the livery resplendent in the afternoon sheen. This was most unusual; this was a Blue Zone. Yellowstone never delivered here. Danny hummed. 'Mrs Lister, is that for you?'

'Jesus, Danny!' the older woman said, surprised. She turned to the Yellowstone driver. She grabbed the parcel from him and shoved the electronic clipboard into it. 'Sign what you want, just get out of here! He's my bloody neighbour, for christ's sake!'

The driver hummed and walked lazily back toward his van. 'I… I… I didn't see you there?'

'I didn't expect to see…' Danny trailed off. He didn't need to say any more. His neighbour's eyes were bulging.

'Yes well… I'll…' Mrs Lister said, scrabbling back into her house. Her front door banged shut as the Yellowstone van drove away.

Danny shook his head and walked over the bone-dry green, under the willow and toward Henry's car.

'Hey,' Henry said as Danny clambered into the car. 'You

ready?'

'She's not happy,' Danny replied, buckling his seatbelt. He laughed as Henry watched. 'I remember your driving from the good ol' days. Not taking any chances.'

'Shut up,' Henry said, and the car scooted away.

'Nice to see one of our hopefully new employers gallant steeds,' Henry remarked, seeing the Yellowstone van pull away in front of them. 'What? Not impressed?'

'I always had her down as a nice woman, Mrs Lister, I can't believe…'

Henry laughed. 'What, all that poppycock? Who bloody cares anymore? You know it's the future, don't you? The end of the Commission is in sight. No more Blue Zones. Freedom. And we're going to ride that wave, you and me.'

'You talk like you've already got the job.'

'Haven't we?'

'You saw how quickly that email got approved. They're probably approving everyone. Anyway,' Danny said, fidgeting in the seat, 'What's with the getup? It's a recruitment day, not your best friend's wedding,' Danny said as he looked at his friend. Henry was dressed to kill in a razor-sharp suit with not a thread out of place, which was a slight contrast to Danny's open-neck check shirt atop blue chinos. Henry was shorter and wider, though Danny had always been lanky. His hair was combed and greased into gentle waves; Danny's was just curly brown. Henry nodded, the cool spring wind ripping at his loose auburn hair.

'Who's the lucky girl then? Not your nan!'

Now it was Danny's time to laugh. 'Piss off. Get the tunes on then, has this thing got all the stations?' Danny reached for the glossy screen in the centre console of the electric car. The interface wheeped and whooshed.

'See mate,' Henry said, 'everything you could ask for.'

'So what made you go for the job?'

'Had to do something. What Yellowstone are doing… I think I can be a part of that. No, Danny' Henry said, lifting a hand from the wheel. 'I can be more than a part of that. I think I can *drive* that.'

'Like you're driving this car? Fixed the bugs in the autodrive? Wasn't that another one of Laurie's successes, from what I read.'

'Media paranoia,' Henry said. His smile vanished. 'Installed the new ParkerDrive update a month ago and it's been smooth as glass.' Henry caught Danny's sceptical eye. 'I'm serious. Yellowstone are going to be like a tidal wave that washes away the crap we've all seen. You remember at uni?'

'I do,' Danny replied, his face now also serious.

'You don't want that to happen. And we're not getting any younger.'

'I'm twenty-seven!'

'And you want to be stacking shelves or flipping burgers at thirty? Or worse? I mean look at your nan…'

'What's that meant to mean?' Danny said quickly.

'At her age, doddling along at Mertons?' Henry said, scoffing. 'Please. We've had this chat before, you and I. *Many times.* I'm gonna rescue you, Danny, from that shit. If it kills me.'

'Who says I need rescuing?' Danny said.

'You want me to answer that? Country went to shit while we are uni, remember,' Henry said. 'Couldn't leave our rooms for days, all this hoo-haa about that contamination…'

Danny scowled. 'I remember. I was there. With you. Unfortunately.'

'And what happened to you particularly was rough—'

'Careful,' Danny said. 'Don't get personal.'

'Stating a fact, really. You're a smart guy, Danny, and a top fella,' Henry said, clenching the steering wheel with the strength of feeling. 'I've seen too many people – less capable people – piss away opportunities. Maybe I care, alright?'

'Maybe you do,' Danny said, unable to stop a smile cracking across his face. 'You're full of the soft shit! Let's get this done then.'

'So, future or past?'

'Watch it,' Danny said. A silence filled the car. There wasn't even an engine to drown it out. 'She does well.'

Henry inhaled hard. 'If you say so. You wouldn't be with me if you wanted that… *pedestrian* lifestyle. You remember what we said at uni, yeah? Yeah?'

'I do.'

'Danny Price and Henry Archer, champions of the world.' Henry watched Danny nodded. 'Let's go make that happen.'

Danny looked out the car window as the leafy suburb he called home transitioned into built-up areas. He let the anonymous waves of music rush over him from the car's surround speakers. Danny watched as the suburbs dissolved, the roads threading around impressive steel and glass edifices as the stature of the city imposed upon them.

***

Eventually the car came to a smooth stop.

'I think this is it,' Henry said. 'And what a site to behold, don't you think?'

In front of the car stood the Yellowstone campus. On one side, lush, manicured and verdant verges lined the riverbank around a plaza thronging with people.

Henry brought the car to a stop at a barrier. Beyond this, a queue of cars led down a ramp into the maw of a tunnel that gently descended underneath one of the grassy banks.

An attendant in a yellow uniform tapped on the window. 'You're here for the campus day, are you?'

'We most certainly are.'

The attendant thrust a rectangular tablet into the car. 'Attendance codes please. They should pop up on your phone automatically. Does this car have ParkerDrive?'

'Of course,' Henry said, leaning over Danny.

Danny produced his phone from his pocket. Lo and behold, the squiggle of machine-readable characters had appeared, as if by magic. Once scanned, the codes flashed green with a smiley emoji and evaporated. The attendant then left to see the car behind.

'Go, then,' Danny said. 'Where do we go?'

'Ah!' Henry snickered. 'Look. It's hooked into ParkerDrive. Cool upgrade.' He drove forward and down a ramp along the side of the building, descending underground. 'Only for EVs, mind. Parking space six-forty-eight. It even shows a map of the car park. Isn't that amazing?' Henry took his hands off the wheel. The car continued without pause.

Danny couldn't help but smile. 'That's some far-out tech. All just works.'

'You see, this is why this company is the future. I just can't wait.'

'Slow down, mate,' Danny said. He looked across to his friend. The car park was immaculate; the tarmac and cement floor has no skid marks or scratches. The walls almost gleamed; there was no chipped concrete or eroded paint anywhere. Above them in the middle of the passage, a beam of light tracked along a path in the ceiling, glowing green. Danny let his seatbelt come off as the car glided into the parking space. 'Let's go get hired first, eh?'

'Sounds capital!' Henry said, and they leapt out of the car and took their first breath of Yellowstone's air. There was no scent of engine oil or coolant, the usual smells of a place like this from years ago. 'They even air-conditioned down here!'

The pair walked along the passageways in the car park toward a gleaming glass and steel lobby. The car park was filling up.

'How many d'you think they're interviewing today?' Danny said. 'There's dozens of people here! And how'd you expect us to get hired out of—'

Henry stopped and stood in front of Danny. He placed both hands squarely on his friend's shoulders. 'Danny, listen. You've not done your background research, have you?'

'Well, I watched the—'

'That's not good enough,' Henry said. 'I've spent days, weeks, whole nights looking at how Yellowstone works. It's how I'm so sure of what I… *we* can offer these people. They don't work like those mum and dad jobs you've done and failed at. This is a whole new culture, it's something we needed in this country years ago. There's none of this *oh, hello, my name is; yes, sir, no, sir; here's my CV; oh I'll hear from you in a week if I'm shortlisted* rubbish. Anyway, come on. I don't want to be late for the induction.'

Danny followed his friend. 'As I've said a few times before Henry, we've not been hired yet!'

They strode toward the door from the car park to the main lobby. The doors swished open and cool, fresh air-conditioned air hissed out like a mist, pulling the two through from the concrete floor to tiled ceramics. Danny's feet squeaked on the shining tiles.

'Hey, hey!' a voice called. Danny turned, but Henry turned quicker.

'Can't you bloody leave me alone?!' Henry hissed at the young woman who stood before them. Compared to him and Danny, she wore loose jeans, an even looser top and her hair frizzy. She carried a shoulder-bag that looked full. In her hand, a slender circular device with a bulbous, glassy front.

A camera.

'Hi Danny!' she said. 'You remember me, don't you? I'm Hailey, Henry's *dear sister*.'

Danny smiled. Even though Henry mentioned her, he never showed her in person. In fact, Danny had never been to the Archer home. Henry was always too happy to pop round, pick him up, take him to the pub with Georgy, Ken, and the others. 'It's nice to meet you,' he said politely, holding out a hand. She took it and shook it.

'That's quite enough,' Henry said. 'How'd you get in here?'

'I applied too,' Hailey said. 'You can't take all the glory. Mum and dad were quite insistent I apply. Dad, mostly. And I needed it, I really did.'

'You could've at least, you know…' Henry said, waving up and down. Hailey stood there with her strawberry-blond hair in a frizz atop a hoodie and her jeans. 'Put some effort in?'

'Hey, they don't judge by appearance. You look like you're about to wait tables at Uncle Ester's golf club.

Danny laughed. 'I thought he was dressed for a wedding. Going by how this one's been banging on, it's like he's about to get married to that pillar over there, he's studied it so much in advance.'

'You two!' Henry said loudly. The giggling between Danny and Hailey stopped. Their faces dropped in mock sadness. 'This is important, not some playground game.' Henry took a glance at Danny. 'Let's go.'

'Alright boss,' Danny said. 'Are we late?'

'No,' Henry said, his face wrinkling up, 'I just—'

'Henry drag you along for the ride?' Hailey asked.

'I said no more lip.' Henry spat. He moved his head. 'Go on ahead, Danny, I won't be long. Just need a word with this one.'

Danny took a few steps forward. Others were filtering in through the car park. Beyond this part of the lobby a column of light beckoned from high above, but the view up was restricted by the overhang of the building. Yellowstone reps were shepherding the recruits through the passageway and toward the light.

'Henry, stop!' a female voice shrieked. 'You can't stop me!'

Danny stopped. He pivoted. He saw Henry pulling at Hailey's bag, but she didn't let go.

Henry lent into his sister's face. 'You'd better bloody behave! None of your stupid online silly bollocks, you hear me?'

'You can't stop me. Anyway, I'll tell dad.'

'Whatever,' Henry said, walking away from her. Henry turned; his face twisted into a snarl. Danny caught his glare. It was like a toilet flush, the red colour of Henry's face dissipating. Danny saw his friend's face crack with a false smile and Henry followed on, though his sister let the crowd swallow her up.

He joined Danny.

'What was all that about?'

'Nothing, she just likes to embarrass her brother. Let's go. I don't want to be late.'

'Queue's that way,' Danny pointed. Henry scoffed.

'You think I'm going to queue? Come on, Danny. Follow me and you'll follow me to greatness,' he said, pushing through the crowd.

Danny followed.

CHAPTER 3

'Henry, dear,' Lucia Archer said over the breakfast table. 'Which car will you be taking tomorrow?'

'Sorry mum,' Henry said, running the knife through the egg perched atop his toast with a chink of ceramic. 'The green one. With ParkerDrive. I want to make an impression when Danny and I arrive.' Lucia nodded. *The green one* didn't bother her. They had three. 'Hello dad,' Henry said as the kitchen door opened.

Immediately, the atmosphere in the airy kitchen wavered into something new. Henry' dad, Robert, brought a colour to the room that leeched saturation into the cool white and grey surfaces.

Robert didn't sit down. Instead, he slapped the head of the table with the rolled-up newspaper.

'Big day tomorrow, son. Let's start. How many territories is Yellowstone operational in?'

'Eighty-six, expanding to ninety-seven in the next eighteen months,' Henry reeled off.

'Grayson Laurie founded Yellowstone in the state of California. How old was he and what motivated him to do so?'

'He was twenty-seven and wanted to provide a firm platform to expand in the future. His grandfather's car crashed because of a faulty part. If the garage had had that part in stock, he might've survived the crash. Instead, because of poor logistics, the part was delayed by seventy-two hours. That inspired him to create the ultimate in logistics and customer care.'

'Not bad. What was Yellowstone UK's annual sales last year?'

'Four-hundred-and-six million pounds.'

'How much tax did they pay? Percentage only.'

'Zero point zero four.'

'And that was too much. Last question: if a Yellowstone executive offered you a job today, what would you say?'

'That I'm proud to be part of the future not just of *this* company,' Henry said in one breath, then took another: 'but that the Yellowstone founding principles are exactly what the United Kingdom needs to be the bastion of commerce. Yellowstone is the answer to the question we've been afraid to grapple, and I am proud to be part of that solution,' he said, gasping. 'I hope that was alright.' Henry glanced at his father's stony face.

The rock face cracked. 'Good.'

Henry's phone buzzed on the table. He glanced at it, then at his dad. 'It's Danny.'

'Ah yes,' Robert said, pulling the chair out and finally sitting down. 'Daniel Price. You're quite the odd couple.'

'He's a nice guy,' Henry said. 'Even when he is kicking my arse at cricket.'

'Didn't say he wasn't. Coffee please, Lucia,' Robert said. Lucia got up on command. 'But don't let him drag you down. You know what this is, don't you?'

'A job? At Yellowstone.'

Robert rolled his eyes. 'Well, yes, but more than that. All this,' he gestured to the expansive kitchen. 'Built not just by skill but by status.'

'Your status.'

'Indeed. Thank you,' Robert said as Lucia set a glass mug full of steaming coffee down in front of him. She knelt down and they pecked on the cheek. 'Love you. Now, it's imperative you impress the Yellowstone executives.'

'Dad, I've pretty much memorised the rubrik for the aptitude test. It's not an interview, they basically award points and the top eight per cent get hired. That's not changed.'

'Indeed, it's a good system. But I don't want you at the bottom of that eight per cent. Your starting salary depends on it.' Hailey bustled in and sat down between the two. She reached toward the last piece of toast in the rack in the centre of the table.

'Go and help your mother,' Robert said with a growl. Hailey retreated.

Henry laughed. 'I don't think it's a problem.'

'Listen to me,' Robert said. The kitchen went cold with the icy glare between father and son. 'It affects everything. Hit the ground running and the family business will hit the stratosphere.'

'Dad, I don't think it works that way.'

'Become a connection, son. Make me proud. That's all I ask. Your success will make me proud.'

Henry examined his now empty plate. He blinked, then looked back across the table to his father. 'I'll make you proud,' he said. 'Prouder than you ever have been of me.'

'Son, this opens doors wider than just working for… I mean *with* me could! If you didn't apply to the company I rightly foresee as the future of this country, and build a real future not just for the country but for your family… well, could you even call yourself an Archer?' Robert glanced to Henry, and then motioned a fork at his empty plate. Hailey was distracted.

He met Henry's gaze. Henry's fork moved and the last slice of toast in the rack disappeared, landing on his plate with a clatter.

Hailey looked up. 'Hey!' she said with outrage. 'I was going to eat that.'

'Good boy,' Robert said, leaning back.

'But the company has been yours for—'

'You'll be the way it really succeeds. Look, I know it'll be strange to work for a boss who isn't your dad. But you'll triumph in that culture. It surprised me they waited this long.'

'What for?'

'That application was targeted. All part of their system.'

'You pay the Yellowstone Prime bill, dad.'

'Forget about that. I've raised an intelligent and talented son. I want you to turn those talents into the future.'

'Alright, if it'll make you happy.'

'That's a good boy,' Robert said, and took a sip of his coffee.

Henry left the table and went upstairs to his room to prepare for the day ahead.

Next door, loud music came through the wall.

'Hailey, please, can you keep it down in there?'

No answer. Henry put the phone down. No new emails. *No rejections.*

'No way! That was so fast!' Hailey yelped from next door, giggling. Henry rolled his eyes.

'What game are you playing?' he called. Footsteps across carpeted floor followed, then a terse knock on his bedroom door. 'Enter.'

The door opened. 'No game, look,' Hailey said, pushing her phone into her brother's face. 'It's an email. From that company. You know the one, the one dad's got a massive crush on. Yellowbond.'

'Yellow*stone*,' Henry said before he cast his eye down onto the email on the screen. His pupils scanned the first few lines. 'Piss off, Hailey, that's not funny.'

'It's real!' she said. 'That test with all the shapes? I did it. I thought I did rubbish but clearly I didn't.'

Henry shook his head. 'That *test with all the shapes* was an aptitude screening test.' He glanced at her monitor. 'Why are you applying for that Yellowstone thing?'

'What, doing the Yellowstone pub quiz?'

'Yeah… wait! It wasn't a pub quiz!' He strode over to her chest of drawers, his eyes picking out the canary yellow emblem. 'Where did you get this?! Is this my letter?!'

'Rude!' Hailey swivelled and leaned, stealing the letter back. 'Came the day after yours. I applied last night. I've listened to you and Dad all week. Thought I'd give it a go.'

'And they didn't accept you? The process is fast, Hailey. Really fast.'

'So I've heard.'

'Does Dad know about this?'

'Sure.'

'Christ,' Henry hissed. 'Why'd you do this to me? It's almost as if you're trying to make me look bad in front of Dad.' Henry gasped, pushing himself away from the desk and over to the other side of his expansive room. He let the sun back in and closed his eyes. The radiant heat warmed his eyelids.

'Was it something I did?' she asked, walking past the threshold into the room.

'It always is, you know. You didn't do any of the research, did you? Not the work I've put in. Yet again, perfect little Hailey swoops in and achieves in a microsecond what I, Henry, worked so hard for.'

'Hey, now, I don't think that's totally fair. It was dad's idea.'

'Bollocks,' Henry said. He pivoted around. 'You've known for weeks that this thing was coming. Dad knew they were sending the letters. He was checking that postbox every damn day. That postman's never lived so well with the money stuffed in his hand. You know I've been applying. The letter was bound to turn up. Only a matter of time; personally, I thought a letter was a bit old hat but it's about the symbol of strength. To hold it in your hand. But no, you want all the glory.'

'Henry, you're… you're wrong,' Hailey said. 'This isn't what all this is about at all.'

'No, you don't get to tell me, Hailey. Can you cancel the application? Stop it?'

'No, and I wouldn't! Jeez Henry you need to sort your shit out.'

'Me?' Henry said in mock outrage. 'Oh, no! Can't have poor Hailey thinking on her own now can we.'

'Henry, shut up and stop being bitter and hateful.'

'Me? Please,' Henry said. 'Why don't you go work at the family firm. You'd fit right in.'

'And what's that meant to mean, you little bastard?' Hailey retorted. 'Look, you always get in a right mood whenever I do something good. Or is it because this makes you look less the blue-eyed boy in front of Dad?'

'Because you're like a bloody little shadow! Oh, Henry has joined the football team. Next thing, Hailey joins the football team. And with all that TubeView stuff…'

'Ah!' she said. 'Knew it. Once I hit twenty thousand subs you started to show an interest.'

'It won't amount to anything. Dad's been saying that for years.'

'He's seen my ad revenue, big brother. It's amounting to more than nothing. He's asking me about getting Archer Construction on TubeView already.'

His chest inflated, and his eyes closed. He wasn't going to rise to it. 'This isn't just about a job, Hailey, don't you understand? No, you don't. You don't know the first thing about Yellowstone.'

38

'I've got an account!'

'And so do I? Doesn't *everyone*? We live in a nice house in a nice Yellow zone. Mum and Dad pay the Yellowstone Prime and everything's just beefy.'

'It isn't, though, is it?'

'Go away,' Henry shrugged. 'You've… you've spoiled everything.'

'Aren't you happy that your little sister will be there with you at this thing?'

'No. I was quite happy when you weren't around.'

'Henry! Oh, forget it, alright,' Hailey finally gave up. 'You be a sour little bastard, alright. I tried. You can't control my life.'

'Like I said, you'd fit right in at the family firm, if you took actual work seriously,' Henry said. 'You could make dad's tea for a start.'

'Piss off, Henry,' Hailey said. 'I'll probably just be *better* than you, that's what you can't stand. You're the oldest, you're the boy. I'll probably end up your supervisor.'

'We'll see,' Henry said, glancing at Hailey's phone. It had remained silent through the entire exchange. 'See, they're rejecting you. They messaged me almost instantly. Maybe, just maybe, the Universe isn't going to hand Hailey something on a plate.'

'Sod you, Henry.'

Henry waved, turning away from her. 'If you don't mind, I've got tomorrow's recruitment day to get ready for. Go video some frogs or something, that's what you do, right?'

Hailey let the door slam on her way out.

'Hey, you two! Behave!' Robert called from downstairs. Henry ignored it, and he kept reading the forums until day turned to night.

The next morning, Henry's phone trilled, pulling him from

sleep. Rays of golden sunshine filtered through the glass. Getting up from the edge of the bed, Henry picked it up. It was Danny. He'd been accepted. Same date, same time.

```
See you there mate. You and me
are going to smash it. Can't wait!
```

Smiling, he put the phone down and thought. Being top of that eight percent wasn't just a goal for his dad's pride, but a personal goal to finally get one over on his annoying sister.

That morning was a brilliant summer morning. If birds still lived outside they'd no doubt have been tweeting their song to filter through the window.

Besides Henry Archer's bed, the alarm on his phone blared. He dozed, grabbing for the device off its wireless charger to dismiss the blare.

8:45AM. Yellowstone were to meet him at two. Time to begin the transformation.

Pushing the duvet aside, he got up, placing his feet on the carpet of his bedroom. The door knocked, then opened.

'Son, you up?'

'Yes, dad.'

'Good.' Robert paced over, placed something with a metallic tinkle on Henry's bedside cabinet, and retreated.

With a stretch, Henry went into the en-suite bathroom, clapped so the light turned on, and began the work to knock Yellowstone dead with envy.

He emerged into the garage. It was a wide space, a double width opening with tool benches and workstations around the periphery. Hardly any of this was used; rather, this was just what one would expect to find in a garage.

Stepping down onto the concrete floor, Henry brushed minute motes of dirt from his jacket. He approached the blue car, the one he usually drove. He reached for the door, the lock disengaging with a click as he got nearby.

He reached into his pocket and found the fob that his dad had left on his bedside table. He closed the door to his car and walked around with an abbreviated, but not hurried pace.

He pushed on the rubbery button on the fob. The grey car–a more substantial construction, with swept angular lines and gleaming chrome and steel – woke up: the interior lights rose to illuminance, and the driver door slid open, just as Henry approached it. He smiled, sliding in through the opening which swept closed as he sank into the plush seat.

Henry finally removed the fob from his pocket and pushed it into the console in the middle of the dashboard. The flat panel display lit up:

Welcome, Robert.

Henry laughed once and swept a finger across. He tapped on his name on the touchscreen.

Welcome, Henry. That was better.

Gripping the wheel, Henry pushed his shiny shoe down onto the accelerator. The garage door opened silently, and Henry emerged into the glorious morning sun and toward, he could only hope, was the start of the rest of his life.

A life to make a car like this really his, and not something he borrowed.

CHAPTER 4

The auditorium quickly filled. Danny glanced around the room. Five hundred people were in this one room, which was scalloped, shell-shaped, with tiers of seats above and around their heads. They'd found seats in the middle, directly in front of the wide stage. At the back was a screen that displayed the Yellowstone logo and nothing else against a slate grey backdrop.

'You ready?' Henry asked. 'This is so exciting.'

'I just want to see what all this is about.'

'It's not an interview. You read the literature, right? What I sent you?'

Danny had. 'I did.'

Then the lights extinguished and the whole auditorium hushed.

The screen behind the stage flickered.

Ladies and gentlemen, thank you for your attendance. Please welcome on stage the founder of Yellowstone, INC: Grayson Laurie.

The crowd collectively held its breath. The screen parted in the middle.

'Welcome, friends!' Grayson Laurie said, emerging through a mist that was pumped up from below the floor. 'I'm so glad to see you!' The silence was swept away by rapturous applause and hollering. After a few moments, his cheeks flushed red, Grayson Laurie patted down the applause with his hands. In jeans, a T-shirt and a jacket, he looked effortlessly cool, though a few beads of sweat glimmered in the spotlight that lasered down upon him.

'Thank you for that welcome, initiates! Today is an exciting day for you all. At Yellowstone,' he started, 'we look for the best and the brightest. This company means so much to me. I can't tell you. I'm humbled,' he said, patting his chest, 'that you want to be a part of this. We have a Yellowstone way. Back when myself and Aaron, my dear friend, founded this company, we set a clear way for how we wanted to be as a company. We're not just a corporation, but a collective of friends. This is in Yellowstone's very DNA. It's gone through iterations and generations over the years, and now we reach the latest apex. To introduce this, let me welcome and introduce you to one of my most trusted friends and executives who has made this company have such an amazing impact on this wonderful country.'

Please welcome the head of Yellowstone UK: Wendy Tunt.

A woman wearing a mustard-coloured blouse and skirt emerged from the side of the stage. Her hair was jet black and styled in a tight bob that looked like a Viking helmet. Her face was plastered with makeup, but her mouth was a line between two smears of lipstick. As she emerged from the wings, the spotlight followed her.

Danny could just tell by her stance next to Laurie that, unlike him, she'd have preferred the ground to open up and swallow her than be there.

'Initiates,' she said in a tight cadence, 'what Grayson says is true. This company is the foundation of the future, not just of this sector but this country. Now, in the next forty-five minutes, my team and I will introduce you to how we plan to assess you and place you. As you're aware, we hire the top eight per cent of the initiates we evaluate. So be prepared for a long day with various sessions, which you'll find have been emailed to you.'

'There's a reason,' Grayson interjected, 'that we chose that number, Aaron and I. Sure, it seems arbitrary. But look,' he said, pointing to the screen. 'Turn the number eight over and what does it become? The symbol for infinity. That's because, at Yellowstone, nothing is impossible. Everything you do today will be judged, graded and input into our system,' he said. 'To make hard decisions, we use hard tech. And that tech is all around you.'

'The way we succeed,' Tunt continued, clearing her throat. Clearly, that interruption hadn't been planned. 'We succeed through ruthlessly cutting our overheads. That's not to say your remittance won't be generous. We reward those who show us commitment. But where we really innovate is in our automation. Even today's process is largely automated.'

The screen on the stage erupted into light. Danny recognised the images: the Yellowstone Distribution Centre with its myriad of robots on tracks going left, right, up and down, zipping around a cavernous hall. Some carried clothing, some carried groceries. The image flicked to a van being loaded by one of the robots and a smiling Yellowstone driver, uniform crisp and immaculate, taking it out of an equally pristine yard.

Danny compared this to the Mertons store where his nan worked. He'd seen the diesel powered lorries reversing into the tiny yard, strewn with litter and rubbish. Piles of rotten wooden pallets threatened to topple over. The store itself was just as bad: threadbare shelves, scuffed and rusty, with tired and scruffy employees looking overworked and underpaid.

The future, here, versus the past, there.

'Let me show you about some things we're working on,' Grayson said. 'And let me introduce you to Parker.'

Hello! a chipper but acutely synthetic voice buzzed from the air itself.

'She's not happy!' Danny whispered to Henry, nudging him with a shoulder. Tunt had visibly tensed up.

'Just a tool, right, Grayson?' she said. 'One we should keep until later, perhaps.'

Grayson paused. 'Perhaps, Wendy, perhaps. He's just an experiment, after all.'

'Right,' she said through pursed lips.

The presentation zipped by. Danny didn't know if he should be taking notes. He glanced around the auditorium. The audience was enthralled, but Yellowstone employees lined the periphery.

In his pocket, his phone buzzed. Glancing around, he took it out, and glanced at the stage, too. He wasn't missing much by having a quick glance.

```
Danny. There's some jobs here at Mertons.
Good jobs. I think they'll suit you.
Hope it goes well, we'll talk later.
Love you. Nan.
```

'You're not seriously going to consider that, are you?' Henry said. Danny jumped and flicked his phone away. The screen went dim.

'No, don't be silly.'

Henry scoffed. 'To think, they actually think people still *go out* for their shopping and don't just have it delivered.'

Danny took a breath and pocketed his phone away, letting the future sweep around him as the presentation came to an end. Afterwards, he and Henry went their separate ways, following their own regimented timetable.

'See you at lunch?' Danny called as his friend disappeared into the crowd.

'Oh, sure,' Henry said. 'Don't wait up!'

Danny emerged a couple of hours later into a wide, expansive hall full of tables and chairs. He walked over to a table. Henry was just eating.

'Nice of you to wait for me,' he said.

'Go get yourself some food,' Henry said, eating. 'Over there, look,' he pointed.

Danny followed his friend's gesture. A queue formed at a servery. His stomach rumbled. The morning had been tough. He joined the queue and a few minutes later, a plate of fish, chips, peas and tartare sauce was on his plate and he carried it back to Henry.

'How'd you think you're getting on?'

'That first session was tough,' Danny said. 'All maths problems and puzzles. Really took me back.'

'Don't worry,' Henry said. 'It all feeds into the algorithm.'

'When do we see the first league table? It must be soon; they've been collecting the results all day. Not like them to keep us waiting.'

'Look around,' Danny said to the full room. 'Quite some number crunching going on.'

'Oh,' Henry said, grinning. 'It shouldn't be a problem. I hear there's some far out tech working all this out.'

Danny demurred. 'I think at four they'll publish it. What's next?'

Danny consulted the timetable in his email. 'Like being back at school, this. Not even uni was this regimented.'

'They've a lot to pack in.'

'I'll say.'

'What next for you? What does your timetable say?' Henry repeated.

'Customer Function and Problem Solving,' Danny said. He looked up, holding his fork in mid-air. Beyond the steam from the cooked fish, Henry smiled wickedly.

'That was a lot of fun. Basically, showing off to the big I-ams.'

'Hey you two!' a trill voice said from behind. Danny recognised it, as did Henry, whose face fell.

'Hey Hailey,' Danny said. 'Join us!'

Hailey moved to sit down.

'Jesus,' Henry muttered.

'What was that?' Danny asked.

'Nothing.'

'What a morning!' Hailey said, immediately getting to work on her lunch. 'Gonna make some great TubeView content, this.'

'What?' Henry said. 'You're not live-streaming this, are you?! Christ, Hailey, you could—'

'Oh, just you wait,' she said through a grin.

'Hailey, at least take this bloody seriously, please. What if they work out we're related?'

'You think they don't know already? I was telling them all about how wonderful my big brother was.'

'Exactly, so if you could—'

'Wow,' Danny said. 'Lighten up, you two.'

Henry swallowed hard.

'That's better.'

The restaurant then hushed unexpectedly. Danny turned in his seat. 'What's going on?'

Henry pointed to the door. 'Someone's coming.'

Footsteps. A collective intake of breath.

Then a woman in a dark yellow suit emerged.

'It's Wendy Tunt,' Henry said.

48

'Wicked!' Hailey grinned, reaching into her bag. She pulled out a camera and thrust it forward.

'What the hell are you doing?!' Henry hissed at her.

Hailey stuck her tongue out.

'She looks smaller than she did on stage,' Danny said. He wasn't wrong. Tunt's diminutive frame looked dwarfed by her surroundings, but a steely look across her face told Danny that the look may be deceiving. 'Christ, she could cheer up a little.'

Tunt was wandering around the restaurant, shaking hands with the initiates. Smiling, just for a fraction, then back to pursed lips curled inward. She shook the hand of the person she was targeting with her stare and then withdrew in horror.

'Big day. Didn't expect her to come and see us,' Henry said. Danny pivoted in his chair.

'You know, considering how much of a boffin you are about this company, that surprises me.'

'Shut up,' Henry said fast. 'Look, here she is.'

Tunt approached their table. Danny wasn't sure whether he needed to stand up. He fumbled in his seat.

'No need to stand,' Tunt said. 'I'm not royalty.'

Her hand shot out. Danny had watched her. He only had a second. He grasped it for a moment. 'Danny Price. Pleased to meet you.' He let go. The hand shot back in.

'Likewise,' she said. 'Thank you for your attendance. You're doing,' she said, turning her head to the assistant next to her. 'Well. You're doing well, Mr Price.' She pivoted to Henry.

'Henry Archer, Ms Tunt, I can't tell you how lovely it is to—'

'Quiet,' Tunt said. She turned to her assistant, who followed. 'Where's *he* on the list?' She glanced at the tablet they carried. She bit her lip, just a bit. 'Mr Archer, room for improvement. You have potential, boy,' she said. 'Don't waste it. Are you filming, young lady?'

'Oh, no, no!' Hailey said with mock surprise.

'Focus more and you might make today worth a damn,' she said.

Danny stifled a laugh, watching Henry's eyes nearly pop out. Tunt greeted Hailey about as warmly as she'd greeted him. Then she left.

'Oh, I will,' Hailey said.

'Not a word, you!' Henry said to her, flustered. 'There must be a mistake. Wrong me. I aced that portion.'

Hailey laughed and shot a glance at Danny.

'Maybe not,' Danny said. 'But she's a weird one. Not exactly exuding the Yellowstone ethos, you'd say.'

'Well, you try running a company like this, in a country like, well, this,' Henry countered.

Danny hummed. He could hardly imagine.

'D'you think we'll see him?' Hailey asked. 'Not her, sour old bitch.'

'Hey!' Henry interjected.

'Who'd you mean?' Danny asked.

'Grayson Laurie. You saw him on stage. Wonder if we'll get to meet him? I wonder if Aaron Moore is here too. You heard him mention him in the speech?'

'I did. I thought it all went south back when –'

'It did,' Henry said. 'He's not mentioned his name for years. So, something must be going on. I wonder if we'll get to ask him directly?'

It was a question Danny was thinking all too well himself.

Danny finished his lunch and left with Henry and Hailey. His timetable directed him to a conference room on the twentieth floor. Climbing into one of the glass-fronted lifts, he whizzed up.

'What do you think we'll get on this one?' one of the initiates said. Danny swallowed.

Another one of the initiated in the lift answered. 'My mate said this was the easiest part. Just smile and nod politely.'

'Really? Someone I know said it was one of the toughest. That's the absolute worst thing to do.'

'Oh. Well, it sounds easy.'

'Maybe it's meant to?' the other said.

'Guys,' Danny said. The rest of the lift turned around. 'Let's wait and see what we walk into.'

The lift pinged and the door opened.

***

'Ladies and gents, come in please,' one of the staff members said, throwing open a set of double doors that opened into what looked like a standard lecture theatre. 'Find a desk, that's it. Great. Now, please,' the staff member said above the hubbub of conversation. 'Settle down. This is one of the most important parts of the evaluation. This is where we tweak and probe you - alright!' he said as some people giggled. 'That's enough. You may have had your practical skills evaluated. Some may be waiting for that pleasure. But this is where we test not just your skills and abilities, but your mind. If you like, we test your soul to see if it fits in the vision.'

'Toby, thank you, that's a great introduction,' a voice called from a darkened corner of the room. Seventy-five sets of lungs took a great inhale of breath at that voice. They'd recognised it.

'Thanks, Grayson, for that!' the staff member, Toby, said. He glanced at the initiates. 'I think they want to meet you.'

Dressed in the same jeans, T-shirt and jacket, Grayson

emerged. 'Toby's been working in our Delaware division for the last eight years. He's a great trainer and one of the finest. Without him, well… Yellowstone may never have gotten into Delaware. It may not have ever left, either. Wendy, you too,' Grayson called.

Emerging, Wendy Tunt joined his side. 'Initiates, what does success mean to you? Because what you're doing to learn, and what we're going to pull out of you, is how you can further the Yellowstone success factor. By that I mean—'

Grayson Laurie cut her off. 'The success factor is our story. How can we make this a better society? How can the Yellowstone family, of which eight per cent of you will join today, make this better?'

'The key to that success,' Tunt said, clearing her throat again. Danny recognised the tic. She was obviously irritated. 'Total market saturation. We want to be everywhere we're not, and where we are, we want to be… not just number one, but the only number on that chart.'

Grayson turned his head and looked at Tunt, who met his gaze. He blinked twice. That was enough. Then he turned back to the lecture hall. 'We have an opportunity, with you at our side, to write the next chapter of that story. I'll leave you with Toby who'll do the business and hopefully by the end of today we'll have our eight percent.' Grayson finished to an applause from the initiates. With a wave, he made for the door and left. Tunt scuttled behind.

'Right, party time's over. Let's get to work,' Toby said.

Three hours later, Danny emerged. He messaged Henry.

That was interesting.

                              How's your head?
**Swimming. I couldn't tell
you how that went.**

**Meet me down in the
atrium. They're about
to publish the list.**

Danny trooped to one of the lifts and felt weightless as he descended to the atrium. Quickly, he found Henry by a potted tree that stretched up with green fronds to the rafters. Outside, the evening sun was filtering across the city skyline.

'That Tunt's quite a character,' Danny said. 'Talk about up her own arse. Wonder who she blagged a job out of.'

'What happened at your session?' Henry asked.

'Grayson Laurie showed up, gave us a pep talk.'

'No way! We had Tunt for most of ours.'

'She showed up, followed him around like a bad smell.'

'I wonder why he came to your group,' Henry asked through narrowed eyes.

'Who's to say?' said Danny. 'Maybe he flipped a coin and we won.'

CHAPTER 5

The lights in the atrium darkened.

'Christ,' Henry said to Danny. 'Here we go.'

'They're not going to do this publicly, are they?'

'Probably. They do that in the States.'

'Bit vulgar, that,' Danny said.

We will be sending you your placements in sixty seconds. Please open your Yellowstone app to receive your results. All decisions have been adjudicated and are final. If you place lower than the top eight per cent, you will be able to reapply again to us in six calendar months.

Everyone got their phones out on cue. It was the longest sixty seconds in the world.

'What's going on?' Hailey said, meandering through the crowd to the tree planter her brother and Danny were propping up. 'Do I need my phone out?'

'If you want to find out if you've got a job, yes!' Henry hissed.

'Easy,' Danny soothed.

Then his phone buzzed. The whole atrium went silent in comprehension. Some hoots of joy. Some moans of aggravation. 'That's… weird?'

'What did you get?' Henry asked.

Danny held up his phone. *Go to floor 88.*

'I got that too,' Henry said.

'Where's Hailey gone?'

'Oh,' Henry said. 'She left. Don't think she got on with it.'

'Did you have anything to do with that?'

'What, me?' Henry said. 'No idea what you're talking about.'

'But Hailey…'

'Enough about her! Jeez, I don't need you running around like a little dog like she does. She's unimportant.'

'If you say so.'

'Come on then, Danny,' Henry said. 'The lift!'

The lift doors closed behind them. The lift descended.

'Hey!' Henry said. 'Where are we going now? I thought we were going up!'

'Shh,' Danny said. 'I'm sure there's a reason.'

The lights in the lift went out, and the capsule was shrouded in darkness. For a moment, only the sounds of mechanism and whirring outside penetrated.

I suppose, a voice started. It was Grayson Laurie. *You're wondering quite what's happening. Floor 88 isn't at the top. It's about half a mile underground.*

Henry's mouth opened, but no words came out.

You're the top of the class. So we have something to show you. I hope you're ready.

The lift stopped with a clank. Then it moved sideways for a minute before stopping again. The door opened to a clinical, crisp, white corridor.

In front of the door a Yellowstone agent waited.

Henry stepped out first. 'Where are we?' he asked.

'Follow me, both of you,' the agent said, and proceeded down a corridor for a moment. The corridor ended at a door to one side. The agent pushed it open, revealing a concrete staircase.

'Where are we going?' Henry repeated his question. 'Where are the rest of the eight-percenters?'

'Shut up, and you might find out,' Danny said.

'I was only asking.'

'Well, if they wanted to tell us, they'll tell us. Look…'

The agent had reached the bottom of the staircase and pushed open another door.

'Through here and get into the transporter.'

Henry looked at Danny. Danny shrugged.

'Beam me up,' Danny said, emerging through the door. He looked. No floor pads. No teleport. But a sleek, white-and-yellow car with darkened windows sat in the middle of the room. It had doors open that revealed a plush, golden interior.

'Subtle,' Danny finished, climbing in. The car rocked just a tiny bit. 'Come on then, princess.'

Henry scowled. 'Button it, alright.'

The doors swept closed, and the car rumbled, then stood still. Outside, the lights of a tunnel pulsed past, faster and faster.

'Jesus,' Henry said.

You're probably wondering what's going on, Grayson's voice said. On a screen opposite the seats, his face appeared. *Welcome to ParkerRail… or at least, the only part of it so far finished. You're speeding at over three hundred miles per hour on a personal maglev train to our Hertford operations centre. I'll see you soon and show you everything you could have…*

Danny glanced to Henry.

'Maglev?' Henry started

'Three hundred miles per hour?'

'Hertford?'

'Je-fucking-sus,' Danny said. 'Get comfortable, I guess.'

They didn't have long. The maglev came to a stand eight

minutes later. The doors opened. An identical room came into view as Danny and Henry stepped out.

'Have we even moved?' Henry asked.

Danny didn't answer; instead he moved outward toward the door opposite.

The door opened by itself to a deserted corridor. Expansive glass windows that wrapped around dominated the far wall.

Danny approached and glanced through.

'Wow,' he said. 'It's bloody vast.'

'So this is how they do it,' Henry said. 'This is the future,' he pointed. 'What they're working towards. This is the fully automated Grid.'

Danny glanced down. A square pattern of pearlescent boxes filled the whole floor. A network of stainless steel rails marked the edges. Zipping in and out from cubbyholes just out of view on the edges, robots gripped the rails and danced around the Grid. The boxes filled with Yellowstone-branded boxes and bundles. Once full, a box vibrated, and the packages tumbled through a chute.

'Want to see what happens after?' a voice called. Danny glanced left. Grayson Laurie stood at the corner of the corridor. 'I'll show you.'

'Gray… Mr Laurie!' Henry yapped.

'That's my name,' he said. 'Don't wear it out. Call me Grayson, please.'

'What did you want to show us?' Danny asked, walking to wards Laurie. 'There's not a soul here. Nobody.'

'That's what I want.'

'Won't that cause massive job losses?'

'Smart cookie,' Grayson said. 'You're Daniel, right?'

'Danny, yes,' he corrected.

'I'm Henry,' Henry added.

'Yes,' Grayson said. 'yes you are. Now come on,' he said. 'Lots to show and not much time.' He spun round and pushed through a door that led to a concrete spiral staircase going down. Danny stopped just in the doorway.

Something caught his eye in the window.

A flash of colour. A flash of fabric. A flash of hair.

It couldn't be —

'Did you see anything?' Grayson asked.

'I… no,' Danny said.

'Don't keep the man waiting, Danny!' Henry harrumphed.

'Alright,' Danny said, following, the door slapping closed behind him.

***

The three emerged at the bottom of the staircase and through a door that led to a cavernous space of concrete and steel. The space was lit from above, where the bottom of the plastic tubs rested on structural members. In front, though, on floor level, a tangled nest of somersaulting and careening conveyor belts took piles of parcels from where the plastic bins deposited them away through a warren of passages and pillars. Flashes of red light strobed all over the place. There was a massive din of hissing air and snapping mechanisms. The packages seemed to pirouette and dance across from belt to belt, some with such regularity that it seemed as if they flourished wildly in mid-air.

'This is the other side of the Grid,' Grayson said. 'Each pulse is a barcode scanner. All linked up to an artificial intelligence that knows where each package goes.'

'Sounds… standard,' Danny said.

'Danny!' Henry admonished.

Grayson laughed. 'It's all done on the fly. That's the difference. See, I could…' he started, moving toward the guard rail and leaning in. He caught a package. 'I can just throw this back in, and the system will sort it!' He did so, tossing the small box over his shoulder. It seemed to hover until it disappeared into the mix. 'This system increases reliability to over ninety-eight per cent!'

'Amazing stuff, Mr Lau… Grayson,' Henry clapped.

'It's a very good post office,' Danny said.

'More than that, Danny,' Grayson said. 'This technology can be used anywhere. We're finally cresting the wave.'

'And what of all the people? Isn't this going to just make unemployment worse? I can't find a job for love nor money!'

'Well,' Grayson said. 'That's not strictly true in your case, now, is it?'

'What did you say?'

'We redeploy our crews to make sure our customers – who will enjoy faster shipping, lower prices and the utmost in convenience – are as happy as happy can be.'

'So what would we be doing in all this?'

'You two can manage the rollout of this project. I want you to meet someone. Come on, come with me.'

Danny and Henry followed Grayson Laurie as he disappeared back into the corridor and into a side room a few moments away.

They followed into a room with nobody in it beside Grayson Laurie, who stood over a table in the middle of the room.

'Mr Laurie,' Henry started. 'There's nobody—'

Laurie pivoted, revealing a squat, metallic dome that shimmered with lights around a rim. 'Here he is!'

'Here's who?' Danny said.

Grayson nodded at the dome. 'Say hi, Parker!'

Hi, Parker! A voice – synthetic and saccharine – trilled from the dome. *It's nice to meet you!*

'This,' Laurie said, his voice bubbling with excitement, 'is the real future of Yellowstone. Parker will control everything the company does. You will be working directly for me on this project. You're too bright to be doing anything else.'

'Are you sure?' Danny asked. 'Isn't this all a bit of a jump?'

'Go big or go home. Did Wendy discuss your results?'

'Yes,' Henry groaned. 'I hate to ask but… am I in the right place?'

'You are, Henry,' Grayson said. 'The algorithm isn't quite fool-proof yet. You're here. Let that sink in. How does *that* sound?'

'Sounds great!' Henry said. 'This AI tech… how far to go?'

'You've read lots, I imagine, but I'll tell you the situation. We're still beta testing,' Laurie said. 'Here, let's give Parker a crack of the whip. Parker,' he said.

Yes, Grayson? The orb on the table answered.

'You've got the floor. Route all Hertford processing logic through you.'

Yes, Grayson. Interfacing now.

Grayson stood back, beaming, his arms behind his back, all the more the proud dad.

Nothing happened.

'Mr Laurie,' Danny asked, 'if this… thing takes over… what about all the people?'

'What about them?' Henry snipped. 'Adapt or die. Am I right?'

'Don't worry, nobody's going to… lose their job or anything,' Grayson stuttered. 'it'll be a managed transition. Business optimisation. That sort of thing. They'll be found, well, something. Based on loyalty and service, of course.'

'I see,' Danny said, not seeing at all.

Outside, clattering carried through. Footsteps. Raised voices down the hallway. Raised voices saying not very nice things.

'Excuse me,' Grayson said, leaving the room. The door closed.

'Well, what do you think of that?'

'Isn't it wonderful?' Henry said, his voice buoyant. 'All that rubbish about unionising in the States. All dispensed with. Those robots are the future, Danny.'

'I wouldn't be so sure if I was working here. You really think this isn't going to just ruin thousands of people's lives?'

'I don't follow, Danny. I told you, this company is the future.'

'Mertons is hanging on by a thread? That my nan works for?'

'Hey,' Henry said. 'That's their fault, not Yellowstone's. Adapt or die, that's the motto, isn't it?'

'They employ thousands. Until this... thing makes them redundant!' he pointed to the Parker dome on the table.

'No, he just said...'

'He said nothing, Henry! God, you're such a bloody idiot sometimes.'

'Stop it, Danny, just bloody stop it, alright! God, if anyone could hear... you're going to throw away the opportunity? They had this exact discussion a year ago when Yellowstone bought Cheepr.'

'Yes, I remember. Four thousand people were fired overnight by a spreadsheet, Henry.'

'And yet, despite all the moaning, Cheepr is better than ever.'

Danny didn't answer. The conversation had been done before. 'A lot of people might not have opportunities soon,' Danny said. 'You might be lucky enough not to know what that feels like...'

'Don't, Danny!'

'What, touching a nerve, am I?'

'You're wrong! Just wrong!'

'I don't think I am! Because, like it or not, I've been there and you bloody haven't!'

Outside, there were shouts. Henry and Danny looked at each other.

'What the hell is going on out there?' Danny went for the door first, pulling it open. The corridor was empty, but noises came from all around. 'Come on, let's see what all this fuss is about.'

They rounded the corner back to the undercroft of the Grid. Flashes of red scanners erupted, but the space was filled with smoke.

'Turn it off! Turn it off!' a Yellowstone worker yelled through the space.

'I'm trying! We've lost control!' another screamed back.

The noise stopped abruptly, with just the tinkling of metal against metal filling the silence.

'What happened?' Danny asked.

'You two,' a sharp female voice said from behind. 'Get out of there!'

Danny pivoted. 'Who's that?!'

'Do I need to repeat myself?' the voice barked. 'Out. Now!'

'It's Wendy Tunt!' Henry said, scrabbling away. Danny followed. Tunt's angular shoulders emerged from the gloom.

'Don't tell me, you got adventurous,' she said.

'We heard…'

'Everything is under control,' she said. 'Can someone please turn that bloody siren off?!' The siren, as if it heard her, hushed. Tunt looked beyond Danny and Henry. 'We've been compromised. Have we found the intruders?'

Henry stuttered. 'We were invited down here—'

'Not you two! The people that broke in?'

'Yes, Ms Tunt,' another Yellowstone drone said.

Tunt strode between Dany and Henry, pushing them aside like the bow of a supertanker pushes aside the waves. 'Show me. You two,' she said over her shoulder, her head not moving. 'With me. See how we work here? You've come this far.'

Danny and Henry followed Tunt and her acolyte into a small room down another warren-like passage. A bank of screens lined one wall. An operator in a Yellowstone uniform – like everyone, it seemed – pivoted in a chair.

'Ms Tunt, watch here,' the operator said, scrolling some of the footage on one screen back. In reverse, against a backdrop of machinery and blinking lights, three shaggy-clothed people trotted into the frame.

'Fascinating. And that one,' Tunt pointed at the screen, 'what're they carrying?'

The operator rolled a trackball on the desk. The image zoomed, maintaining clarity. 'It's a female. A young woman. Bag under one arm, camera in the other.'

'Christ,' Tunt said. 'Bring 'em in.'

'Working on it,' the operator said, leaning to pick up a handset from the desk.

'You two,' Tunt said, 'this is how we deal with industrial espionage. You wait and see.'

'What's she doing?' Danny asked. 'How did she get in?'

'It doesn't matter, Danny,' Henry said, stealing the breath out of Tunt's mouth. 'Whatever she's doing, she shouldn't be here. Who knows whether that feed is live or not?'

Danny watched Tunt's face harden at the word live.

'I only hope for her—' Tunt started.

'Got 'em,' the operator said, holding up a hand. 'They're coming here.'

'Excellent. I want that camera destroyed.'

Outside, footsteps squealed on the hard floor, followed by laughter.

'I can't believe it,' a shrill voice giggled. 'Nearly bloody saw the lot!'

'Hey,' Danny said, glancing to Henry. 'Doesn't that sound like—'

'I bloody hope not!'

The door opened and Henry' fears were confirmed.

'Dear brother!' Hailey said, wriggling in the grip of two Yellowstone agents. 'Fancy seeing you here!'

'Hailey?' Danny asked.

'Hailey!' Henry spat with palpable menace. 'What the hell are you doing? And how the fuck did you get here?!'

'Both questions I'd like answered,' Tunt added. 'The camera. Hand it over.'

Hailey beamed. 'Why?'

'You don't want to say no to me. I'll have you arrested. Trespassing, for starters.'

'For starters,' Hailey said, her smile dissolving. 'I could have you arrested for what *you've* been doing, Ms Tunt.' Tunt gulped. 'Brutalising workers. Cutting back on their rights. Really turning the screw. Shall I continue?'

'Add libel and slander to the list of charges. You can't prove a thing. Our legal department will make mincemeat of you.'

'Hailey, shut up and just get out of here!' Henry said. 'Before you say something stupid.'

'I've found stuff, dear brother. This whole company is rotten. And it's down to her.' She pointed right between Tunt's eyes.

'Enough!' Tunt shouted. 'Get her out of here.'

'Hold on,' Danny said. 'I want to hear what she's got to say.'

'Ethics, Danny. She,' Hailey said, bucking her head toward

Tunt, 'doesn't even know the meaning of the word. Where's Grayson Laurie? Does he know?'

'I said get her out of here!' Tunt yelled. 'Another word out of her and it's not just a gagging order I want. I want her lips sewn shut.' Leaping from her chair, Tunt scrabbled to be nose-to-nose with Hailey. 'I'll do it myself if I have to, you little bitch. Believe me,' Tunt snarled, 'I see even a *hair* of you around a Yellowstone property again. Maybe I'll sew them shut myself.'

'Big words, shoulder-pads.'

Henry was the next out of his seat. He grabbed his sister and, with the help of the Yellowstone goons, pushed his sister out of the room. The door snapped closed, leaving just silence between Danny and Wendy Tunt.

'Now,' she said, 'let's get down to business.'

'Wait,' Danny said. 'What's she talking about?'

'Daniel,' Tunt said, 'she's the problem this company has.'

'I think she's right. I think you're going to just fuck everyone over.'

'My *plan*, with your help, will be to take this company to the stratosphere. We'd offer you extremely generous recompense for your aid, if you meet my target.'

'What is it that you want? All I have is a degree, and people keep thinking I'm special.'

'Way to really sell yourself, Danny,' Henry said with a sigh.

'I want you on my acquisitions team. We have one coming up that would suit your… talents, hands down.'

'Talents? I got a 2:1 in my degree. Like I just said, I'm nothing special.'

'Telemetry says otherwise. The 2:1 is by-the-by. You're something special, Danny. And you're just what I… we are looking for.'

Danny sat back, tenting his hands and staring into his lap. The microchips in his brain were pulsing. He looked up. 'Target, you say?'

'We completed with Freshco six months ago. The integration is nearly complete. It went textbook.'

'I said,' Danny repeated. 'Who is the target?'

'Mertons,' Tunt said. She saw Danny's eyebrows raise. 'Surprised? Their board is holding out, but we think you can help us get a better offer.'

'Christ,' Danny said. 'What do you want with Mertons?'

'They're withering on the vine, surely?'

'They still, somehow, have a foothold in regions we can't crack, despite their creaky operation. So we're bringing down the hammer.'

'Wait, how?'

'We want to buy them. Is this business you can't stomach?'

'I've family… my nan…' Danny looked up at Tunt. 'She warned me about you.'

'I know,' Tunt said, then stopped, as if she'd said too much. 'I mean, it's change, right?'

'She'd never forgive me.'

'But look at the *opportunity* for you, Daniel. You could achieve true greatness here. Let's cut the bull: Mertons is the past. High prices, an outdated business model… and you want to hitch to that? You want job security? The country needs job security. And given all that's happened recently… Yellowstone is the only thing that can do it.'

'That's a very persuasive argument but…'

'I don't like *buts*, Daniel.'

'I… I don't think I can do it. After what happened—'

'Your brother? Your mother?' She snapped her lips shut. 'Shit. Besides, consider it a patriotic duty. The country needs you, and so does Yellowstone. The duty may be one and the same.'

Danny waved his hands and lent forward. 'What do you know about Lewis and mum?'

Tunt took a bigger breath. She was distracted. 'You need to decide what's more important to you. Family by blood or family by contract.'

'I don't know what you're talking about. But has this got anything to do with my nan?'

'I…' Tunt trailed off. 'She could be a problem, yes.'

'A problem? How? She's all I have left.'

'You've lived with her for six months, Danny. Before that, you were surfing sofas. I'm sorry if our offer means breaking some eggshells.'

'I've got a funny feeling. If I say yes,' Danny said, 'this is going to hurt her, isn't it?'

Tunt spun her eyes. 'She… works for… we could try to preserve…'

'More waffle words,' Danny said. 'You'd lay her off. You wouldn't bring this up otherwise.' He saw Tunt relax. 'You hurt my nan, my last bit of family, you hurt me. I can't do it,' he said.

'There's time to reconsider,' Tunt said. 'I want you on my team. I want you to be the future. Your nan is wedded to the past.'

'What are you offering, anyway?'

Tunt pulled a letter from her briefcase. She pushed it, facing down, to Danny. He flipped it over. A big number in big letters flew from the page.

'Blimey.'

'Think carefully, Danny,' she said.

'I…' Danny said, trailing off. The letter was barely legible lines of legalese. 'Am I selling out my family for this?'

'We can't guarantee there won't be redundancies once we

complete on Mertons. You'd need to be ready to make tough decisions. Obviously, the details are confidential, Daniel; I can't just tell you anything without some commitment the other way.'

'At the cost of what, even more jobs? More people on the streets.'

'I'm not making myself clear, am I? It would be… unwise to refuse this. We know about your mum. Your brother, Lewis.'

'There you go again. What the hell do you know about Lewis, about mum?'

'We did a comprehensive background check—'

'Don't you dare. Don't you fucking dare,' Danny snarled. 'You've lost me, right there. I want a job, yes, but I won't be your slave. You dig around, looking up my dead family to guilt me into a job where I might have to give my own nan, the last family I've got left, the sack?! God, does the word *ethics* mean nothing to you?!'

'Tough words. That's the most generous the offer gets. You've got five minutes, Danny, or we'll be a lot less generous.'

'I don't need the time,' Danny said. He took the letter and screwed it into a ball, tossing it to the floor. 'There's your answer.'

Tunt tutted. Danny got to his feet and stamped on the letter. 'No more questions.'

Tunt shook her head. 'You'll live to regret that one, Danny, much like—'

'One more word about my mum or Lewis,' he growled, 'and I'll shove you through that damn machine. And I don't give a shit who you are. You leave them out of it.'

And he stormed out, up the stairs and onto the cool, cloudy street above. The breeze pushed him to the train station, and he sat on the platform, not sure how he got here but damn sure it'd take him a longer time to get back.

CHAPTER 6

'Sit down, Archer,' Tunt said as Henry entered the office alone.

'I think we're into double digits,' Henry said, pulling the chair out and taking a pew.

'What're you talking about?!' Tunt said.

'Double digits. Of words said to me. By you.'

'I could have you out of that door quite as quickly as you came in,' she hissed back.

'You won't, though.' Henry smiled.

Tunt gave a brief, bewildered expression, which dissolved after a moment. 'Enough, I've had enough playtime from Mr Price back at Hartford. The train back was a nightmare. And don't think I've forgotten about your errant sister. Today has been nothing but trouble for me.'

'He didn't look too happy either, after what happened. As for Hailey, I am deeply sorry.'

'You should be, for her. Mr Price, however? He's made a decision,' Tunt said. 'Let's leave it at that. But I want to discuss your future with Yellowstone. I want to ask you a question,' she said, reclining, her shoulders relaxing. 'What does loyalty mean to you?'

'Oh, it's paramount,' Henry said.

'Loyalty to who, though?'

Henry glanced at the logo above the desk. 'I suppose Yellowstone,' he said.

'You suppose. Mr Archer, you're going to have to make me believe you want it more.'

Henry swallowed. 'I want it.'

'You've not even read the offer,' Tunt said, pointing to the un-opened letter that he held. 'Sure?'

'I don't care about the offer. Or the money. Or anything. I want this more than I've wanted anything.'

'Why?'

'Because I think Yellowstone can be the—'

'No,' Tunt said. 'Why do you *really* want this?'

'Because,' Henry said, 'I think it's my…' he trailed off. 'No, it's not my destiny. After all those years of being a name. I'm more than that.'

'There's something else, isn't there?'

Henry bit his lip. 'To make my dad proud. To make him love me. To finally show my sister I have that pride. That I have that love.'

Tunt sat back for a moment. 'Interesting. You'd prioritise the goals of this company above your friends? Your family?'

'I'm not. I'm doing this for the family. Dad would… his words…' Henry stumbled. 'Who needs them when you have this kind of opportunity? I want to change the world. That's what my dad taught me. It's what he expects of me. To change the world. Not be a passenger. Despite the price.'

Tunt smiled. 'Don't we all? I could give you that opportunity, Henry. Are you sure you want it? What makes you the man who's got what it takes to stand at my side when the going gets tough? To really show your father what he expects of you. You're not his son. You're his name.'

'I… realise this.' Henry sat back in the chair, mulling over what he thought Tunt was about to offer him. The look on his dad's face. The look on Hailey's. He chuckled. 'I think I do. Is this to do with the, er—'

'Oh, no, no,' Tunt said. 'Nothing so mundane. You have a bigger part to play in our plans.'

'I see.'

'You're aware of the current… political situation, right?'

'Was there any truth to what Hailey said?'

'Smoke always comes from a spark. Is firefighting a problem for you? Regardless of where the wick lies?'

'Was it a problem for Danny?'

'I need someone to extinguish the fire. Choke it. Suffocate it. Will that be a problem? Are you seeing what I mean, Henry?'

'Not a problem, not for me,' Henry said, his forehead creasing. 'Not a problem at all.' Tunt cocked her head. He continued: 'Company like this could really swoop in. Government's at its knees. Burned-out hulk. Selling the family silver to the highest bidder.'

'Opportunities are presenting themselves,' Tunt said.

'I feel there's more to this. Something I can do that Danny can't.'

Tunt grimaced. 'Mr Price has made a decision. We expected it in a way, but let's not talk here.'

'But this is your office,'

'What I want to propose to you is outside of the parameters of this office. And what we will discuss certainly doesn't *leave* this office. Are we clear?'

Henry raised his eyebrows. *Outside the parameters of the office?* 'Crystal.'

Tunt produced a business card and scrawled an address on the back, passing it to Henry. 'We'll meet here. Closer to you out of London, tomorrow. Away from prying eyes. Alone. Well, you will be. Our legal counsel will be there on our side. Are you ready for this?'

Henry glanced around the office, circling his head around to Tunt's position. In his mind's eye, her form transformed into his. *Yeah*, he thought. *I could fit right in.*

'Yes,' Henry said. 'I am.'

'Excellent,' Tunt said. 'I look forward to it.'

Henry left his house the next evening, easing the electric car into the cloying summer heat once again.

At the end of the road, he faced the T-junction. Left or right.

Left: the status quo. Right: the future.

He turned right.

The suburban clamour turned into thick trees synonymous with the Home Counties. The roads the sat-nav led Henry down were anonymous in their appearance – unloved trees and shrubs lined the pitted road.

The events of the past few years had really spared no parts of the country. The outbreak had decimated the economy; the government and the people simply gave up. The weather had stripped the roads of their lustre.

Eventually, the road widened into the sleepy riverside town. Henry parked up in a car park shielded from the dying indigo of the day by the walls of an abandoned pub. A famous chicken chain had once owned the property, but it now stood empty, the funky lettering patchwork and decrepit.

He exited the car park and stood on the corner. His phone buzzed.

'This way,' a voice called. Henry swivelled. Beside his car, a man in a long coat had appeared at the edge of the car park, beside a dark alley.

'Are you—' Henry asked.

'Shh!' the figure hissed. 'This way, please. In through the back door.'

'Why, who are you?' Henry walked forward.

'Why are you asking questions?'

'I don't usually meet strange men in a back alley. *Usually*.'

'Look,' the man said, 'd'you want to keep Ms Tunt waiting or not?'

Glancing over his shoulder one last time, Henry followed the man back into the car park and down an alley between buildings. A door in the wall next to some bins squealed open. The man in the coat stopped by the door and ushered Henry in.

'Thanks,' he muttered. *Exotic locales*, he thought.

Passing through a service entrance and past a kitchen that looked in use but was devoid of cooks, Henry entered the restaurant. It was empty.

A woman sat at a table with a man in the middle. The rest of the tables had been cleared away to the side of the room. She looked up. 'Hello, Henry,' Tunt said.

'Ms Tunt, this is, er…'

'Needs must. This is Grady, my legal representative,' Tunt nodded her head in the man's description. The thin, gaunt man with the wiry glasses showed no emotion; his skin was almost as pallid as the suit he wore. 'He's here to make sure this is all… in line with the plan. Sit down.'

Henry did so. Tunt nodded past his shoulder. A waiter glided to Henry' side.

'And for the gentleman?'

'Oh, er,' Henry said. He fumbled for the menu. He pointed at an item at random. Something about this whole setup didn't inspire his appetite.

'Excellent choice,' the waiter said, vanishing.

'So, er,' Henry said, trying to break the ice.

'Show him,' Tunt said.

Grady knelt down and pulled a tablet from a leather case nestled next to his seat. It thudded just a little as he placed it on the table. He swiped the screen and images appeared. Someone's house.

'I think I recognise that house,' Henry said.

'You should,' Tunt said. 'Carry on.' Grady flicked the screen another time. 'How about that now?'

From the second picture, the house was very familiar. He'd dropped Danny outside there not long ago.

'That's Danny's house?'

'Hopefully not for much longer,' Tunt said. 'We want to buy it.'

'Why?'

'The owner presents certain… logistical and political challenges to our future plans.'

'You mean Danny's nan.'

'Yes,' Grady said.

'Why?'

'She's well connected to one of our last competitors. We want to buy them out. We're planning on a big push for a new bill in parliament,' Tunt took over. 'She could be a fly in the ointment of the plans.'

'And how can I help?'

'Danny may be attracted to potential offers from the competition. His loyalty is with the family, and that loyalty will no doubt transfer to Mertons in short order. Especially if he learns his provenance. The company is his for the taking, and it's a risk we cannot take.'

'Really, Danny could be privy to the sort of wealth that… well, my dad'll be having a fit if that was him.'

'There's been years of smoke-and-mirrors to keep his mind

pure,' Tunt said.

'I know things changed a lot after his mum died. And Lewis, too,' Henry said, remembering conversations at university when Danny's mother and brother had died in that accident.

'Terrible,' Tunt said, breaking eye contact.

'It was. It messed him up something else. I was there, he cried into my shoulder. This news could set him up for life.'

Tunt glared, her head shooting up.

'Don't even think about it.'

'Mr Price,' Grady added fast, 'must not find out in any which way or fashion about this.'

'I don't want you as a postman, Henry,' Tunt said. 'I want you by my side. The riches and fame and *power* you could have would dwarf any inheritance Daniel Price could or couldn't get. Remember,' she said. 'We're the future. He's chosen the past.'

Henry sat back for a moment, the cogs in his mind whirring. *A bigger inheritance than even his father could dream of. A whole company, the size of Mertons.* 'What do you want me to do?'

'You can have all of what we offered Mr Price, but you must do one thing. Stop him from realising what he is legally entitled to.'

'You mean Mertons?'

'And then some. Believe me. They don't know quite what they're sitting on. We want it to get it out of the way.'

'But he's a friend. We've been through… what happened with his mum. And Lewis. It nearly broke him. He needed me then.'

'That was then,' Tunt said. 'And what would your father think? I appreciate your… affinity for your friend, but his actions show he doesn't know what he wants. Not really. But you, I think, do.'

'I… I need some assurances.'

Grady reached below the table and produced an envelope that

bulged, just a little.

'Will these be enough? Share certificates. You won't just be an employee, Henry. You'll be a partner in all we plan together. Danny could've taken on more than he ever dreamed of.

'I… wow, I see,' he said. 'But…'

'Think about it. Before you say one more word, think about it.'

Henry took a drink from the glass of lukewarm water in front of him. *Could he really? But Danny had been an idiot. Idiots need to pay for their mistakes. It's what father always said. They won't miss what they never knew they had…*

Swallowing, Henry reached his answer. 'Alright. I'll do it.'

Tunt reclined in her chair. 'Excellent,' she smiled. 'I think this partnership will be fruitful.'

'How do I start?'

'First,' she said, pushing up from her reclining position. 'You're going to don the blue and get us some facts.'

CHAPTER 7

Danny stared at his house as Henry drove away. Dusk erupted from above the gable roof, dark angular shapes against the streaky ochre sky. After taking a couple of deep breaths, he walked up the little path towards the big blue door. He reached into his pocket, pulling out his keys and opening the door.

He stepped into the living room; the door clunking behind.

'What did you do?' Jane asked.

'I said no to them.'

Jane's eyes widened. 'I'm… I'm surprised.'

'They wanted me to… well, you always talk about mum and dad. And Lewis, too,' Danny began. Soft rock hummed through the speakers. 'They made me realise what matters more than a job.'

'And what's that?'

'Family. They… I don't want to go into it.'

'Danny,' she said. 'Tell me.'

'They know something about you. I don't know what. But it's something to do with work.'

'Christ,' she said.

'They also mentioned about mum. And Lewis.'

'Those bastards! What did they ask you to do?'

'Something I felt uncomfortable with. Like, sure, the money would've been great, but there's more to life than money, right?'

'Right.'

'I just wonder about Henry.'

'Why's that?'

'His family is different. All through university, he pushed himself.'

'He achieved,' Jane said. 'So did you.'

'It's like he was scared, though, like it was a competition. Everything was, right? We used to go out drinking, even stuff like that. But I overheard him a couple of times. His dad…'

'I know him,' Jane said, cutting Danny off with a scowl. 'He built all those houses. The ones that fell down in the flood in Kent, for starters.'

'Oh,' Danny said with a gasp. 'Don't mention that around Henry. It's a sore point for the family.'

'It should be. That stuff nearly got people killed.'

'He's terrified… not of his dad, per se, but the feeling that his dad is disappointed in him,' Danny said. 'You're not disappointed in me, are you? Means I'll be bumming around at home some more. Maybe I made the wrong choice.'

'No, Danny, you didn't. Big corporations like that… they just want one thing. And you know what that is?'

'Money?'

'And what is money?' she asked.

'Money is… happiness?'

She laughed, but her face remained serious. 'No, think bigger than that. Power.'

Danny hummed. He couldn't disagree. 'I still don't understand how they knew about… our family.'

'What do you mean?'

'They knew about Lewis. And mum.'

'Jesus,' she said.

'It felt invasive. And wrong.'

'It is,' Jane said.

'Though I have a question.'

'What's that?'

'What happened with mum and Lewis…'

'Whatever they said was wrong, Daniel. Absolutely wrong. And I don't want to rake over all this now. Or ever again. Do you understand me?'

'But they know—'

'They know *nothing*, you understand me? They don't understand what I had to do. I had to go down to a grotty morgue and identify my daughter and grandson. I won't forget that. Now please,' she said, her voice faltering. 'I don't want to speak of that.'

'Oh,' Danny said, 'I'm sorry, Nan.'

She sniffed. 'Not your fault. They put the idea in your head. Look, it's a long day. How about your old nan treats you to a burger from the grill?'

'Are you sure?'

'Positively,' she said, reaching out and touching his bare hand. 'One hundred per cent.'

Danny smiled. 'Alright then. I'll drive.'

Danny drove back with the smell of friend potato and meat filling the car. He turned the car into the final road, up the hill toward the green and their home again. Soon, the dark form of the house was next to the car. Danny got out first, followed by his nan.

They walked up the little path toward the cottage.

'Stop,' Jane said. 'Someone's been here.'

'What do you mean, I only swung by to get the key—'

'No,' Jane said. 'Curtains. Not how I left them. And you don't touch them.'

'Want me to call the police?'

'No point,' Jane said. 'They won't come, even if you're dying in the street.'

Danny knew from the news she wasn't being hyperbolic. 'You want to go inside?'

'Can't stay out here all night,' she said.

'I'll go first.'

Danny put his key in the lock and turned. The latch clicked. Then he pushed the painted door. It creaked. He stepped inside. The floorboards rattled. Normal sounds. Inside, he turned into the living space and dining room. It was one big space. Opposite on the other wall was the staircase upward. The dark stained wood blended into the dark wall in the evening light that streamed through the window.

He turned the light on. 'Come in, Nan,' he said.

'That isn't as it should be,' she said, shadowing Danny. She pointed. 'The rug's skew-wiffed.'

Danny hummed. 'Anywhere else? Check the kitchen,' he said, pointing past the dining table. The net curtains against the French doors danced in the breeze. Jane stepped lightly toward them. Danny turned to the living area. The coffee table had a pile of leaflets and papers.

'Danny!' Jane called. He spun.

'What?'

'Door's open.'

'Did you lock it?'

'Silly question,' she said. Danny nodded. It was.

'These yours?' he said, picking up the leaflets?

'Where'd they come from?' she said. Danny palmed through one. He stopped at one of the flyers. Canary yellow ink and a logo he wanted to forget.

Don't forget to subscribe to Yellowstone Prime, Jane! It read. For

*all the latest services in one place! We'd love to have you back. It'll
be good for you.*

Danny crumpled the leaflet and pocketed it. Clearly, the postman was making personal deliveries.

'Just bills,' Jane said. 'Maybe I left the door unlocked.'

'And I had my big day.'

'You did.'

'Maybe,' Danny said. 'We'll have to be more careful, I suppose.'

A couple of days later, Danny drove Jane to Kier Wood. He
pulled up in the car park. He left the engine running and his seat
belt buckled.

'Danny, come in,' Jane said, getting out of his car. 'There's
someone in here I want you to meet.'

Danny killed the engine and got out. He was surprised. Usually when he left Jane at Kier Wood he never hung around. He'd
spent his childhood in that store with his parents and Lewis, but
since he'd come back from university... there was just a presence
emanating from the two sets of double doors that prickled the
hairs on the back of his hands. He just didn't want to go in.

'Alright,' he said, swallowing his feelings.

'We'll cut through the store,' Jane said, entering first. The store
was a tired wreck – aisles filled with scuffed racking where shelves
had been, most of it empty. A few hardy shoppers braved these
aisles, but most of the traffic was people in royal-blue polyester
with carts full of things.

Danny lingered, his eyes dancing into the rafters. Ducting
rattled.

'Careful!' one worker said, his trolley nearly careening side-on
into Danny.

'Nearly!' Danny jumped.

'Sorry mate,' the man said with a heave. 'Thing weighs a ton.'

'No worries.'

'Danny! Get over here!' Jane called.

Danny followed her across to the back of the store to another set of double doors that blended in with the once-white-now-cream decor. This place hadn't been refitted in years. The paint was chipped and worn in patterns that only years of hand-rubbing would do. Beyond that door, a passageway led around to another door. Beyond this, a stairwell going up. Finally, Danny followed his nan across the canteen floor. She said hello to some of her colleagues. Danny felt out of place in his civvies; everyone else was wearing the white and blue Mertons uniform.

Jane knocked on a door just past the canteen, not waiting for a response before she opened it. Danny followed.

'Danny, this is Brian. He's one of the senior managers,' she said. The man in front of him was balding, slightly chubby.

Danny reached out to shake Brian's hand. 'Good to meet you. You manage this store?'

'Not quite,' Brian laughed. 'I manage the region. Six stores in this zone, and I oversee all the zones in the region. It's a task, alright, what with the transition?'

'Transition?'

'Kier Wood's one of the last where the public come in. We're trying to change our model. Delivery only.'

'Right,' Danny said, glancing at his nan. 'What can I do for you?'

'We think you're just what we need,' Brian said. 'The competition is really getting dicey. I don't suppose you've heard, have you? The shop floor is a write off, but it's in the delivery space we're finding it hard to compete, and there's one in particular.'

'Yellowstone?' Danny asked.

Brian laughed again. 'That's a word we don't want to talk about. They're exerting enormous pressure, yes. Moving into our space, what has been our space for fifty years. And like you saw, we're trying to adapt the existing property. But we don't think they're the real cause of the acute trouble we face.'

'Tell him about the vans, Brian,' Jane said. Brian took a sharp intake of breath.

'Nasty business,' he said to Danny. 'Delivery vans making normal drops. Then they're accosted by a gang of… well, have you ever used Deliverangel?'

'Yeah,' Danny said. 'All the time at university. They're going after your vans? Why? To steal them?'

'It started off as boisterous stuff, but it's escalated. Last two weeks we've lost eight vanloads across the region. It's unsustainable losses.'

'What do you exactly mean by *lost,* Brian?'

'You familiar with western movies? The roads have become the Wild West. And we just can't get the drivers. Or the vans, for that matter. We're scraping the bottom of the barrel.'

'So you want me to drive your clapped out old vans in this lawless wilderness outside your door? Surely in the blue zones you should be safe. There's rules, right?'

'Like I said, it's not Yellowstone. They wouldn't do that. We think there's some kind of organisation with the Deliverangels. Hence, they're harassing our staff, damaging our vans, intimidating our customers. And the drivers are quitting. They see what's happening. And it's the old guard too. They just want a quiet life. The losses will tally up, and, well, look at this place. Well worn and rugged, right?'

'How can I help you, though?' Danny said.

'It's…' Brian said, glancing at Jane, who gave a subtle shake of her head. 'Your youth, for a start.'

'Did you apply for this job for me, Nan?' Danny asked Jane. He then turned to Brian.

'Not in that sense…'

'Nan, you brought home a form for me. I don't remember filling it in. Certainly not to be a punchbag for some punks on scooters. I just want some cash, bit of pocket money on top of my Basic.'

'She also told us you were interviewing with Yellowstone,' Brian said quickly. 'And you're fresh out of uni, barring that spell at Freshco's. The board is clamouring for new blood.'

'Did she now?'

'I did, Danny.'

'Anyway,' Brian said, taking hold of the conversation again. 'We think we can make you a better offer.'

'They put a lot of zeroes on a cheque in front of me, Brian. I don't mean to be rude, but this is all a bit embarrassing, really. My nan getting me a job. I'm twenty-seven years old.'

'It's more than the money though, isn't it? We want to look after our staff. They're valuable to us, especially now. We know you said no to them. Do you think they're just going to take that lying down? We're under pressure from all sides and yet we try, Danny. We try to give the Mertons experience people remember. What people know us for. What people might be prepared to pay for. A way of life,' he said, ending with a sigh. 'At least, that's what I tell myself every morning before I come in to firefight every day.'

Danny reclined in the chair. 'Certainly a different kind of pitch,' he said. Regarding the room, he saw photocopied notices, scuffed tables, a cathode-ray tube television with burned in branding from a decade of training presentations.

'Danny, give it a chance, at least,' Jane said. 'Come and work for us here.'

'You can be given your own office at a store of your choice, Danny,' Brian said. 'Through the graduate programme we have, we can—'

'I don't want you to make up a job for me,' Danny responded. 'The answer's no, Brian.' Brian's mouth fell open. Danny continued: 'I want to start at the bottom. Like everyone else. You need drivers, right?'

'Danny, no,' Jane said. 'It's too dangerous!'

He laughed. 'Nan, I don't need wrapping up in cotton wool, I'm not…'

'Think about it Danny, don't rule the graduate scheme out. It might be worth your while. But please take some time, Danny. But we can only wait a couple of days,' Brian said. 'Is that enough?'

'I think so, yes.'

***

That night the Cranston Arms pub was heaving with bodies.

'Come on, Henry,' Danny said over the din, 'get the drinks in!'

Henry fumbled for his phone. 'Trying,' he said.

'Could just go up and get 'em. Might be quicker,' Danny said. Henry looked up. 'Was it something I said?'

Henry scooched out of his seat and pocketed his phone. 'Twat. Oh, great,' he said, seeing Hailey appear in the doorway. She mooched over to their table. 'I'll go to the bar.'

He got up and sidled past his sister.

'Jeez,' Hailey said. 'Did he sit on a pin? Or something happen at cricket?'

'You heard, did you?'

'Big hotshot job at Yellowstone. And what happened to you?' Hailey said. 'You threw it in their faces.'

Danny sucked through his teeth. 'I had my reasons. Sometimes you have to stick with your guns and stick with what you know.'

'And what is that, Danny?'

'Nothing, for now. I've had another offer, though,' he said.

'Well, that's good,' she said.

'You had a lucky escape. Did they take the camera?'

'Yeah, but it was all backed up on the fly. It'll take a while to piece together,' she said. She glanced toward the busy bar. Henry was dancing on his tippy-toes, waiting to be served. 'He was pissed off. Thought I dragged the family name through the mud. Dad does that well enough on his own, but let's not talk about that.'

'Let's not, eh?'

'It was all bollocks, Danny,' she continued, unable to stop. 'Once you scrape past the big thick corporate icing on that cake. I think this is all surface level, anyway. For now. What about you?'

'Yeah, it looked great at first glance, but I dunno... I'd rather make a choice than have my arm twisted.' He caught Hailey's curious gaze. 'The offer was more a threat than an opportunity.'

'You and I could get on,' she said. 'Still, Yellowstone's great for ordering from,' she said. 'Just look at this cool bangle I got. And it was dirt cheap, got to mine within a couple hours.' She pulled up her sleeve. The metal ring around her arm reflected in the foggy light of the pub. 'I know they're evil, Yellowstone,' she said, 'but a girl's gotta have it from time to time, right?'

'How'd you even get away with that? I know where you live, Hailey. You're in a blue zone, just as I am. That's not possible. And how do you put that beside whatever it is you've found out about them?'

'Who says I have them deliver it in a van? We get Pro Plus on our Prime. Dad insists on it,' she said. 'They deliver by drone right to the doorstep. And anyway, like I give a shit what the neighbours think. Watch out,' she said, spotting Henry pacing his way back to the table. 'Here comes trouble.'

Henry placed the drinks on the table and resumed his seat. 'Bloody had me waiting,' he said, picking up his glass of wine.

Danny sipped his cider. 'Real tragedy,' he said.

'Let's not talk about tragedies,' Henry said. He didn't look at Danny. 'I'm disappointed, Danny. You could've really embarrassed me.'

'Henry,' Danny said, putting his drink down. 'Give over, alright.'

'This is what I don't get from you,' he said. 'You could've had it all at Yellowstone.'

'You have it, then,' Danny said. 'I don't think you can really lecture me about how much all this means to you.'

'They made me an offer,' Henry said. He smiled, his face an epithet of smugness. 'Not made any decisions yet, mind you.'

'Better or worse than what they offered me?'

'I don't know what they offered you,' Henry said. 'You wouldn't even open the letter.'

'I should've rolled it up, would've made it easier to stick it up your arse…'

'Guys!' Hailey snapped. 'I don't want to hear another word about this fucking job, alright?'

'Easy for you to say,' Henry said. 'Look, whatever. I'm gonna take a leak,' he said, getting up again.

'Sorry,' Danny said. 'It's just…'

'They made you a crappy offer, right?'

'It's not about the money, it's about… does family mean anything to you?'

Henry pitched his head toward Hailey. 'Believe me, it does. Back soon.'

'More than it does to him,' she said, 'but I get you. You didn't want to be a small cog in a huge machine. Neither did I. Not there, anyway. You saw what happened. He's not told dad yet, but when he does…'

'You had something to do with all that business? Hailey, shit, that's deep. Don't you know what you're doing?'

'It's going to go viral once I post it. I can't wait to see the look on his face. He was like a cabbage when I went over seventy-five?'

'What's that, subscribers? He told me about your Tubeview thing.'

Hailey laughed. 'Seventy-five *thousand*. The First Plaque is within my grasp. This expose on Yellowstone…'

'Wait, what?! What do you know?!'

Hailey hushed. 'Not now.'

'What about the company?'

'That's the point,' Hailey said. 'Henry thinks I'm stupid, but I know this is all some bullshit thing for Dad's attention. Dad's been taking a real interest in my TubeView thing. I thought he was an old fart, but show him some good numbers.'

'I've never met your dad. He seems terrifying to Henry.'

Hailey laughed. 'My dad? Terrifying? Nah. Henry just wants approval. Classic bigger brother. I came along and suddenly there're rations on dad's love.'

'Wow,' Danny said. 'I didn't know it was that bad.'

'So tell me,' Hailey said, straightening herself in the chair. 'This new offer? Anything good?'

'Mertons,' Danny laughed. 'I'll be taking my nan to work, it seems. And without being threatened in an interview.'

'You could do a lot worse,' she said. 'Look, take my number at least. If anything spicy comes up.'

'Spicy?'

'I'd like to talk to you about this, Danny. Without my brother around. See what happens,' she said, lowering her head. Danny saw a glimpse of her teeth as her lips curled just upwards.

'Alright then,' Danny said with a glint of a smile. They exchanged numbers.

Henry took his seat again. He took a sip of the now-warm drink.

'Danny,' he began.

'Something you want to say?'

Henry didn't rise. 'Sorry about all that, it's just…'

'Families, eh?' Danny said, raising his glass. Hailey chinked hers. Then Henry.

'Yeah, families,' Henry said, taking a glug. 'Next round's yours,' he said to Danny.

'Fine,' Danny said. 'We can celebrate my good news. And yours!'

'What's that?' Henry said as Danny got up to go to the bar. 'I don't want you to make a big deal out of what you might have heard—'

'I got a job offer. From Mertons. And I think I'm going to take it. Same again, yeah?'

CHAPTER 8

Margaret Hudson thought that day was just like any other day. She came down the stairs in the home they'd shared with their husband Martin, glancing at his photo on the mantelpiece.

Part of her daily ritual.

He was always the first thing she looked at. The second was the kettle in the kitchen. It was half full, enough for a couple of cups of tea. She flicked the switch,

'That's weird,' she said. The light on the kettle didn't come on. 'Come on!' Margaret said to the kettle, rocking the switch back and forth. Nothing. It was turned on at the plug.

Merry the cat mewed from the stairs as Margaret paced toward the front door. She ignored the pile of letters for now.

'Hey Gloria!' she called from the front garden to her neighbour who was in the adjacent garden in a dressing gown. 'You got electric there or not?'

'Everything's fine here, Margaret,' she said. 'Maybe check that card?'

'What card?' Margaret said. Gloria pointed to a card on Margaret's front door. 'Oh, right. Thanks Gloria.'

'You're welcome,' Gloria said as Margaret let the door close behind her.

MRS HUDSON – YOUR YELLOWSTONE PRIME HAS LAPSED. PLEASE USE THE YELLOWSTONE APP TO RESOLVE THIS

SITUATION AT ONCE.

Margaret screwed her face up. This must've been something to do with George. She reached for the cordless phone on the kitchen wall. She knew just enough to access the phonebook, but she couldn't find George's number. She pressed for a dial tone. None was forthcoming.

A serene but sinister synthetic voice trilled instead:

Please contact Yellowstone Telephony customer service to restore your service.

'George!' Margaret hissed. He'd set this up. She knew it. No power to brew a cup of tea. Now no phone. All connected to that Yellowstone company that had taken control three months ago. *I thought they just delivered parcels...*

Margaret pulled herself back upstairs and turned into the bathroom. She let the nightie droop around her saggy body into a pile on the floor. Her wrinkled hands turned the tap.

A gurgle of air came where the water should before a solitary, pathetic drop heaved itself over the crest of the tap and into the dry bathtub.

'Margaret cursed, 'This can piss right off!' Finding some clothes, she dressed herself and went back downstairs. She opened the front door again.

Gloria was still outside.

'Margaret,' she said.

'Gloria, I've got a bit of a problem. I can't get the electric to work, the phone's down the spout and I've got no water. Mind if I...'

'Oh,' Gloria bowed her head. 'I'd love to—'

'But?'

'We can't, sorry. It's all connected, you see.'

'To what?'

'Yellowstone Prime. Our account. It's for our personal use only, we get a big fine if—'

'What if you're neighbourly? This is ridiculous.'

'Sorry,' Gloria shrugged.

'Alright, alright,' Margaret said. Gloria scampered back inside her house. 'Bloody woman. What rubbish all that was.'

Margaret fished around the lounge for her bus pass. She knew there was money on that. She glanced at the clock. Twenty minutes until the next bus to town. Then she'd be able to call George and tell him what he could do with this Prime thing. *He can get rid, is what he can do.*

Then she looked at the pile of letters on the doormat that she'd stepped on. Bending down, she picked them up.

'Yellowstone Bank?' she said. 'What's this?'

Margaret opened the letter. Red numbers howled at her from the printed page. 'No, this can't be right?!' she said to herself, the words unable to hold on inside her mind.

The letter fell from Margaret's hand. She reached for her pass-key and shoved it into her bag. George had some explaining to do. She gathered the bag and slung it over her shoulder and went through the door. She pressed the key card to the lock pad on the outside of her front door. It buzzed like it always did when she left, then clicked resolutely closed.

Margaret checked her watch. Fourteen minutes. She hurried to the bus stop at the bottom of the road. She waited, eyeing the bend in the road where the bus would appear from. A digital board attached to the lamp post counted down the minutes, though most of the panel was just an advertising space.

Scan here to buy this on Yellowstone today! The ads all said.

Margaret wouldn't be scanning them, not after that.

The bus arrived and glided to a stop. Margaret climbed on.

'Tap there,' the driver pointed. Margaret did so. A red light and a hounding *bzzt*! Other people on the bus looked around.

'Sorry,' she said.

'You're not on Prime,' the driver said. He gestured to a sign below the cab door. *Prime Customers Only.*

'Please, look, I'm sorry—'

The driver held out a hand. 'Sorry. Rules are rules. Now if you don't mind…'

'Fine.' Margaret held her hands up. 'Poke your stupid bus!' She backtracked and stepped back on to the kerb. The doors to the bus closed, and it slid away with just the rumble of rubber on pavement.

Margaret put her card back to her front door. George would have to come round. Somehow. She'd write a note to that bag, Gloria.

Her card buzzed. Margaret pulled down on the lock. It didn't move. She looked, pressing the card again. The pad glared red.

'Great, now I can't get into my own bloody house,' she said. 'Just bloody brilliant.'

***

'Are you sure this is a good idea, sir?' Heaton McCall, Grayson Laurie's personal assistant, said with a tinge of reservation.

'Of course! I've heard great things about how the Zones are working.' Grayson Laurie said, throwing the last of his things into a slim leather bag. He draped the hoodie over the other hand. 'Come on,' he said.

Stepping outside the office, Grayson Laurie nodded to Wendy Tunt. 'Who's this?'

'Grayson, meet Grady from legal. He's coming with. You're going to be thrilled with how things are going in the Yellow Zones,' she said with a smile. 'Prime subscriptions are up nearly six-hundred percent, and—'

'Stop, stop, Wendy,' he said. 'I want to see it, not hear it.'

'As you wish,' she said. They entered the lift and descended into the depths of the building, and in a few minutes a gleaming Yellowstone corporate car careened out of the garage and onto the streets of the city, through the motorway and into the suburbs.

'How is our plan for enhancing the Prime offer?' he said to Tunt as the city disappeared in a blur outside the window.

'Good, we've got some meetings with the parliamentary committee in the diary.'

'Nothing untoward, I hope?'

'A formality,' Tunt smiled. 'Soon the test powers we bid for will be permanent, and we'll be able to go forward. You won't see a single citizen of this country without a Yellowstone branded something.'

'Any problems? Bumps in the road?'

'None whatsoever,' Tunt said. 'You can take that assurance to the bank.'

The corporate car slowed as it entered the neighbourhood, letting Laurie bask in the glory. The streets were pristine, with no litter or loose stones. Hedges immaculate. Houses brightly painted. A few joggers in lurid lycra sped past the car. Some pedestrians walked the other way, stopping to admire the car.

'Is that…?' one mouthed, pointing across the street.

'It can't be…' the other responded.

'Put the window down,' Laurie said. The driver lent forward. The window slid into the door.

'It is, I told you! Hello!' one of the pedestrians called.

'It's nice to see you,' Laurie called from the car. 'How're you finding life in this zone?'

'Fantastic, things have never been better!' the pedestrian said.

''Thanks,' Laurie said with a grin. 'You have a good day. And thank you for being loyal customers.' The window went back up and the car moved again. 'Find out who they are and give them a ten pound credit. For their enthusiasm,' Laurie said.

Tunt nodded at Grady, but neither wrote anything down. She tapped her tablet. A graph appeared on the screen. 'Performance has increased month by month. As has satisfaction and profit from subscribers.'

'And overhead?' Laurie said. 'Come on, Wendy, it's not like you to hide away from the bad news like that.'

'Up fifteen per cent. But given how we've taken over most civil functions…'

'Yes? You have an idea of doing it better?'

'Well, reduce the amount of human workforce for automation.'

'I'm not sure,' Grayson said. 'Big increase. And the tech's not flawless. I don't want this impacting how people see Yellowstone. Future replaced by robots everywhere?'

'It's the direction of travel.'

'I think we've a conversation to have that on another day,' Grayson said. 'Let's continue though.'

'Left please, driver,' Tunt said. The car turned at the end of the road into another immaculate street, though there were no pedestrians to be seen. No other cars. It was as if the street was asleep.

'Quiet today,' Grayson said. 'Almost too quiet. Is everyone at work?'

'I don't know,' Tunt said. 'Probably.'

'What about that woman? Look, she's sat on her front step,' Laurie said. 'Pull over. I want to talk to her.'

'If you're sure,' Tunt said through a frown.

'Might I advise we don't interact directly with the customers…' Grady hummed, shaking his head.

'I agree,' Tunt finished.

'Wendy, what could possibly go wrong?'

Laurie got out of the car and smiled toward the woman. 'Hello,' he said, offering out his hand. 'I'm Grayson Laurie, president of Yellowstone…'

'Right,' the woman said, shooting to her feet. 'You can tell me why I can't get in my house. Ever since that Prime thing… now I've got no power, no water and I can't go anywhere. Bloody bus driver said I had to have Prime to get the bus to town.'

Laurie took a step back, aghast. 'I'm… I'm sorry to hear that, miss…'

'Margaret Hudson. Bloody cheek, coming here in your fancy car. Even your bloody bank says I have no money. And I'm a pensioner!'

'Come on, Grayson,' Tunt urged. 'Let's go.'

'Er,' he said. 'We'll send someone to help!'

'Don't make promises!' Grady hissed, but the advice bounced off without hitting home.

'Will you, now?!' Margaret said. 'I'll tell you where you can poke that help, you—'

The car door slamming shut stopped her hectoring. Skidding away, Laurie glared at Tunt. 'What the hell was that all about?!'

'Mr Laurie,' the secretary said as the group walked through

the lift door, 'the committee are ready for you.'

'Great,' he said, stopping. He glared at Tunt. 'My office, afterward.'

'Let's not be hasty…'

'Are you trying to pull the wool over my eyes?'

'I don't know what you mean.'

'Fix it,' he said, walking into the room, but missing Tunt's icy glare boring into the back of his head. 'Grady,' he said, 'with me.'

The door to the boardroom opened.

'Hello gentlemen,' Laurie said, opening his arms. 'It's wonderful to see you.'

'You're chipper,' one of the men said, not getting up. 'I don't think it'll last very long.'

'Have we met?' Laurie said, letting his hand linger in the air, pointing at the man. 'I don't think we have, have we? Grady, do the honours.'

'This is Hector Steel, he's from the committee.'

'Which one, there's so many?'

'The Business and Regulatory Reform committee, Mr Laurie, and we have some… *concerns*.'

'Concerns? Please, tell me,' he said, sitting down.

'We've polled the Yellow Zones you're increasing your Prime rollout into,' Steel said. 'These charts are not encouraging.' He pushed some printed paper across the desk. Laurie pulled the sheets toward him.

'Are these charts bad?'

'Look at the titles. We think that while the consolidation of services from insolvent local authorities is admirable… you're creaming these people for all they have.'

'That's not true, I was assured that our pricing was fair and

100

competitive for the package offered. This,' Laurie said, pushing the chart away, 'I don't believe.'

'We know you're only recently ingratiated to the UK scenario, so we'll cut you some slack,' Steel said. 'This can't go on. The commission was founded to ensure equality. The Prime rollout as it stands seemed geared to lock people out if they don't buy in to you with all their worth.' Laurie nodded. 'We can't condone this, your vertical domination of the market is going to kill people.'

'Let's not talk in melodramatics,' Grady said. 'I don't think it'll come to that.'

'Have you provisioned for the lower-paid, or the less able?'

'Should we have?' Grady responded.

'Well, wait a minute,' Grayson held up a hand. He swivelled in his seat. '*Of course* you should have. Prime Lite? If what Steel is saying, the Prime rollout in Yellow Zones is price gouging. That wasn't the intention.'

'If there's a plus,' Steel said, taking a deep breath, 'the service quality is good. Very good, in fact.'

'I'm pleased,' Grayson said. 'We try to innovate.'

'We can't endorse your latest proposals, though,' Steel said. 'What you're proposing isn't fair. People are entitled to a basic standard of living, regardless of how much they contribute to you. When it was the previous system, some services were deemed necessities, and now people can't access this.'

'If I may,' Grady said as Laurie took a breath. 'All this was allowed,' he said. 'You didn't have a problem with this when we agreed to this stage of the transition.'

'Parliament won't have it if you carry on,' Steel said.

'We'll just see what Parliament has, shall we?' Grady said. 'The Basic Income plan has come close to bankrupting this country, has it not?'

'I'm not here to discuss—'

'And I think you'll find we're totally compliant on all tax and compensation rules, too. As you *always* seem to bring that up.'

'Excuse me just a moment,' Grayson said. He leant toward Grady. 'What was that? I thought it was agreed that there'd be some basic access. For those that Mr Steel here is talking about.' He leant in and growled at Grady. 'Like what I saw about an hour ago, need I remind you.'

'It was that model that led the local authorities to where we are. We're just enabling your vision, sir,' Grady said, sitting back in the chair. 'Apologies for my… vigour in defending our vision to these people.'

Laurie turned to Steel. 'I take your feedback on board. We'll… we'll sort it.'

Steel smiled, relishing the moment of seeing one of the world's richest and most powerful men squirm. 'Excellent,' he said. 'I'm glad I could impress that upon you.'

'The pleasure is all mine,' Laurie said, following Grady and Steel out. Steel made for the lift and disappeared. The hallway was empty. Beyond the plate-glass windows, the sunny vista of the city streamed into the lobby. 'Do you have *any* idea how embarrassing that was for me?! For this company?!'

'We simply followed your orders.'

'Followed my orders?!' Laurie said. He threw open the door to an empty office and bundled Grady inside. 'You made up my orders and made me look like a right ass! Now I don't know who gave you the set of balls you so stupidly showed in that meeting, but if you don't cut that out, it'll be yours I'm after. Are we clear?'

Grady swallowed, the lump travelling down his throat. 'Perfectly, sir.'

CHAPTER 9

Brian smiled as Danny entered the office above the store. 'Danny,' he said. 'I'm glad we could come to an agreement.'

'Me too,' Danny said.

'So, we need to go over the details. You probably saw my email.'

'As I said,' Danny waved. 'I don't want the special treatment. I'm still not sure why you're offering to fast track all this…'

'Er, as I told you, we can give graduates additional steps in their careers. In fact, we've already had a couple step on. I know I broached this with you?'

'Yeah, well, I want to go in at the bottom. As if I was anyone else. Which I am, by the way,' Danny said. 'I'm not above doing the donkey work. Relax,' he said, seeing Brian about to speak. 'A crap job is a job.'

'None of our roles are, as you say, crap,' Brian laughed. 'I like you, Danny. Obviously, your pay will be…'

'The same as everyone else's.'

'You sure? I know we can't match the offer you had from—'

'I said I want what the others have. No more. No less.'

Brian shrugged. 'Suit yourself. Come and meet Elaine, who'll get you all set up.'

Danny followed Brian into another room, where a frumpy blonde lady sat at a desk. 'Here's your uniform, two name tags and your Mertons ID,' she said, pointing to a pile of plastic-wrapped items on a chair. 'Welcome to Mertons,' she said.

'Thanks,' Danny said, scooping up the uniform and lanyard.

'Danny, go into the locker room here and change. Meet me in a bit in the canteen and we'll introduce you to your service leader.'

'What, no induction for me today?'

'You can sit and stare at that television if you want, but we both know that's not necessary now, is it?'

Danny laughed. 'Start as we mean to go on.'

***

Emerging a few minutes later resplendent in blue and grey polyester, Danny walked into the canteen.

'Very nice,' Brian said. 'Now, as for your nan,'

'Please,' Danny said. 'Don't say it like that.'

Brian chortled once. 'She's just another colleague here. We don't scorn at family relations, but neither do we want accusations of… bias. Impropriety. That sort of thing. Hurts what the customers feel about us. And that matters.'

'Right.'

'Now, about your role. We need you on the delivery team. High risk, so you get an extra quid an hour.

'I'll do it. No questions asked.'

'Great,' Brian said. He looked across from Danny to a man with a goatee who'd just entered the room. 'Hey, Rick!'

Danny turned his head. A goateed man in a navy shirt was walking toward him.

'This Danny?' the man said. 'Hi, I'm Rick, the service leader for you. I hear you're going to be joining our delivery team,' he said.

'Yeah. How'd you know already?'

'Brian gave me the lowdown. Just a bit about you. It's hard to keep hold of people these days. Shall we?' Rick gestured.

'Danny, Rick'll look after you. We'll catch up soon.'

'Come on,' Rick said. 'I'll introduce you to the lads.'

Danny followed Rick out of the canteen to the shop floor. It was a cavernous, dark space filled with racking.

'Not much in,' Danny said.

'Times are tough. I've been here thirteen years and never seen it so bad. We're lucky we have what we have. This all used to be regular shelving, but like Brian probably told you, the company's trying to play catch up.'

'You're trying to match Yellowstone?'

'Don't say that word!' Rick said, stopping on the spot. 'They're the enemy. I saw this place years ago, before all the stuff happened. People pushing trolleys. Our guys in with them. Now it's all online, it's like it crept up on us. Now,' he said, walking again. 'I'll show you to the hub. You'll meet your partner, who you'll be delivering with. They always go out in pairs now.'

'Why's that?' Danny asked.

'I don't want to scare you, but for reasons that make this job difficult. A bit dangerous too.'

'The missing vans?'

'We've lost twelve over the last eight months. Stuff coming in and coming out. It's the drivers we're losing I'm worried about. Good people giving the job up. I won't lie,' Rick said, walking along the racking, 'it might happen to you. Hey,' he called, reaching the end of the corridor. Plastic boxes stacked with bags of groceries and sundried lay on wheeled pallets. 'Sparky! Get over here!'

A man in a bright high-viz jacket turned and walked over. 'Piss off Rick, think you're the boss of me,' he said jovially. 'Who's this?'

'Danny, meet Sparky,' Rick said. 'And, Danny, I am your boss, as good as. You about ready to head out?'

'Sparky?'

'His real name is…' Rick started.

'Don't you dare!' Sparky said. 'Sparky's the name I go by here. You're the Danny I was told about.'

'Wow,' Danny said. 'It's like I'm famous.'

'Or stupid to take this job!'

'Only two vans?' Danny said, counting the vans under the shelter just outside.

'We have the vans we have,' Sparky said. 'Just gotta finish loading up and we're on the road.'

'We?' Danny said.

'Yeah,' Sparky said, slapping Danny on the shoulder. 'you and me, Danny. Let's load up.'

'Sparky'll look after you, thought it best we throw you right in,' Rick said. 'Sparky, a word?' he gestured.

'Danny,' Sparky said, 'just wheel those dollies out and we'll crack on. Won't be a minute.'

Danny did so. He noticed the plastic trays were filled with a variety of goods and packages, some plastic bags, some cardboard boxes with branding he'd never heard of.

'I thought Mertons was a supermarket?'

'I dunno what it is any more,' Sparky said, hefting one of the trays into the van. 'Now we deliver for all and sundry. Those that don't wanna pay the tax. It pays the bills.'

Danny wanted to ask about *the tax,* but thought better of it. *A Yellowstone thing.* 'Do you know what any of this is?' Danny said, heaving the next tray and passing it to Sparky.

'Not my job to know. Just to get it to people. That's what they pay for.'

108

'Can you believe that?' Sparky said as he and Danny trooped down from the block of flats they'd just delivered to. 'Did you see the label?'

'I thought that sort of thing was meant to be hidden for modesty?'

'Her face, mate!' Sparky laughed. 'She'll be doing a lot more than smirking later.'

Danny laughed, getting back into the van with a sigh. The doors clattered closed once more. Sparky turned the key, the engine bursting into throaty life.

'Next job?' he asked.'

'I'll punch it in,' Danny said, leaning forward. His high-viz jacket crinkled. The little screen beeped. Sparky drove, and the van soon crossed onto the open road.

'Great weather, right?'

Danny had retracted the window. 'Do you remember what it was like? What was it, eight years ago?'

'Don't remind me,' Sparky grimaced. 'Whole thing was a massive pain in the arse. You couldn't have been long outta school?'

'I'm old enough to remember,' Danny said. He sat back in the seat, watching the little chevron on the chunky GPS map move around the screen.

But something twigged his ears, and he sat up. 'What's that?' He glanced at Sparky, whose face had already frozen.

'Trouble,' Sparky said. He nodded at the side mirror. 'Look.'

Streaks of pink appeared behind the van.

'Who are they?'

'The competition,' Sparky said, gripping the wheel. A cacophony of tinny, buzzing engines erupted from behind. It chased the van and four streaks of pink zoomed in front.

'Deliverangels? They're the trouble?'

'The very sort,' Sparky said. 'Hold on.'

'They look harmless.'

'Don't be silly,' Sparky said.

Splat! Splat-splat!

The van whinnied.

'Whoa!' Sparky said, gripping the wheel. The tyres whined. With a squeak and a heave of the little electric pump, the screen turned from a cloudy, eggy mess to something remotely see through. The van bobbed as Sparky pulled over, lashing it onto the kerb. 'Bastards!'

'You alright?' Danny said.

'Fine,' Sparky hissed, pushing the door open. 'Could've been way worse. Let's clean this up and get moving.'

The delivery run with Sparky was hard work, but rewarding, and the six hour drive sped by. By sunset, the van purred back into the yard and backed into the loading bay.

'You did good today, Danny,' Sparky said. 'Couldn't have managed that sixth floor flat at Chivron Tower without you. Big old bloody box, that was.'

Danny laughed. 'Pisstake there being no lift.'

'Classic council, though, right? Why fix the lift if there's still stairs? That old dear looked like she hadn't left for weeks. Not even our patch, but Rick and Brian want us to go over and above. Ever since…'

'Since what?' Danny asked.

'Upper Hedingbury. I knew people there. It was rough.'

'What happened?'

'I'll… tell you some other time.'

Danny nodded, not wanting to probe an obvious sore point.

The van stopped under the shelter. Danny got out. 'Hey Rick.'

'Danny!' Rick said, coming down a tiny flight of metal steps from the office. Rick looked at Sparky. 'He did good?'

'He did good,' Sparky confirmed.

'Top man,' Rick said. 'Look, you remember what we talked about earlier? About tomorrow?'

Sparky laughed at Danny. 'Sacking you already, sunshine.'

'What's happening?' Danny asked.

Sparky went *ugh*. 'Ask him,' he nodded at Rick.

'You're needed elsewhere. I've been on the blower. It's got worse,' Rick said, this time just to Sparky.

Danny watched Sparky's face drop. 'You going to tell me where, then? You didn't mention that earlier.'

'Elsewhere.'

'Lower Crayford,' Rick said, holding out his hands. 'I'm sorry, I'm sorry.'

'You'd better be!' Sparky said. 'That place is a tip. A real dive. Sorry, Danny,' Sparky hummed.

'Stay here for a couple of weeks. Learn the ropes. But you'll be over there in a fortnight. Shit's hit the fan, Brian's orders. Hands tied.'

'How long for?' Sparky said.

'As long as it takes,' Rick said. 'But hopefully a few days, max.'

Sparky walked out back onto the shop floor. Danny followed. He hadn't heard of Lower Crayford. 'Where's that?'

'Other side of the city. Riverside. Usually getting into shit. And…'

'And?'

'There's usually trouble. And we usually are the ones to fix it. Come on,' he said, 'we've got a job to do.'

Danny walked down the path to his car. A few specks of rain fell from the sky and onto his skin. 'Great,' he said. 'Of all the days.'

He got into his car and felt his phone buzz. He pulled it out, smiling. A text from Hailey:

You free to talk tonight?
About the stuff?

                              I'm still interested.
                                After work today?

Sounds good.

He pocketed his phone, still wondering what Hailey was digging about, then set off for Kier Wood.

Sparky was waiting by the staff entrance as Danny walked round from the car park. 'Don't bother going in,' he said. 'We're going over to Lower Crayford right away.'

Danny followed Sparky into the building. 'You sure they won't miss a van?'

'It's all cleared. This sorta shit doesn't happen on a whim,' he said. 'Get in, I'll drive.'

Danny did, and the van roared out of the yard and down the ramp onto the main road.

'I tell you,' Sparky said, 'that nice weather wouldn't last. Had to cancel my holiday.'

'Were you going anywhere nice?' Danny asked.

'Family had a place down the coast. Down Selsey way.'

'Wasn't that hit by the—'

'Not quite, Danny. Selsey missed the worst. Not that it matters anyway. I get to spend my time away at another arsehole of the world.'

'It can't be that bad,' Danny said.

'Just you wait.'

Forty minutes later, the van rocked to a stop. 'We're here,' Sparky said.

Danny regarded the store he stood in front of. 'What a dump,' he said.

'Rick told me last night that there was some new store manager, found the place in chaos. First thing he did was the hive plan.'

'What's that?'

'We all pitch in to pull the store together. Until it happens somewhere else. It's like a cycle.'

'Seems inefficient.'

'Yeah, but written into bones of the company. All one team. Anyway, let's go inside.' Sparky led the way through the car park.

Lower Crayford was built of bricks lined with sheet panelling that, at one point in the distant past, was white; now it was stained with grime and fumes. The entrance stood on the corner of the store under a metal and glass greenhouse. Danny glanced up as he entered and made the awkward turn through the doors and around a sharp two-seventy pivot into the store, past people pushing trollies of goods out. The glass was filthy, caked with grime and moss.

Sparky walked forward to the security podium. 'Alright boss,' he said to the guard. 'Where's the fire?'

'Good to see you boys,' Rick said.

'Must be bad if they've got *you* over here, too.'

'Watch your lip, or I'll let him drive,' Rick said.

'Really?' Danny said back.

'Don't see the harm. It's a van, not a battleship.' Rick laughed and looked at Sparky. 'Go up to the training room. Henry'll assign you.'

'Who's Henry?'

'Rick said that a hotshot graduate was filling in for a couple of weeks. Quite a character. Fits right in.'

Danny followed Sparky up into the private area of the store.

'Wait here,' Sparky said. 'Gonna use the facilities.'

'Alright,' Danny said. Sparky disappeared into the cloakroom. Down the corridor, he heard a voice on the phone.

'Dad, it's not a demotion. I told you…' the voice said. Danny paced toward an open door down the corridor. The voice got louder. Clearer. Danny rounded the doorway.

'Blimey,' he said.

'I've gotta go!' the voice said, putting the phone down.

'What happened to the big new job, Henry?' Danny laughed. 'How the mighty have fallen. Graduate programme shoved you in at the deep end?'

'I'm filling a hole temporarily, and anyway, just shut up,' Henry said, 'and get to work!'

Danny laughed, turning. 'I'm going, don't you worry.'

'That someone you know?' Sparky said.

'You could say that. Friend of mine. Surprised to see him here, of all places.'

'All about the new blood,' Sparky said. 'Let's load up and get out of here. They've just showed me the manifest. Fourteen thousand items.'

'Blimey,'

'All picked, waiting to hit the road. Might be bumpy, Danny,' Sparky said. 'Not like yesterday.'

'Guess we'll cross that bridge when we come to it,' Danny said.

The loading dock was awash with a chaotic cacophony of containers.

'What a fucking mess,' Sparky said. 'Not the first time this has happened, Danny. It's why I'm glad you're here,' he heaved, picking up one of the crates destined for the van they'd be taking. 'Fucking shithole, the whole place. Right, you good to get those last few on?'

Danny heaved himself. 'Yeah. Beats the gym, this,' he said.

'Definitely. Right,' Sparky said, eyeing up the last crate on the dolly. 'That'll do us.' He lifted it roughly.

'Careful,' Danny said. Sparky walked forward, missing the empty dolly that rolled in front of him.

'I'll be - fuck!' Sparky yelped with a crack of bone. The tote dropped with a thud, clattering to the floor. 'Fucking hell!'

'Christ,' one of the other guys said. 'What did we tell you, Sparks?'

'Shut up,' Danny said. 'He's hurt. You alright?' he asked Sparky who had tumbled to the floor.

'Back's killing me,' he said, trying to get up. He failed.

'That's more than a bloody bad back! Did you not hear that crack?'

'Fuck,' Sparky said. 'Missus is going to kill me for this.'

'Why?'

'She's been telling me to take it easy for weeks,' he moaned.

'Stay there,' Danny said, picking up an empty crate and upending it. He helped Sparky sit against the wall on the end of the crate. 'Wait there.'

'We've gotta go,' Sparky winced.

'You can't go anywhere,' Danny said. He cast his eyes around the loading dock. 'Anyone wanna help?'

The four guys shrugged.

'We've got our own vans, sorry man.'

'Fine,' Danny huffed, picking up the dropped crate. 'I'll do it myself.'

The other lads *ooooohed*.

'Danny, don't!' Sparky said. 'It's a rough run. It needs two people.'

'Well, I'll just have to deal with it, won't I? Seeing as no other plank's willing to step in.'

'Hey,' one of the other lads said. 'It's not like we don't want to! But you need to be signed off to drive on one of those.'

'And you've not been signed off, Danny, not yet anyway,' Sparky said. 'It's not worth the risk.'

'You talk like it's going into war. It's driving a van,' Danny said. 'Rick said I could drive, anyway.' He heaved the last tote into place and banged the door shut. 'This shit's gotta go out. What was it the company stood for again?'

'Shit,' Sparky heaved. 'Guess you're right, Danny. He did say. But be careful. Keys are in the ignition. You sure?'

'Got the sat-nav, the manifest, and my brain. I'll be fine,' Danny said, clambering into the cab. 'Cheers guys,' he said. The engine roared to life in a vibration of diesel energy. 'See ya when I see ya.'

'Watch yourself, Danny,' Sparky said. 'Roads are funny at this time of day.'

The van roared out of the dock and onto the slip road.

***

Danny threw the van doors closed later that day. It was getting empty. Danny cruised the van down the road. In the rear-view mirror, the setting sun glowed orange, disappearing behind the horizon. The light filtered into the cab, casting a rusty glow over the synthetic plastic. Tinny music popped through the speakers in the door.

Reaching for his phone mounted to the centre console, Danny swiped. Next track. No traffic.

'Crap,' he said, sitting back up. Shadows appeared in the rear-view mirror.

Turn left, then next right. Your destination will be on your left. The sat-nav next to his phone trilled through a collection of assembled clips. Danny lent a finger on the indicator stalk and clicked. The light flashed with the *blink-blonk* of the repeater. He slowed the van, the diesel engine roaring as his foot pressed down on the clutch.

Rounding the corner, Danny glanced in the side mirror. The shadows had disappeared. He crawled along, looking for the house. No lights on. A lot of the houses had patchy, overgrown front lawns. Litter everywhere. Plastic toys strewn among the long grass. Dirty siding and cladding, with the occasional missing roof tile.

'Nice part of town,' Danny mused to himself. 'Maybe I'll move in. Here we go.'

The van stopped. Danny killed the engine. The not-so-silence of a suburban evening filled the void the throaty roar of the diesel engine had left behind. Distant planes flying overhead. The movement of the wind. Fuzzy, far-away TVs blaring through block-work walls.

Danny opened the rear of the van, looking at his manifest. Eight crates to drop. *Easy*, he thought. *Last job of the day.*

The metal trolley rattled as it hit the tarmac. Heaving, Danny managed to get four of the crates onto it. He heaved even more, trying to get it up the kerb, but managed it, pulling it up the weeds toward a front door that desperately cried for a paintbrush.

It swung open.

'Wozzat?' the grisled woman in a tracksuit uttered. Her hair moved in a tight ponytail. The light shone off the grease.

'Delivery,' Danny said. 'Sorry, we didn't have—'

'Useless, you lot,' the woman said. 'Go on, go get the rest,' she ordered to Danny. 'Mercedes! Alfie! Geddown here!' she called into the dank pit of the house beyond the door.

Danny needed no encouragement and turned the trolley down the path back toward the van. He swung the door open and climbed in. The other four crates looked lonely. They rattled as he manhandled them out of the storage shelves and scraped along the floor.

The scraping shrouded the high-pitched buzz as the shadows approached.

Danny turned at the threshold of the van door. A rabble of six shadows on mopeds stood waiting.

'Can I help you guys?' Danny asked, jumping down. He turned back to the van to pull one of the crates out.

'Leave that right where it is,' one of the helmeted figures said. 'It's ours now.'

Danny laughed. 'What're you on about?'

'Look at him, Iceblue,' one of the riders laughed. 'He must be greener than he is blue!'

The helmeted figure in the middle stood forward, pulling the hard, round helmet off. A shock of dark hair erupted from the helmet. The figure wore a dark covering across his face but a pair of icy blue eyes shot out in the evening sun.

Danny regarded the face for a moment, seeing shadows and lines across the visage. He placed this man at about ten years his senior.

'Like I said,' Iceblue said, 'that lot's ours.'

'Quick! Get inside!' the woman said to her son, throwing her door closed with a bang. The rest of the street stood deserted.

'Nah, not today,' Danny said. 'I'm doing a job.'

'So are we,' the figure said. 'Bailey, Angel,' he said over his shoulder. Two of his comrades moved. 'Start us off.'

Danny ducked as the two riders pounced on him but missed the ground. He was caught on the first rider's fist. 'Fuck!'

'You two,' Iceblue indicated to his other comrades. 'The van.'

'No!' Danny called but was greeted in response with a kick. Squirming, he watched. The four goons tore the crates out of the van, upending them on the street. The contents spilled. Liquid - milk, laundry fluid and soda pop, burst into the gutter. 'What're you doing this for?'

Iceblue turned. 'You picked the wrong team. I've been doing this longer than you, kid. You want my advice?'

'Not really,' Danny said.

'Have it anyway. Free gift. Get the hell out here and learn your lesson. Because things just get *worse* from here.'

'Whadda ya wanna do about this,' Angel yelled. He held up the manifest. 'Could be useful?'

'Keep it,' Iceblue murmured. 'But torch the van. You've got the stuff.'

Angel jumped down as the others pulled the van apart inside. He walked to his parked bike and pulled a soda bottle through of light yellow fluid. Walking back, he made contact with Danny.

'Don't try anything heroic, man,' Angel said, laughing. The fluid stunk as it coated the inside of the van. 'Do it, Bailey.'

Danny looked past the group to the house. The door was open. Alfie and his mother cowered.

'Call the fucking police!' Danny yelled.

Iceblue pivoted to face the door. 'Don't you dare!'

The door slammed shut.

The other rider pulled a silver lighter from one of his many pockets and flicked it. Once. Twice. On the third strike, the flame emerged, and the square of metal flew through the air.

Danny leapt up, wincing. The five riders cackled as the flame erupted from the back of the van. He launched at the back of Iceblue, pushing him down. *Thwack!* Iceblue's forehead hit the metal step on the top of the van.

'Fucking hell!'

The four others stopped.

'What did ya just do?!' Angel yelled.

'He scored against Ice,' the other said.

Iceblue wailed in pain. 'Fucking teach him a lesson!'

The four others pulled Danny to the ground. The punches rained down like a summer shower. His face. His legs. His arms. His chest.

Danny saw the world turn from the orange of sunset to the static grey, fading in and out. His head throbbed. His face was blowing up. Eventually he slowed, the will to fight back seeping out.

Distantly, sirens blared.

'Scram!' Iceblue ordered. The four others dropped their implements and ran.

Iceblue rounded on Danny, visible through what was left of his eyes. He knelt to Danny's prone level.

'You think you're pretty clever, huh? Learned a lesson, right?'

Danny hissed through his teeth, but didn't say anything. Instead, he swallowed, hard. 'What's that?' Iceblue continued, 'got something to say?'

Danny did. He sniffed hard, hocking back and opened his

mouth. With a wet slap, the ball of spit hit Iceblue right across what was visible in his face.

The sound of plastic and laminate burning, the scrabbling of feet on the rough tarmac, even the wind and the sirens… all of that paled into silence.

Iceblue wiped his face. Then he hauled Danny to his feet before dumping him on the pavement. His fist filled Danny's view.

'If I weren't told not ta,' he growled, 'I'd fucking *end* you for that.'

'If you weren't such a bitch,' Danny said, 'you'd do it anyway.'

Iceblue's eyes widened. The cobalt colour burned like plasma.

'Don't do it, Ice!' Bailey called. 'He ain't worth it. None of those scum are. He's just a punk kid!'

'That's right,' Iceblue said. 'Just some punk chancer. Remember what I told you, kid. Learn from this one and maybe I won't see you again. Might be better for you!' Iceblue gave Danny a shove, hard, backwards onto the pavement before mounting his scooter and disappearing into the sunset from whence he'd come.

CHAPTER 10

Sparky peered into the brown sunset. The violet night was fast creeping over Kier Wood. 'He's still not back,' he said. Past the ramp, down to the street, the night swept across the road. 'Something must've happened.'

'Easy,' Rick said. 'Let's not jump to conclusions.'

'He was travelling through a rough part of town,' Sparky said. 'Alone. I told you this would happen. It's too dangerous now.'

'He was brave, going out like that alone,' Rick said. 'He knew the risks of what's out there.'

'Will you shut up, Rick, talking about him like he's dead?'

'I'm just saying.'

'Yeah,' Sparky said, 'but if anyone's started on the kid, I'll be the one to finish it.'

'Come on,' Rick said, peeling away from the view down the ramp. 'Whatever's happened, he'll walk away from it. If he got jumped… we've not lost anyone that bad. Not yet.'

'You hope so,' Sparky said, continuing to lean on the metal barrier. 'You better bloody hope so. There's something about that guy,' he murmured. 'He could play it big.'

'How'd you mean?' Rick asked, peering carefully at his colleague. 'What's he said?'

'Nothing. Just a feeling, ya know. World's going to shit, but Danny? He's a good guy, and we need to look after people like that.'

Hailey paced around her room, phone in hand. She'd left the messages app open, the draft sitting there unsent.

She'd not heard from Danny all day. Her messages had remained on one grey tick.

The phone buzzed. A picture message appeared. Hailey's stomach dropped. She erased the draft and her fingers fused across the glass surface, tapping wildly.

`Where are you?`

> `Ward A6, St Helga's Hospital.`
> `I'll be okay.`

`I'm coming to see you.`

> `No need.`

`No stopping me.`

Hailey cringed. *Too strong.* Then a few seconds passed. Three animated dots appeared on the screen.

`Ok.`

***

The imposing form of the hospital loomed on the murky skyline. Years ago, it'd once been painted white; now the finish, tarnished by decades of pollution and grime, flaked off in plasterwork scabs. The structure was a filthy iceberg in an ocean of pitted and undulating asphalt.

Hailey parked as close as she could and trooped under a walkway into an entrance on the side of the building, punching through its very side. A wide corridor led straight ahead. Dirty lights shone the beige paint to almost yellow, with the green high-lights muted almost to brown. A-wing was at the far end, and she started the brisk walk.

'Typical,' she said, seeing the OUT-OF-ORDER sign taped to the scuffed lift door. 'Are you alright for the stairs?'

She followed signs that led to a great, wide stairwell that wrapped around and began the climb up six floors of anticipation.

She arrived on the sixth floor and followed the door. A variety of beeping noises replaced the echoing footsteps.

'Can I help?' a nurse said from the station just opposite the ward door. 'Visiting hours are about to close, but I can…'

'It's okay,' Hailey said. 'Danny Price. He texted me, said he was here. His nan's making her way up the stairs.'

The nurse looked through her papers. Her hair was unkempt, and her smock creased. 'Forgive me, it's been another day.' She then stopped. 'Yes, Danny's in bed 7. What relation are you to him, his girlfriend?'

Hailey's mouth was agape for just a moment. 'Yes, that's right. I'm his girlfriend.'

She followed the little flag signs on the doors until she reached a room containing four beds, only one of which was occupied.

Bed 7

'Hey,' she said to the bruised figure. 'You look rough. What happened?'

'Just a scrape,' Danny coughed. 'Oh, who am I kidding? They beat the shit out of me. Torched the van, too.' Danny tried to laugh but only ended up wincing through deep-rooted pain. 'Guess I'm out of the cricket then.'

Hailey approached the bed. 'I was so worried when I heard you'd not made it back. Everyone was. Well, almost everyone.'

'Did they send a search party out?'

'Henry said that guy you work with…'

'Sparky, yeah?'

'Yeah, him. He wanted to bust out and go find you. But they told him no. Then when the police…'

'Ah, yes,' Danny yawned, suppressing the wince of pain as he shuffled in the bed. 'Our faithful servants. Took them an age to turn up, and even then they were clueless.'

'They showed up though. That's something.' Danny hummed at her sceptically. 'Look, Danny… I think there's some serious shit going on.'

'Yeah? Look,' he said, leaning forward. 'Mind puffing my pillow.'

'Sure,' she said, doing so. Footsteps approached outside.

'Danny!' Jane said, sweeping into the room. 'My goodness, what happened?!'

'Bad people, Nan,' he said. 'Look,' he said as his nan approached. 'Give me and Hailey a minute before you start making a fuss.'

Jane's mouth hung open, but no words came out. 'Okay,' she said.

Danny watched her leave before turning back to Hailey. 'You were saying?'

'Yellowstone are about to fire a load of their workers. These gangs are terrorising the blue zones… where does it end?'

'Where indeed.'

'I think they're connected,' Hailey said. 'Random gangs on bikes don't do that, shit. Someone's paying them.'

'Did you bring your tin foil hat?' Danny laughed. 'That'd make good TubeView content.'

She laughed too. 'I mean it.'

'I know,' he said. He yawned again.

'How long are they keeping you?'

'Couple days,' he said. 'Till the bruises go down.'

'Okay,' she said, getting up. 'I'll let you sleep.'

'No, please,' Danny said, trying to sit up but collapsing into the pillow. 'Come back. Tomorrow.'

'Okay,' she said. 'Want me to just come and sit with you?'

'That'd be… that'd be nice.'

'Has Henry offered?'

'Not that I know.'

'Okay. See you, then, Danny.'

'Wait!' he called again as she rounded the door. 'Maybe once I'm better…'

'You'd want to hang out?'

'Yeah, if you want to.'

'I want to, Danny.'

'Okay then,' he smiled, and she disappeared from the ward.

Outside, Jane caught her.

'A concerned friend, right?' she said. 'My eyes are on you, lady.'

'Honestly, Ms Price—'

'My name isn't Price,' Jane corrected. 'It's complicated.'

'Aren't all families?'

'I suppose,' she said. 'I'm just looking out for my grandson.'

'And a fine job you're doing,' Hailey said. 'I've not known Danny that long, but believe me, I want to look out for him, too.'

Jane nodded, not knowing how else to react, before rounding the corner into the ward.

Danny was waiting outside the Pizza Champion restaurant after finally getting out of the hospital. She smiled as he approached.

'Hey.'

'Hey yourself,' Hailey said. She glanced up and down. Underneath the hoodie and jeans was purple flesh and puffy eyes obscured by a messy do of hair. 'You look…'

'Like I've been beaten the shit out of. I know.'

'Better than when you were in the hospital,' she said.

Danny laughed. 'I'm dying to eat, shall we?' he pointed to the door.

'Yeah!'

They walked in and sat down. The place was just a hair over subdued. A third of the tables were empty - not even set for customers.

'Things are getting bad,' she said. 'Everywhere.'

'Well,' he stretched, wincing. 'I know all about things going from bad to worse. Go get a nice little job and I end up with the shit beaten out of me. You're allowed to laugh, you know.'

Hailey's cracked face erupted. He smiled too.

'Look,' Danny said. 'Place to ourselves, almost. Romantic. Working on that girlfriend position, after all?'

'What?!'

'Don't worry,' Danny said. 'My nan told me what you said to the nurse.'

'She didn't did she?!'

'It's okay.'

'I mean, maybe?' Hailey hesitated. 'We're new friends getting to know each other. You and Henry both have new positions. Maybe we'll see where things go.'

'Good,' he said. 'I like that. I dunno why Henry hid you away. Wish we'd met sooner.'

'That's my brother for you.'

'Ah, yeah…'

'I wind him up,' she laughed. 'Which is probably why we haven't. He wasn't too keen on tonight.'

'Just friends getting to know each other,' Danny said.

'Right!'

'I think he's pissed off with me. We had a… philosophical disagreement. Over the whole Yellowstone business.'

'Yeah,' she said. The waiter placed two pizzas in front of them. 'Did you speak to him?' she asked.

Danny gave a quizzical look. He winced. The motion hurt. 'Shit!'

'Sorry!' she said, but Danny laughed.

'He spoke to me for a couple of minutes. I think I pissed him off.'

'By taking the job?'

'By losing the van.'

'I think he should marry it, personally,' she said. Danny laughed again. 'I'm surprised he gives so much of a shit.'

'Why'd you say that?'

'He's desperate to please dad. Like, palpably. It's almost sad in a way.'

'Aren't you?' Danny asked between mouthfuls. 'Wanting to please your dad?'

'Sure, but I don't try as obviously as Henry. I think it comes down to us being kids. He hated me taking dad's attention from him.'

Danny's eyes widened. 'Henry is Henry after all.'

'He is,' Hailey said. They finished the meal over chatter about anything that wasn't her brother. Games. Films. Books. Goofy videos on internet.

'I'm stuffed,' he said, pushing his plate away.

'Me too,' she said. A few minutes passed. The table was

cleared, and the waiter presented the bill. Hailey reached into her little bag for her purse.

'No,' Danny said. 'Let me.'

Hailey laughed. 'Nah, I'll pay. It's not a date if the woman pays, now, is it?'

Danny shook his head to hide his grin. 'It ain't, is it? Maybe…'

'Yeah?' Hailey said. Their eyes met. 'Maybe, eh, Danny?'

'Maybe I'll get the next one in, is what I was going to say.'

They exchanged long looks. Hailey felt her stomach do somersaults, and not just because Danny had ordered pineapple on his pizza.

BZZT. BZZT. BZZT.

Her phone trilled, breaking the mood. She reached into her bag and pulled it out.

'What do you want?'

'You home yet?' Henry said.

'I'll be home when I'm home.'

'You know the rule.'

Hailey hung up. The clock on her phone blared into her retinas. 'I suppose we'd better end this.'

'That's a shame,' he said, getting up with a heave. 'I've really enjoyed this. And we haven't even mentioned Yellowstone.'

'You're right,' she said. 'We need to talk about that soon. Like, really soon.'

'I think we can work that out.'

'You need a lift?' she asked.

'I'll be fine, parked round the corner.'

'Danny! You shouldn't drive!'

'Why not? How else was I gonna get here? Look, we should do this again,' he said as he pulled his jacket on.

'Yeah,' she said, following him to the door. 'We should.'

Exiting the restaurant, a cold breeze snapped down the high street. They walked along the street toward the car park. Railings lined the roadway to the right, with a dimly lit theatre to the side. It was boarded up, having not survived the recent crisis.

'Shame,' Hailey said. 'I heard the Playhouse was lovely years ago.'

'Not anymore,' he said. Danny froze, his ears picking at something in the distance.

'What is it?' Hailey asked.

'I recognise that…' Danny started, his head darting, searching for the source of the sound.

It was a distant thrum, like a gnat's wings, but… the sound became clearer.

This gnat's wings were motorised with petrol engines.

Then came the hollering.

Danny dove behind a large wheeled bin, pulling Hailey with him. She cried, confused.

'What the hell!'

A group of four mopeds rode past down the empty street, swerving all across the painted markings before disappearing back around the one-way system into the night.

'Sorry,' Danny said. 'Bad blood comes with those bastard things.'

Later, Hailey sat on her bed, phone in hand. No texts from Danny. Her fingertip hovered over the stylised speech bubble on her home screen. *No*, she said. *Play it cool. If that's how you want to play it, anyway.*

She'd shower and let whatever threads of energy were running around her mind settle down and pull into a big ball of yarn and unthread them tomorrow.

She grabbed the pink Bluetooth speaker and turned it on. It activated with a chime, signalling it had reached out to her smartphone and they were talking. Her father had been in his study, not to be disturbed. Mum was already snoozing on the couch. Henry… well, Henry was just Henry.

Sometimes it felt like the only things in this house that *did* talk to each other were her phone and the Bluetooth speaker.

She left her room with a pop tune thrumming through the wireless speaker. The tune ended. She'd resumed it near the end.

She put an ear to Henry's door. Muffled voices. But they stopped. Footsteps. She backed away.

'Can I help you?' he said, flinging the door open and poking his head out of the maw of darkness.

'Nothing I was…'

'You know where the bathroom is, dear sister. Down the hall. Unless you have something you want to ask me?'

'No…'

'Then stop skulking outside my room.'

The door closed with a clatter.

Shaking her head, she moved down the hall, closed the bathroom door and pressed play on her speaker over the sound of the water coursing from the shower, hoping to wash this weirdness down the plughole.

CHAPTER 11

'Well, I still think it's too soon for you to go back.'

'Nan,' Danny said. 'It's been over a week. I feel fine.'

'I still think you need to be more careful—'

'Nan!' he said, sitting up. 'You wanted me to work, so let me work.'

She paused. 'Be careful, Danny,' Jane said, kissing her grandson on the cheek. He winced a little. 'Still sore?'

'A little, now stop,' he said. 'I'll be late.'

'You be careful,' she said. 'No more trips to Lower Crayford. I could've told you that place was trouble. Always has been, always will be. Kier Wood, right?'

'Right,' Danny said, letting the door click closed behind him.

Jane moved to the bay window overlooking the road. Danny disappeared in his car, around the bend toward Kier Wood.

She wished she could sigh, but she couldn't. The postman would be here soon. With more bad news. Jane busied herself in the kitchen, washing the bowls and plates from breakfast. She'd had toast; Danny had had cereal. Cheerios. Honey Nut flavour.

The postman was always prompt at ten-twenty, and today was no different. The letterbox rattled. Papers fluttered to the doormat.

'Oh god,' Jane said under her breath, but the house was empty. She tottered out of the kitchen, through the main room, and into the little snicket of doom toward the front door.

Just one letter in a yellow envelope. She picked it up and

turned it over.

The label had been hand-printed by someone in an office, not by a machine. This one was personal.

She opened it with her finger.

Jane Greene,

You've been ignoring us. Let's go old-school, shall we? No risk of a spam filter interrupting what I have to say, or letting you ignore the truth any longer.

That's alright, entirely your right to do. You can't escape the truth. We're going to get the power you're frightened of, and it's only a matter of time. You know what we want and we aren't going to give up. Your Yellowstone Prime is going to expire today. A Prime Enforcement Agent is going to call to persuade you to resubscribe and accept the terms and conditions included with this letter.

If you have any questions or concerns, please contact my office directly by scanning the code at the top of this letter.

WT

Jane balled her hand, feeling the letter crumple. The envelope wasn't empty. She'd read the *terms and conditions* before, each time rejecting them with silence.

They wouldn't take what she worked so hard for.

This *Prime Enforcement Agent* sent a chill down her spine. Someone coming to the house. The house creaked. Maybe they were already here? She heaved and bolted the door. Then she ran through to the kitchen, to glance out of the French doors. The hedgerows that backed on to the orchard behind the house stirred with the wind. Not worth the risk.

There was still an odd rattling. The sort of noise the house never usually made. Upstairs. Jane moved to the stairs, taking a tread up.

The door knocked.

'Christ,' she said, freezing halfway up the stairs. She turned so she could view the outside of the house through the net curtain in the bay window.

Smiling, she recognised the man. Mr Frankton from the private school. He walked along the flowerbed outside the bay window, saw her and knocked on the window.

Jane moved to the door and unbolted it.

'Hello Henry,' she said, letting out the wind in her lungs.

'Just letting you know I was mowing the lawns. You don't work today. Did I… catch you at a bad time?'

'What makes you say that?'

'You're white as a sheet, and it looks like I scared you half to death knocking on the window.'

Jane's eyes darted. *Shit.* 'No, it's nothing, Henry, just I'm, er, expecting someone.'

'Oh,' Henry said. 'I'll leave you to it, then.'

'Thanks,' she smiled, closing the door. Turning, she re-entered the living room and screamed.

Thudding on the door.

'Jane?' Harold Frankton called; his voice muffled by the door. 'Are you okay?'

'Not a word. Are you Ms Greene?' the man in the yellow over-all said. Jane nodded through tremors. 'Good.'

'H-how did you get in?!'

'Easy,' he said. 'I was always here.'

Jane watched him move to the cupboard under the stairs. 'What're you doing?'

'Enforcing your Prime. You do want to accept the terms, yeah?'

'No!' she said. 'Never!'

'Well, we'll have to remove certain privileges, you see. First,' he said, 'we're cutting the electric power.'

'You can't!' she said. The workman lent into the under-stairs cupboard.

'We can,' he said, his voice reverberating through the brick. 'You've not played ball. So we need to motivate you.'

'But this… you're in a Blue Zone! I don't even have your poxy Prime thing! This is illegal, you know that.'

The workman poked his head out of the cupboard. 'I'm well aware of what zone I'm in. As is my manager. We're going to make an example of you.' He lent back into the cupboard, breathing as he bent into the space. A few seconds later, there was a clunk. Then silence. The man in the yellow overalls scrabbled out of the cupboard. 'Now, you *know* what we need from you.'

'You'll never get it,' she said. 'It's… it's not even here.'

The man shook his head and walked back to the kitchen. 'You're telling lies again.'

'What're you doing now?' Jane said.

'Water next.'

'Oh, come on!' she said. 'I'll… I'll call my grandson! He'll sort this mess out. You can't leave me without water! The police!'

'We can,' he said. 'All you have to do is sign the agreement. I believe you have a copy. I believe you have lots of copies of lots of things that would be very helpful to us.'

'Never,' she said. 'Never ever. You'll never get a *thing* out of me.'

'Well,' the agent said. 'I'll carry on then.'

'You bloody won't!' she said, advancing on the man. 'Get the hell out of my house!'

'Ms Greene, you're acting irrationally.'

'Irrationally?' she yelled.

The door thudded again. 'Jane, are you sure you're okay?!'

'We can make things easy or hard for you, Ms Greene. Do you understand?'

She ran forward, arms splayed out, but the man in the overalls caught her hands.

'You can behave. For once. They told me about you.' He pushed her away. 'Just sit down and think about what you've done.'

The thudding on the door turned to tapping on the window.

'Jane, are you…' Henry said through the glass. 'is that…'

'Water man,' the man said loudly. 'Nothing to worry about. Isn't that right?'

Jane nodded.

Harold Frankton disappeared, putting a hand into his pocket.

'What's that?' Danny said. 'They did what? I'll be home right away.'

'What's up?' Rick said as Danny entered the delivery office.

'Trouble at home. Bloody neighbours. Someone's… broken into my house, with my nan there. Or something.'

'Get out of here, Danny,' Rick said in a serious tone, 'and get home. The job'll wait. Family comes first at Mertons.'

The car zipped out of the car park at Kier Wood and onto the main road. The drive home was ten minutes in easy traffic, fifteen in challenging.

Today, the drive home was in easy traffic, but that was the only part of the evening that would prove easy.

Approaching the green, Danny saw the flashing lights of the police car reflected on the walls of the houses before he crested the hill.

'What the…' he mouthed, slowing down to enter the road past the green. The police car was outside his house.

Danny got out of the car after parking up roughly on the kerb.

'Nan?!' he called. Two policeman on the doorstep of his house turned. 'What the hell's happened?'

'Do you know her?' one officer said.

'I'm her grandson,' Danny said. 'Now let me into my own house.'

'Good, she's been waiting for you. Come with me.' The officer went forward. The house was pitch black, so a body-worn LED torch lit the entrance. The house felt like it was missing its soul.

'Danny,' Jane said from her position by the stairs.

'Nan!' he said, moving quickly. She got up and they embraced, then parted. 'What happened? Why aren't there any lights?'

'It's… complicated,' Jane said, exhaling with a hiss.

Danny cocked his head to the first police officer. 'Can you explain any of this?'

'It seems someone masquerading as workman—'

'It was Yellowstone, I'm telling you!' Jane interjected. 'He was one of those bastards,'

The officer turned back to Danny. 'Someone got in and disabled the electricity and water supply.'

'Why'd they do that?' Danny asked.

'Your nan won't say. Do you have anywhere to stay?'

'There's an electrician and plumber coming tomorrow, Danny,' Jane said. 'Get this fixed, I hope.'

'I've got a mate,' Danny said, pulling out his phone. 'He'll surely help.'

'Thanks again, Mr Archer,' Jane said on the doorstep to the Archer household. 'Kind of you to agree to take us in.'

'Not at all,' Henry' dad said, ushering Danny and his nan inside. 'Happy to help.' He closed the door. 'Guest room is upstairs, third door on the left. Would you like anything to eat?'

Jane shook her head. 'Maybe later. You've done enough.' She heaved at her heavy bag. 'There's more.'

Danny heaved to the doorway, plopping a large plastic sack and a beaten old briefcase on the doorstep. 'Sorry, she doesn't travel light.'

'Nonsense,' Mr Archer said, waving her away from her case. 'I'll get that taken up for you.' He turned his head over his shoulder. '*Henry!*'

'You are most kind,' she said.

'Come in,' Mr Archer smiled through clenched lips and turned away. Danny followed his nan upstairs. The guest room had two single beds at opposite ends, with two identical level chests of drawers between them.

'Don't get comfortable,' Jane said, sitting on the farthest bed.

'So,' Danny said, letting the door close behind him. 'You want to explain what happened? Yellowstone? Why'd they want anything to do with us? We're in a Blue Zone after all.' Jane avoided his gaze. 'What's been happening?'

'Look, Danny, you're dear to me,' she said.

'But?'

'But nothing, alright. Nothing I can't solve myself.'

'We're in my mate's guest room because a bloke got into your house - *our house* - and threatened you and cut off the power and water. Are we going to have to move because of this? What are you not telling me?'

'No,' she spat. 'We'd never move.' She then swallowed. 'I'm being totally open with you, Danny.'

His eyes narrowed. 'This isn't a chance thing is it?' he said.

141

'Danny…' Jane moaned. 'Just…'

'How are they so hot on you? I don't even have Yellowstone Prime, it just doesn't make any sense,' he twittered.

'Danny! I don't want to talk about it, please! It's… it's not a big deal.'

'You're lying. Tell me what's happening, please, Nan, I want to help.'

"I know you want to help. But I can't let you. I can deal with it.'

'What's next? Some bloke's going to come back to the house again? And do a lot worse?'

'No…'

'Or worse, more of them? A whole damn gang of shits? Breaking in? Smashing the place up?!'

'Danny please!' she snapped. 'I don't… I'm doing this for you. Really.'

'How?'

'Just, please,' she said, lying down on the bed. 'It's for your own good. After what happened to your parents. To Lewis.'

Danny's eyes widened at the mention of his brother. His *dead* brother.

'Don't you trust me?'

'Of course, love,' she said, reaching out for his hand. He snatched it away. 'Danny, I want to tell you everything, but I have to protect what's left, the company—'

'Is this to do with Mertons? As well as Lewis and mum?' Her face wrinkled but she said nothing, instead averting from his gaze and sucking air through her teeth. 'I'm going to have a shower,' he said, pulling off his top. He left the room.

'Oh!' Hailey said, covering her eyes. 'Hey. Sorry, I'm trying not to look.'

Danny didn't laugh. 'Bathroom?'

'That way,' she pointed, scrunching her eyes shut.

'Cheers,' Danny said. 'Sorry, it's not that bad, you can actually look at me.'

Hailey pulled her hands from her face and looked at Danny. He smiled at her. And she smiled back.

'See you at dinner then,' she said, walking back to her room.

'Nonsense,' Robert Archer boomed from the head of the dinner table. 'I'll have my finest chaps round by the weekend. They'll put your house right again.'

'That's very kind,' Jane said, her fork hovering in mid-air. 'I'm sure they'll do a… fine job, yes.'

'It's a shame my *son* isn't as proud of the family as I am.'

'Dad,' Henry shuffled in his seat. 'You're embarrassing me.'

'Pass the sauce, dear,' Robert shook his head at Lucille. She passed the porcelain bowl with a spoon sticking out of it. 'I've told you for twenty-odd years, son, it's the little things that matter.'

BZZT. BZZT.

Henry's eyes shot to his pocket like lead weights. His hands followed.

'Can we have no phones at the dinner table, *please*?!' Robert boomed, making the question more a demand.

'Who's texting you?!' Hailey giggled. She turned back to her dad to continue the story. 'Yeah, little things. Like grades, right?'

'Shut up, Hailey,' Henry said, not looking up.

'I told you—'

'I'm not texting anyone!' Henry grunted.

'Then what *are* you doing, you little squirt—'

'Now, children…' Robert said. 'No need for… histrionics.'

'Did you ever tell Danny *how* you got into the Thameside University.'

'I thought it was a scholarship?' Danny said, catching Henry's eyes. They were buried beneath his rutted, rage-filled forehead.'

'Danny,' Hailey said, 'he *did* get a scholarship…'

'*Dear sister*,' Henry growled. 'I'm warning you…'

'Hailey, please,' Lucille mewed. 'This is dinner, we have guests we don't have to…'

'Let her speak,' Jane said, swallowing her mouthful. She wagged the empty fork at Henry. 'He's been wriggling all night.'

'I don't want to talk about it,' Henry said, not looking up from his plate. 'And I don't want anyone else, either.'

'It was—' Hailey continued.

A hand clapped down on the table. '*Silence!*' Robert cracked. 'No more of this rubbish, please! Henry,' he nodded in one direction toward his son, 'you know how I *feel* about this. You know what I *expect* of you to do better. As for you,' his head turned to the opposite direction. 'You know better. I *expect* better. From both of my children. Is that clear?' No answer came immediately. The table wobbled again under the slam from another fist. '*Is that clear?!*'

'Yes dad,' Henry and Hailey said in monotone unison, and the rest of the dinner was eaten in cold, uneasy silence.

Plodding up the stairs, Jane stopped.

'Nan, please,' Danny said. 'I need to sleep.'

'One night, it's all I want in this place.'

'Why?'

'That Henry. There's something off about him. Fidgety.'

'He and his dad—'

'They're more similar than you think. One night, Danny. One night.'

'Okay,' he said, watching his nan walk up the stairs in front of him.

＊＊

Danny woke early the next morning. A few feet away, his nan snoozed in her bed. He checked his phone. 7:18. Just about right.

Quietly, he snuck the T-shirt on from the previous night over his tall, slim frame and opened the door. 'Wah,' he jumped.

Hailey giggled. 'My turn, I guess. You want breakfast?'

'I wouldn't mind,' Danny said.

'My mum'll be down at eight.'

'Nan usually wakes up about seven-thirty. Think I got in early.'

'Cool,' Hailey said, holding onto the handle for her bedroom door. 'See you in a bit.'

'Okay,' Danny said. The door to the guest room opened behind him. 'Hi, Nan.'

'Which way to the bathroom?'

'That way. Breakfast is at eight. Oh, and Danny?'

'Yeah?'

'Unlimited hot water here. Enjoy yourself.'

After breakfast, Danny and his nan gathered their bags and walked downstairs.

'Thanks again,' Jane said. 'That was very hospitable,' Jane said to the elder pair.

'Our pleasure,' Mr Archer said. 'Hopefully the last of that… business. If you need any work done in future,' he reached into his pocket and pulled out a card, 'here's my number.'

Jane regarded the card for a moment as it hung in mid-air. She took it without looking. 'Very kind, thanks. Now, Danny,' she said.

145

'Let's go, not keep these… lovely people any longer.'

'Guess I'll see you later,' Henry said. 'You going straight to work?'

'Probably,' Danny said, heaving his rucksack over his shoulder. 'Might take this one home first,' he nodded his head to his nan.

'This one,' she repeated in mockery. 'Watch it, you.'

Danny laughed and headed to his car, popping the boot lid. He placed his rucksack in first, slipping it off his shoulder, then put his nan's bag in.

'Home?'

'Yeah,' Jane said. 'Their tea was bloody awful.'

'Priorities!' Danny laughed, reversing out and into the drive. The Archers waved twice before going back inside.

In the rear-view mirror, Danny saw nothing. Just other anonymous cars going about their business. A couple of Mertons vans, doing their duty deep in the Blue Zone.

He didn't see the moped following four cars behind edging out into the middle of the road every so often, just to check.

Arriving home, he pulled up. Jane got out.

'Don't you need your uniform?' she said.

'Nah, got another set in my locker,' he said. It was true. 'You sure you want me to go in?'

'We've gotta keep up appearances,' she said. 'I ain't letting whoever that guy was win.'

'You sure you—'

'Danny,' she said, her face serious now. 'Go to work. I'll have your dinner ready when you get home. Just like before. I'll start tidying up. Did you order that safe for me?'

'Yeah, just after dinner,' he said. He recalled the conversation with his nan. Important documents in the house and needing somewhere to put them. He'd ordered a safe for her, but she'd refused to entertain ordering it from Yellowstone. It was going to take time to arrive, and the delivery fee had been a killer.

'Are you going in?'

'No, no,' Jane said. 'I'll wait. Get tidying. See what Robert Archer's men have done, make the tea.'

Danny shrugged and moved the car, turning round and going to the edge of the road. The usual turning toward Kier Wood. He made the turn in a gap in the trickle of traffic.

He didn't see the moped driver on the other side of the junction, holding his phone to his helmeted head, taking a photo of the house through the zoom lens and then raising the handset to his head.

CHAPTER 12

The moon rose in a clear sky above Henry Archer's house. Inside, there was snoozing from his parent's bedroom, and mellow musical vibes from Hailey's.

Henry wasn't ready for bed, though; instead, he was slipping into a set of black jogging bottoms with a navy blue hoodie. He opened his door gently, knowing where the hinge squealed. The gap was narrow but enough for his svelte frame to slide through. He pulled the door closed equally cautiously, the door only bumping just slightly in the frame.

The carpet on the stairs softened the sound of his socked feet going down. Once at the bottom, Henry put on his trainers and entered through a doorway into the garage. His hand felt along the wall just beyond the doorway, rubbing the rough, unfinished brick. The fluorescent light turned on with a thrum. He walked through the space to a switch on the wall which clacked under press.

He nodded to himself, then left the garage and out the front door. The safety light that would usually illuminate the driveway stayed cold and dark. He'd flicked that switch before when he had to sneak out. It worked every time. Walking down the driveway, Henry glanced over his shoulders. No twitching curtains. An understated yellow glow. Soon he was beyond the driveway and down the lane.

Their house was down a private road that wound through trees past sleepy domiciles. Henry opened his phone as he approached the gate that separated the private road from the public highway beyond.

At the old bus stop.

Henry smiled, the glow of the phone reflecting off his shiny teeth. He let himself through the gate on the pavement. Cars whisshed past with the roar of rubber on asphalt. To the left, woods that were shrouded in night. The figure on the moped was nearly invisible in the abandoned bus stop a few score feet away.

'On time,' Henry said.

'Yeah,' said the rider. 'You got the money?'

Henry rolled his eyes and reached into his pocket. 'Seven-fifty. Split it between the five of you.'

'You promised us a grand. Where's the rest of it?'

'Listen, Iceblue,' Henry said, 'you were sloppy.'

'We got the van, like you asked. Gave the guy driving it a right scare. Little bitch.'

'Yeah, but you beat him black and blue. There's gonna be re-percussions.'

'No police found us, boss. No-one.'

'Well, be more careful.'

'We found out where he lives, too.'

'You did?! Who told you to do that?!'

Iceblue read off an address. 'We're thorough like that.'

'That's his address, alright.'

'You knew already? Why couldn't you just tell us?!'

'I did. The guy's Danny Price, mate of mine.'

'Like you and I are *mates*, eh?'

Henry ignored the comment. 'Were you seen?'

'Of course not,' Iceblue said. 'We ain't amateurs. You wanna remember that, kiddo.'

'We'll meet up soon to discuss the next target.'

Iceblue coughed. 'We ain't doing the old bird yet?'

Henry shook his head. 'Not yet. We'll play it cool. Then you'll have a chance to earn that two-fifty you blundered away.'

'Now you're talking,' Iceblue said, grinning to let the moon pick out his teeth. 'Say, you want her out, right? So we can get in?'

'What are you thinking?'

'Seen the weather forecast?'

'No,' Henry said, leaning in to listen to Iceblue's plan.

***

'W? Yeah, it's me. We need to talk,' Henry said into his phone.

'Meet at the restaurant,' W said. 'Two hours.'

'Okay.'

The phone call ended in three terse bleeps from the handset. Henry came out of his room.

'Son,' his dad said. 'Thought you'd cocooned yourself away in there. You off again?'

'Er, what makes you say that?'

'Well, you're staring past me and out that window, for starters.'

Henry huffed. 'You got me.'

'Is it a girl? About time, if you ask me.'

Henry rolled his eyes as he walked past his dad. This was his dad's *second* favourite subject. 'No...' he began, then thought. It kind-of was, if the definition was stretched to its limit. 'Work and pleasure, shall we say?'

'Your mother and I were talking. You're getting toward twenty-five. Things need to get motoring in that life of yours.'

'I have a great job,' Henry said.

'I've seen the colour of those grotty, horrible uniforms,' his dad said with a sneer. 'Hardly worth the pennies they cost to make in some godforsaken dump in China. You know, I'm still disappointed you didn't get the job.'

'What job?'

'Yellowstone, of course! Starting to wonder if you really are a son of mine.'

'Dad!' Henry retorted, spluttering. 'I thought we went through this. They told me what they wanted—'

'About experience? Oh yes,' Robert said. 'I remember the conversation clearly.'

'Then you'll remember,' Henry said, feeling his body tense. He was about to *disagree* with his dad. 'That I needed some experience. Mertons is the past. I need to get with the past before I can embrace the future. Yellowstone's not off the table yet, Dad.'

'After all we went through? I find that… a tall tale. Are you sure this isn't like before? If you just *didn't get the fucking job* I'd be more understanding.'

'Dad,' Henry said, with just a hint of panic in his voice. 'I'm sorting it.'

'Button it,' Robert said. 'Must be a woman.'

'Why'd you say that?'

'You're dressed up. You only get that sort of getup on for a woman or a job interview. I'm still perplexed you turned down Yellowstone.'

'Eh,' Henry said. 'Never say never with them.'

'I'd have thought you'd have bitten their hand off. And I thought they didn't do repeats. You had one chance, Henry, and you blew it.'

Maybe I did, Henry thought with a wicked grin. 'Look, I'm going to be late.'

'It's not Stevie again? You know I don't approve.'

'No, it's not,' Henry said. *If fucking only. Shame about all that… business between them.* 'You don't have anything to worry about that.'

'Good,' his dad said as he walked down the stairs. 'The Archer name carries a lot of prestige, and I want to keep it that way! And Henry?'

Henry stopped midway down the stairs. 'What?'

'Can you at least remember to turn the floodlight back on next time you disappear on one of your escapades? Nearly rammed your mother's car last night.'

The blood dropped from Henry's face. 'Yes, dad.'

Henry walked into the restaurant, but it was a contrast to the clandestine meeting after the day at Yellowstone. For one, the place was packed.

'Can I help?' the server said. 'Are you here for someone?'

'Yes,' Henry said. 'Er?'

'Do you have a name?' the server slicked. Henry's face tightened, then relaxed.

'He's with me, thank you,' Wendy Tunt said, approaching from the dining room. 'With me, you.'

Henry followed and sat down at a crowded, claustrophobic table. 'Don't bother ordering,' she said, looking up. 'This isn't a social call.'

'What?' Henry said. 'We're going to get seen!'

Tunt laughed once. 'Don't expect me to book out the whole place just to make a song and dance for you. I've heard, by the way.'

'About what?'

'The histrionics with the van. Bit crude, considering what we're paying you.'

'It's the campaign I inherited. Your guy screwed up.'

'How do you possibly come to that conclusion?'

'Trying to cut off their gas and electric? It'd be all very double-oh-seven if it wasn't so hapless.'

Tunt ignored the remark. 'Are you mixing work with pleasure?'

Second time that phrase has come up, Henry thought. 'Things are getting… complicated.' Tunt gestured for him to continue, rolling her hands horizontally. 'The target seems to be getting close to home.'

'What do you mean?'

'My sister. She's spending more time with him, and the trip to the hospital only made it worse.'

Tunt couldn't contain the laugh. 'Why are you worried? You're focussing on the wrong thing. We don't have time to deal with your family drama.'

'Your guys did the hit, right?'

'Shut your mouth! You can't tie that to me, or the company, for that matter. They didn't know he'd be driving the van, or he'd be stupid enough to go out alone.'

'Maybe your guys don't know Danny Price that well.'

'Is Hailey going to be more of a problem?'

'She's my sister, and what I'm doing goes completely underneath the foundations of—'

'Listen and listen good. None of that matters. We're on a tight deadline, as you well know. I want the Mertons acquisition done before that stupid robot gets going.'

'You mean Parker?'

'Yes, thank you. Before Grayson bloody Laurie hands over the levers of the company to a bunch of microchips.'

'That explains it,' Henry said. 'Still, this whole thing with my sister…'

'You're getting cold feet because the heat's coming a bit close to home? Poor you,' Tunt said. She took a sip from a tall glass full of transparent liquid. 'It's water. Not drunk a drop of alcohol in eight years. Clouds the vision. You certainly could do with some clarity.'

'What do you mean?'

'For someone as supposedly intelligent as you,' Tunt said, 'you're dumb sometimes. Leverage.'

'Leverage?'

'You've been friends for how long?'

'We went to uni together. We go way back, to when we were kids.'

'Good. Get yourself inside his house. His nan is keeping information somewhere that could undermine Mertons. Your job is to find it. Because, lord knows, we haven't yet.'

'What makes you think I can do what all your money and power hasn't been able to? It's one house, not a castle.'

'We've tried the stick with the old lady. Shook 'em up.'

'What were you looking for?'

'Thanks, Les Dennis,' Tunt said.

'Who?' Henry asked.

'Ask your parents. She's sitting not just on property we want. The neighbours will fold once we take over the zone. Plop a convenience store right on the green. No, she has knowledge from Mertons that would reduce the price and the risk of the acquisition quite considerably.'

'I… that seems…'

'Sketchy?' Tunt sat back. 'Possibly illegal? All a matter for the lawyers, though with a government this weak we'll make the law soon. But if you can use your family connections to get what we need, well… to the victor, the spoils.'

Henry sat for a moment. The din of the restaurant - the babble of conversation, footsteps on carpet, the creak of furniture, the clink of crockery against cutlery - faded into white noise. A grey blur between his ears. *The spoils.*

'If that's what it takes,' he said. 'I'm already working on it.'

'Excellent,' Tunt smiled. 'You're going to fit right in once this deed is done.'

CHAPTER 13

Entering the canteen at Kier Wood, Danny felt a presence as everyone there fell silent from their conversations, lunches, and chats.

He gulped. Clearly, what had happened at home had got out. They'd been talking about it all week. And then some.

Danny was an unwilling participant in the parade through the canteen, now feeling like a catwalk. He avoided eye contact with anyone until the doors to the stairs and the shop floor beyond were right in his face, then parting, then revealing the off-white corridor beyond.

Entering the relative gloom of the delivery annex, Danny sighed.

'Alright, Danny,' Sparky said. 'You alright?'

'Felt like a goldfish. Upstairs.'

'Oh,' Sparky said, putting the crate on the floor. 'I guess we heard about…'

'Yeah,' Danny said, breaking eye contact with Sparky. He wheeled a dolly of crates to his colleague.

'Worried about Jane, we are.'

'Why?'

'She's been a big part of this store. Oh, look,' Sparky said over Danny's shoulder, 'Here's trouble.'

Danny turned. 'Brian,' he said. 'To what do I owe the honour?'

Brian tried to laugh, but the humour wasn't there; instead it was a more hoarse cough. 'Sorry about what happened, Danny.'

Danny shook his head. 'Can you all stop treating me like someone died, please? It was a thing, but we're getting through it.'

Brian looked to his feet for a moment before looking back at Sparky. 'Can you give us five, please?'

'Sure,' Sparky said, walking out. He slapped Danny on the shoulder.

'I… I…'

'Spit it out, Brian,' Danny said.

'Your nan, she's… a big part of the culture of, well… the store. The company, even.'

'Right. She's been coming here for twenty years. Probably since before I was born.'

'I hope she can feel right to return soon.'

'Why wouldn't she be? Am I missing something here?'

Brian clawed at the air, trying to grasp the words. 'It's… complicated.'

'Why say anything, then? Look,' Danny said, 'I appreciate your concern. I really do. But I'm a bit insulted, in a way, at how you're all treating me with kid gloves. All bloody week!' He turned back to the dolly and put his hands on the top crate to propel it away.

'Danny…' Brian started. Danny kicked the dolly. 'Danny! Please! I… only wish I could tell you more.'

'I just want to get on with my work,' Danny said. 'This work, for starters. Look at the state of this place,' he said, regarding the disarray in the loading annexe. 'Shit everywhere. I spent the last two days just sorting this shit out, and I feel I've got nowhere.'

'You've only been here a few weeks! Who made you boss?' Brian couldn't hold in the genuine laugh. 'Suppose you're right.' His face turned. 'We lost a couple more crew while you were away.'

Danny glanced at the whiteboard. Two conspicuous clean

spaces where names used to be. 'Christ. Another attack?'

'No,' Brian said. 'They walked. You've been here six weeks, Danny. I wouldn't blame you if you jacked it in too.'

'Nah,' Danny said. 'I've lost jobs for many reasons, but not getting chased out by some shitty kids. Where's bloody Sparky? Van's due out.'

'For someone who's been here a month, you seem to have got the grips of our operation.'

'Yeah,' Danny said. 'I have. It's good work. Tough but good.'

'Beats the gym, right?' Rick laughed. 'He teaching you well?'

'When he shows,' Danny laughed. 'I'll take this one out if not. Nearly time anyway.'

'You think it wise to go out again after that other incident?'

'Brian,' Danny smiled through a sigh, 'that shit's just how it is. And if we give into that, it's just going to get worse. I'm here to do a job, and if we don't do it, we might as well all walk, right?'

Brian nodded, pursing his lips before slipping out the way he came.

***

'I know what those kids do, Danny,' Sparky said as the delivery van motored down the ramp and onto the road.

'Oh yeah?'

'You're not the first, and you won't be the last. Believe me.'

'There must be some, like, reason for it? Apart from anarchy,' Danny said. The engine roared in front. 'I know that punk said we'd picked the wrong team. But why? Why'd some thugs on a load of mopeds want with one of our vans? Well, they didn't even want the van. They trashed it.'

Sparky took a breath as he drove. 'You're the latest, Danny.

You won't be the last. We've been asking this ourselves for months. Things are changing, fast.'

'How'd you mean?'

'The deliveries are going to dry up, you know. If we lose the blue zones. Last play the company has.'

'Lose the Blue Zones? What do you mean?'

'Matter of time, ain't it? Yellowstone is going to turn the screws on that commission. You know, that panel that does the zoning. They're only human. They'll bend soon enough. We shoulda seen 'em coming years ago.'

'That,' Danny said, thinking back to that day at the Yellowstone recruitment event. His mind came to the conclusion very rapidly. 'That wouldn't be beyond them, you know.'

'Really?'

'I interviewed with them before I…'

'What made you turn down all the money you'd ever need?'

'Sometimes life is worth more than just what you earn at the end of the month,'

Sparky laughed. 'Tell my ex-missus that!'

'I lost most of my family years ago,' Danny said. Sparky continued to drive, remaining silent. 'Nan took me in, gave me a home… it felt weird but it's all I have left.'

'And what did they want?'

'Yellowstone was making more threats than job offers. They knew about my brother and my mum.'

'Reckon they know about my ex?' Sparky said, laughing. 'They're welcome to her.' Danny laughed too. Sparky continued. 'Surprised they don't just buy the company, really.'

'Who, Yellowstone?'

'Yeah. I mean I would. If I had to choose that option. Which I don't. They're a cold lot, Sparky, let me tell you.'

'They still benefit from the vans. Our sat rating,' he said, refer-
ring to the customer rating that went into the Commission. It was
a big factor in the zoning reviews every twelve weeks. 'We're tank-
ing. Things might look good, Danny, but even if the slots are
there, people'll go where their shit's likely to come without the
threat of a bunch of ragtags with them.'

'You really think so?'

'Wouldn't you? Imagine I was some big fat businessman. In
the same game. But laced up with rules. If I couldn't buy the last
great opposition,' Sparky said, 'I'd just want to make their life difficult. One way or another. Each van we lose, each customer who
gets scared off,' Sparky said. He turned to Danny. 'Zip,' he winced,
drawing a finger across his neck.

Danny sat back in his seat for the moment as that sank in.

'First drop,' Sparky said after another couple of minutes.
'Don't you get too comfy in that seat!'

Danny woke, throwing the duvet away. It was still night time.
He squinted, feeling something cold and damp on his face. Rubbing his nose, he felt the drip of water.

Danny reached for the lamp beside his bed and fumbled for
the switch on the cord. It always seemed to get stuck somewhere
between the bed and the piece of chipboard furniture.

The light flicked on.

'Shit,' Danny said, scrabbling out of his bed. He glanced up.
The ceiling was weeping, just above his bed.

The thin window rattled in the frame as the wind pushed on
it. Rain splattered against the glass in irregular bursts.

Danny pulled a crumpled T-shirt on and left the room.
Downstairs, he heard the television blaring.

'Nan?' he called, but with no real effort. He trod downstairs, just enough to see the Western movie on the flat panel television against the corner of the living room, with his nan astride the couch opposite.

Danny thought about going down, but a gust of wind prompted him to turn around. Now the landing ceiling was rattling. *The loft hatch. Of course.* He turned on the landing light and saw the square of ceiling jittering.

He swallowed. It'd been years since he'd been up there. Not even to get the Christmas decorations, which had mysteriously appeared in the shed one year. In living here so long the hatch had become anonymous, blending into the very fabric of the ceiling, despite it making no such effort to shroud itself.

Danny reached for the handle. It didn't budge. 'Ah,' he said, spying the keyhole next to the handhold. *Where did she keep the key again? It wasn't the bathroom... the spare room was full of junk... ah.*

Danny put his hand on his nan's bedroom door and pushed down on the handle. The latch groaned. He took a deep breath through his teeth and pushed it the rest of the way slowly. The door creaked too. Danny's nose wrinkled as the scent of musk and perfume puffed out of the crack in the door. He slipped inside, trying not to gag, though his nose adjusted quickly.

The furnishings were in immaculate order, just as he remembered it from when he was a kid.

The years between that had been a maelstrom of events. Danny shook his head, dispelling the recollection. He turned the light on. The bed, fashioned of tired brass, without a crease out of line on the duvet. Beside it were two off-white side tables with fancy brass handles. Danny paced. Past the end of the bed was a dressing table with glass pots of jewellery and other things women collect over the years. Hairbands, clasps, brooches. A tri-fold mirror with dated moulding stood proud in the dead centre of the dressing table. Some photos dotted the space in little oval frames.

Nan, in her youth. Granddad. Then a couple of photos that Danny found most arresting. His mum and brother, Lewis.

He gulped and looked away, just as the light reflected off one of the pots of gold jewellery. *That wasn't an earring...*

Danny picked up the brass key on the end of the short cord of fraying string. He nodded and slipped out back into the hallway.

Those strange feelings from being in his nan's room dissipated with the rough vibrations of the wind on the loft hatch. Just beyond, the rain hammered on Danny's bedroom window. He reached up, twisting the key into the little lock. It stuck. He pushed once more, gently. The key wobbled, then the tiniest of clicks tapped through. The hatch dropped a couple of inches with a clatter. Danny pulled it down fully, a ladder unfolding with it. The aluminium ladder scraped just a little as it came down and made contact with the beige runner on the landing that covered the dark wood floor around it.

Danny pulled himself up, feeling the wind from outside.

The loft was shrouded in darkness except for a criss-cross pattern of indigo light - the colour of the night sky through the gaps in the tiles and timbers. Danny sat on the ledge of the hatch, trying to catch a pull cord that buffeted in the wind. He caught it after a few tries and tugged. An old, dust-encrusted lightbulb burst into life to fill the space with dirty yellow luminescence.

Boxes and cases filled the loft - a lifetime's accruing of nick-nacks, old items shoved up here for another day that'd never come.

It was also full of wind and flecks of rain on Danny's face. He glanced up. No hole there, but he looked to the space of the roof above his room. The shape made by the purple night sky was dancing around.

'What on…' Danny said, trudging over. The joists had just a bit of give in them, and the plywood boards sagged too. The hole in the roof grew larger as he approached. 'Huh,' he said, pushing a hand upward to reach the missing tile that was hanging on like a loose old tooth. The wind realised what he was doing and blew harder, throwing rain into his face. His grip faltered as the wind tugged at the tile, now held on by the rusty vestiges of a lone old nail.

'Crap!' Danny called, losing the battle. The tile slid out of his hand and down the roof with a scrape, then followed by a muted *tssh* as it hit the paving outside.

He had to get something to plug the hole, so looked around. The boards around his feet were wet, and he could see his bedroom light through the sagging sheets of plasterboard where the material had just given up, turning soggy, drooping under its own weight.

He saw the briefcase he'd lugged into Henry's house for their brief stay.

'How the hell did this get up here?' he asked the wind. *No way she got this up the ladder by herself.*

Danny glanced at the small keyring in his hand and noticed the second key made of dark metal. He slid it into the keyhole and turned. Latches clicked, and the briefcase fell open.

Wind caught a plastic bag next to the briefcase. He glanced, seeing flashes of blue and grey uniform through motes of dust. An old Mertons uniform that hadn't been used in years.

He looked back to the briefcase, seeing papers, browned with age, flapping through the irregular light. He bent down and started to read, though the wind kept trying to yank the pages from his hands.

The briefcase contained decades of old Merton's paperwork, but as he continued to scan, the words seemed… not real. How'd all *this* get *here*?

Danny got to his feet to look around. Whatever this was… it wouldn't plug the whole.

Then he saw his nan by the hatch.

'Hello, Danny,' she said, with none of the warmth he'd ever have associated with her.

'Nan,' Danny said. 'I thought you were asleep, there was—'

'No,' Jane said. 'I thought we said you wouldn't come up here. Have you been to my room? You must've been, to find the key.'

'Well, yeah, but, look,' Danny pointed to the hole in the roof. 'What're we going to do about this?'

'We?' she said. 'You're not going to do anything. You're going to go downstairs and go back to bed.'

'How did this get up here? I didn't bring it up, I—'

'Don't worry about what I do in my own house, Danny,' she said, not meeting his eyes.

'And what about all this stuff?' Danny asked. 'There's all sorts. About mum, dad… Lewis too.'

'You shouldn't be up here, Danny,' Jane said, taking a step forward. 'There's things you aren't meant to know. About all of those things. For your own good.'

'What happened?' Danny said. Jane's face twisted. 'Please, Nan. I feel like I know next to nothing. Is there something?'

'Danny…'

'*Tell me.* Have you been *lying* to me?'

Jane rolled her eyes. 'Danny… love,' she started. 'I'd… I'd love to, but… I can't tell you.'

'Why not?' Danny said, as the wind thrust more rain into the loft. 'What happened then? You wouldn't keep all this forever if you—' Danny was cut off by the wild whistling of the wind and the creaking of timbers. The roof vibrated, as did the rest of the house. The hole in the roof opened wide, the tiles, joists, and rafters unzipping. 'Nan!' Danny leapt past the pile of boxes toward his nan, who ducked out of the way. 'The roof's going!'

'God,' she called, 'not again!'

'Downstairs! Now!' Danny shouted.

Jane wailed. 'No, we have to save the—'

'What is that stuff, Nan? Why do we have to save it?' Danny shouted over the thunderous wind.

'It's important,' she shouted too. 'We need to keep it.'

'You know what it is, don't you?' he shouted, turning to grab the bag. 'This is old Merton's shit,' he said. 'Why'd you wanna keep it all?'

'It's not *old shit*! It's very important stuff, stuff the company's let me keep. It's my job to keep this away from people,' she said, waving for the next bag. 'Quick, the rain's really coming in now!'

Jane wasn't wrong; the hole in the roof was the size of the dining table. Outside, the wind turned to thunder, forks of pure natural energy coursing down from the sky with the sheets of rain. Danny pulled the case now toward her.

'Even this?'

'Especially that!' she yelled. 'Over here, quick,' she said, dragging the briefcase with her to the opposite end of the loft space where the roof remained intact. 'There, good,' she said, patting the pile with some relief.

'It won't stay there,' Danny said. 'If you really want to keep that stuff, it has to go down.'

Jane's eyes bulged. 'Fine, downstairs.'

Danny heaved the first bag and let it fall through the void left by the hatch. The bags thudded on the landing floor with the hiss of folding plastic. Then it was just the briefcase. Jane held onto it with a vice-like grip.

'I take this,' she said.

'You sure?'

'I'll go down. You pass it to me.'

'Alright,' Danny said, moving to the hatch. Jane went down first, standing at the foot of the ladder. 'Let's get you out of here.'

'Pass it to me, Danny!' Danny did so. 'Got it! Right, down,' she said.

Danny slid down the ladder.

Jane pushed past her grandson to push the hatch closed, locking it with a click.

'Don't think that's going to do anything, really.'

'Get the stuff in my room,' she wheezed. The adrenalin had dissipated in her bloodstream and all of her sixty-seven years now caught up with her again. 'You're freezing, nan,' he said as she whimpered through her bedroom door. Danny followed with two of the bags.

'Alright,' she said, 'Put those things there.'

'You want me to stay in here?'

'No, please, Danny,' she said. 'You did well.'

'We can't stay here,' he said, pushing the loft hatch closed. 'That whole roof could go at any minute. And the wind's getting worse.'

'These things will be safe,' she said. 'That's the main thing.' Jane fell back onto the immaculately made bed with a sigh. 'Danny, go to bed,' she said.

'Don't you want to get out of, oh,' Danny replied as Jane's eyes closed with the exhaustion of the experience. The room was silent, even with the maelstrom whipping at the remains of the loft above.

She was fast asleep, and whatever secrets she held would remain sentinel for now.

Danny left the room and crossed the landing into his room. It was destroyed. Remnants of the ceiling festooned every fitting, and the wind howled through the collapsed ceiling. He turned, heading downstairs, the door blowing closed behind him, finding the settee. He sat on and pulled from beneath his T-shirt, tucked into the waistband, the article about his brother, Lewis.

His eyes opened.

CHAPTER 14

Tunt scowled across her desk. The sound of water trickling down an artificial wall filled the space. The cool breeze of conditioned air pushed at fronds of potted plants.

Henry hadn't seen such overt luxury in an office before.

Tunt broke the spell, clearing her throat. 'Well, what do you have? Is this really it?'

'Look,' Henry flustered. Papers flew across the table. 'Oh, shit, I'm sorry.'

'No, no,' she said, leaning back in her office chair. Henry scrabbled to pull the papers together from their chaotic arrangement on the table. She swatted his arm away as it crossed toward her zone of the table. 'Bloody stop that. I'm the one who should be sorry.'

'Why?'

She lent back with a sigh. 'Clearly, we've promoted you too fast. You've lost your bottle.'

'I've been focussing on my work,' Henry said. 'That's not fair.'

'The acquisition has stalled. The board is not biting. I told you to find something that might help me… *us* convince them. And so far, you have nothing!'

'I've got a whole operation!'

'Yes,' Tunt said, 'and you've done nothing with it. You're pushing paper, Archer. Big time. And time is one thing we don't have!'

'I'm sorry.'

'You're apologising again. I know Price has a whole cache of documents *somewhere*. They're not online, of course they're not. And we didn't find them at the house.'

'Look, Wendy…'

'Don't *Wendy*, me!' she hissed. 'Get out.'

'No,' Henry said, gripping the chair.

'Unless you can magic me up the stuff I need, you're no bloody good to me. If I wanted a lapdog, I could've easily got one at a tenth of the salary you're being paid.'

'I'm not a lapdog either!' Henry protested.

Wendy Tunt got out of her chair. 'Aren't you? You have one job, and it's only because Daniel Price spat in my face you even have that. And I don't have time to waste.' She plodded over to the window that gave a vast vista of the city below. 'This is all supposed to be mine…'

Henry paced over. 'It still can be.'

'Are you still here?'

'I'm not giving up, Wendy. And you aren't going to give up on me. Look at this place,' he gestured. 'I could earn an office like this.'

'You really think so? Then do better. I reward the risk. And unless you can get me some actual dirt… well, never mind. I was a fool.'

'A fool?'

'To place faith in you. After Mr Price turned his back on us,' she sighed, her shoulders relaxing in resignation. 'My timescale doesn't wait for you. Find me what I need, or I'll put you out and get someone who can. Do you understand me?'

Henry approached the doorway, then stopped. 'I hear you.'

'Final warning,' she said. 'Don't make me regret it.'

'Stormy last night, wasn't it?' Henry said.

'What?!'

'Did you see the weather?'

'Are you off your chair, Archer?' Tunt said. 'And why are you still here?'

'Lots of rain. Might've, shall we say, flushed out some new info.'

'What do you mean?' she asked, but Henry didn't answer. He headed down the stairs and out onto the street. His phone buzzed. He smiled, once, at the text message he'd received. Swiping, he danced his fingers over the glass panel.

```
Sure, usual old pub, yeah?
Get the guys. It'll be nice.
```

***

'Good to see you, mate,' Henry said to Danny as the latter fell into the busy pub.

'You too,' Danny said. 'Sorry, was a right 'mare getting here.'

'I bet it's all been go for you. Don't worry, I'll go get the drinks in.'

'Cheers,' Danny said as Henry got up and went to the bar. He returned a couple of minutes later, the glasses clinking on the counter.

'What's come over you?' Danny said.

'What d'ya mean?'

'All this,' Danny waved. 'You're being… nice.'

'Danny,' Henry said, 'after the week you've had, you could use a friend to cheer you up. Like the old days at uni, right?'

Danny smiled. 'Right.' He took a sip of the amber cider. 'Definitely needed,' he said with a contented sigh.

'How's the house?'

'Worse than we feared,' Danny said. 'That whole side of the

171

roof is cream-crackered.'

'Shit,' Henry said, leaning back. 'Expensive?'

'Nan had some kind of insurance policy. Told me not to worry about money. We're looking at five figures though at the bottom of the bill.'

'You don't need a place to stay, right?' Henry said. Danny shook his head, but smiled.

'Too kind, mate,' he said, 'but there's a sheet over the hole. Scaffolding going up next week.'

'Need anywhere to put stuff? I've a spare garage or two, you know I do!'

'Nah,' Danny shook his head again. 'Nan's got some stuff she wants to keep on her. You'd think she was holding onto the secret sauce recipe for those burgers from McDeckers,' he said.

'Is it?'

Danny laughed. 'Nah. Old work stuff.'

'Old work stuff?'

'From my nan's time at Mertons. They gave her some big suit-case or something of paperwork. The way she freaked out,' he said, 'during the storm, you'd have thought about it being a case of bloody diamonds.'

'Is that so? And where is this stuff now?'

'Oh, we've put it away, back at mine. It's not that interesting, really.'

Henry nodded, but the conversation with Danny faded into mumbles. His mind was focussed more on what Danny had told him about.

The evening wore on, eventually the crowded pub thinning out. A bell rang out, smashing Henry back to the clarity of the evening.

'Last orders all!' the publican hectored over the hubbub of

warm conversation. 'Drink up, lads!'

'Come on,' Henry said to Danny as he slumped in his seat. 'Home time.'

'Can't walk…' Danny slurred as Henry got up. He heaved.

'Gotcha,' Henry said. Danny wrapped an arm around his friend. 'I'll give you a lift.'

'You sure?'

'Stayed clean, just in case,' Henry said. 'Pepsi all night.'

'Pepsi?' Danny wrinkled his face up. 'Rather drink my own piss than that shit.'

'Could've been worse.'

'Worse? How?'

'Dr Pepper?'

They both grimaced at the thought. Then, they staggered toward the door, Danny proving to be more of a dead weight than anything on Henry's shoulder. The door opened.

'Shit,' Henry said. Outside, it was pouring.

'Looks like God's taking a piss on us tonight. Just like last night.'

'Yeah,' Henry murmured. 'Lucky us. Car's only over there,' he pointed. Henry's car stood in the gravel car park about fifty feet away. 'Think you can manage it?'

'Me?' Danny said. He laughed. 'Sure thing, you!'

Henry opened the car and got in. Danny laboriously followed. The door closed behind him.

'Ready to go?'

'Sure! You're good, Henry. You're a good mate. Just know that.'

'Just fulfilling my promise,' Henry said. 'Danny and Henry – champions of the world. I mean that.'

'I know,' Danny said, leaning against the window. He continued to murmur. 'I know…'

Henry smiled weakly, driving out of the dark car park and onto the little street.

'Remind me,' Henry said, his eyes peering into the sleepy streets bathed in moonlight. 'What number are you again?'

'That one,' Danny pointed, seeing the row of houses appear on the crest of the hill, behind the green. Timber frames surrounded one house where the roof ended with jagged shapes against the night sky. 'You've been before, remember?'

'Yeah, but not in the dark.'

Arriving at Danny's house, Henry stopped the car.

'You got your keys?'

'Sure!' Danny said. Henry clenched his teeth. *If he says sure one more time…*

'Come on, let's get you in.'

Henry followed Danny up the short path toward the dark door.

Danny fumbled with the key in the lock.

'Need a hand?' Henry asked, pulling the key from his friend's hand. Henry turned the key in the lock. It clicked. The door creaked open.

'Lock that,' Danny said, his feet clopping on the hardwood floor.

Henry ignored it. 'You gonna…' Danny made for the stairs. '… take your shoes off?'

Danny shrugged. His feet thudded up each stair. A door opened with an elongated squeal. Then there was a yelp and a crack.

'You okay up there?' Henry called. No answer. He rolled his eyes for the climb. 'Jeez…'

At the top of the stairs, he saw Danny astride his bedroom

174

floor, splayed out on the floor.

Then he turned, leaving his friend. The door perpendicular to Danny's took more attention.

Henry rattled the handle. It turned in his hand. The door swept open against a threadbare old carpet.

'Christ,' he said to the stench of musk and time that escaped from the room. He gasped.

This was clearly an older lady's room. He scanned it. No sign of the cache of documents Danny had mentioned. He knelt on the rug, pulling out the drawers. Linen and sundries. He looked under the bed, casting the frilly duvet cover away.

Musty paperwork. He smiled, casting his phone torch over the papers.

The old Mertons logo. He reached in, wanting to palm over the creased paperwork. He pulled out one of the papers, the light casting a warm glow on the softened-by-age paper.

But he didn't. A creak punctuated the space.

Henry froze. There were footsteps outside. And humming. He shoved the drawers, pushed the paper into his pocket and sprang to his feet and strode toward the open door.

He was right under the frame when an old lady appeared.

'Can I help you?' she spat; her voice venomous.

'I brought Danny home.'

'Wrong room,' she said. 'And I don't think you're staying, are you?'

She watched Henry roll an eye to examine the house. 'No...'

'Sorry if my old house disappoints you. Now as I said,' she paced the floor. 'Wrong room. You've been to the pub, haven't you? And you drove him home! The state of you! Now go.'

Henry nodded, skidding out of her room. She went in with a huff, the door snapping closed behind her. A latch clicked in the jamb.

Henry looked at Danny, just once, before bolting down the stairs and out of the room.

Someone would be very happy.

***

'This is good work,' Tunt said, pushing the paper back to Henry. 'Fantastic work!'

'You've changed your tune,' Henry said, pulling the file back from Tunt. She resisted with her tented fingers for a moment before relenting. 'I thought you'd be impressed.'

'A daring little operation. How did you know that the roof was going to come off?'

'Remember that storm?'

'Clever boy! Tell me,' she said, leaning back in your seat. 'How do you feel about Grayson Laurie?'

'Should I be feeling anything?' Henry asked.

Tunt laughed. 'What I mean is, do you think this company could succeed… let me think of a way of putting it. Do you think this company can succeed despite… no, let me try a third time…'

'Do you want to know if I think his… credo, his idealism, is stifling things?'

Tunt's eyebrows arched. 'Impressive.'

'I'm loyal not to him but to the company.'

'Some would say he *is* the company.'

'Is he, though?'

'This is the question I've been pondering.'

'Have you, now?'

'Enough,' Tunt said.

Henry took a sip of his drink. 'Why'd you ask?'

'I've many plates spinning. Mertons, the Commission… even the Private Innovation and Enterprise Act itself.'

'Do they all play in tandem?'

'You could say that.'

'I'm glad I just did.'

Tunt laughed. 'Grayson may not approve of our… methods. Of securing market dominance. He may need to be… neutralised. You do understand, do you? I think he'd be bad placed to have any reservations to the detail of the plan I'm working on. Many plates to spin. So let me ask you again, Henry…'

'Ask me what?'

'Who are you loyal to?' She raised a finger. 'Don't say the company.'

'To… you?'

'Good. Because Grayson may not be in the picture once the plan starts to rise above the surface.'

'Can… wait? What are you saying?'

She didn't elaborate on that point. 'My legal team has a procedure in place. He won't know what hit him.'

'Yellowstone legal?'

'My legal team,' she said. 'On reappraisal… your work here has been good. You're proving valuable at last.'

'I only hope,' Henry said, putting his glass down, 'that I have excelled despite those reservations you had.'

'Carry on like this and you will be. I'll need a deputy. No, better. In the event of any ascendancy… you can be the Director of UK Operations nationwide. It doesn't stop here, you know. The company has seventeen divisions. One by one…' she said, flicking her fork in her hand. 'They'll fall into line once they see the true power of what I've created.'

'You want me at your side?'

'Can I count on your loyalty? Forget your friends, your family… all of that isn't relevant. What I need is your total loyalty. And your total loyalty, to act without question… well, you'll be paid the world for it.'

'It's an offer I couldn't possibly refuse.'

'Wise boy,' she said. 'Now we go to the next stage. And the information you've provided will be most valuable. Now we need to acquire certain… *individuals*.'

'I think I know where this is going.'

'I bet you do. This isn't enough. We need all of it.'

'Can't we just burgle her house?'

'We could,' Tunt said, reclining. 'But that's not the full story. No, we don't have time for another bungle. Too risky, no time. Instead, we acquire the *individual*.'

'Are we thinking of the same individual?'

'I think we are. Jane Greene. I'll tell you why.'

Henry lost his composure for a second at the words.

'Something wrong?' Tunt asked.

Henry shook his head and smiled. 'No. Go on.'

She lent forward and began to explain. And Henry began to listen.

CHAPTER 15

I need you to do me a massive favour,' Henry said to Hailey as they coasted down the road.

'What's that? Never good when a ride starts with you asking me favours.'

'Can't a dutiful brother offer his dear sister a lift? Who were you meeting again?'

'Nobody you know,' she said. 'What's the favour?'

'Danny.'

Hailey's face swelled. 'What about him?'

'I, er… want to make sure he's not getting ripped off.'

'By who?'

'The builders doing his new roof. Why he didn't just ditch the house is anyone's guess.'

'Er, maybe because it's not his. Why are you so concerned? Didn't he tell you it was all insured or whatnot?'

'He did,' Henry said, 'but I'm looking out for a mate, right? Can't I do that? Why are you so shocked?'

'I'm not,' Hailey said, then realised she was. 'I… guess I am, really.'

Henry laughed. 'See if you can get the insurance details, too.'

'Isn't all this with his nan?'

'Yes,'

'Did Dad put you up to this at all?'

'No! I can do things without asking our beloved father first, Hailey,' Henry said, his face crinkled with mock outrage. 'Though

I'm a bit surprised he didn't ask.'

'Like I said,' Hailey repeated, 'all to do with his nan.'

'Maybe she's got some paperwork. Look,' Henry nodded, 'keep it all hush-hush. Call it a good friend doing Danny a favour.'

'You want the papers? I think I heard Danny talking about some stuff she keeps in her room. Something about the Mertons insurance she has.'

'Really? Christ, that must be ancient. I don't need the originals,' he said. 'Photos of them would do, I guess.'

'Henry,' she said. 'There's another way.'

'What's that?'

'You ask Danny?'

'I want to surprise him. Be a good mate. Can't you help me out this once, dear sister?'

She grimaced, knowing it was bad when Henry called her *dear sister*. 'It'll help dad, too. He wants to help, but he needs to know what he's up against when he pulls in the quotes. That house is worth a lot.'

'This seems pretty cloak and dagger, Henry,' she said. 'Does it have to be one of us?'

'Dad said yes. I'd do it, but I don't think his nan likes me much.'

Hailey laughed. 'I got that impression from dinner, yeah.'

'Yeah,' he trailed off. 'You'll do it, then? *Please?!*'

'I guess…'

Henry held his tongue. He wanted to tell her exactly where and what to look for, but didn't. *Too creepy*. He drove on for another couple of minutes.

'How're things going with Danny? You've been seeing a bit more of him?'

'You're doing it again,' Hailey laughed. 'Showing an interest.

180

When do you care about my boyfriends?'

'Oh,' Henry said, 'he's your *boyfriend* now, yeah?' He glanced at his sister, who had turned beetroot red. 'You've done a lot worse, believe me, Hails.'

'Shut up,' she said, 'and drive before I grab the wheel and crash us both into a bridge to shut you up.'

Henry said nothing and drove on.

After a few minutes, he broke the silence.

'We had a good time at the pub. I'm worried, though, Hailey.'

'You, worried?' she said. 'Are you feeling alright?'

'Hey, now that's not fair,' Henry said. 'His house is a wreck.'

'Dad won't put him up, if that's what you're asking. Danny won't leave his nan home alone. They had… a thing happen.'

'What sort of thing? How'd you know?'

'I asked already. And she was spooked. Some bogus gas man tried playing silly bollocks with her.'

'Did you, now?' Henry asked. 'We've got the garage, haven't we? Dad never parks his car outside.'

'You want to rent out the garage to Danny and his nan to store their old stuff?'

'Hey,' he said. 'Just an idea.'

'What's in it for you?'

'Do I need to have something in it for me?'

Hailey laughed. 'I'm your *dear remember?* I know you. You wouldn't get out of bed for something if it didn't benefit you somehow. Let me guess – a work thing?'

Henry's face fell with outrage. 'Where'd you get that idea from?'

Hailey laughed once more. 'Like I said. I'm your *dear sister*. I know you better than you know yourself.'

'I worked for Mertons on a contract basis, as you well remember. Now, a nice man I met called Claggett runs a distribution warehouse. It's totally buttoned up.'

'Why's this of interest to me?'

'I know you're all for this citizen journalism stuff,' he said. 'Thought you might like to know.'

'Mertons is a family company. It's what they built their brand on – the family blood. Unlike the Yellowstone hippy commune, that image is as real as rock.'

'Is it, though?'

'What are you saying?'

'Nothing. Just something you might want to look into someday.'

Hailey's face crumpled. 'I don't buy this, Henry. I'll need some proof before I risk my network on this. If this is a fool's errand…'

'It won't be.'

***

'I'm glad you could come at such short notice,' Henry said.

'You said you had a party for us,' Iceblue said at the end of the private road. 'Where's it at?'

'Not yet, not yet,' Henry said. 'Are you willing as we discussed to…'

'I've got teams ready, man,' Iceblue said. 'You got what I need?'

Henry did. He reached into his jacket pocket and pulled the creased white envelope out.

Iceblue snatched it, pulling it open. He held the bundle of notes to his face and inhaled hard.

'Love the smell of cold, hard, cash,' he said. 'This'll do nicely.'

'How many men have you got?'

'Enough,' Iceblue said. 'Enough for this rodeo. We've got

people coming in from Sheffield, Leeds... they're all up for a shindig. You going to tell us a venue yet or not?'

'All in good time,' Henry said. 'I just need to arrange the headline act. Get my ducks in a row. Is that alright with you?'

'Well, boy,' Iceblue said, taking a step back toward his parked moped. 'Don't keep it too long. The boys are getting antsy. And we'll get better offers,' he swung around. 'There's a demand for our, shall we say, services.'

'That won't happen,' Henry said. Iceblue stopped. 'A better offer doesn't exist.'

Iceblue swung around. 'What're you saying, man? You saying I can't get a better price?'

'For this kind of work? I could get my own stooges.'

'Hey, hey! No-one goes using that kind of word with me, man! I ain't no stooge!'

'No, of course,' Henry said. 'You know too much to be a stooge.'

'Right.'

'Good. But don't play hard to get. I know people too. People with deep pockets who know some deep shit, too. We got an understanding?'

'I get you,' Iceblue said. 'But I've pulled out a lot of stops for this. Don't make me waste my time. Or even the deepest of daddy's pockets won't save you.'

'Of course,' Henry said. 'I think we're done for now, don't you think, Ian?'

Iceblue winced. 'We're done. Just get me the party that was promised. Maybe we'll meet in more... intimate circumstances.'

'I don't like your tone, Ia—'

'Posh boy,' Iceblue hissed, 'I know more about you than you think. Nice evening for a stroll down a private road. Might say it's close to home. You get me?'

'Don't even think about it.'

'Hey,' Iceblue said, raising his hands in mock alarm. 'Remember how we, shall we say, *became acquainted*? Remember who you're in league with, is all. Your dad did.'

Henry did. *Bloody dad and your contacts…*

'Alright, it'll get sorted.'

Henry watched as Iceblue resumed his seat on his moped, disappearing into obscurity down the road. He turned back to walk up his drive. He laughed. Empty threats.

CHAPTER 16

Henry peered right down the crease. The sun had been brutal that afternoon. He gave a sniffle underneath the helmet and reached to scratch the sweat from the back of his neck, but the glove on his hand wouldn't slip inside the elasticated neck.

'Bugger,' he said, squinting. The sun was right in his eyes.

'You ready, Archer?' one of the other players hollered from behind.

'Yes, yes,' Henry waved. 'Let's do this.' *One more over for the game*, he thought. The other side cheered. 'Oh, great.'

'Come on, Pricey!' the rabble at the other end of the cricket pitch roared. A tall, slender white figure approached the opposite stumps, obscuring them.

Just twenty-two yards.

The bowler yelled once, then pitched. The dark maroon spot approached on the prevailing wind. Henry lifted the bat, feeling the weight of the carved willow. He lifted it beyond his back, then swung, clamping his eyes shut.

Impact.

Thwack!

He opened his eyes to see the ball arcing against the aquamarine-blue sky.

'Run, dammit!' a voice barked. Henry did so, but wobbled. Danny glanced past on the left.

'Move it!'

Henry pounded, but caught a foot and tumbled, watching his vision turn from blue sky to green grass to dirt, then darkness.

He opened his eyes to cheers. He spat out the clump of grass in his mouth, pushing himself up. He looked over to see the players clapping Danny on the back.

'Bastard tripped me!' Henry protested.

Danny turned around and held out his hands in mock protest. 'Not me!'

'Yes,' Henry heaved, 'you did, with your bloody lanky legs.'

'Relax,' Danny said, slapping Henry on the shoulder. 'All fun and games.'

'Come on, Henry, let's hit the pavilion!' one of the other players said. 'Game's over. And wipe that salty mug off, too!'

Henry growled and followed the other guys toward the slanted roof of the pavilion. His feet clopped on the concrete floor and into the locker room.

'Where's Danny?' he said.

'Oh, out the side,' one of the lads said. 'I think his girlfriend showed up.'

He left, following the cement path round to the corner of the building. He heard giggling. Mutterings of sweet nothings. Taut breathing. Henry paused at the threshold where the bricks ended.

'Can't wait,' a voice mumbled, the cadence laced with saccharine happiness.

Henry followed the voice around the corner. He gasped.

'Henry?!' a shrill voice said.

'Jesus!' Henry said, surveying the scene before him. Danny was propped up against the wall, his arms like stanchions against a svelte female figure. The face looked guilty and familiar. 'Is that… my *sister*?!'

'Er, surprise?' Danny said, smiling awkwardly. His eyes darted to Hailey. 'I'm… I wish there was a…'

'Don't act so shocked, *dear brother*. I thought you knew.'

Henry looked over his shoulder, his glance following a rumble of sniggers. He turned back 'Whatever happened to… discretion?!'

Henry shut his eyes.

Opening them again, he was in his car with Danny beside him, and his sister behind in the back seat. His mind blotted out the painful, vexatious, and embarrassing scene. He'd turned, tail between his legs, to get away.

'Henry, you've not said anything,' Danny ventured first. The road ahead was consumed under the bonnet of the car.

'Think yourself lucky,' Henry breathed, not taking his eyes off the road or his hands from the wheel. 'You're not walking home after that humiliation…'

'Mate, it was a cricket match…'

'Don't *mate* me, Danny Price,' Henry growled, flecking spittle onto the vinyl and synthetic. 'Was that display totally necessary?'

'Hey!' Hailey repeated. 'Don't get arsey because you're bad at cricket.'

'You me look like a *fool*. All a good laugh, we all laughed, didn't we?'

'Henry…' Danny said. The car streamed to a stop at a red light. 'Don't be like that. You know it's all a bit of fun.'

'I'm glad you do,' Henry said.

'You should see him, Danny, after a match like that. He'll be in a mood for hours. Can't wait to endure *this* one, *dear brother*.'

'Another word from you,' Henry coughed, swallowing the bundle of anger that lumped in his throat, 'and you'll walk home, okay? I'm doing you a favour.'

The rest of the car ride to Danny's house passed in uncomfortable silence.

'Want some tunes?' Danny asked aloud, ostensibly to both companions, but really only to Hailey.

'Nah,' she said. 'Unless you want us to hit a tree or something.'

'Okay then.'

Eventually, Henry saw Danny's house on the brow of the hill. The car came to a near-silent stop.

'Thanks for the ride,' Danny said, unclipping his seat belt and opening the door. 'Look, sorry it didn't go well. Maybe catch you when you're less crazy.' Then he turned his head and toward the back of the car. 'Chat later,' he said, his voice carrying much more warmth. The door closed, and the light turned green. The car skidded away.

'Well, that was fucking awkward,' Hailey said. Henry ignored her. 'Don't bullshit me and tell me *that* was all about cricket—'

'So,' Henry said. 'You and him are an item, I see.'

'We are.'

'Didn't you think to tell me? What are the other guys going to think?!'

'Who cares, Henry? Did I need your permission? We're all adults. Maybe you should start acting like one.'

Henry heaved and gripped the wheel. *Hold steady.* 'Of course not,' he said. 'I'm sorry. Look, I couldn't be happier.' He glanced in the rear-view mirror. It had worked. She looked... confused. 'You're a nice couple. I just... wish you'd told me. Before. Then I wouldn't have made an arse of myself in front of our friends.'

'Well, *dear brother*, consider me pleasantly surprised.'

'Oh,' he laughed, '*dear sister*, the pleasure's all mine.'

Henry awoke a few days later to an ochre sunrise. Rays erupted from behind a scattering of clouds.

He smiled, looking down the garden from the bay window in his bedroom.

Next door, he heard giggles.

He remembered, and his face crumbled.

'Screw you, Danny. Screw bloody you.'

This was the day, whether they were ready or not.

He glanced at the clock. Early. But for today, he needed to be early. He quickly dressed after a brief rinse in the shower before stealing out of the house.

'Quiet,' he said to himself as he edged his car out of the drive. 'Bloody gravel.'

He breached the threshold between his empire and the world outside. He paused before merging onto the deserted main road.

'You there?' he said into his phone. 'Good. I'll be along shortly. We're good to go. Focus on the secondary target, as discussed. I'll meet you at the primary in forty-five minutes.' He hung up. Then he drove.

The town was sleepy, evidenced by the lack of traffic. He crossed the hill and slowed. On the other side, going down, was the town. The street snaked through houses and under a railway bridge.

Henry glanced to the left. The house he was after was down a little street on the other side of the green. He pulled up, wheels lazily hogging across the pavement and the kerb, digging into the soft earth. Just a little bit of give, but it didn't matter.

Henry glanced at the digital clock. Just on time. A figure emerged from one of the houses, dipping into a car and driving away. He reached for his phone.

A few notifications lay on his home screen. Offers. Emails. Game updates from apps he'd sidelined years ago. With over two terabytes of storage, what was the point of deleting them?

Then a text from Hailey:

Dad wants to know where you are.
He was expecting you.

Henry closed his eyes, breathing deep. Another text, from another contact, only stored with an emoticon of a snowman.

You ready? Say the word.

Opening his eyes, he looked back at his phone. His fingers drifted, and he opened PhotoGram. A feed of filtered pictures materialised on the screen. He swiped down, the synthetic inertia bouncing the images down.

And there he saw it.

Hailey, her arms around a lanky, thin figure whose face was unmistakable.

Danny Price.

The caption below was a single, red heart.

Now Henry finally saw red.

He couldn't stand her. And he couldn't stand him for siding with her. He shook, the juvenile side of his brain overflowing with emotion.

'You bastard,' he growled to no-one, and flicked his fingers on the glass screen, leaving trails of grime in their wake.

PhotoGram disappeared, replaced with the message list. The snowman's thread came into view; a litany of terse, one-word or one-phrase messages. Never more than a line.

A virtual keyboard appeared. Henry danced his digits across it.

Showtime

190

He tapped **Send**, and the message whooshed out into the ether around him.

And then he waited. He settled in. They'd take a while, but they had all the time in the world.

Twenty minutes passed, with the sun's rays lapping up the dashboard like the tide at the beach. In the distance, a harsh noise that disrupted the calm.

Buzzing.

Henry smiled before opening his eyes. They were on time alright.

The buzzing sidled up. Henry opened his window.

'Confirm the number?' Iceblue said. 'My crew are here.'

'Fifty-two. Go in when you're ready. I'll park up. Away from here.'

'You're the boss.'

Henry raised the window and turned the key. Symphonic chimes trilled, and the car lumbered back on the road as he turned the wheel. He followed the main road, glancing once in the rear-view mirror to see six mopeds proceeding down the road by the green.

He turned at the next junction on a side road, seeing a gravel-paved layby. That'd do. The car stopped with a wheesh. He got out, feeling the morning air on his face. Direct sunlight hit his skin. Radiant heat warmed it. It was all rather pleasant.

Then he retraced his steps up the hill and over the green toward house number fifty-two.

And then he walked through what was left of the front door toward the sound of screeches, thudding, and wails of despair. Raised voices. Glass breaking.

The threshold approached. He stopped, just before the doorway.

'I didn't think you'd want to get your hands dirty,' Iceblue said as Henry paced up the path. 'Bit risky, you being here. Standing there. Where people can see you.'

Henry didn't respond. He knew what he was doing was irrational. He was going to defile Danny's sanctuary like Danny had defiled his family. With one big deep breath, knowing this couldn't be undone, he stepped into Danny Price's house.

CHAPTER 17

Right, Sparky,' Danny said, 'where we off to now?'
Turning round, Danny didn't see Sparky. He stepped forward, through the flappy doors into the delivery annex. It was deserted. He glanced, side to side. Nobody. The place had been abandoned; dollies of crates were where people'd left them.

A door opened to the left. Danny glanced.

'Get in here, Dan,' Sparky hissed. 'Get in here and quick!'

Danny sped toward the tiny flight of metal stairs and barrelled into the office. Six of his colleagues were huddled around a computer. Tinny voices, distorted by static, could be heard.

Danny pushed through. He listened in.

'This is…' a voice said, clearly in distress. 'We're at… Lower Crayford… there's bloody dozens of them…'

'Who's there?' Brian said. 'How many? Can you tell us what's happening?'

'Bikers… no, mopeds,' the voice said. In the background was the sound of thuds. Many thuds. Then the tinkling of glass. 'They're bloody Deliverangel drivers! What the hell!?'

Danny didn't need to hear any more. 'Sparky, I know who this is. Must be the same lot that ran me off the road,' he said.

'Are you sure?'

'I remember the logos. Can you get back in touch with them?'

'Nah, sorry,' he said.

'Tell them if you can,' Danny said, striding from the office, 'tell them we're coming to help.'

'Danny,' Brian said. 'You can't go and be the hero, you know that.'

'Call the bloody police then, though we all know a fat lot of good that'll do.'

'We will.'

'How many over there? Jeez...' Danny trailed off. 'This is exactly the sort of stuff I'm meant to be working to stop. And here I am,' he said, kicking the trolley of crates with a clatter, 'doing this shit.'

'It's important,' Brian said. 'We've got to keep our rating.'

'Fucking rating,' Danny said. He caught Rick's face. 'Where's Brian?'

'Don't do it, Danny,' Brian warned. 'We can't go vigilante. Then we're no better than they are. Are we?'

'I guess not,' Danny relented.

'Good. And anyway, people rely on us to keep our word. Regardless of what's happening eight miles up the road.'

'Okay,' Danny said, walking away. 'No problem.' He left the door and out into the sunshine of the yard. He walked toward Sparky, who was just closing the roller door on the side of the van.

'Mate, what's come over you?'

'With me,' Danny said, pushing back into the store. He grabbed one of the BOXNET terminals and started poking it with his finger.

'What are you looking for?'

'Tools,' he said, not looking up. 'Found it.' He sprinted away, into the expanse of the floor. Sparky followed.

'What have you got planned, Danny?'

'You'll see,' he said, halting in front of one rack. He pulled on the scuffed plastic box and reached in. 'This'll do.'

'You can't take that,' Sparky said.

'Why?' Danny said, examining the cricket bat as he tore the tags off it. 'Might just come in handy. You want one too?'

'I guess I'd better.'

Danny reached in and chucked a second bat toward Sparky, who caught it. 'Let 'em take it out of my wages.' Then he ran back to the loading bay.

'What now?!'

'Get in,' Danny said with a low rumble, opening the driver's door.

'You driving today?' Sparky said.

'Get in,' Danny repeated.

Sparky did so. 'Everything alright? I've got the manifest here for—'

'Keep it,' Danny said, starting the van with a rattle and a splutter of diesel. The van roared down the incline toward the main road.

'Danny, are you sure?'

'Don't worry,' he said back. 'I know what I'm doing.'

'What do you mean?' He asked Danny. The van turned right. 'Danny, that's not the right way!'

'We ain't going that way,' Danny said. 'We're going to Lower Crayford.'

'You're mad,' Sparky said. 'You can't go and stop them. Danny! Think rationally! *Stop this bloody van right now!*'

'We can't lose another one,' Danny said. 'You heard what they said? Losing a whole store would drag the ratings down. And the Commission is looking right now at us to do the right thing.'

'And what about what we're carrying?'

'It's an impossible choice. Either way, the Commission will fuck us over for what happens today. If I had to choose…'

'You actually believe that?' Sparky said. Danny nodded. 'You really bloody do, don't you?'

'If you want to go home, or think it's too dangerous, that's fine. I appreciate that,' Danny said. 'I'll drop you off. You've got a wife. Kids. People who need you.' Sparky looked at his lap. 'Honestly, I'll do it alone.'

'Danny, it's a job. You don't need to risk yourself like this for a job, it's crazy.'

'It's not just a job. This place means something to what little family I have left.'

'Shit, your nan!' Sparky said. 'Honestly, that woman is amazing. She's been here for years, feels like one of the family.'

'There's that word,' Danny said. 'Family. Job family, work family. Mine's one and the same.'

'Mate,' Sparky said. 'That woman has helped us all more than you'd imagine.'

'You can tell me all that over a beer sometime.'

'Gladly.'

'Now, if you're worried, I will drop you at home. Is that understood?'

'Nah,' Sparky said after a few moments. 'Last time I left you, you got the shit beaten out of you. You're a damn fine guy, Danny. I won't let that happen again to you. Let's do this. Like you said, we've got to do this or our jobs depend on it.'

'Not just that,' Danny said. 'It's more than our jobs.' He drove down the ramp in a rattle of engine noise. 'It's about the team. We're all dedicated, right?'

'Yeah,' Sparky said. 'I could get a job anywhere else. But with Mertons… I feel like I'm valued. Even if sometimes the hours are shit, the loads are massive and if the missus is on a right bender. I've had a lot worse.'

'Excellent,' Danny said. The morning sun glinted outside. 'Call in. Let them know we're coming.'

Sparky lent forward and grabbed his phone. He dialled and held it to his ear, then placed it in the phone cradle that hung from the vent.

'Who the hell is this?' a voice crackled.

'This is—' Sparky said.

'I'm Danny Price, delivery driver from Keir Wood. We hear you're in trouble and are coming to ass—'

'Are you mad?'

'No, sir—'

'How many drops?'

'Eighteen.'

'Then you know what you need to do.'

'But—'

'We will hold our own. Maybe see you on the other side.' The voice said, then the connection dropped.

'They're duty bound,' Sparky said, 'and so are we.'

'Fine,' Danny said, gripping the wheel and pushing his foot to the floor. The diesel engine roared throatily in response.

***

The Huntermill Creek estate had a name that belied the reality of the location. The watermill hadn't existed for fifty years; instead, it had been replaced with a warren of identical looking houses fashioned of the same yellow brick and white fencing.

It was an improvement on the sixties concrete of some other parts of their patch, but something felt false about it. The houses had no character or warmth to them. Just the same design repeated over and over.

'Always lovely to find ourselves here,' Sparky said as Danny brought the van to a crawl. In front of him was a turning. Just before that, a row of parking spaces beside an overgrown children's play area. 'Those two big old boxes, wasn't it?'

'That's it,' Danny said. 'Number fifty. The name rings a bell, doesn't it? Show me,' he said.

Sparky passed the crinkled paper manifest to Danny. This was the eighth drop. Halfway through. 'That's her, there,' he said, pointing just left of forward. A front door opened and a woman with her hair in rollers had pottered out.

'Looks nice,' Danny said.

'She is nice,' Sparky said. 'Just makes me wonder.'

Danny brought the delivery van to a halt in the empty row of parking spaces and killed the engine. Some kids rode by on their bikes, music blaring from a speaker dangling from the handlebars. The van rocked with a few hard thuds. Danny watched the kids laughing as they passed by, waving their hands. Shaking his head, he got out, walking to the back of the van. 'What makes you say that?'

Sparky opened the cargo compartment door. 'Why'd you stay in a place like this?' Then he disappeared into the van. Danny hefted two large boxes down on to the pavement. Sparky jumped down and reached for one of the boxes.

'Stop,' Danny said, holding a finger to his mouth. He trod carefully. At the end of the road was a bush overflowing a little wall that he crouched behind. Around the corner, tyres approached, but no engine noise. Sparky appeared behind Danny.

The sound became visible as another van emerged from the right-hand side of the T-junction and pulled to a stop. It was high-sided, the angle at the front acute and sharp, painted in nondescript white paint, with no other markings. Not like the boxy van that Danny had driven. The van mounted the kerb with a hump and rocked before stopping. A couple of employees got out, but they weren't wearing uniforms; instead, T-shirts and jeans. One wore large aviator-style sunglasses beneath cropped hair; the other, shorts and a baseball cap

'Seen that van?' the one in the cap asked.

'What van?' the man with the sunglasses and cropped hair said.

'Swore I saw a Mertons van around here,' the first man asked.

'Find it,' the first man said. 'They can be the first to the party.'

Danny glanced over his shoulder. The van was *right there. How could they miss it?* He turned back to listen in.

'You didn't, idiot,' the first man said. There was a clunk of a latch and then the sound of bearings rolling along a track. The man was opening a roller door on the opposite side of the van to the one Danny could glance at. 'You guys alright?' the man asked. Some grunts followed. Then the door slid closed again. The first man got into the unmarked van first, then joined by his colleague. The tail lights lit up and the van crept forward, bumping off the kerb and toward the bend at the end of the street. Danny watched the Yellowstone van turn, watching the driver.

'Coo-ey! Hello there!' a voice cracked from across the street. 'What're you lovely young boys doing there?' Danny's head turned. It was the woman from number fifty. Now she was waving at them. 'You got my bits and bobs in that van of yours?'

Danny got up and smiled. 'Yes, yes we have.' He looked to the left, down the street. 'Fuck,' he said under his breath. The other van had come to a stop, and he stared right into the twin lenses of the driver's sunglasses for just a moment. Then the van raced away behind another row of identical houses. 'We'll be over in a moment,' he said, waving to Sparky.

'What's happened?' Sparky said as Danny walked toward the

stack of crates.

'That other van looked fishy, didn't you see?'

'I saw,' he said. 'Not one of ours. What's it doing around here? This is a Blue Zone after all.'

'Well, whoever they were, they weren't making a delivery,' Danny said. 'Watch yourself,' he sighed at Sparky. 'Don't want your back going again.'

'Piss off,' Sparky said with a smile that Danny matched. Danny led.

'They were looking for us. Soon as the driver saw me, he bolted.'

'Well weird.' Sparky said. Danny shrugged. 'Let's not give them any time to find us.'

'I get the feeling,' Danny said as they walked up the garden path, 'we may have been rumbled. Hello,' he said to the customer. 'Lovely day for it today, isn't it?'

'Thank you, boys,' the old lady said. 'Mind bringing those two big boxes into my kitchen? These old bones,' she said, holding out her pallid, thin arms, 'can't carry like I used to.'

Danny looked at Sparky, who raised his eyebrows. Then he turned back to the customer. 'Sure, for someone as nice as you.'

They took the boxes through the door. The hallway was dark, the paint peeling. From upstairs, the offensive scent of decay lingered down the stairs.

'Sorry,' the old lady said from the first room on the left. 'Leave them here. Got a nice grandson who can unpack them.'

'Is that so?' Danny said, his head pivoting as he looked at the sweet old lady. To Sparky he said: 'come on, we're all done.'

'Definitely.'

They trooped back and forward a couple more times until the pile of crates was empty.

'Can I offer you a cup of tea?' the old lady asked.

'Oh, no,' Danny said, 'we're a bit behind now.'

'Oh,' she said, crestfallen. 'Maybe next week, then.'

'Maybe. See you.'

Danny walked quickly out. Sparky was waiting. 'Not a bloody word, you.'

'First time on the estate, there's nice ones and nasty ones. She's,' Sparky said, glancing over his shoulder. The front door to number fifty lay open. 'She's a bit special. Means well, but we're buggered for the next drop.'

Danny pulled the van keys from his pocket and got into the van. Sparky closed the door and assumed his seat.

'That was weird,' he said. 'Very weird.'

'Let's get out of here,' Sparky said.

Danny agreed and the engine roared as he turned out of the layby.

The van rocked past number fifty and around the bend.

Danny turned onto the next road through the rabbit warren of estate streets. His colleague nodded and lent forward.

Danny fumbled for the key and the engine gurgled. He tapped the accelerator. The engine wheezed, only barely over an idle. His feet skipped on the pedals, depressing the clutch. He clicked the gear lever into first.

Then it happened.

His foot slipped.

The van bucked forward, the engine gunning.

'The hell was that?' Danny asked.

'Company!' Sparky yelled.

Danny glanced in the mirror as the van leaned into the next turn. Mopeds. A couple. But there were no doubt more. 'Bad company!'

'Keep moving!' Sparky called, leaning forward in his seat. The van lurched again. 'Danny, where the hell did you learn to drive?!'

'I'm trying! Wasn't expecting this bastard to handle like a cabinet!'

'What're these losers doing?!'

'The same thing as before!' Danny shouted. The zip-zip noise of the moped engines buzzed like mechanical hornets behind them. 'I've gotta stop!'

Sparky looked up. They were at a junction. 'Go straight on.'

'Where've they gone?' Danny lent to look in his side mirror. 'Can't see 'em.'

Thuds along the side of the van racketed into the cab. 'There they are!'

Danny growled along with the engine, turning the van into the main road. The traffic was sparse. This would be a problem. There would be nowhere to hide. After a few seconds, the buzzing sound of the mopeds came alongside. Danny glanced. The rider was laughing at him while bashing the side of the van with a gloved fist. It made a noise but had little effort.

'We're not going to outrun 'em, Danny—'

The van veered to the side of the road with a screech of brakes. There was a gritty rumble and a hiss of moped horns.

'Fuck, Danny. You nearly ran 'em over!'

Danny held a finger to his lips to hush his mate. Two riders appeared in front, parking up.

'Here we go,' Danny said. 'Get the—'

Sparky thrust the cricket bat into Danny's hand. He held one too. 'Good thing you packed these!'

'I prefer to hit balls with 'em.'

'I didn't know you played.'

'Didn't just sit on my arse at uni. We all have hobbies. Now move!'

'Sparky!' Danny called, but his colleague had got out. Danny followed.

'So,' Sparky said, 'just the three of you this time. I see. You guys want to party with us?'

The three riders stood astride their mopeds, silent. The middle one looked from side to side, nodding at each. Then he pointed at Danny before taking his helmet off.

'You,' Danny said, feeling his blood chill. 'Iceblue. Of course.'

'You remember,' Iceblue said. 'Unlucky for you today isn't it?'

'Who's this guy, Dan?' Sparky said through the corner of his mouth.

'Me and this twat have some history,' Danny said loudly. 'We met once before, didn't we? Maybe things will work out differently.'

'I won't put you in hospital this time, kid,' Iceblue said. 'I'll put you in the grave.'

'Tough words,' Danny said. 'I found some of your shit online. On TubeView.'

'Did you?' Iceblue said rhetorically, hardly able to suppress the gleeful smile. 'You like what you see?'

'This ain't a job to you, is it? You're sick. You actually enjoy this shit you do.'

'A job is a job,' Iceblue said. 'Gotta love what you do. And I do. I *love* what I do, and I love what I get for doing it.'

'Who do you even work for?' Danny asked. Iceblue laughed. 'Come on, tell me already. Why keep attacking delivery vans? There was a Yellowstone van a while ago.' Danny smiled. Iceblue's eyes opened, just enough. Danny knew he was onto *something*, even if he didn't know what *something* was. 'Why not go after

203

that? It's probably carrying better gear than this clapped out old thing. We're just carrying milk, eggs and stuff for old folks. That Yellowstone van… imagine what all those gadgets are worth. What,' Danny held out his hands, 'have I not made a point?'

'Cute weapons,' Iceblue laughed. 'Right, time to party. Sorry, whoever you are—'

'Danny. Danny Price. And you are *not* going to party on my watch again.' Danny held his cricket bat out horizontally, pointing right at Iceblue.

'You,' Iceblue said to the rider on his left. 'Start us off.'

The rider dismounted and approached, flexing his knuckles in his gloves. Beneath the visor, he grinned. Then, with a *thwack,* Sparky's bat made contact with the helmet.

'Touch it and I'll break your- ow!'

The second rider had thrust himself on Sparky, who writhed on the floor.

Danny swung his bat toward the first rider. It hit him square in the side of the chest. The rider collapsed. Sparky was fighting with the second. Danny shoved the bat into the second rider's kidney. He collapsed too, to a heap.

But Danny gasped in agony, feeling a pinching at the nape of his neck.

'You think you're so cute, don't you, prick,' Iceblue hissed. He reached into his jacket and started to pull out a long metal club. 'Well, take a load of- oooh!'

The pain in Danny's neck subsided, but it ached. He turned around. Sparky wrestled with Iceblue before landing a punch on the rider across his face. Sparky pushed himself up and poked the bat into Iceblue's mid-chest.

'Drop it,' Sparky said. 'Fucking drop it, or I swear to god…'

'Alright, easy tiger,' Iceblue heaved. He released his grip. The club rattled to the ground. 'Happy? We all friends now?'

'Piss off,' Danny said.

'Good party,' Sparky heaved. Iceblue wiped his mouth, which had started to seep blood. 'But we expected you. Bring more friends next time.'

'Gah! You fucked with the wrong people,' Iceblue said.

'Tell me who you work for.'

Iceblue laughed. 'You're fucking stupid, you know that?'

'I'm not the one about to get fucked up with a cricket bat. What was it you said? You weren't going to put me in hospital, you were going to put me in the grave?'

'God damn,' Iceblue hissed. 'Work it out yourself if you're so bloody clever.' Danny raided the bat above his head, baring his teeth in unrestrained rage. 'Shit!'

'Danny, no!' Sparky said. 'You're better than that shit.'

Danny lowered the bat, then recanted, whacking it into Iceblue's side.

'You're wasting your time,' Sparky said, getting up and kicking Iceblue, who writhed once more. 'He ain't going to talk.'

'You wouldn't like the answer,' Iceblue hissed in pain. 'I found out some plenty strange stuff from my boss. Someone I think you know well.' He laughed and said no more.

'The hell's that meant to mean?' Sparky said.

'You can come with us until you do decide to talk,' Danny said. 'Open the damn door, Sparky.'

Sparky did so. 'Danny, be careful—'

'I am,' Danny said with a heave. 'Get him in.'

Sparky heaved too, and they threw Iceblue into the back of the van. His writhing form landed on a pile of packages with a thud. Underneath his form, streaks of blood and dirt clung to the surface.

'Don't you dare think of causing any shit,' Danny said into the darkness in the back of the van, just as Iceblue lifted his head. 'You got something to say?'

Iceblue gurgled, his limbs slipping. He managed to, with a tremor, extend a hand in a fist, which he rotated before raising just the one finger in the middle. Then he laughed, but the cackle was cut off by Danny slamming the door shut.

'Shit,' Sparky said, 'what're we going to do?'

'Get out of here, for starters,' Danny said, snarling with anger as he walked to the driver's door. He clambered in, pulling the door closed behind with a clank. Sparky did the same in the passenger side.

Danny started the engine. The van sputtered. 'Come on,' he said, trying again. The van complied. He turned back into the road, swerving past the three parked mopeds and their bested riders.

'That wasn't serious,' he said to Sparky.

'What do you mean?'

'Before, there was five of them. And before there was none of that theatrical stuff.' Danny swallowed. 'They'd have just gone for the van. That's what they want.'

'I hope you're right. What about the rest of the packages?'

'Don't worry,' Sparky said. 'Let's go. Let's get him back to base before he makes any more mess in the back.'

'What about the others?'

'Choice we have to make.'

'Okay,' Danny said, guiding the van into a sloppy turn, back toward Kier Wood as the summer sky turned to sunset.

CHAPTER 18

The van raced through the streets toward Kier Wood. Rounding out of town and toward the bypass, Danny saw an ominous sight above the treeline.

A column of smoke rose against the orange sky.

'Christ,' Sparky said. 'What the hell's going on there?'

They were about to find out. Danny brought the van to a stop at the final set of lights. The bypass was deserted but he still had to wait.

The lights changed, and the engine gunned.

Danny drove up the ramp but came to a sudden halt.

'That's not good,' Sparky said. The gate was closed, barricaded shut.

'I'm going around the front,' Danny said, wrenching the wheel. He drove the van along the service road and stopped again. He felt lashings of heat through the cab of the van. 'Jesus Christ.'

The car park was sparsely populated with cars but filled with at least a dozen mopeds that Danny could count. They whizzed around the paved space in chaotic circles. A few of the old trolley storage bays had been smashed and fires set in them, smoke filtering through the smashed plexiglass.

Another group of the riders were against the foyer doors while a few pushed against the glass doors.

Danny crawled forward to peek a bit further. He couldn't see beyond the glass of the doors. The low sun in the sky opposite reflected off the glass.

Some of the riders stopped. They'd clearly seen Danny.

'Shit.'

Danny pushed the gear lever into reverse and nudged the accelerator. The van was slow to react, but lurched backward after a couple of moments.

Two staccato buzzes of static erupted from beneath the van.

Stand clear! This vehicle is reversing! Stand clear!

Danny closed his eyes for a moment.

'Here they come,' Sparky said. Danny looked forward. About ten of the riders ceased their laps of the car park and made a beeline toward the van.

Danny grinned and pushed the gear lever back.

'What're you doing?' Sparky said. 'Danny…'

'Shh,' he hissed as the diesel engine in front roared. Then, with a click, Danny selected first gear. His foot jabbed upward off the clutch. The van skidded before gaining traction.

'Danny!' Sparky shouted again, grasping for the handle above the passenger door. 'Don't do it!'

Danny didn't listen and gripped the steering wheel. His knuckles turned white, and he glared forward at the group of riders that approached. He shut his eyes instinctively. The front of the van made thudding sounds, and the group appeared to split just as the last moment as the windscreen cracked with the impact with the mopeds.

'Shit!' Danny ducked, but the glass didn't cave in. 'Where'd they go?'

More thuds came from all around. The buzzing sound of two-stroke moped engines followed too, all getting closer to form an arc of bodies around the cab.

'We've gotta get out of here,' Sparky said. 'We're a sitting duck!'

'You're not wrong,' Danny said, reaching for the door handle. He clicked it. The door pushed open a crack. Then he pushed the door. It squealed as the van rocked under the bombardment of concrete and cement pieces. Danny glanced over his shoulder. 'Sparky?'

Sparky wasn't there.

'Danny!' Sparky appeared in front of Danny. Danny glanced left and right, puzzled. 'Quick!'

They pounced to the rear of the van and opened the door.

'Get him outta here,' Danny said, leaning in with Sparky to pull Iceblue to his feet. The guy made no effort to stand on his own, so was a complete dead weight. Danny and Sparky slung him between them.

They stumbled to the corner of the building. Danny looked down the front toward the foyer, which jutted out a hundred feet or so away. There were seven semi-circular windows, all pockmarked with damage. Cracks spier-webbed across the glass. Inside, metal security shutters blocked the view inward.

'Can't stay here,' he said. 'Gotta get in.'

'They seem to have lost us,' Sparky said. 'Let's try to get past 'em, get in the back. This douchebag weighs a ton.'

'Okay, good plan,' Danny said. He heaved. 'And he does!'

'Follow me,' Sparky said. They crept around the corner, down the path that Danny had driven the van from. The colleague door beckoned. 'Got your pass?'

Danny patted his chest and pulled out the piece of plastic. 'Yep.'

'Tap it,' Sparky said. Danny did so. The pad buzzed. The row of three LEDs glowed carmine red.

'Bollocks,' Sparky wheezed. 'They've locked the store down.'

'Can't blame 'em,' Danny said. 'What about the yard?' Just a few feet away was the massive gate to the delivery yard. The structure was at least forty feet tall, most of that netting to keep birds out. Danny shook the gate, which wiggled along its form. 'Oi, anyone there?'

Noises came from the other side of the gate. The scraping of shoes on the cement. Metal clinking together. The gate vibrated, then yawned as it opened inward.

'Danny, Sparky,' Rick said. 'Just in time.' He pointed at Iceblue. 'Who the hell's that?'

'Special guest,' Danny said. 'The hell happened?' The yard was a mess of disarray.

'Absolutely. They've been rampaging through the whole place.'

'Christ,' Sparky said. Danny hummed. He heard hoots and hollering as the yard gate closed behind them and the sound of mopeds grew. It was getting closer.

'Quick,' Rick said. 'Get inside!'

Danny and Sparky scampered inside, just as a handful of the yobs erupted from the other end of the yard on their scooters and bounded toward them.

Inside, the noise of the riders echoed in and became deafening. A group of three or four rider shouted; the atmosphere chaotic. At the front of the store, loud thudding music pushing and vibrated the walls and glass doors. Then there was a crash of breaking windows.

Danny and Sparky dropped Iceblue to the ground against a wall.

'Sparky, tie him up,' Danny said. Sparky disappeared to find some nylon rope, reappearing and lashing Iceblue to a column.

210

'Has anyone called the police?' Danny asked.

Rick shrugged. 'No reply.'

'Useless anyway,' another retorted.

Danny rounded into the delivery annex and up the three metal stairs into the office. The whole room was asunder. He reached for the phone on the desk, jabbed his index finger into the keypad.

'Hello? Police? This is Mertons Kier Wood, under some kind of, well, attack. We've got dozens of trespassers it seems, they've… oh, right.' Danny's face contorted. 'You don't have the resources for this one? What a fucking shock. Well…' Danny trailed off. A tinny voice offered worthless platitudes. 'Well, *officer*, thanks for your help. Bye.' The handset clattered.

'Told you,' Badger said. 'Useless bunch.'

Whooping and hollering came from outside. Danny stepped out of the office ad through the racking. The yelling got louder.

'Hey, you!' a voice called. Danny looked sharply up. A rider was hanging from the barrier to the metal mezzanine floor above the warehouse. The metal rail rocked. It wasn't permanently fixed; this was where forklift trucks lifted pallets of merchandise to the upper floor. The horizontal barrier began to spin as the rider pushed and swayed on it like the paddle-wheel of some old time showboat. 'Come join the party!'

'Don't!' Danny shouted, running from the racking aisle into the open walkway, but the barrier rotated, and the rider lost his balance, falling with a smack to the concrete floor of the warehouse.

Then the flappy doors to the sales floor banged. Six or seven other riders emerged from the bright lights into the gloom of the warehouse.

'Crap,' Sparky said. The riders saw their fallen comrade writhing on the floor. Then they looked to Danny in the open space.

'You,' one of the riders snarled. 'Look what you did to Polygon.'

'Polygon?!' Danny mouthed. His eyes darted. A couple of the new riders went to help the fallen youth to his feet. 'Look, that was nothing to do with me.'

'Like shit it was,' the rider said, stepping forward.

'Watch it, Swatch,' one of the others urged. The rider who challenged Danny glanced over his shoulder.'

'You watch it, punk. We gotta teach this one,' he pointed at Danny, 'a lesson for wrecking our party.' He nodded in Danny's direction. Three of the riders joined Swatch and advanced on Danny.

'I told you, nothing to do with me!' he shouted. 'But you lot shouldn't be here. Just piss off.'

'Ooh,' Swatch said in mock outrage. 'Now he's getting antsy. Right party-pooper. Let's show him the way out.'

The three riders advanced, and Danny backed, but they formed an arc and the way back into the warehouse was blocked.

'Run,' Sparky shouted. More riders appeared, the sound of the heavy music erupting through the doors. Danny cast an eye about. A huge set of speakers mounted to a trolley blared the music into the space, creating a total cacophony that echoed around the airy warehouse.

Danny couldn't run, but was backed further into the warehouse. 'Argh,' he winced, feeling a sharp pain in his ankles. The metal stairs up to the mezzanine! Danny scrabbled upward. The riders pulled from their waistbands crowbars, and eased brass knuckled fists into a waiting palm.

This was going to be bad.

The mezzanine floor creaked as Danny ran onto it. Footsteps

followed fast up the stairs behind him. The mezzanine was almost empty. Just some piles of old cabinetry. Rolls of paper. Irregular stacks of supplies that went back years, quietly forgotten. The ceiling above closed in on the floor.

'Come out, come out, wherever you are,' Swatch goaded. 'We'll find you. You'll pay for what you did to Polygon. And them some.'

'Yeah,' one of the other riders cackled. 'Something alright!'

The footsteps stopped.

'You two,' Swatch mumbled. 'Spread out and drag that fucker out.'

'Yes, boss,' the other squeaked.

Danny held his breath, daring not to move an inch. His hiding place wasn't very convincing. The floor creaked all around him. The stairs wailed too. More people were coming. The music still blared from downstairs.

He tried to move to get a better view, but the floor gave a long, horrific *yaaaawwww* as it creaked.

Silence. Even the music seemed to fade to nothing.

'Over there,' Swatch said. 'You hear that noise. Over there.'

There, Danny realised, was where he was. He glanced around. The ceiling and metallic walls were closing in.

But then he smiled, seeing the concertina gate to the other part of the mezzanine that he'd forgotten existed. His eyes darted, waiting to see the looming shadows getting closer. One was climbing up the wall.

'Swatch,' the voice said, really loudly and clearly. The top of the rider's head appeared above the parapet of the old products. 'He's here.'

And then Danny sprung, pushing the rider away and onto the floor with a crack and made for the gate, praying it wasn't locked.

'Hey, punk!' the rider hissed. The floor behind Danny thudded with a thunderous rapture of footsteps.

The door filled Danny's vision, and he pushed. It didn't move. 'Crap!' Then he saw the pad beside it. Fumbling in his pocket he pulled out his Mertons swipe card and tapped the pad.

The door didn't open.

'Shit,' Danny cursed. He felt two hands digging into his shoulder, then tumbled back.

'So,' the rider, Swatch, spat. 'You wanna be the hero? Chance has gone, pal.' Swatch laughed, dragging Danny back onto the mezzanine area, the particleboard floor creaking with every step and grunt of effort.

Danny squinted, his face aimed directly at one of the flourescent lights dangling from the ceiling.

Then he stopped.

'What do you want done first?' Swatch asked. 'Is Polygon gonna be okay?'

'Yeah,' another rider said, 'But we have to sort this fucker out.' Danny looked. He saw the goods lift with the heavy metal concertina door. His eyes narrowed even more. 'This'll do, boss,' the other rider said. Danny heard the racket of tape being torn off a roll.

'get up,' Swatch said, dragging Danny to his feet. 'You know what I'm gonna do to you?'

Danny laughed. 'That's stealing, that is,' he said, nodding toward the second rider before ducking, pushing into Swatch with a thud.

Swatch went limp as he fell backward, but scrabbled on the floor.

Perfect, Danny thought. He backed toward the goods lift, putting one hand behind him.

'You little shit!' Swatch called. 'Curly, help me!'

The other rider came forward, but Danny was ready. His hand found the handle of the goods lift door. It wobbled. The two riders advanced. He pulled, feeling the door's weight.

'Come on,' he hissed through gritted teeth. 'Come on!'

The door opened, revealing a void where the lift car should be. Danny's face screwed up as the door heaved open with a wail of metallic friction. He saw the piece of cardboard in the frame that had been overriding the safety switch. *Just as well.*

Curly tumbled forward, not expecting the door to open, and disappeared into the shaft with a yelp, then a crash. It didn't take long – the shaft was only a storey tall, and the roof of the car broke the guy's fall.

Swatch wasn't so foolish, so teetered on the threshold. He spun, grasping Danny with both hands, naturally pulling him forward.

'You don't wanna do that!' Danny said as Swatch overbalanced. With both hands, Danny pulled at Swatch's gloved hands, disentangling them. Swatch continued to teeter, his focus slipping from pulling Danny to stopping himself falling.

It was enough. Danny took the upper hand and grabbed the rider's uniform. He felt a bulbous pouch in his front pocket slip. Danny watched the glass screen – a phone of some kind – fall in the struggle to the floor, just avoiding the lift, but landing with a crack.

'Shit!' Swatch said, his eyes darting to the floor. 'No!'

Danny heard footsteps outside. Curly was coming back upstairs. He took the initiative and shoved. Swatch fell backward with a yell. Danny ducked, picking up the phone. He turned, hearing the door beep!

'Anyone here?!' a voice called. Danny recognised it and smiled.

'Brian!' he yelled, running toward the door. He glanced, seeing Curly tumble back through the regular door, but Danny was bursting with momentum. He fell through the emergency door and pushed closed again with a roar.

On the other side of the door, Danny planted on the white flooring of the staff corridor.

Danny heard raised voices.

'Get him!' Swatch called. 'Bust that shit down!'

Danny scrabbled to his feet. The reprieve was temporary, and he darted away. Metal rended and squealed, and more noisy footsteps followed. Danny grabbed the shelving of this part of the warehouse. It jittered. He pulled on the shelves. Boxes atop wobbled, but more so, before tumbling.

'Get him!' the riders called, but Danny was already past them and out of the door and into the stark, off-white corridor outside.

Danny stood on the apex of a staircase.

'This way, Danny,' Brian said.

Downstairs, toward the shop floor, the sounds of crashing anarchy and disorder.

Across, past a battered door, cries and moans.

Brian pushed the door open and squeezed through.

Danny followed. 'Jeez, what's happened here?!' Danny pushed into the canteen. Tables had been upended and a tired sofa lay in front of the door, which is why it'd produced the struggle. 'The hell's happened?'

'They've been here hours,' one colleague said as Danny picked his way through the chaos. 'We couldn't stop them getting in.'

'Where'd they come from?' Danny asked. He helped the colleague to her feet. 'Are you alright?'

An older colleague wheezed and got up from behind the barricade. 'They've trashed the place, Danny. It's all ruined.'

'Didn't you try to get out? Through the warehouse? That's how I got in.'

'It was too risky,' the colleague said. 'Some tried, I don't know what happened. They were everywhere.'

'The police are useless,' another added between sobs. She was a middle-aged woman, her figure bullish but hearty. *Mumsy*. Danny blinked heavily as he listened. 'Twenty bloody years, I can't see a way back.'

'Don't say that,' Danny said. A weird silence befell the canteen. He looked around. Thirty colleagues had hidden here. The sharp noise of metal wailing snapped Danny to attention. He ran to the window that overlooked the yard. The riders careened about the space like a pack of hyenas. 'I called them. They're coming,' Danny said to the colleague, meeting her gaze. Hers wobbled. Danny wasn't sure if he was convincing himself or her. He pursed his lips, hoping he was right.

The door to the rest of the staff area at the far end of the canteen creaked.

'Brian,' Danny said. 'Impeccable timing.'

Brian sighed, catching his breath, his shirt in tatters, his tie loose around his neck. Soot and dirt marked his face. 'Danny, I'm so glad I found you…'

'Why?'

'You've got to get out of here, Danny,' Brian said with a deep, gasping wheeze. 'You've got to go and make sure they don't get—' he stopped himself.

Danny relaxed his shoulders. 'Is this anything to do with my nan?'

Brian shrugged. 'Yes. She's… the company…'

'Is this to do with a big briefcase of paperwork she's sitting on?

As in, literally? She nearly freaked when our roof nearly came in.'

Outside the canteen, footsteps rocketed up the stairs.

'They're coming! Hide, everyone!'

Everyone did, with a couple of people pushing the sofa back against the door to the shop floor.

'Danny, with me,' Brian said, dragging Danny with him into the training room. The same room where he'd been offered the job those weeks ago. Brian fell into a chair with a harsh scrape. 'You've got to go. Right now.'

'I can't leave you guys to deal with this.'

'Danny, as your senior manager I've gotta be firm. You can't help here. We have a contingency. A backup,' Brian said, combing his hands through his thinning hair. 'We knew this day'd come eventually, the vans... this was the escalation. But to attack and ransack a store... *multiple* locations, all within a few days... this means one thing,' Brian said, lifting his head up. The glassy look in his eyes had disappeared behind a steely glint. 'This was co-ordinated.'

'By who? Are we thinking the same thing?'

'I...' Brian started, but the sentence never finished. One of the captive colleagues bashed through the door. 'Time to go, yeah?' Brian said past Danny.

'Yeah,' the colleague said.

Danny's phone buzzed. He pulled it from his pocket. It was home. He swiped his finger, leaving a trail of sweat on the glass screen.

'Nan,' he said with a hoarse breath. He held the phone to his ear for a few seconds. 'I'm coming. Call the police. Bolt the door.' Then he pocketed the phone again and turned to Brian. 'They're at my house. *My house!*'

'Fuck,' Brian said with a big sigh. 'Go, Danny. She's more valuable than you could realise.'

'You can explain later! Look after the guys,' Danny said. 'I'll make a distraction as I go. Get as many of them out.'

Brian nodded. 'You do your job; I'll do mine.'

'We'll get through this!'

Danny had started to realise, but he parked that thought as he pushed up from the laminate tabletop to his feet, nearly wrenching to door off its hinges and into the corridor. The smell of smoke and sorrow nearly dragged him back into the maelstrom, but flashing lights filtered through the window out to the world at the far end of the corridor.

Dashing into the yard, his face fell when he saw the column Sparky had tied Iceblue to was now devoid of a figure at its base.

'Shit,' he said. Then he realised where Iceblue might've gone. 'Shit!'

He ran, and he could only hope he'd get back in time.

CHAPTER 19

Nestled in the Hertfordshire hills, the unassuming country pile had seemingly been there since time immemorial. The weather of the past century had softened the red-brick facade into the terrain.

The mansion was a contrast indeed to the high-tech steel-and-glass pile that symbolised the most powerful commercial enterprise on the planet, but the man responsible and who symbolised everything the behemoth did needed an anonymous place to secrete himself at this most trying of times for the company.

But the face of tradition was skin-deep. On the other side of the walls, a bedroom bedecked in opulent, smooth shades of grey beckoned, with flashes of chiffon yellow around the dados at the top of the wall.

From a greyscale duvet that covered the super-king-size bed, Grayson Laurie emerged.

'Parker,' he muttered. A synthetic tune trilled from beside the bed. 'I'm awake.'

Welcome to another wonderful day, Mr Laurie, a false American male voice emitted from the ceiling. *Everything is super in your world today.*

Grayson Laurie smiled. Parker always woke him up with this optimism, just as he had programmed him to.

'Good,' he said, putting foot onto the light grey carpet. A grid of lights in the ceiling flashed yellow as he moved around the room toward the en-suite. He stepped in, dropping his pyjamas and swished a hand toward the expansive shower cubicle. The door glided open.

Crossing the threshold, the water coursed from a rainfall head, forming a curtain of water at a perfect temperature that he stepped into. The light followed above, illuminating the oblong frame of the cubicle. Tranquil notes of music followed for eighteen blissful minutes. Grayson held his head back and let the water rinse over him.

After eighteen minutes, Parker toned down the music and reminded Grayson of his day:

Mr Laurie, you have fourteen appointments today. First: ten twenty-five AM with…

But Parker stopped there. The serenity and anonymity that brought Grayson Laurie to Honeydew House was shattered. First by shouting, then by the *thwack-crack* sound of objects being hurled through the gate and smacking on the ground.

Grayson leapt from the shower and glanced through the window above the sink, which overlooked the drive. The end of the drive was a couple of hundred feet away.

'Parker,' he said, hurriedly donning a towel, 'call security. What are those people doing?'

Sir, I cannot reach the security system. Shall I call for manual backup?

'What do you mean, you can't reach the security system?'

Martin Hennessey has not logged in.

Grayson's eyes widened, and not with pleasant surprise. He rushed, letting the towel fall, back into his master bedroom.

'Switch the cameras to my personal monitor,' he barked. Parker did so, a cliff-face television opposite the bed illuminating into a grid of camera views.

Outside the gates to Honeydew Mansion, a rabble had arrived.

They knew he was here.

They knew where he lived.

How the fuck did this happen?!

Grayson reached for his phone from its place on the bedside table. He slid through the menus into the contacts, scrolling to the one he wanted. He jabbed a finger into a green *dial* button and held the phone to his ear.

'Where the hell are you?' Grayson barked. A man in his position could skip the pleasantries when the situation demanded it. *This one did.* He never arrived at Honeydew during the day; always under the cover of night. The house was owned by a labyrinth of holding companies arranged to obfuscate the nosy or the unwanted.

Yet he'd been *found*. And not by friends.

Grayson listened to what the voice on the other end of the phone had to say before terminating the call. He'd heard enough. He slipped into some of his casual clothes - hoodie, jeans, to appear on-trend, and then made his way down the opulent staircase. It had once been fashioned with stained oak and a regal red carpet runner, but it followed the aesthetic of the rest of Honeydew: greyscale wood with flashes of yellow down the bannisters. Some had called it clinical, some masterful, depending on who they were and whether Grayson Laurie had subsumed their media outlet into the Yellowstone conglomerate.

Sir, you shouldn't exit the grounds unaccompanied, Parker trilled, his ever-present voice following Grayson around the house. The yellow light that trailed him now hung around the hallway of Honeydew Mansion.

He reached to the sideboard and pulled his watch from the side. The satin-finished puck of anodised steel and glass slid onto his wrist. The display lit up with a smiley face.

Are we going for a walk, sir? The voice now came from the watch.

'I know what I'm doing,' Grayson said, pushing the latch and opening the door.

The crowd at the bottom of the driveway was louder as Grayson let the natural air enter his ears. A variety of electric vehicles beckoned next to him, but he walked the length of the driveway as the clamour got louder and uglier.

'Please,' he called, knowing he'd be in earshot. The rabble stopped for a moment, almost shocked. They looked at each other, waiting for *someone* to take the first step in this meeting.

'You fucked up my whole life!' one man said, smashing the silence with his ugly words.

Grayson smiled. 'Please, friend,' he started, approaching the gate, 'tell me what it is I can do for you?'

'Fuck off and never come back,' the man spat. 'Take your slimy American arse and fuck off back to wherever it is you come from.'

Danger, sir! Parker trilled. *Extreme danger!*

Grayson's smile faltered just enough. Then he ducked as the first egg smashed against his jeans with a thwack. Then the missiles followed in a volley all around, pockmarking the driveway with smashed shells and their runny contents.

Grayson turned and ran, his face flushed with blind panic. He glanced only a few times over his shoulder, seeing the crowd boil over. They wrestled with the gates, which wailed and wobbled.

Finally, Grayson Laurie had returned to his castle, trembling with panic and confusion.

Heads would roll for this, he snivelled, as belatedly, sirens cauterised the cacophony on his doorstep.

A storm emerged from the lift in the Yellowstone campus in

the form of Grayson Laurie.

'Sir,' Heaton McCall said as Grayson walked toward the office door. 'Good morning, we were beginning to—'

'Shut up,' Grayson barked. He pulled the door open violently. 'Get in here.'

Heaton followed. 'Sir… Mr Laurie, what's happened?'

'Near enough a damn riot at my house, Heaton. Who told them that Honeydew was my English pad, exactly?'

'No-one did. I don't know what you're… a riot? What happened?' Grayson pointed to the dried egg on his shoulders. 'That's terrible.'

'I want legal on standby,' Grayson said. 'Pull the whole damn thing apart if you have to.'

'Sir, that'll take time. You deliberately made it a complicated affair…'

'Clearly not complicated enough!' Grayson said. He took a deep lungful of air. 'Sorry, you were saying?'

'The Commission is here. They're waiting for you.'

Sir, you've six new additions to your calendar, Parker beeped. *Would you like me to tell you who's-*

'Shut it, Parker!' Grayson cleared his throat and pulled the hoodie off, tossing it over a chair. 'I'll go in as I am. Good news?'

'They didn't say,' Heaton said, 'but they looked pissed.'

'We'll see,' Grayson said. His shoulders relaxed. 'Sorry, Heaton. It's been… quite a morning.'

Heaton smiled. 'I bet. Here's the data,' he said, pushing a tablet computer toward Grayson, who took it. Grayson smiled. Green charts were always good.

'What room?'

'Boardroom sixteen.'

Grayson laughed. 'We have sixteen?'

'More than!'

The door to Boardroom Sixteen was at the end of a long corridor about midway up the building. The corridor had no windows; it was a dead end. The white walls seemed to close in as Grayson walked. He'd glanced at the tablet but not studied it. He didn't have the time. Even the wealthiest man in the world knew better than to keep the Commission waiting longer than they needed to.

A pair of double doors punched through the wall. Grayson held onto the gunmetal handle, pushed, felt the latch click. The door opened with a swish.

They were waiting.

'Thank you, Mr Laurie,' Grady said, getting up and ushering Grayson to an empty chair on one side of the conference room. He sat down next to Wendy Tunt.

'Wendy,' Grayson mumbled as he scraped his chair back into place.

'Grayson,' she mumbled back. Her face was like cement. She darted a glance at the dried egg on his shoulder. 'Should I ask?'

'No, you shouldn't.'

'Well,' the first man said, clearing his throat harshly. He was a thin, uptight man with skin taut against the structures of his neck. 'I'm glad we can finally get this meeting into order.'

'I do apologise…' Grayson began. Heaton ducked to meet his ear.

'Ben Steele, head of the Commission, That's Anthea Franklin and that,' Heaton nodded at the blob in the third chair, 'is Arthur Gravey.'

'Right.'

Steele held a hand up. 'No time for that, Mr Laurie.'

Grayson's eyes darted. He wasn't expecting that. 'Well, did you want to go over the Prime successes or—'

'No, we don't.'

Franklin spoke up. She was an older woman whose features had slowly collapsed into rolls of skin beneath her chin. 'We're concerned about some operations in Blue Zones. We want to know if you've any idea about them?'

'Blue zones?' Grayson laughed. 'What would I know about Blue zones? Apart from their substandard public services, held together by the last vestiges of—'

'Enough,' Steele said. 'We don't need the sales pitch.'

'We just want to know the truth from you.'

A third Commissioner piped in. 'It's better for you if you tell us now. We take an extremely dim view of dishonesty to us.'

Grayson didn't know who to look at. 'Well… what trouble is it you're talking about?'

Steele nodded at his colleague. The screen at the end of the conference table showed photos. Mopeds riding around an estate. The burned-out remains of a Mertons van. Terrified children.

'Where's this?'

'Upper Hedingbury,' Gravey said. 'Show the map now.'

The collage of grainy photos became a map of the United Kingdom, overlaid with shaded blotches, Grey. Blue. Yellow. About roughly equal size. The blue was concentrated toward the North, but not totally. The yellow swept in from the West. The grey pockmarked the two.

It was a map that Grayson Laurie was familiar with. He glanced at Tunt, who was also looking at the map, her face not saying a word.

This was the Battle Map. Tunt's job was to turn it completely yellow.

'You see,' Steele said, gesturing to the map. A wave of dots appeared to pepper the image. 'These are all reported incidences. Do you see a pattern emerging?'

Grayson swallowed as the pattern was clear to all in the room. The dots appeared only on blue areas of the map. He took a breath. 'Might I just say…'

'Please do,' Franklin interjected. 'The next slide, please,' she said, and the image shifted, 'shows the planned rezoning distribution.' Most of the blue zones with the most dots had turned into hatched yellow. 'The pattern further develops.'

'I… I… I don't quite know what you're inferring,' Grayson said. 'This is news to me,' he finished. It really was.

Ben Steele turned to Grayson, peering down his nose and through his glasses, his pupils like laser beams. 'We're putting you on notice. None of our planned work will go ahead until a full investigation of this. We play fair, Mr Laurie,' the commissioner said. 'And we want to make sure you do, too.'

'We'll reconvene in six weeks,' Franklin said, getting to his feet with his colleagues. 'Until then,'

'You can't,' Tunt said, her first words of the meeting.

'I assure you,' Gravey said, stopping to catch breath from the effort of getting up. 'We can and we will.'

'The parliament…'

'They appointed us, and our word is beyond their legislation. Read the standing orders,' the Commissioner said. 'Or better, ask your legal team to.'

'Look, look,' Grayson said, painting a smile across his face. 'This is all… a big misunderstanding. There's no ill will here. We have an ambitious timeline and we'd hate for this to intercede with these grand plans, which we're dying to tell you about.'

The three Commissioners remained stony-faced.

Steele started. 'We may be more forthright should your organisation assist our enquiry. We'll leave it there. Your legal team should be more than capable of acceding to our request.'

The Commissioners left the room without even glancing at the Yellowstone delegation, disappearing into the corridor.

The conference room door clicked closed.

'Do either of you two,' Grayson pointed at Tunt and Grady, 'want to fucking *explain* what just happened in there? What the hell is going on with that map?' He pointed to the chart on the screen. The dots across the blue zones hung like filthy fairy lights on an incriminating Christmas tree.

'Rest assured, Grayson,' Tunt said as Grayson took deep breaths in his chair, his form rising and falling. 'Our plan to consolidate our operations is completely above board. Ask Grady here if you doubt me. Do you doubt me, Grayson?' she said lower. 'After all the work I've done for—'

'No, no, of course not, Wendy,' he said, breaking his gaze with her. 'Any idea who these punks are?'

'We do,' Tunt said.

'They're Deliverangel operatives,' Grady said.

'They made a hasty retreat in the states when Yellowstone really exploded.'

'Yeah,' Tunt said. 'Now they're here and causing trouble. I think,' she said, 'that they're trying to pin their bad behaviour on us. They're non-affiliated, probably trying to get out of the doldrums of the grey zones. Of course,' she smiled at Grayson, 'we'd *never* work with them. Not in a million years. The reputational damage would be...'

'Yes, far too great,' Grayson trailed off.

'We're working on the Mertons acquisition, too,' she said.

This was news to Grayson. 'Good,' he said. 'Keep up the good work. And keep me informed, of course.'

'Of course,' Tunt smiled as they motioned toward the conference room door. 'Lunch?'

'Sure, Wendy,' Grayson said. 'I'll join you in a minute.' He watched her walk down the corridor. 'You,' he said, turning to Grady. 'Get in there.'

'Sir,' Grady said, clearly surprised. 'Whatever's the—'

'What's this about a Mertons acquisition? That'd never get through the Commission.' Grady didn't blink. 'Tell me what's happening and you'll have either the best or the worst days of your career. And I'm sorry, sorry that I have to threaten you here.'

'Sir,' Grady the lawyer said, 'I don't like it either, but I do what I'm told. By Ms Tunt.'

'You realise this is *my* company, not Wendy Tunt's?'

'Sir,' Grady said again, avoiding Grayson's gaze. 'This puts me in a most impossible position.'

'We've worked together for years,' Grayson said, trembling. 'Are you sure you want to do this?' Grady nodded. 'You're fired, Grady. I'm sorry.'

But Grady didn't react at all to those words. *You're fired.* Grayson twisted his neck in intrigue.

'So am I,' Grady said, 'but I'm afraid you can't do that.'

The lawyer brushed past the richest man in the world as if nothing had happened.

Grayson turned to watch Grady walk away from him. His face trembled with anger. But then he took a deep breath, feeling his whole body relax.

Instead, he laughed.

'Time for daddy to check on you,' he said to thin air.

He disappeared into his own building, slipping into a nondescript door in the basement that led to a ladder going down into darkness.

'Mr Cube,' Grayson said in a murmur that still echoed against the rough walls of the cavern the ladder entered.

'Sir,' Jacob said, pivoting from a terminal.

'How's he doing?' Grayson asked. He cast an eye around the dark space. Lights twinkled, and if he squinted to let his eyes lose focus, it was almost like a starlit night.

'He's… behaving, today.'

'Better than yesterday,' Grayson Laurie hummed. 'You getting everything you need? Remember what I told you at the start? You ask, you get. No questions asked. By anyone.'

'Fine,' Jacob said. He looked, seeing Grayson disappearing into the racks of equipment. 'Sir, are you okay?'

'Fine, fine,' he said, but was lying. He turned with a sniffle. 'I just wanted to see how he was doing.'

'Sir,' Jacob said, 'what this room represents is going to change the world. We'll get it right.'

'I know,' Grayson said. 'Are we still on schedule?'

'Next code refresh is due in an hour. Should improve the metrics we discussed last time we reboot it's—'

'Jacob, we agreed. Parker isn't an *it*, he's a *he*. What we're creating, he's more than the sum of his parts.'

'Sir.'

Grayson picked up a circuit board. 'A silicon dream. Now becoming reality. This is what it was all for…'

'Sir,' Jacob repeated. 'Are you okay?'

Grayson turned, his face pinched in. He nodded in the affirmative, though wasn't. 'Keep it up,' he said, moving past Jacob and toward the ladder. 'I suppose I'd best go have lunch.'

'Good luck, sir,' Jacob said.

'I'll need it.'

CHAPTER 20

The house was completely dark as Danny approached. He pulled up and scrambled out of his car.

The scent of burning wrinkled his nostrils. He glanced up at the ruins of the roof. Wisps of dark smoke rose against the azure blue sky. Then he glanced down.

The front door was open, reduced to a deep black maw. The bay window was smashed, angular shards of glass cutting inward.

A door to the right clicked. Danny sprang up, but stopped. It was Mrs Lister.

'Oh, Danny,' she said. 'It was horrible!'

'Is she okay? What happened?'

'There was a big gang of them. They came up the path,' Mrs Lister said, gesturing to the green. It was marked with brown ruts leading to the doorway. 'They tore up the grass on their scooters. Look, they left one outside.'

Danny walked slowly through the evening gloom toward the tiny front yard of his house. The scooter was in silhouette. He peeked, seeing a flash of pink. It was enough. He recognised it. He knelt down, putting a hand to the engine block. It was warm, or at least not as cold as it should've been had it been here a while.

He swept around, back to Mrs Lister's porch. 'Stupid question, but have you called the police?'

'My husband, Alan did, yes,' Mrs Lister said.

Footsteps came from within the house. A bearded man appeared on the doorstep next to Mrs Lister.

'You must be Danny,' a bearded man in a polo-neck and glasses said. 'Alan Lister.'

'I'd say it was nice to meet you,' Danny said.

'They were tearing up the street. Bloody bastards.'

'Look, I want to go and see if my nan's okay.'

'You sure? You don't want to wait for the police?'

'No,' Danny said. 'Those mopeds… I know who they're from.'

'They anything to do with this lot?' Alan asked, disappearing for a moment before reappearing, his hands full of glossy paper. He thrust it to Danny. 'Pesky bastards keep flyering the damn street.'

Danny glanced. The flash of pink and the Deliverangel emblem was enough.

'These are the guys, yes.'

'We got it all on camera. See?' Alan pointed to the camera on the door jamb.

'Good. Show me it later. I need to go and check.'

'You not waiting for the police?' she asked. 'They could still be inside.'

'Why wait for them?' Danny responded rhetorically. 'Fat lot of good they've been with these shits.'

Alan stepped forward. 'I'll come with you.'

'No,' Danny said. 'Don't risk yourself. These people aren't just thugs. They're organised. Bad news. You smell that?' he sniffed. Alan shook his head. 'Petrol and rubber. Yeah, I've got a good idea who's here.'

He hurried back into the littered ruins of his front garden and walked to the front door. Splaying his fingers, he pushed on the painted door.

It creaked and opened, without a key.

Danny stepped inside. His feet clacked on the floor.

First thing: the carpet runner was crumpled into a mess at the opposite end of the entrance hall. He turned. The main room was asunder with upset furniture and possessions thrown about. At first glance it was the result of some natural disaster. But upstairs footsteps clomped.

'Where is it? Where've you hidden it?' a voice called, muffled through the ceiling. 'We won't go until we find it!'

Danny clenched his fists, wanting to run straight for the stairs. But he held his breath behind his teeth which he pushed together. The breath carried a roar, and he didn't want to let it out. He stepped further into the ruins of his house.

The floorboards groaned. Danny stopped, glancing right into the kitchen.

Tyre tracks led through the kitchen across the lino floors. Beyond, through the doors, four mopeds were parked up on the grass.

Danny pushed the door open. It gave little resistance.

Examining the bike, he saw the sticker on the fuel tank of one of them. An ice cube.

'Shit,' Danny hissed. *He was still here.*

He put a hand to the engine, feeling subtle warmth.

Then he turned, walking back into the house, not bothering to close the door behind him.

A silhouette of a figure appeared in the doorway back into the living room.

'Thought you'd turn up,' the figure mumbled.

'You,' Danny said. The figure emerged from the kitchen into the gloom of the dining are. 'Iceblue. Like a fucking shadow,'

'And you, whose name I don't even know.

'I told you once,' Danny said. 'Danny Price. And I told you

that if you fucked with me—'

'Yeah, yeah,' Iceblue said. Those petrol-blew jewels in his eye sockets glimmered in the gloom. They glanced at the ceiling. Thudding rang through. The scraping and heaving of furniture being moved. 'We've looked everywhere,' he said. 'We know it's here.'

Danny's face hardened. 'Fucking lay a finger on her…'

'Whoa, whoa! The only person I'm going to lay a finger on is you,' Iceblue said, hobbling forward. 'For your little stunt earlier.'

'Thought you were down for the count.'

'Yet again, you thought wrong.' Iceblue heaved, wincing.

'No good,' Danny said. 'You're knackered.'

'Not gonna let you keep me away from the motherlode,' Iceblue hissed, meeting Danny's glance.

'Stay the fuck there,' Danny blurted. 'Want me to finish you off?'

Iceblue laughed, smiling a twisted grin.

'What's so fucking funny?'

'You,' Iceblue said, before shrieking as he bent over and barrelled into Danny, who went flying back. The floor clattered.

Danny stared at Iceblue who scrabbled over him. Then he felt the blackness and the pain as the punches fell on his chest, arms. Then his face. His head felt like broken glass.

The patchy view of the ruins of his dining room faded away with the pain. Danny's head rode on a lake of needles, buffeted by Iceblue's punches.

But they grew less regular. The delay grew, imperceptibly at first, but became a few milliseconds. Then a second.

Danny felt the blood rush to his head, between the impacts.

He growled, opening his eyes against the pain. Iceblue was above him, heaving for breath.

That was his chance. Danny's growl turned into a roar, his arms pushing him up from the prone position.

Now Iceblue, surprised, tumbled backward onto the hardwood floor. The bandit winced hard, sliding away.

Danny scrabbled forward, pulling at the rug beneath Iceblue. He spun like a turtle stranded on its shell, baffled by the motion. Danny strained, trying to get to his feet, but this gave Iceblue the chance to roll, knocking into Danny's legs like skittles. He fell again, with a definite clatter and an eruption of pain from his lower back.

The floor wasn't helping.

'Come here, you fucker...' Danny hissed hard through his teeth, grappling for Iceblue's taut leathers, but the surface was slippery and his sweat-drenched fingers and palms just couldn't get the purchase. Instead they grappled for the blonde hair of Danny's assailant, yanking at the locks.

'Try harder, pretty boy,' Iceblue managed, smiling widely.

Danny glanced from those crazy eyes to the balled fist racked to the side, then prepared for the-

Oooft!

Danny's head rolled and his neck clicked. He collapsed to the floor once more.

Above him, Iceblue got up, feeling his bruised ribcage.

'Nice try, twinkletoes.'

'Sod you,' Danny spat into the floor with a gob of bloody phlegm. Iceblue didn't answer as one of the other riders emerged from the stairs.

'What do you want done with him,' the rider said to Iceblue.

'Nothing, leave him where he is.'

'Right, boss,' the rider said.

'Did you find the—'

'Nah, it ain't here.'

'What?!' Iceblue said, grasping his comrade. 'What do you bloody mean?!'

'She won't say. We've turned this place over. Whatever they want—'

'Fucking hell, we were *told* it'd be here. Boss himself was here, he said so!'

Danny's ears pricked at that statement.

'It'll show—' the rider began. Iceblue didn't let go.

'It had better,' Iceblue relented, and moved out of Danny's sight. 'Or we're in mad trouble, bro. Or we've been fucking *had*.' He turned his gaze back to Danny. 'And *nobody* would want that, you get me?'

Danny kept his eyes closed, but couldn't hide the grin from spreading across his puffy face. He knew what they were looking for. It wasn't here. The smile didn't last long though. He heard a woman shouting. More chaotic knocking on the floorboards of the stairs.

'She ain't coming,' the rider said.

'She will,' Iceblue said from the landing. A door clicked. A few more footsteps. The door closed again.

Mumbled voices filtered through the door, the floor, and the raging inferno of pain that spread through Danny's body. He scrabbled, pushing himself up. He got to his feet. He stumbled drunkenly into the kitchen, pulling at one of the drawers. It rattled. He picked up what he needed. The pain was subsiding. In the light he cast a glimpse at himself. He was trembling. The adrenalin beat through his bloodstream, his heart pounding like a drum at full pelt in his head.

The chair looked nice, but no time to sit down. The knocking from upstairs resumed. The door clicked open, with muffled voices coming into clarity.

'Where's Danny? Where's my grandson?!' a voice hollered.

Danny felt a crackle of energy burst down every neuron and nerve in his body. The tingling had every hair standing up.

'Nan!' he breathed, wobbling out of the kitchen into the dining room just as Iceblue emerged from the stairs.

'Get her out,' Iceblue said to his comrades. Four of them emerged from the stairs with a bundle around them.

The bundle had legs and feet. Female feet, bare, with withered old skin.

'Stay there,' Danny shouted, 'and don't move a muscle!'

Iceblue pivoted. 'You don't know to stay down, do ya, punk!' His knuckles white, Danny drew the knife toward his face. It glinted. 'And now it gets serious, yeah?'

'Yeah,' Danny said, levelling the knife at Iceblue.

'Danny? Danny!' Jane screamed from underneath the pillowcase that had been fashioned into a hood. 'Danny they're—' her words were stopped as one of the riders held a hand over her mouth. Now she scrabbled, trying to breath.

'That's enough!' a voice roared into the ruined living room. 'Get the hell out of this house!'

Iceblue scowled. 'You're mixing in serious shit, old man. Don't be a hero.'

Danny turned, wincing with effort. He saw Alan in the hall doorway, a long slender object levelled on his outstretched arms. 'Alan? What the hell?'

'I said,' Alan repeated, clicking the gun. 'Get the hell out.'

'He's got a gun, Ice!' one of the riders gibbered. 'He's got a fucking gun. Screw this,' they said, scarpering with the squeal of boots on the shiny floor.

'Alright,' Iceblue said. 'Easy, man. No need to take my head off.'

'Leave him,' Alan said. 'And leave her.'

'Okay, okay…' Iceblue paced carefully toward Alan. He looked past the neighbour, to his other rider who held the blanket-bound figure. 'Let her down… *now!*'

'What? Oof!' Alan sighed as they pushed him to the floor next to Danny.

'Get her out!' Iceblue shouted. 'Now, before he—'

Danny saw Iceblue's glowing eyes meet the maw of Alan's rifle. He gulped, feeling time slow down.

The gun clicked.

But there was no boom.

Iceblue hung in mid-air, suspended by the expectation of death.

Then he laughed. 'It's a dud! Come on, let's get her out of here!'

The two riders cackled, following Iceblue out and pulling Jane with them.

Danny looked at Alan. 'What the hell happened?'

Alan gave a toothy, embarrassed grimace. 'It's just an air rifle. And it's not even loaded. Sorry.'

'Never mind,' Danny said, pushing himself back to his feet. 'I've gotta get after them.' Then he toppled, Alan only just managing to catch him.

'You're going nowhere, son,' Alan said. 'Now, is there anyone I can call?'

Danny rolled his eyes, admitting defeat to the bumps he'd taken. He gave Alan one number.

***

Hailey didn't take long.

'Get in,' she said. Danny heaved the door open and fell into the passenger seat. 'Christ, Tasha said it was bad, but you look beaten up. Where to?'

'They took my nan,' he said. Hailey drove. 'Everything I had. All gone.'

'They call the police?'

'Yep, think they might actually turn up.'

'Waste of time. And no, Danny, you haven't lost everything,' she said. He gave her a glance. 'Your nan's tough. I know that. Remember when I came to dinner? You've still got me.' She lifted a hand from the steering wheel and grabbed Danny's bruised mitt, giving it an affectionate rub.

Danny smiled. 'You're right. Not everything.'

'D'you want to speak to the police?'

'Is there any point?' Danny said with a yawn. He watched three policemen in tattered uniforms running around the car park. A lone fire engine joined them, dousing the ashes of the fires with impotent streams of water. 'They've got their hands full.'

'Don't say that! This isn't a parking fine, it's a bloody kidnapping! They can help. They have to.'

'No,' he said. 'I wanna believe you. But now it's just me. If I want to actually make a difference, I've gotta help myself. Isn't that obvious?'

'Danny!' she said. He nudged into her shoulder for a moment. She placed a hand on his cheek.

'Where're you staying?'

Danny didn't know. They had trashed his house. He couldn't stay there. 'I don't know.'

'Sure you don't want to go to the doctor?' she said, her eyes drawn to the scuffs and scrapes across Danny's face, surrounding the pits of his eyes.

Danny sighed a tremendous sigh. 'Fine. Let's go there.'

'You won't be alone,' Hailey said. 'I'll stay with you.'

'Thanks. How's Henry?'

Hailey's face soured. 'Being Henry.'

'I won't expect him at my bedside, then.'

'I can be persuasive.'

Danny laughed, the giggle turning into a painful cough.

The hospital loomed as the sun finally gave up for the day and went to slumber. Patchy white walls six stories high, weathered and wizened by the years. The sign was just as worn.

St Helga's Hospital.

'A&E's packed,' Hailey said, seeing a stream of headlights outside the main entrance to the hospital.

'Just park up,' Danny said.

Hailey pulled up in the patch of tarmac that formed the car park. The side of the hospital loomed up a gentle slope. Behind the facade that faced the road were three towering blocks filled with grey windows.

'You sure you can make it?' Hailey said. 'I'll wheel you in if you want?'

'Nah,' Danny insisted. 'I'd rather hobble.'

'Danny, don't be stupid,' she called after him. He waved her off.

Hailey shrugged, following Danny down a narrow, dimly-lit path. On one side was a sheer brick wall leading to an outbuilding atop a slope. A few glass light sconces hung from the wall but didn't erupt in light. To the left was a scrawny garden. Danny stopped to examine a sign on a boarded-up pergola that led inside the patch of dirt.

'Friends of St. Helga's maintain this garden,' Danny read.

242

'Doesn't look like the old girl has many friends now, does it?'

'Come on,' she said, leading him away. The path opened out onto a road. To the left, the road spilled out into the street beyond. Just in front, round the front of the hospital, a couple of ambulances unloaded under a concrete awning.

Worn paint led to the right, underneath a bridge that linked the main hospital to the block atop the slope.

Beyond the road, a pair of concertina doors opened and closed as the lost and the dispossessed meandered in and out, taking wonder at the evening air and then seeking the shelter of the cloying heat inside once again.

'You sure? I could take you to our doctor, they'll—'

'No.' Danny held up a hand. 'This'll do fine. Our finest, really. I don't want to become a burden.'

Hailey grasped his hand. He smiled, then took the step off the bobbly tiles that marked the road crossing.

Danny became one of the mass, shuffling through. The main corridor was like a runway of shiny vinyl the walls teal and magnolia. Hailey followed.

'You alright there?' a nurse in faded teal overalls that matched the walls asked, scratching his bearded chin. 'You look rough.'

'Y—' Danny began, before his legs turned to jelly and he began to fall to the floor.

'Careful!' the nurse said, but Danny missed his outstretched arms with a sigh and a clatter. The nurse pulled him back up to his feet. 'Whoa,' he said, placing Danny into a wheelchair and glancing at Hailey. 'What happened to him? Where's the trauma?!'

'A gang broke into his house,' Hailey said. 'They did this to him. They've been harassing him for ages.'

'So this isn't the first time?'

'No…' Danny lent back, exhausted in the chair.

The nurse wheeled Danny down the corridor. His vision blurred and scurried around, the end of the corridor warping into a mass of swirling colours, like it never ended.

'You brought him in just in time,' the nurse said, though the voice sounded like it was miles away. Underwater. The cadence crackled and throbbed all around. A door rattled, then the strange silence of the corridor was washed away with the chaotic hubbub of the waiting room.

'He won't have to wait,' the nurse said.

'Good,' Hailey answered. Danny shook his head. The room was still spinning.

More voices. The wheelchair scurried across the floor. Motion. They flopped Danny onto a bed.

'Who's this?' a voice said.

'Danny,' Hailey said. Danny smiled.

'And who are you?' the voice said again. 'He needs pain relief. What the hell happened?'

'He was… oh,' Hailey said. Danny felt them wrench his work top up his arm. The scratch from the needle followed. Then the pain seemed to ooze right out of him. 'He's my boyfriend. He's been very brave.'

'Brave?'

Hailey explained, and all the time gripped Danny's hand. He felt the warmth in the palm of his hand. He squeezed back. She smiled.

Either the morphine or the euphoria of hearing that took the pain right off and Danny blinked to wipe the dew from his eyes.

CHAPTER 21

'Terrible news, isn't it, all this?'

'I don't know what the world's coming to.'

'An army of ruthless hoodlums laying siege to a Mertons store,' Tunt lent back in her chair, holding the tablet and caressing it with a finger. 'Unthinkable a few months ago. Even weeks!' She smiled. 'Good work.'

'Nothing to do with me,' Henry said, holding his hands up in fake outrage.

'Good,' Tunt said. 'I trust no evidence was left of our involvement.'

'The boys were thorough, alright,' Henry said. 'Nothing on the bikes, uniforms, or anything to suggest…'

Tunt put the tablet computer down. 'Property damage will be considerable for Mertons. The Commission won't fail to notice their ratings drop too. The store was completely knocked out of action. That's a whole zone that will be forced to call us in to service them.'

'I was thinking,' Henry said.

'Dangerous start,' Tunt retorted. 'Carry on.'

'Why not go for the distribution centres? The depots?'

'Stop there,' Tunt said. 'Our people wouldn't get near them. Too risky, for now.'

Henry moved in his chair. 'How'd you mean?'

'We had to act quickly, so your piece of shock-and-awe did us a favour,' she began. Henry nodded for her to continue, though she'd planned to, anyway. 'It just shows that only we are the solution to the problems facing this country. Take a look for yourself,' she said, pointing to the display behind her. 'It's like a plague across the blue zones. But the yellow zones, as you'll see, are clear. Everything is functioning as it should.'

'What are those dots?'

'Reports of vandalism against Mertons property. Raids.'

'Right,' he said. 'And the yellow zones—'

'Ones we control, of course. The population pay their Prime subs, we provide infinitely better public services, and they get more films and game downloads over their giga-wire broadband that we provide, and everyone is, as they say, quids in.'

'What does this have to do with Mertons?'

'We're bypassing the Commission. Mertons will join the fold one way or the other, through acquisition or through amalgamation. They want the status quo. Not good enough. It's not in line with our vision for Yellowstone.'

Henry lent in. 'Yours? Or Grayson Laurie's vision? And what about Parliament?'

Tunt sat back and blinked. 'Ours, Henry. That's all you really need to know. There's little time, so we must act quickly.'

'Why?' he asked. She reclined in her chair for a moment.

'Parker.'

'Parker?'

'It's been a thorn in my side for as long as I remember.'

'It's a useful little tool.'

'Grayson's pet. It's more than an assistant. It's going to become a firewall to my plans for this company.'

'Your plans? A firewall?'

'Do pay attention,' Tunt sighed. 'He wants to go live with the 2.0 upgrade of ParkerNet.'

'I see,' Henry said. 'Thought that was just a backend system.'

'So did I,' Tunt shook her head. 'But he's adamant about bringing all company functions under it.'

'And that's bad?'

'I like the idea of streamlining,' she said, 'but not when it threatens my position. Or my access.'

'Can't you stop it?'

'Yes. That's where you come in. We cripple Mertons like we have, show them that Yellowstone is the solution. We pass the Act and take over the functions of the government. But there's going to be collateral.'

'That's not remotely aligned with Grayson Laurie's vision, is it?'

'And Parker will be a barrier to the tools and resources we need.'

'A company within a company?'

She smiled. 'Of sorts. There's plenty for you, though, if you show your loyalty.'

He drew forward. 'I've come this far. You're the only thing I've got left to be loyal to.'

'Not your family? Your sister?'

'No,' he spat. 'You're planning on, what, integrating Mertons into the Yellowstone system like you did Freshco?'

'No,' Tunt said, leaning forward, 'Frescho integrated well into our operation. We turned them into dark stores, feeding Yellowstone Grocery. But Mertons is too far gone. We're going to turn them to dust.' Henry sat back, taking a heavy breath. 'I hope you've the stomach for this, Archer. The country could change by this time next week.'

'Do I have much choice?' he asked. She raised an eyebrow. 'I want to know I'm backing the winning horse. What I think you're planning is going to turn some heads. Powerful heads. I'd hate to lose, and there's a lot to lose, if you get my meaning.'

Tunt remained still for a moment before smiling. 'Of course. The reward for loyalty will be… considerable for you. We've taken mitigation to limit our involvement. Keep our necks dry. You're a big part in that, you realise.'

Henry smiled. 'I appreciate the responsibility.'

'But,' she lent in again, her face forming a storm. 'But let me remind you. Fail and you're history. The one we blame. You'll be public enemy number one, believe me. We're too close to stop now, and you're the scapegoat if everything goes awry.' He gulped. 'I'm glad the arrangement we've made is crystal clear.'

'I won't let you down.'

'Excellent!' Tunt lent back in her chair. 'You know, I had my doubts about you, Archer.'

'Why's that?'

'You were too keen at your interview. Too good, almost. You were trying too hard. If I wanted someone to kiss my arse,' she laughed once, 'I'd have asked one of the many lackeys I keep on staff for that purpose.'

'I'm glad I'm exceeding your expectations, then.' Henry grabbed the seat.

'I am too. Losing Danny Price put a temporary halt to our plans, but you helped bring in a bigger prize.'

'What's that?'

'Our crews don't just answer to you. My people have contacts. You are just one driver. We steered them in the right direction once everything was in motion.'

'Kier Wood was gutted, you said.'

'Honestly, Kier Wood means nothing to me. A backwater. Couldn't even find it on the map. But you revealed something we didn't know.'

Now it was Henry's turn to laugh. 'Don't keep me in suspense all day, Wendy. Where are you going?'

'Me? No, *we*,' she said, waving for him to get to his feet. Henry did so automatically. 'I'll show you the real prize for all your work. Follow me. I'll show you the key to your success in the society we want to build.'

Raising his eyebrows at those heady words, Henry followed her out of the corridor and down. They emerged in the garage and Wendy moved to a car, a Yellowstone rep opening the door just as she swooped in.

Henry followed. The door swooped closed. The car moved out into the daylight and toward the future.

'Welcome, Ms Tunt,' another Yellowstone rep said as the car drew to a halt. The door opened, the rush of outside air buffeting the conditioned atmosphere inside the car.

'Where are we?' Henry said, stepping onto virgin concrete. His ears twigged the sound of running natural water.

'The new facility on Riverside. Home away from home,' she said, already striding toward the imposing grey building. Henry followed her inside and through some stairs, heading downward.

Bare concrete tunnels and shafts led through a rabbit warren of corridors and passages. Pipes and ducts lined the spaces with a harsh electrical thrum all around.

'Why're you taking me down here?' Henry asked.

'It's where we keep the rubbish,' Tunt said, her taut syllables echoing around the space. 'Keep up. Time is money in this business.'

Tunt stopped in front of him next to a door that blended almost completely into the tan brick wall of the basement tunnel. If

Tunt hadn't stood there, he'd have not even known it existed.

Perhaps that was the point.

'You ready?' Tunt asked. 'This is the real point of no return stuff, Archer. Once you go in, you've committed fully. So,' she clicked the latch down. It echoed on the bare, desolate concrete. 'Final chance.'

Henry felt himself wavering, but that was the cold. Gusts of air seemed to run rampant in these passages. His face hardened. 'Let's do it.'

Without saying another word, Tunt opened the door and Henry entered the darkness within.

The door closed behind him. Silence. Breathing. Shuffling of feet on a cement floor. The rattling of delicate metal chains. A switch clicked. The lights sparked into life, fluorescent tubes humming into luminosity.

'Hello,' Tunt stepped forward toward the centre of the room. 'Enjoying our hospitality.'

'No,' a voice spat. Henry recognised it. The voice belonged to someone who had been in his house.

'I want you to meet Mr Archer, Ms Greene,' Tunt said. 'He's a good colleague of mine.'

Henry's face dropped as Tunt moved aside.

There was Danny's nan, Jane Green, her hair asunder and her skin pallid, tied to a plastic chair like those he'd sat on in school. She was staring at the floor, avoiding Tunt's gaze, not even giving her the dignity.

It was a courtesy she gave Henry, though, but it was not welcomed. 'You.'

'You,' he said back.

'Took us into your home,' she spat. 'Played the doting friend to my grandson,' she said, taking a deeper breath. 'All the while you were selling us out to these abject miseries?!'

Henry hesitated, his mouth open.

'I should've known. I knew your father was a cold fish, but he brought up a toerag of a son.'

'You don't know what you're talking about.'

'I see Robert Archer's son. And believe me,' she said, 'the apple didn't fall far from the tree.'

'You don't know anything about me or my family.'

'I know more than you could imagine. I know your dad's a conniving, grease-haired bastard… and he's out for one person only. And it's not you.'

Henry stepped forward and pointed a finger at Jane. 'You're wrong.'

'I'm not,' she said. 'And here I am, with his rat of a son—'

'I'm no rat!' Henry said. He cleared his throat, seeing Tunt's dismissive glare. 'Just shut up! You don't know anything!'

'Why?' Jane hissed, her tongue snakelike. 'Touch a nerve? How is your dad, anyway? When did he last look at you and not grimace?'

'That's enough!' Henry said. 'Danny made the mistake. This could've all been ours. He let me down. He embarrassed me. Then they made me an offer, one I couldn't possibly refuse.'

'Ha!' Jane snorted. 'Let *you* down? What would you know about that?'

'I knew a good thing. I thought it'd be just as good for Danny. Like we'd always planned at uni. Danny and Henry, champions of the world.'

'And here you are in a basement, seeing what your ambition does,' Jane snorted.

Tunt interceded. 'Have you reconsidered our generous offer? If you hand over the documents. You'll save everyone a lot of bother and us a lot of money. Money we could use repairing your house.'

'By bulldozing it into flats, you mean?'

'Repair includes redevelopment. I hear it's been badly damaged.'

'That was you…' Jane said at Tunt. 'No,' she pivoted. 'It was *you* wasn't it?'

'It didn't have to be this way,' Henry said. 'Danny made the wrong choice. Sadly he's paying the price for it.'

'Listen to yourself,' Jane said. 'You actually believe all this,' she sighed, turning to Tunt. 'Never. I'll never give you what I swore on that man… You'll have to prise it from my cold, dead hands before I'll give it to you.'

'We can wait,' Tunt said, stepping around. 'It won't take long. The landscape's changing. Rapidly. A week. Three days. Who's to say?'

'You're not going to do this,' she said. 'This is illegal. None of this is right. You simply can't have that kind of power?!'

'We're sweeping the old world away to form the new. You either evolve or erode away. We've found the new path. We're cutting you out. Come on, Archer,' she nodded toward the door. 'Now you've seen our most valuable asset.'

'Yeah, take that pathetic little git away. Or tell his dad.' Henry stopped. 'See, I hit a nerve. My, my,' she smiled. 'What would he think of *this*?'

'Don't…' Henry trembled. 'Don't you even dare.'

Tunt barked at Henry. 'Archer.'

'… don't you ever call me that. I told him the truth. He didn't believe me.'

'You really believe that, don't you?' Jane said. 'You really do?'

'I don't need to explain it to you,' Henry said, turning away.

The door opened, a patch of light appearing in the wall as the lights in the room disappeared.

'He'll never forgive you, Henry. And I'll never forget. You're just a… useful idiot!'

The door slammed closed.

'Well?' Tunt said.

'I… did that?'

'Your fine work did, yes. Now, enough. Lunch.'

'Where's lunch?'

'Up, top floor,' Tunt said, striding past Henry toward the lift.

Tunt had walked into one of the open lift doors and it swooshed shut just behind Henry. He exhaled as the lift glided upward through the atrium. He watched the associates busying around the open floor, getting smaller until the lift punched through the ceiling into the lift shaft proper.

'Remember,' Tunt said, 'you're ingratiated now. Totally.'

'How many people know about…'

Tunt held up a hand, splaying the fingers. 'This many. And you're one of them.'

'Is Grayson Laurie one of your fingers too?' Henry asked. She didn't answer.

'She'll cave,' Tunt said. 'We'll turn up the pressure.'

'We will?'

'You will, that is. She's stubborn. We need something to heat her up, make her pliable.'

'Won't be easy,' Henry said. 'Considering she's our prisoner.'

Tunt swivelled. 'Nobody said the word *prisoner,* Archer. She's a guest in our revolutionary new accommodation. It's just that access in and out is… restricted to opportune times for the company.'

'I see,' Henry said. The lift came to a stop so smooth it was almost impossible to ascertain.

'I'm glad,' she said, stepping out into a vista of light. The floor outside the lift was bathed in natural light from curtains of glass that surrounded the floor. Tables were dotted around the edges of the wall.

'Ms Tunt,' an associate said as the pair approached.

'Our usual table? Is…'

'Waiting for you, Ms Tunt.'

'Excellent,' she smiled. 'Come on, Henry. There's someone I want you to meet. This is where the great and the good at Yellowstone have lunch.'

Henry stepped forward, past the threshold. Airy, classical music trilled softly from speakers above the gentle trickling of running water. Rounding the corner, Henry saw the impressive stone water feature. Rough rock formed the outside of a large circle of shimmering water. From the centre, a spout of water trickled from a height back into the basin. He stopped to take the spectacle in.

'That's from the Yellowstone National Park, in the States,' Elroy said. Henry jerked. 'Easy, tiger,' the older man said. 'Come and eat. I hear you've done some wonderful work.' He beckoned Henry past the sculpture and into the restaurant.

Ivy hung from the lattice-work ceiling and Henry's shoes clopped on the marble floor. A large table in a secluded alcove came into view around a corner. Tunt was sitting down.

'This is seriously impressive,' Henry said. 'Nothing like what we saw in our orientation. No tennis tables, no poles, no—'

'Please,' Tunt said. She reached for a tablet computer on the table, selecting menu items. 'I've ordered lunch. Those trappings,' she pointed at Henry, 'just aren't becoming a professional workplace. See that,' she indicated out of the window. The City of London outside looked like a toy town. 'That'll all be ours. We'll own every one of those towers. It'll be glorious.'

Henry nodded, but was interrupted from any further imagining.

'Has Wendy explained your next assignment?' Elroy said.

'Danny Price has to come into the fold.'

'That won't be so easy. We're not going to be able to kidnap him so easily.'

'Henry, we don't like to use *that* word,' Elroy said fast. 'That would be too blunt an instrument, anyway. Wow, that was quick.'

'Here you go, folks,' an associate appeared with a tray of food. 'Ms Tunt, it's a pleasure to see you.'

'Thank you,' she said from her side of the table, peering at the associate's name tag. It was pinned across his heart. 'Elroy. That's just kind.'

'My pleasure,' Elroy said. He didn't move. Tunt's eyes rotated.

'Was there a…'

'A message for you, that's all.'

'Who from?' Her smile was dissolving.

'Number six.'

She shuffled out of the booth. 'Keep it warm,' she indicated to her lunch. 'I'll need it. Elroy, with me.'

'Er, sure…' he said, following Tunt as she strode away.

'Number six, eh?' Henry said. 'Must be someone important.'

'Henry, it could be you one day,' Elroy said. 'We've got a bold plan for this company.'

'Doesn't Grayson Laurie?'

'I'll humour that,' Elroy said. 'You're with us now. You report to Wendy. If Wendy isn't there, you report to me, right?'

'Right.'

'Grayson Laurie isn't going to stand in the way of our superior vision for Yellowstone in the UK, Henry. And if he can't stand in the way,' Elroy finished, picking up his fork, 'Neither can you.'

'Hasn't my loyalty already been proven?' Henry said. 'Sorry, I think my appetite's going.'

'Eat,' Elroy said. 'It'll be good for you. Serve us well, and you'll eat here every day. But betray us, and it's an awful long fall.'

'Okay,' Henry said, relenting. 'Okay.'

'Attaboy!' Elroy said, finally grinning. 'We're just making sure we're absolutely certain. Nothing can stand in our way. And you'll stand on the shoulders of giants. I think you'll fit right in.'

Tunt re-emerged. 'Sorry Elroy.'

'Wendy, no sweat.' He looked to Henry, who smiled, but not comfortably. 'I was just making sure we had Henry on board. For everything.'

'And do we?' Wendy Tunt asked directly of Henry.

He gulped and swallowed, but was penned in. 'You absolutely do,' he said. 'One hundred per cent.'

CHAPTER 22

'You must be Ashley, right?' Danny asked as he entered the large warehouse. He looked around. Racking was everywhere, filled with scuffed and worn plastic bins. A dribble of Mertons workers scurried around with little metal cards, grabbing items from the bins and careening around the space.

This was not Kier Wood.

'Come in, Danny. We heard what happened. Who's this?' the manager, Ashley, said to Hailey.

'She's with me,' Danny said. He slipped through the door from the main floor to the quiet colleague area. 'What is this place?'

'The future. Or so we thought. One of our new fulfilment centres. Was to be the rebirth of the company. Until—'

'Yellowstone,' Danny said.

Ashley nodded. 'Follow me. Both of you.'

Danny and Hailey followed.

'I heard about Kier Wood. Dreadful,' he said. Danny and Hailey followed wordlessly. 'Just down the road. I can't believe those bastards did it, and so quickly.'

'Danny was a hero,' Hailey said. Ashley hummed.

'Hailey, please…' Danny said, squeezing her hand.

'No, she's right,' the manager said. 'This way.' He pushed a door open to a wide space filled with pairs of eyes.' Danny stopped dead in the opening. 'Everyone,' the manager said, 'he's here. Danny, the hero of Kier Wood.'

The room filled with applause. Danny felt his cheeks blossom ruby red. Hailey squeezed his hand.

'I… I…' he said.

'Come on, Danny,' the manager said. 'This way.' He walked toward to pass through the room.

Danny followed. He felt claps on his shoulder.

'Thank you, Danny,' one colleague said. 'You did great.'

Danny smiled nervously and nodded. I didn't do anything.

'Love,' an older lady said, 'your nan would be proud of you. This company means everything to her.'

Danny felt his eyes glisten, then a squeeze on his hand.

'We'll find her,' Hailey soothed. 'We're in the right place.'

Danny swallowed and looked at the lady. 'Thank you.'

'Danny,' the manager said, as the room grew vocal with murmurs of admiration. 'Come on, we've stuff to discuss.'

'Okay,' Danny said, following into a side room. The door sucked closed behind the three.

'Are you increasing security.' Danny asked, not even taking a seat.

'Not as simple as that,' Ashely said. 'The Commission put a big hold on bully-boy tactics.'

'Why's that?'

'All in the name of playing fair. They're too slow to react to something like this, though. We're on our own.'

'Nah,' Danny said. 'We've got to work together. We're all one big family.'

'Orders have increased in the last three days, since Kier Wood…' Ashley trailed off. 'Sorry. I understand you were there for the brunt of it.'

'It was like a warzone, honestly,' Danny said, putting his hands through his hair. 'That place actually meant a lot to me. Grew up there, now working there. Not quite what I had planned, but it was the cards life dealt me.'

'You said on the phone,' Ashley said, 'you had clues. The Deliverangels? Where are they operating from? Do you know?'

'Danny,' Hailey said, 'tell them what you think.'

'Not my first rodeo with them,' Danny said. 'Look at this.' He fished the tracker from his pocket. 'Can you do anything with this?'

'What is that?' Ashley asked.

'One of the riders had it. Think it clips onto the moped. He was wearing it and I grabbed it.'

'Then what did you do with him?' Ashley asked.

'Pushed him down the goods lift?' Danny shrugged.

'Danny!' Hailey scolded.

'The bastard will live.'

'Fascinating,' Ashley said. 'I think this is what links them in with BoxNet. The big logistics backbone. Basically, anyone who's not Yellowstone hooks in. We've been working on it too.'

'Can you get into it?'

'Maybe,' Ashley said. 'One of my guys can. Follow me.'

Danny and Hailey did so, following an electrical whirring and dry heat through a warren of angular corridors.

Ashley opened a door into a darkened cave of a room. Opposite was a bank of blinking lights and the silhouette of the server racks that held them. 'Adam, you in here?'

'Yes, boss,' a voice said, the accent thick with Scottish brogue. A swivel chair creaked. Footsteps approached. A man, clad in a hoodie and with thick brown hair and thick-rimmed glasses, emerged from the gloom. 'Who's this?'

'I'm Danny. Take a look at this. Can you crack it?' Danny pushed the module into Adam's hands.

Adam looked at the device through squinting, inquisitive

eyes. Then he looked up, through his glasses, at Danny. 'Where'd you get this?'

'It doesn't matter,' Ashley said. 'Will it plug into your… thing?' He waved at Adam's desk, which was festooned in wires around the base of a monitor that provided the only light in the room.

Adam sighed and sat down. 'Probably,' he said, and pushed the connector into the socket on the module. The computer monitor jumped. 'Hey, this is juicy.'

'If you could get some GPS data out of that,' Danny said, 'that would be sick.'

'BoxNet doesn't quite work like that,' Adam said.

'What can you get me?'

'Box codes. It'll take me some time. Gimme fifteen minutes?'

'Okay,' Danny said.

'Come to my office, Danny. We'll wait there.'

'Guys,' Adam said, emerging into the office. 'I've cracked it.'

'What've you got?' Ashley said. 'Quickly!'

'I'll show you.' Adam said, leading the three back to his office. He sat down at his terminal. He pointed. 'There's seventy box codes.'

'Blimey,' Ashley said, 'they've been busy.'

Hailey leant in. 'A lot of repetition. Can you filter this?'

'Sure.' He clicked a few buttons. The codes rearranged themselves into groups.

'That top one… can you turn that into a location?'

'Not for a while,' Adam said. 'The flow only goes one way.'

'That could be their main base,' Danny said. 'We need to know where that is!'

'Don't worry,' Hailey said, reaching across with her phone and snapping a photo of the screen. She tapped a few times. 'I think I know some people.'

'Know some people?' Danny said.

'As part of my big expose on Yellowstone. Let's just say… I know *some* people, alright. You'll be surprised what you can find on Cheepr these days.'

'Especially since Grayson Laurie bought it.'

'Get all sorts, like I said.'

'How long do you need?'

'Couple hours at home. That alright?'

Danny smiled. 'It'll have to be.'

'Are you sure we can trust some script kiddies on Cheepr? Especially if it's anything to do with Grayson Laurie?' Ashley said. 'I don't trust him. Not after what happened.'

'What happened?'

'Jeez,' Adam said, 'he's going to go off about—'

'Upper Hedingbury.' Ashley spat. 'Damn right. Used to be our turf. Damn right should still be.'

'What do you mean it *used to be* our turf?' Danny said, catching Ashley's gaze. 'The Commission?'

'Yellowstone. Four months ago. We had an old store there. It didn't make much money, which is probably why it was prime for rezoning. Anyway, we had to abandon it pretty darn quick.'

'How quick?'

'You ever seen a rezone, Danny?'

'No.'

'We had a weekend. We ended up burning records in the yard. I was there. The place was stripped bare. None of us have been there in weeks. It's as yellow as yellow zones get. We had a few holdouts, but they didn't last long. Not with the amount of citations from Yellowstone's service people. You couldn't stop a Mertons van at a red light without it breaking some kind of rule or regulation. Emissions, roadworthiness… all bullshit.'

'They can do that?'

'Danny, you're so naïve. When was the last time you set foot in a Yellow zone?'

'I interviewed for Yellowstone,' Danny said. 'Central London.'

'I should throw you out just for that fact alone,' Ashley laughed, but there was a shortage of humour behind the huffs.

Danny didn't detect any sincerity in the expression of humour.

'Yeah,' Hailey said quickly. 'But you saw what they were planning. I've heard on the underweb… all it takes is one ReCheep and I can have people staked out.'

'People?' the manager asked.

'She's doing a thing for TubeView, aren't you?'

'Tell me more,' Ashley said. 'Something about Yellowstone?'

'We've been piecing it together for months. Maybe it's connected.'

'And maybe it isn't,' the manager said. 'Why did you turn down Yellowstone, then? You could've been kissing Grayson Laurie's arse by now. And if it's not, I'm colluding with hackers and undesirables. There's a legal implication if this all goes south. I'm putting fingerprints right on it. And as you can see, I've a flock to protect.'

'I didn't take the job. They were asking too much. I'd have to sell my soul to agree to what they wanted me to do.'

'Well, I'm glad you didn't do that,' Ashley said after a few moments, letting the mental gears whir. There was a knock on the hollow door. Danny glanced. A face appeared on the gridlined glass. Ashley waved the face in. The door opened and the face was attached to a thin body.

'Boss, trouble.'

'What sort, Stan?' Ashley said, leaping to his feet. 'A van?'

'How did you tell?' Ashley said. 'We've had one radio in. It sounds bad.'

'It's your department. Danny, with us. Take me down to the office,' Ashley said.

'You Danny Price?' Stan said as they walked through the corridor back onto the busy shop floor.

'That's me,' Danny said. 'Seems I'm quite famous round these parts.'

'Nah,' Stan said. 'Not famous. Useful. You've seen how this lot operates. You can help us fight back.'

They entered a small backroom office with a bank of cloudy, worn computer monitors against a wall. Paperwork, keyboards, wrappers, and mice were strewn across the counter. The edge of the laminate was worn back to dimpled composite wood by the passage of time and elbows.

'Report,' Stan said into a radio handset. 'Where are you, over?'

'We're…. We're trying to lose them but more keep coming along behind us,' a voice crackled from the radio.

Danny gestured to Stan for the handset. 'How many crewed are you?'

'Two of us. Who's this?'

'Doesn't matter. You on your way out or back?'

'Four drops left.'

Danny held the handset down and looked at Stan. 'They'll be faster with fewer drops left on the van.' He picked the handset back up. 'Right, that's good. You'll be faster. Keep in traffic, they might just lose interest if they can't find a quiet spot to pick you off. Hope that helps.'

'Cheers,' the crackly voice said. 'We'll stay in touch.'

'Are they coming here?' Stan said. 'That van's got to return to base eventually, and they're faster.'

'They are,' Danny said, catching the glimpse of the two beneath his furrowed brow. 'But let's be ready for them.'

Stan looked at Ashley.

'Let's give something back.'

Then Danny looked at Hailey. 'I need you to go. Get me an address. Please.'

She nodded. 'You going to be okay?'

'I hope so,' he said, his lips wavering. 'I really hope so.'

Danny emerged from the backroom into the store with Ashley and Stan.

'Danny, with me.' Ashley said. 'We did prepare for this eventuality, to a degree.'

They strode through the store, Ashley accosting what colleagues he came across, telling them to batten down the hatches - the gates outside would be barred and locked.

'Good call,' Danny said. They left, passing through the quiet space of the store that had quickly emptied.

'What's going on?' the colleague asked. He was trembling. He knew, alright. 'Is… is everything okay?'

'It's what we trained for.'

'God, what happened to Kier Wood?! No, I've gotta…'

'No,' Danny said, stepping forward. Around him, customers wheedled their way out. 'Look at these people. The people you serve. They depend on you. Your team. They need you too. To defend your livelihood.'

'They had a guy at Kier Wood, Danny something…, some hero, related to Jane Greene, from what word says.'

Danny rolled his eyes. 'I'm Danny. She's my nan. But - wait,' he started, holding up a hand as the colleague's mouth opened, 'I'm not a hero. I just stepped in. Can you do that for me, too?'

'Sure, Danny,' the colleague gave a nervous but sincere grin. 'What do you want me to do?'

'Check the fire exits and make sure they're barred,' Ashley said. 'We may not have long to prepare.' The colleague scampered away. 'That was a good pep talk, Danny.'

'I meant it. I'm no hero. I just don't want shit to go down. Where's the weakest point in the store's security? Where are they most likely to come in?'

'This way, I'll show you to the delivery hub. If they follow a van in and it's easy to get right in from there.'

'That's where we'll make our stand,' Danny said. 'Repel them at the door. Then maybe something good will come of this.'

'Come on then,' Ashley said. 'Take up positions.'

Danny followed. The warehouse opened into a yard surrounded with twenty-feet fences. The gate out to the two-lane street outside whinnied closed, rattling in the wind.

'Van's coming,' a colleague hollered to Ashley. 'Do you want us to open it?'

'Yeah!' Ashley called through cupped hands. 'Let our boys in!'

The colleague nodded. At the upper end of the street, a diesel engine grunted. Buzzing followed it. As predicted. Then the gate opened as the blue and grey van skidded in.

'Close it, close it now!'

The gate wobbled as it began to sweep closed just behind the delivery van's bumper. Then it stopped. Moped engines revved, the occupants braying.

This was the crucial moment. Danny rushed forward across the yard as a quintet of Mertons colleagues pushed against the crowd on the other side. The gap in the two gates was less than a metre. A tyre stuck through the gap, skidding on the concrete pad.

Danny heard engines roaring overhead. 'They're going up the ramp!' he shouted.

'They won't get far,' the colleague said with a glint. 'All locked up.'

'Called the police?'

'Yeah,' the colleague said. 'They're on their way.'

Danny scoffed. 'Don't bet on it.'

'They said they had no choice. Too much shit going down.'

'We'll see.'

Rattles of chains followed. Wheels screeched down the other ramp.

The big gate whinnied and wobbled but didn't move. The tyre retracted and the gap closed with a shudder.

Danny sighed, and he wasn't the only one.

Stan re-appeared and nodded to Ashley. 'Call for you. Hey, Danny,' he called across the yard.

Danny was already treading across the yard. The van crew emerged, sweaty and shaken but triumphant.

'We beat 'em,' the driver said.

'Don't celebrate yet,' Ashley said. 'We can't stay buttoned up like this. No delivery. No company. This ain't good. Come on, you,' he pulled toward Danny, 'let's see what's what.'

Danny followed back inside.

'In here,' Ashley said, leading Danny into a dark back room. He heaved at a heavy sliding door. It squealed on its track, resting against the dark brick wall.

'Christ,' Danny said, his face scrunching up. 'Stinks in here.'

'The waste room's down the hall. Used to be cold storage.'

'But now isn't.'

They entered the room. Danny saw Hailey already sitting there with her chaperone, Stan.

'Right. Sit down, Danny,' Ashley showed him to an old office chair. 'Go home, you deserve it,' he said to Stan, who skidded out. He pulled it over as Danny came into the room. The chair rattled on the hard floor. Danny did so.

'What's all this about?'

'Ever since you started,' Ashley started, leaning toward an old, scuffed monitor, pressing the switch on the corner. Static burst to life on the screen. 'There's been things about the company you've not been told.'

'I did get that impression.'

'I think,' Ashley said, 'Ah yes, hi Brian.'

'Hello,' Brian said from the screen. His voice was tinny and indistinct, reverberating around the space. 'I see you're something quiet.'

'Danny helped us prepare for a second attack,' Ashley said. 'He did a great job. Losses were minimal.'

'That's good to hear. Danny, how are you holding out?'

Danny squared up to the screen.

'Camera's here,' Ashley said, tapping at the top.

Danny adjusted. 'I'm... worse for wear. Everything bloody aches. They did a number on me at Kier Wood and now I've been running around here like a blue-arsed fly.'

'Sorry to hear that, Danny,' Brian said, his cadence garbled by the lack of bandwidth. Danny could infer the missing syllables through. 'So, we heard about Jane Greene.'

'I think I've a lead. Ashley here told me about the store we lost. In the new yellow zone. I'm going there.'

'Danny...'

'Don't,' Danny said. He held up a hand but couldn't contain

the wince of discomfort from erupting from his core. 'I need to go. I want to find out two things: who they're working for, and where they're holding my nan. Then I'll stop whoever is pulling the strings.'

Brian was silent for a moment. 'I'm going to tell you, Danny, just how important you are to not just your nan - who I've worked with for years, but to this company. Now, that might not sound like they're of equal importance.'

'This company means a lot to my nan. And the people here are ready to fight to defend what they know is right. So don't do yourself down.'

'Fair enough. You may be aware of some documents that your nan was… custodian of.'

'I remember stuff in my loft. When the roof blew off, she went potty.'

'Right. There's a reason for that. And it has to do with your parents. And your brother, Lewis.'

'What about them?' Danny lurched forward toward the television. 'This has something to do with them?'

'Honestly, yes. They worked for us. Your whole family did. Then it happened.'

'What did?'

'Bad people found out about your family connections. Mertons is a family company. Has been for seventy years. Your nan was married to John Merton, the founder.'

'Her surname is Greene. And mine is Price. What does that have to do with that?'

'The colour of money.'

'What do you mean?!'

'She wasn't just his wife; she was intimately wound into the company in its gestation. Kier Wood isn't her first rodeo. She tried

268

to retire. We knew the company would be faced with stiff competition. Freshco. Redsave. They all wanted a piece of the pie they both built from the ground up.'

'So what did she have that was—'

'She had John Merton's personal archives. Some of that company information was lost to time. Never digitised. Some that was, we lost when AXIOM crashed in the nineties. That was all planned, by the way. We didn't want Kegmart getting their hands on it.'

'Kegmart? Weren't they that big American lot?'

'Biggest of the big. Now you never heard of them. Now it's happening again, but we think that the perpetrator wants the archives. They know our secrets. We're chicken feed.'

'Yellowstone,' Danny said. 'They're the only one pushing too aggressively into the market.'

'Worse,' Brian said, 'They're not just taking over the market. They want the country. There's a bill going through Westminster that would allow carte blanche privatisation of the government.'

'Is that legal?'

'The Commission can't stop it,' Brian said. 'If that bill passes, the Yellow zones will become their own personal communities. Yellowstone will just *become* the government. No checks, no balances, just a monthly subscription. We can't let that happen.'

'You're suddenly a big patriot?'

'Your nan is. This company is. We want to stay British. We want to stay independent. You know what happened that summer all those years ago? Promises, buses… all written off as horseshit at the time, but it exemplifies the British spirit. We want to hold on to that. If Yellowstone can buy up whole sections of the government, there won't be much of a country left for the rest of us.'

'I see. So what does this mean to what we're doing right now?'

'The Deliverangels are just the start. Without the Commission holding onto the status quo… they're going to throw everything they've got at us.'

'I find this a bit hard to believe,' Danny said, leaning back. 'Grayson Laurie. Doing it all for the good of mankind. He doesn't seem like the sort to be sitting in a chair stroking a white cat, really.'

'Don't be so sure, Danny. This project,' Hailey said, 'that got you here, the information… Grayson Laurie's a man of a million faces. Don't believe the one he puts on show. Trust me.'

Brian nodded to Hailey. 'I'm inclined to agree. It's who he's got working for him you've got to fear.' There was a great thud in the background. Brian looked about the space, skittish. 'Look, Danny, I hate to lay a load more responsibility on your shoulders…'

'… but I feel you're about to?'

Brian smiled dismissively. 'You've got a choice. Go and pursue your lead, but you need to be careful. There's not much of the family left. Kegmart saw to that.'

'They did?'

'Your parents and brother Lewis were taken on a trip. They never came back. The stink it created finished Kegmart off. Left a void that Grayson Laurie - championed to fill. He's cold, when you dig beneath the surface. But his lackeys are colder.'

Danny's eyes widened. The penny didn't simply drop; it was catapulted like a meteor into his mind. 'You're not saying that…'

'I am, son,' Brian said. He quickly corrected. 'Danny. You're the future of the company. It will always be family owned as long as a Merton - or now a Price - is around.'

'What about my nan? She's neither.'

'She's your nan. That's what counts.'

Stepping outside, Hailey pulled on Danny's arm.

'What?'

'I… I think I know where they might be holding your nan.'

'Where?' She recited address. 'Who told you this?'

'My…' she said, almost finishing the utterance of the word brother. But she caught herself. 'Contacts,' she said.

CHAPTER 23

Rolling up the lane, Danny passed dark, secluded industrial units fashioned out of metal sheeting that matched the sky. It was hard to delineate the difference. The road was lined with twig-like trees, a token effort and nothing more.

This zone was deep blue alright.

His phone had died a few miles back. He stared at the blank screen and pocketed it, not wanting to glimpse his reflection on the glass panel.

'Shit,' he said, pulling over. It had begun to rain, the drops making a pitter-patter on the light material of the car roof. He switched the wipers on, which cast the captive raindrops aside in minuscule rivulets. His teeth chattered. *I just hope this address is right*.

The lane was empty. A few parked cars that looked unloved and untouched. Vans backed in and out of yards, but never encroaching onto the road. The pavements were empty too, bereft of the waifs and strays that wandered these most picturesque of locales.

Danny pulled back into the lane. No good waiting here, under a tree. He turned his car around, but hit the brakes suddenly.

A Mertons van roared past, toward the carriageway out.

He was on the right track and pivoted the car around, accelerating down the road that the lorry had emerged from.

Soon, neon blue lights illuminated the gloomy sky. But closer, a sheet metal sign delineated that this was the place.

Danny turned into the wide concrete expanse and found a space. There was plenty. Cars dotted this apron sporadically, surrounding the hive. A dozen Mertons vans waited outside the gaping maw of a loading dock that sheltered darkness.

'Looks like the place,' he said, grabbing his dead phone from the holder and pocketing it as he got out. He walked through the rain toward the shed.

'Can I help?' a colleague said from a little shack.

'I want to speak to the boss,' Danny said.

'What about?'

'Mertons business.'

'And why,' the gate colleague said, 'should I let you within five hundred feet of this place?' He rattled the cabin behind him and Danny looked past at a very worn and very nasty-looking baton. Probably ex-police.

Danny fished through his pocket with his sodden hands. 'Here,' he said, thrusting his pass into the gate guard's window.

'Right,' he hummed, picking up a plastic phone and humming into it. Danny tried to listen, but it wasn't much good; the din of the rain on the polycarbonate roof of the cabin was too great, and the guard was making efforts. 'Go in. Up the stairs to reception. Ask for a man called Claggett.'

Danny did so and was glad to be out of the rain.

'So,' the man called Claggett asked. 'You're the lad from Kier Wood. I heard what you did that day.'

Danny rolled his eyes. *News travels fast.* 'Yes. I'm not a hero, before you start.'

'I wasn't about to,' Claggett snorted. 'And you think the answer to the punk kids who're responsible is here?'

'I've… been informed of some irregularities. With your box

codes. By someone who knows.'

'Irregularities? Box codes?' Claggett laughed, but his face didn't fill with humour. Danny distinctly thought the portly man's face filled instead with derision. 'What sort of irregularities? You some kind of auditor? Or worse? A little Yellowstone spy?'

'No, I'm just… you know Brian Rose?'

'Brian's known to me, yes,' Claggett said. 'I think I'll call him. Do you mind?'

'Go ahead,' Danny said. Danny looked over his shoulder. He saw a group of burly lads rolling their shoulders as they stood in front of the exit.

'Mighty kind of you.' Claggett reached for the phone from his belt. His fingers danced around the keypad and he pushed the handset to his wrinkled ear. He hummed a few syllables into the piece, then handed it to Danny. 'He wants to speak to you.'

'Sure.' Danny reached for the phone and took it. It was warm and clammy, but he pressed it to his ear.

'Danny,' Brian's voice rung out. 'What in god's name are you doing?'

'I was given a lead by—'

'Claggett is a man I'd trust with my life! And you thought he'd gone rogue? I… I can't believe you'd actually think that's the case… and you didn't get my say-so? Why didn't you ask?'

Valid questions indeed. 'I… I was acting on… other intel.' Danny paused.

'Well, what intel was that?'

Don't say it was your girlfriend. 'I was told to come here by someone who's,' he began forming the words in his eyes, and watched them dissolve in absurdity. 'Been told some things by someone they wouldn't mention, either. Though I suspect I've been had…'

'You should've passed it to me, Danny. You're wasting time! I expected better from you, son, and this is a real disappointment. Now get out of there!'

Danny heard the beeps of the phone hanging it up and handed it back to Claggett. 'Sorry to have wasted your time.'

Claggett hummed. 'Hopefully, young man, we won't cross paths again. I've always been loyal to Mertons, and the family before that.'

If only you knew you were talking to family, Danny thought, but Claggett was already ushering him out. The time had been lost.

The car wiggled on its suspension as Danny got back in. He threw his dead phone away. Outside, the gloomy skies turned ever greyer. Starting off, Danny left the compound and began the long drive back to Kier Wood and where home would be tonight.

***

Danny drove out and down the lane. It was dark - the subtle shades of the streetlights forming discs of pale light on the tarmac.

He edged forward to a junction, looking both ways before emerging. The road was much quieter now. Everyone had clearly got home.

Danny looked forward to being back at home, or whatever counted as home these days. Since the attack, he still hadn't been back to his house. He waited, the lights staying red,

This whole sojurn had been a waste of time.

Time he didn't have to waste.

He pulled over, the rush of traffic buffeting the car. He flicked to his phone. Still dead. He tossed it away with a clatter.

'Fuck your whole fucking family!' Danny spat, exulting in frustration. He knew who was to blame. Danny gripped the steering wheel, his knuckles going white with the effort. He thudded the wheel with a free hand.

Stupid, stupid, stupid!

The car veered just a bit in its lane. Danny took a long breath. *Careful now.*

Cogs started whirling in Danny's mind. His eyes began to glaze. It was still raining, the moisture on the glass windscreen coalescing into rivulets and diffusing the glow from the errant vehicles that passed by intermittently.

The cogs pulled Danny's attention away from the light behind. A buzzing sound, just the one.

Danny tapped his hands on the wheel, following the contours of the road. Traffic was picking up again, slowing his progress.

Coming to a set of lights, Danny glanced in the rear-view mirror. One light. It pulled around to the driver's side of the car.

'Hey, what do you think you're—' Danny said, turning to the right. He saw a helmet. A flash of pink. The visor went up.

Iceblue.

'Shit, you're—'

A black object hurtled toward the window. The glass shattered, bursting all over Danny. He yelped.

'How'd you like *that*, fucker?!' Iceblue growled above the din of the rain.

Danny scrabbled for the wheel, stomping the floor of the footwell. The car veered off, tyres squealing for grip on the wet road. He wrestled with the wheel as the car spun.

'Fuck!' he braced as the car rolled across the opposite lane and into some bushes. A handful of other cars blared their horns. Danny yelped involuntarily. With a thud, the front of the car fell down into a depression and everything stopped.

Silence.

Then the buzzing approached. Danny scrabbled out of the car, pushing the door out of the way. His feet scratched across the damp ground, the rain beating down onto him. Twenty feet away was an alley between some darkened retail units. He dove into the alley and ducked behind one of the large wheeled bins. He held his breath, hearing the buzzing sound of the moped engine.

And the smell. He didn't want to breathe that in.

Then footsteps. Iceblue approached the wreck of the car.

'Come out, come out, wherever you are,' he taunted. Danny remained perfectly still. 'I know you're here, little piggie. You'll never get her back now, you know. Stupid punk.'

Danny looked around from his hiding place, poking out just a couple of inches. He saw the back of Iceblue at the end of the alley. He was chuckling.

Not for long.

Danny's face contorted as he barrelled from the alley, smashing into Iceblue's back, knocking him forward. Danny grabbed the biker's leathers and spun him around, straddling him.

'Give her back unharmed,' he said, slapping the blond-haired biker on the face. Grabbing Iceblue's lapels, he pulled him close. 'I'll end you, got it?' Danny pushed Iceblue onto hard ground.

Iceblue laughed. 'My friends will look forward to taking you, too.'

'What friends?' Danny didn't let go. 'Who the fuck do you work for?'

'You really don't know, do you? You really haven't worked it out?'

'No,' Danny roared. 'Tell me! *Tell me!*'

Iceblue cackled. 'This is amazing!' Iceblue pushed, but Danny caught his wrist.

'Don't think I won't,' he said.

'I know you won't. You'd have done it already.'

Danny let go. In the distance, he heard more buzzing sounds. That was trouble coming. He didn't want to encounter it.

'Sod you, you stupid bastard,' Danny heaved as he got to his feet. He ran, his feet hardly gripping the wet cement and asphalt surface.

'You'll never get her back, mark my words!' Iceblue shouted after Danny, but didn't run after him.

Danny scrabbled through the fleeting rain for what seemed like ages but was about an hour. The bright lights of the commercial strip wound round, up a hill, to a big crossroads.

'That'll do,' he said, looking diagonally across. The train station beckoned. He crossed and entered the concrete building, the rain teeming around him.

'Christ, right night for it?' the bored-looking attendant said.

'You don't know the half of it,' Danny said, plodding to the ticket machine in great, rainy footsteps. 'Ah, shit,' he said to the machine after patting his pockets. They were empty, lacking the familiar bulge of his wallet.

'What's the problem?' the attendant said.

'No money.' The attendant hummed. Danny glanced at the big digital clock. Nearly midnight, with the last train in eight minutes. 'Fancy giving me a break? Can't you see what happened?'

'I don't know…'

'Come on, man,' Danny said, his voice wavering. He didn't want to have to beg, but his knees trembled. They'd take the first step, even if he didn't want to.

The attendant spun on their heels in a slow, swishing motion.

'Where're you going?' Danny explained. 'Alright,' he said. 'Looks like you've had a shit night.' He tapped a pass on the barrier. A green light lit, a friendly beep came, and the gate opened.

'You're a legend,' Danny said, smiling widely at the man. 'A real legend.'

'No worries,' the attendant said. 'You take care.'

Danny emerged onto the platform. Darkness filled the void between that and the other dirtily lit platform opposite. To the left, stairs up to a lattice metal footbridge. Beyond that, darkness punctuated by distant colour of light from the signals. To the right, largely the same, sans the footbridge. The station only needed one, and there was nobody here to use it. He paced along a few feet toward a bench covered in peeling paint.

He sat down and took a deep breath. *So much time wasted. And now not even a car to drive.*

The speakers in the canopy chimed.

The next train from Platform Two is the twenty-three-fifty-seven service. Calling at…

Danny didn't need to listen. He knew where it called. He looked up to see a pair of white lights in the darkness beyond the end of the platform that danced in the gloom, getting bigger. Then the yellow front of the train emerged. It was streaked with dirt and grime, with the silhouette of a glum figure in the front window.

It was deserted, and Danny got up as it wound to a stop. He clawed the rubber dome that operated the doors, which hissed open and clattered at their stops. Finally, he fell into one of the high-backed chairs and sighed. The train jolted into motion.

Twenty minutes later he was heaving himself up from that seat at his stop. His whole body ached, and he stretched to get up, nearly falling out of the carriage and onto a grisly platform. Danny walked through the exit - there a no barrier - and emerged down a ramp into a sleepy residential street. Across the road was the old Tony Carvery, now shuttered and dismal.

Finally, the pain in his body almost unbearable, Danny fell through the door to his rented room and stumbled until he fell onto the little single bed that he'd been reduced to. He lay there for a few minutes, letting his energy recharge.

'Crap!' he remembered - his phone! He slid his hand into his pocket and pulled it out. The screen was chipped, but not staved in completely. He fumbled down the side of the bed for the cable and jiggled it into the port on the bottom of the phone. Then he waited. After a couple of seconds, the phone made a tone and an empty battery icon appeared. He turned over. The phone would need a few moments to charge enough to switch on. He looked up at the ceiling of the bedsit. Damp marks permeated the ceiling covering. Toward the middle, the light fixture hung at a lazy angle.

A couple of minutes went past. Danny just breathed in and out. The shock his body had gone through was starting to fade as the adrenalin was absorbed into his blood.

With some effort, he picked up the phone and unlocked it. His dirty fingers danced around the screen. He tapped into contacts and switched to Hailey's profile. His hand trembled. She'd told him to go there. *Say it wasn't so. Say it was some mistake.* He tapped *dial* and held the phone to his ear.

CHAPTER 24

Grayson Laurie entered the boardroom, the door closing with a clatter.

'Oh, they didn't tell me you'd arrived.'

'We're back,' Steele said. 'Sit down please, Mr Laurie. I think we've been *more* than fair to you.'

He did so. Hunching forward, his face scrunched up. The three commissioners were flanked by Yellowstone legal. They conferred in hushed whispers. He lent back.

'Guys, guys. Are you here about those reports in the media? Look, I've got my best people—'

'That's partially the reason, yes,' Steele said. 'Rather…'

'What you're proposing is going to do away with the Commission,' Franklin said, stabbing the table. 'It's why we couldn't wait another month or more. What the hell are you playing at?'

Grayson sat back. 'It is?'

'Don't play dumb with us, Laurie,' Gravey spat, his chins wobbling. 'What you're up to threatens the whole equilibrium our organisation has brought.'

Grayson's mouth dropped open. He didn't know what to say. Then the door clattered open behind him. He turned in his chair. 'Wendy?'

'Sorry I'm late,' Tunt said, straightening out her jacket and sitting down. It was a shocking pink affair. The colour almost burned against the litany of yellows and corn colours that punctuated the walls. 'Commissioners. I'm sorry we could only slot you in this late.'

'This is an outrage! You don't have the right to do what you want, not like this!.'

'We won't stand for it!'

'It'll never pass!'

Tunt laughed.

'What's so funny, Wendy?'

'Don't you see?' Tunt addressed the room itself, not anyone in particular. 'They're clinging on to the framework of the past. It's out of date.'

'Is it related to the Special Provisions?' he asked.

'Of course it is. You really think the Commission,' Steele interjected, 'will let you get away with this?'

'Quite frankly,' Tunt said, 'I don't really give a damn what the Commission thinks.'

Grayson's glance darted from the plum-red commissioners and Tunt. A smile couldn't help but crack from the corner of her mouth. His gaze settled on Tunt. 'Wendy.'

She turned.

'A word, please?' he turned to the Commission now and gave them a painted smile. 'Can you excuse us a moment?'

'Sure,' Franklin nodded.

Grayson leapt from his chair, sending it thrusting into the wall with a bang. He almost dragged Wendy from hers and barrelled through the door.

'Hey!' she squeaked.

'In here,' he said, pushing open the door opposite. A couple of Yellowstone employees were cleaning the adjacent board room. They nearly dropped their cleaners, seeing Grayson Laurie emerge through the door. 'You two. Out.' They scampered past. Grayson slammed the door closed as Wendy fell through.

She hissed, 'What the hell is that about?'

'I could ask you the same question! The fucking Commission banging down my door! All this business with the Special Provision was meant to be handled by *you*.' He stabbed the air at chest level. She flinched backward.

'It is, Grayson. I don't know what you've been reading.'

'My emails,' he said. 'The portal.'

'What you're reading is false.'

'You saying the other execs are *lying*?'

'Who?' she said, her glance narrowing. 'Which execs are telling you that?'

'These people were hand-picked, Wendy. By *me*. Don't you dare impinge their loyalty. Is it true or not? Our proposal is going to gut the Commission. I don't recall hearing that in the briefings.'

'There's an element to that, yes, to open up opportunities for the company. I'm only doing what you asked me to.'

'I told you to cement Yellowstone as a powerful force for good in the UK.'

'Which is what I'm doing? We'll be the sole operator.'

'What else does the Private Sector Innovation Act do, Wendy? Tell me. I need to know. This is my life's work at stake.'

'You've read the draft?' She didn't wait for an answer. 'A simplification of the system that we've been enslaved to in this country. Why we've let a body set up by emergency powers that are grossly due for expiry is beyond me. But we have the means to get rid of it and build a bright future.'

He stood back. 'Okay.'

'Is that all?'

'Okay. But promise me one thing.'

'Anything, Grayson.'

'That's the truth, right?' She blinked. 'The God's honest truth?

You to me?'

She took a deep breath, her chest expanding in her suit jacket. 'You have my word. Now, let's not delay things. Are you coming or not?'

'Is there any point? You know the details.'

'Fine,' she said, brushing herself off and turning to the door. The latch clicked.

'Wendy,' he said. She stopped.

'Yes?'

'My office in two hours. I want to see quite what it is that you've got planned.'

She hesitated, but just for a moment.

'Whatever you want, Grayson. I'll see you soon.'

Grayson watched as she slipped through the door and through the one across the corridor. He followed, but only out into the corridor. He turned back toward the grand lobby. A panoramic vista of London peeked through the glass.

He reached into his pocket and slipped his phone out. He pressed it to his ear.

'I'm coming up. Are you here? Good, that's just brilliant. No, not my office. Best not,' he said, stealing a glance over his shoulder. 'I'll message you where. We've got a couple of hours.'

Grayson Laurie stepped into the fresh London morning, feeling the breeze on his face and the rush of air around him. He crossed the street. It was quiet. Not many people around. The wide road became a narrow street framed with glass and steel offices. He stepped into this narrow alley, already feeling the lack of radiant heat on his face. The sun couldn't penetrate this deep into this shrine to enterprise. It became a passing observer.

A snicket opened up on the left. Grayson crossed the road

briskly, diving straight down into it.

'Grayson Laurie,' a voice said. 'I thought we'd stop meeting like this.'

Grayson smiled. 'Aaron,' he said. 'Good to see you.' He embraced the man who stood in the shadow. A grin of teeth brightened the alley.

'What trouble are you in now?' Aaron started. 'Don't tell me, trouble in paradise?' He nodded to the Yellowstone campus at the end of the street. 'Do you know how *hard* it was to get here at short notice?'

'I'm glad you came.'

'So tell me. Have you started a fire?'

'Just a bit. Did you get those documents I asked for a few weeks ago?'

Aaron nodded. 'Difficult to decipher, but they're button downed tight. You know, when I left the comp—'

'Don't,' Grayson said. 'Let's not talk about that. Tell me what you found out.'

'The first part gets rid of this Commission,' he said. 'Weird British thing, that. They love having a big government panel to deal with everything for them.'

'Yes, I found out about that about twenty minutes ago. But are there any other surprises I should know about?'

'The language is dense and references itself all over the place. This could clog up Congress for months.'

'We're not in the States, Aaron.'

'Indeed not. Who knows how long the British Parliament has?'

Grayson took a step back. 'Come back to Yellowstone, Aaron. I need you back again.'

Aaron stepped back too and broke gaze with Grayson. 'I… I

can't. I'm sorry.'

'My door is always open, you know that. I want things how they were again so much. Just like old times.'

'But it's not, is it? We're hardly dropshipping like we did before. Me on X, you on Y. It's all very… I couldn't do it.'

'You bailed before even giving it a proper go,' he said. 'Come and see my office, at least.'

Aaron looked at Grayson and then glanced down the street. 'It's been a crazy twenty years.'

'And you're still unofficially part of…'

'Hey,' Aaron said with a bark. 'I did this because I owed you a favour. And, like you said, things go back a long time.'

Grayson looked at Aaron, but only fleetingly. 'Okay. Let's catch up soon. Neutral ground if you like. Man to man.'

'That'd be good.'

'Just remember…'

'Grayson,' Aaron said. 'I do this because I like you. And I want your vision to work. But this can't be called work, okay?'

Grayson stood in the alley for a long moment. Then he smiled wide like a piano. 'Sure.' His phone rang just once. 'I've gotta…'

'Richest man in the world caught in a London alleyway? What will the British tabloids say?'

'They can fuck off, is what I'd say to them.'

***

'She's in your office, Mr Laurie,' Heaton said as Grayson stepped from the lift. He crossed the lobby in a handful of wide strides.

'Is she?'

'She is, sir.'

'Thank you. Wait here. This won't take long.'

He took a step past Heaton and down a passage toward the penthouse office. The trickling of water filtered through the glass, steel, concrete, and aluminium of the building.

Opening his office door, he saw the tree in the planter surrounded by the trickling brook. All false but made to look natural. Then he saw Wendy Tunt behind his desk, her face smashing the serenity that usually filled this zone.

'Wendy,' he said. 'We meet again.'

'Close the door,' she said. Grayson did so. He stepped forward. 'I'm sorry if I misunderstood the—'

'Button it, Grayson. I know what you've been doing.'

Grayson's stance hardened. 'And what's that?'

'I found the list of execs. They're packing their things.'

'Those aren't your people, Wendy. You can't fire them.'

'And,' she said, 'I know about the *drip-drip-drip* to your friend. Your co-founder. The one who walked away. You were with him now. How could you? Demean yourself. The richest, most well-liked person on the planet. Trading rumours down some filthy alley to the likes of Aaron Moore.'

'Hey!' Grayson said, raising his voice. 'Your office has been stonewalling me for weeks. You've been stalling me for weeks. You give it all that,' he said, clapping his hands together in a mock talking gesture, 'but you give me no detail. Do you know how many divisions I've got? And I've not been out of London for six months.'

'Seventeen continental divisions. And you wanted to make London your hub for European expansion. Sorry to have diverted your attention, but isn't what you hired me for?'

'Yes, and now I'm seriously worried. First protests outside my house. Now the Commission is sniffing around because they smell shit, Wendy. None of this happened before you took over. I don't need any *more* legal shit to deal with, and you've dumped a whole load right on me, you stupid—'

'Careful,' she said, leaning forward in Grayson Laurie's chair. 'You could say something you may later regret.'

'Don't you remember the motto? London is a unique opportunity. Given what happened all those years ago.'

'I remember all the bullshit you wrapped the opportunity in. You don't know what you're sitting on.'

'Get out of my chair, Wendy,' Grayson said, striding forward. 'Get the hell out of my building. You're done. I want no part in what scheme you've been concocting while I've had my back turned.'

She leant back. 'I'm not going anywhere. And you're right. You won't have any part in the scheme. Because you're not part of this company, Grayson.'

'I *am* the company, you fucking bitch,' he growled. '*Get out of my chair.*'

She laughed. 'You have no idea, do you? The opportunity here is too big for you to fuck it up. We're taking over the failures of the government, Grayson. You could've had one big, huge Yellow Zone called the UK, all paying Prime, all living like kings.'

'It doesn't work like that. I wanted to create not just a business that improved the world around it, but that brought people with them. You just want them all to be customers. We don't need customers, Wendy...'

'See, that's precisely the kind of attitude that stunted the opportunity. And you were too busy pissing about with that stupid robot *thing* to realise it.' She tossed a dirty glance at the Parker speaker on the desk.

'Look at where you are? Eighty floors up. And still in my chair. I've asked you three times now, Wendy. *Get out of my chair!*'

She smiled a beaming, cattish grin. And finally, she got up and stood around the desk.

Grayson heaved.

'There's your bloody chair,' Tunt said with a dismissive glance at the seat that spun lazily with the latent momentum of her exit. 'Not that you'll do much with it.'

'What have you done, Wendy?' Grayson ran around the desk. He sat down.

'You'll find out soon enough,' she said. 'I'm not going to let your stupid credo miss out on the biggest opportunity this country has ever presented someone. Letting people reap the spoils of our innovation for free? What are you, completely mad?!'

'I told you when we first met that I wanted you to help me change the world.'

'Which is precisely what I'm doing! I'm just being honest, Grayson. I want to make money while we do that. You've gone soft on that, haven't you?'

'But that's precisely what led to what happened a few years ago. Don't you see the folly?'

'Lessons have been learned, Grayson. Now, if you don't mind, I've work to do.'

The door opened behind Grayson, who stood up. 'You're fired, Wendy. You are *fired*.' She laughed. 'I told you, Wendy. I'm firing you. This ends now.'

'I think you'll find you no longer have the authority to do anything, Grayson. Consider it a professional courtesy that I even let you sit in that damn chair one last time.'

'What are you doing?' Grayson heaved. 'Heaton,' he indicated to his aide, who had entered the room. A couple of heavy-set Yellowstone security guards in orange uniforms followed. Heaton's face was quarry-like. 'Good, security. Remove her.' Grayson

291

ordered. No-one moved. 'That wasn't a request! *Do you know who I am?!*'

Wendy smiled. 'They don't take orders from you. Not any more.' She nodded instead to Heaton and gestured with a long finger at Grayson. 'Remove *him*.'

Heaton took a step toward Grayson.

'Heaton… please,' Grayson said. Heaton instead grabbed Grayson's arm and wrenched him to his feet. 'What… no! After all this time, you're—'

'The old management,' Wendy said to the room. 'Show him the door, please. I won't ask again.'

'With pleasure,' Heaton said. He pushed his fist playfully into his opposite palm as he approached the desk. Then he grabbed Grayson and dragged him to the door.

'What are you doing? Don't you know who I am?!' he screamed. 'You dirty bastard, how could you do this to me?! And you, Wendy, you bitch?!'

'Hostile takeover, Grayson. It's not business, really. It's *personnel*.'

'Is this legal? I demand to see—'

'Go play with your stupid toy,' she said, throwing one of the disc-shaped speakers at Grayson. It bounced off his contained body and rattled to the floor, plastic cracking into pieces.

Grayson's eyes followed the device and faltered, watching it break. 'You can't do this!' Grayson shouted as Heaton dragged him out of his own office and toward the lift.

He was dumped on the kerb in the imposing shadow of the building that had once been his, but had now been stolen.

CHAPTER 25

'Danny?' Hailey said as the door to the Archer house opened in her hand. She hissed, clutching the towel close to her body. 'I told you not to come! You can't be here, you'll be—'

'No bullshit,' he said. 'You know something, right?' She hesitated. 'Tell me. I don't have time to waste. Especially after being on a wild goose chase of *your* doing.'

'That's not fair, Danny, I—'

'Tell me then. Tell me *every fucking thing*.'

She paused, then relented. 'Okay,' she said. 'Come in. Before you're seen.'

Danny pushed through the door.

'Come upstairs, quickly,' she said.

'Anybody home?'

'No, but still. We have to be careful. Dad's got the place full of cameras now.'

'People getting wise to him?'

'Everything's going to shit,' she said. 'People keep… turning up.'

'if you say so,' he said, following her up. Hailey opened the door to her bedroom.

'Come on then,' she said. Danny followed. On one side of the bedroom was a desk covered in scrawls and scraps of paper, as well as camera equipment, cables and notepads. 'You've been busy,' he said.

'We're nearly ready to drop the bomb on Yellowstone. I knew

there was something when Henry started there,' she said, rifling through the bits of paper and equipment. 'Now it all makes sense. That dossier was just *too good*.'

'Wait,' Danny said. She looked. 'Henry works for… Yellowstone?'

'Oh,' she said, catching a glimpse of his agape jaw. 'You… you didn't know?'

'And you did?'

'I thought it was obvious. When he knew you'd got the tracker, he knew it'd only be a matter of time until we got the box codes. When I got home, he was waiting for me. I… I…' she said, her face falling, expecting sympathy or warmth.

Danny didn't reciprocate. 'So you betrayed me?'

'No, nothing like that!' Hailey said, grasping Danny's hand. He held on. She smiled, hopeful it was enough. 'But when it's your brother…'

'I get it. He's a bastard.'

'He wanted me to do other things, Danny. He wanted me to find those things of your nan's, and—'

'Did you?'

'No! But that pissed him off. So I had to get back in his good books. I didn't know what'd happen.'

Danny hummed, weighing up mentally whether to believe her. 'Consulting, my arse. Fucking twat. He took the job they offered me. Now, come on!'

'Right,' she said. Slipping across her bedroom, Hailey produced a piece of tattered paper from her bedside drawer. 'I've double checked the address with the research I've been part of. It matches,' she said with a glint of glee at her subterfuge. 'What Ashley was saying about that old Mertons that got abandoned. Here, look.'

She handed him several of the papers. Some were fresh, flat and with no crinkles or crumples.

'Where'd you get that lot?'

'He doesn't know they're missing,' she said, pulling on a loose top. 'He's got lazy the more they've had him… working. But that tracker spooked him. It's why he had me divert you.' Danny was captivated as she clipped the brassiere around her back.

'Do you need any…' Danny trailed off. Soap suds were still streaming into his eyes.

She laughed. 'Easy tiger. Let's get going.'

Hailey led Danny round to the garage. The door thrummed open.

'Wow,' he said as the morning light cast through the opening. He brushed a hand through his hair. He'd washed the grease and the grit from it. 'You sure you wanna take this?'

The sole vehicular occupant gleamed a metallic bronze and brown.

Hailey grabbed the key. 'I'll drive. Least I can do.'

'Yeah, sure,' Danny said. He regarded a rack of tools that looked hardly used, almost decorative. 'This'll do.'

'What will?' Hailey said, then saw the crowbar. 'Well, alright. But keep it off the seats.'

Hailey approached the car, clicking the fob with his fingers. The headlights trilled, lighting up in a ring. The cabin faded into clarity as the visor retracted from the panoramic glazed roof. Then he got in. The new car smell was intense. The freshness of the plastic, the leather of the seats and the scent of newness. 'Has this ever been driven?'

'Once or twice,' Hailey said. 'It's dad's plaything.'

'Where's yours?'

'Got rid of it. Dad wasn't pleased.'

She leant forward, tapping on the touchscreen that was the centre console. Beyond that, the dashboard was treated wood and satin chrome. 'Hold this,' she said, pushing a black polyester case into Danny's lap. 'I'll put the postcode in.'

'What is this?'

'Camera,' she said. 'Not missing this chance…'

The console blipped, and Hailey depressed the accelerator. The car glided out of the garage and down the driveway like a shadow.

'What do you expect to find there?' Hailey asked. 'This… abandoned store? You really think they'd be holding your nan there?'

Danny took an intake of breath through his teeth. He hoped that would be the case, but very much doubted it. 'Don't think so. But I like to think we'll find a clue. They're getting sloppy.'

Hailey hummed. 'Me and a group of friends. We've done some digging about Yellowstone.'

'Is this why I'm carrying this bloody camera?' Danny asked.

'Yeah, and look after it,' she said. 'Maybe for both of us, the jigsaw's coming together.'

They drove for half an hour across pitted streets and past overgrown verges.

'Thing are getting worse,' Hailey observed.

'Yeah, this is the future we've got, I guess,' Danny hummed. The rain returned as a mist across the windscreen. A wiper deployed from the base of the windscreen and wept the water away. Danny's eyes opened, surprised. 'Neat!'

'All the mod cons, this thing,' Hailey said.

'Ready to cross the threshold?' Danny pointed at a sign by the roadside.

Now entering Yellow Zone. The future of progress and tomorrow's community today!

'I thought we already had,' Hailey said. 'Oh, right, that?'

Crossing the border felt like emerging from a portal in space and time. The most immediate difference was a change in the road. The tyres no longer thudded through pitted and worn tarmac; now they glided across the smooth asphalt with barely any noise, just the hiss of the electric motor in the back propelling them forward.

The streetlights changed, too - lamp posts at odd, jaunty angles with glowing orange bulbs became uniformly straight sentinels casting cool white light from modern bulbs. The verges and pathways glimmered verdant in this fresh lighting.

Nothing seemed out of place.

'Quite a change,' she said. 'If only everywhere was like this.'

Danny's face crumpled. 'Is it worth the price, though?'

'What price?'

'Yellowstone Prime - once you're in, you're in. And if you change your mind, that's it.'

'It can't be that bad, surely,' she said.

'Maybe, maybe not,' Danny said. 'How far are we from the store?'

Hailey crouched forward to examine the at nav screen on the centre console. 'Eight minutes.'

'Turn off here,' Danny said. She did so, turning from the brightly lit thoroughfare into a more dimly lit backstreet.

'Clearly it's only skin-deep,' he said, squinting. Hailey pulled on the stalk on the steering column. The street ahead was bathed in electric light. Cracked paving and weeds sprouting. 'The transformation, that is. Can't see a damn thing.'

'Why'd they only do the main road?'

'This has only recently become a Yellow Zone, remember?' Danny said. The tyres bucked on the uneven paving. 'See? Old roads. They've only gussied up what most people see. Keeping up appearances.'

'They'd get to this eventually,' Hailey said. 'Their prices and speed are what most people care about. Everything else is a cherry on top. I was expecting worse.'

'You really believe that? Look at this road,' Danny said. 'Just trees, bushes and abandoned units. Who'd pay to do this up?' He glanced at the closed, darkened industrial units. Hoardings, barely visible in the gloom, advertised a shiny rendering of a futuristic warehouse on the river, with serif fonts labelling it as the *Yellowstone Distribution Centre.*

Hailey nodded, unable to argue.

Next right, and your destination is on the left.

Hailey followed the direction, and the car came to a halt in front of a tall, yellow hoarding. 'This is it,' he said, unclipping his seatbelt.

'Don't leave the car here,' Hailey said. 'Might be trouble.'

Danny nodded, reversing away from the hoarding. A few metres down the road, he found an overgrown driveway. The long branches of the tree squealed against the top and sides of the car. 'You're wrecking the paintwork.'

'Doesn't matter,' she said. 'It's dad's car.'

'Really?' Danny said, his eyebrows arching. She nodded. The car fell dormant, and Danny finally alighted.

Hailey followed. The hoarding was swaying in the breeze.

Beyond that, a large, angular shape against the trees all around. The shape was dark, gloomy and still. A few letters of the Mertons sign remained hanging onto the frontage.

'Acquired by Yellowstone UK LTD,' Hailey read from notices attached to the hoarding. The notices conveyed placid images of a regenerated development - brick-clad flats with anonymous retail underneath, streaks of cars gliding by computer-generated trees. Vapidly gawping people dotted the image, but something about them just seemed… off. None of the people's feet seemed to contact the paved surface, and they all seemed to have expressions devoid of warmth.

'They're also looking in about fourteen different directions,' Danny said. 'This is all fake. They've no plans to do anything here.'

'That doesn't surprise me,' Hailey said. 'We need to find a way in.'

'Already looking,' Danny said, scoping down the hoarding. He felt it as he walked, but the sheeting only went a little. 'If this is a base, there has to be a way in.'

'I'll go this way,' Hailey said, taking the opposite direction. Danny continued, pressing gently on the hoarding for any weak spots. 'Danny!'

Danny pivoted. Hailey waved at him. 'What have you found?'

'A way in,' she said, disappearing into a hole no taller than waist height. Danny followed quickly, emerging into the weed-infested car park. Beyond that, the empty shell of the Mertons store stood before them.

'Now to get in there,' he said. They approached the front doors - once motorised, now sealed. 'No luck.'

'Didn't think so,' she said. She pressed her face to the dirty glass. 'Wow, it's like they've been gone forever.'

Danny did the same. Beyond, he saw dilapidated shelving

units, some with product still on them. The floor was festooned with filth. Old packets, discarded items and more. 'The change of zone wasn't a pleasant one, it seems. They didn't take it well.'

'Change of lifestyle,' she said. 'You've heard about it, right?'

'I've read—'

'Danny,' she said, stopping. 'I've been to these places for my channel. The regime changes overnight. Everything stops and starts again. It only ever goes one way. Those who can't pay – it's all taken away. The whole system is broken.' She tapped her bag with her camera. 'I've seen how it turns lives upside fucking down.'

'It's that bad?'

'You and I are really privileged,' she said. 'You ain't seen it when those that can ride out the change the least get caught in the crossfire.' She swallowed, pausing for a moment. 'Let's go round the back,' she said, tearing herself away from the glass. Danny followed. They followed the footprint of the building until they came to a door that looked rusted shut, but that the wind had been teasing in its frame.

'This'll do,' Danny said, grunting at the door as he grabbed the handle. The wood in the frame splintered, and the door squealed open, suddenly losing all resistance.

'Danny!' Hailey gasped.

'What?' he said, then looked. His hand still gripped the handle. He glanced at the piece of missing door. 'Anyone could've done that.'

Hailey pushed the remains of the door closed behind her.

Inside, the blackness was total. Danny reached for his phone and illuminated the flash on the back. A set of stairs led straight up. To the left of the stairs was a lift that didn't work.

'Wow, this is creepy,' Hailey said.

'This is a lot like Kier Wood,' Danny said as they wound their way up the stairs. 'Maybe this store opened at the same time.'

'Probably,' Hailey said. 'Let's see what's here.'

Upstairs, a corridor went left and right. Darkness beckoned to the left, but an open door went right.

'Right?' Hailey said, reaching for Danny's hand. He gripped it.

'Right,' he agreed, taking the first step.

They walked through into the shattered remains of an office. Bench desks along one side were littered with papers and pieces of litter, the sunset streaming in through the murky windows above. Besides this lay open cartons of glossy flyers, the top layer left askew. Hailey took hold of one flyer.

'Welcome Yellowstone to your Zone,' she read, palming over the glossy paper. '*More jobs, more opportunities, more life for you. All thanks to Yellowstone – working in your interests.*' She snorted.

'Yeah, well, that's the marketing.' Danny dismissed the words she read. 'We need something concrete. Nobody's here, anyway, that's for certain.'

Outside, throaty engines roared nearer. Wood clattered. Hailey stole away, hiding behind the window to outside. 'Don't be so sure,' she whispered. 'Look.'

Danny moved over and crouched, peeking above the ledge. Headlights rolled around the car park outside, having come through an open gate in the hoarding. Four anonymous-looking vans emerged into the car park. People got out, leaving the engines running. From the back of the vans, people in biker leathers and delivery outfits, but without helmets.

'They're coming this way,' Hailey said. The troop of people downstairs headed into the entrance they'd taken. A racket of footsteps filled the staircase. 'Hide!'

Danny looked around, seeing a small cubicle room that faced the corridor outside. He nodded. Hailey's jaw opened.

'It's full of glass!' she said. She was right. The cubicle office overlooked a wrecked seating area and the corridor outside. A small hatch window was jammed half-closed in the wall.

'Quick, it'll do,' Danny said, thrusting forward and diving to the floor under the little counter in the room. Hailey hit the deck too, just as the footsteps passed the window. Danny kicked the door closed as the footsteps entered the office.

The hubbub of conversation filtered through the door.

'You've all got your orders, right?' a voice said. Not one Danny recognised. 'I've heard from our contact. The fugitive is out, presumably accompanied. They're both liabilities,' the voice said, 'and are to be dealt with accordingly.'

'He escaped me at the depot,' a further voice added. Danny recognised this one.

'Iceblue,' he hissed, before pursing his lips together.

'But he can't have gone far. Henry's sister...'

'No names! No real names, may I remind you... *Ian*,' the first voice barked.

But Danny heard enough, the voice now one he recognised. *Henry is involved in this...*

Iceblue growled. 'They've made off. No sign of either of them. Maybe they're in cahoots.'

'And there's a car missing at your place,' another voice added.

'What?!' the first voice said. 'You've been there?'

'I told you that you owe. Consider it insurance. Now, about those two—'

'Love's young dream. Good for them,' the first voice called. 'I'll tell our contact. If you can't trust your family...'

'You can't trust *no-one* in this business,' Iceblue said. 'There's the matter of our payment.'

'What about it?'

'You owe,' Iceblue said. 'Now pay up. We've done your dirty work for weeks. Now the time is due.'

'Can it wait a couple more days once everything's sewn up?'

'No,' Iceblue said. Three footsteps followed. 'It can't.'

A chorus of *ooohh*s followed. Danny shuffled, pushing the door open a couple of inches with his foot. The hinge creaked. He closed his eyes, expecting capture. But he opened them to see Iceblue with his hands against a man in a suit's chest. The light glinted on a piece of metal jutting out from the skin of Iceblue's fist.

'Let's not be hasty,' the man in the suit whimpered. 'We'll get you your recompense before tomorrow's out. How does that sound?'

Iceblue took a single step back. 'Better. Let's not ruin this good thing we've got going on.'

'Where are we taking them?' one of the other bikers asked. 'Iceblue was telling me about the YDC…'

YDC… what's that? Danny thought.

'We moved the primary asset there yesterday. We'll bring them all together there,' Iceblue explained. 'If I'm allowed in, that is.'

'May I remind you,' the man in the tie coughed, recovering some composure, 'that this is the most critical part of the operation. What we're doing is highly… irregular. That's why we meet here. Safe territory.'

'Just say illegal, for fuck's sake,' Iceblue said. 'We're all friends here now, right? It's why I let you into our turf.'

'Turf we've provided for you, remember,' the man in the tie sighed. 'Hopefully that regulatory difficulty will be resolved soon.'

'Your problem, not mine,' Iceblue said. 'Let's go. Maybe we'll find them skulking around tonight. Nowhere's safe for them.'

The room beyond filled with brief murmurs of assent, then the sound of the group filing back out and downstairs. A minute or two later, van doors clicked and clacked open and closed, followed by the abrupt eruption of the engines which disappeared into the darkness.

Danny lay prone, taking deep breaths that made his chest rise and fall.

'The hell was that?' Hailey asked.

'That was too close,' Danny replied. He got up. 'What's a YDC when it's at home? The answer must be here!' He moved back into the office and skittishly looked about the messy place.

'Danny,' Hailey said. Danny didn't respond. 'Danny!' she said, louder. He spun round. 'We're wanted by those people. Who knows what they're capable of?'

Danny stopped and walked over to Hailey, putting both hands on her shoulders. Then he held her head close and put his face next to hers. 'I won't let them do a thing to you. Whatever their beef is, or this plan… it's just me they want. I won't let them endanger you.' He pushed his lips to hers. She reciprocated for a tender moment.

'Come on,' she said. 'The answer must be around here. Let's keep looking.'

They did, but the papers and piles they found were useless. Old Merton inventory sheets. Stock ordering bills. Staff schedules. All discarded in a hurry. In an ideal world this would've been archived, but the relentless wave of Yellowstone left no room for due process.

The exit hadn't been voluntary.

After fifteen minutes, the two drew a blank.

'Sorry,' she said.

'Don't be,' Danny said. He threw a pile of useless paper on the carton of Yellowstone fliers. One flipped over.

His eyebrow raised with inquisition. He moved fast.

'What've you found?' Hailey said.

Danny reached for one flier. On the back was a great yellow and grey metal warehouse. 'Jobs,' he said. 'At the YDC they're building. Up on the Riverside.'

Hailey's eyes widened. 'You think that's where they're holding your nan, for whatever purpose?'

'Must be,' Danny said, pocketing the flyer. 'Let's go. Nothing left here in this dead store.'

CHAPTER 26

Danny and Hailey drove through the sleepy Yellow Zone toward their next destination. The subset finally yielded to night by the time the river's rippling surface reflected the headlights back to them.

'Thameside,' Danny announced. 'Now, to find this place.'

'Can't miss it, really,' Hailey said as the car swooshed down the meandering bankside road. 'Look, there it is.'

Danny squinted, but really didn't need to. The buildings by the side of the road seemed to part in awe of the massive concrete and steel behemoth that not just assumed the space, but claimed it with its presence. 'I'll park up here,' she said, pulling into an empty bay. 'This car's quite conspicuous.'

'Just as well we moved it back there,' Hailey agreed.

Getting out, the space around the Distribution Centre was completely flat and paved with asphalt and concrete. Painted lines shone out, freshly installed and yet to be worn down by the passage of vehicles, feet and time. A tall chain-link fence surrounded the place, creating a barrier a couple of hundred feet around the place.

'Enormous,' Danny said as they approached the fence. 'This must've cost a fortune.'

'Why build it here?' Hailey asked. 'This is prime riverside estate. People would kill for a place here.'

Danny stood at a crossroads. To the left, the riverbank. To the right, the town. A shimmer of yellow and gold came from the left.

He followed it, the building unfolding as he crossed the corner.

'There's your answer,' he said, stopping at the apex of the corner. He glanced at the great cliff-like side of the building.

The Yellowstone logo - completely illuminated - must've been fifty feet tall, as high as the side of the building. The light and colour rippled onto the dark surface of the water. It was part of a massive dot-matric light display so bright Danny had to squint to look directly at it.

'Talk about advertising,' Hailey said.

'It's obscene, really,' Danny said. A tall hologram of Grayson Laurie's smiling face came from the screen. 'Imagine living across the river from that?'

'Across there, you mean?' Hailey jogged her head. 'Nobody home.'

Danny followed her gaze. Some blocks of flats stood opposite the Yellowstone sign on the other side of a condemned bridge. 'Of course. It's a Blue Zone. They must've got sick of this quickly.' He looked at Hailey. 'Now we've gotta get in.'

'How'd you think we'll do that?' she asked. 'We can't go in the front door.'

'We could, but the game would be up pretty quickly,' Danny said. He frisked the chain-link fence. 'It's pretty buttoned up. I can't climb that.'

'Neither can I.'

The road rattled quickly.

'The hell is that?' Hailey gasped. She turned, seeing a huge, angular *thing* blot out the sky. It rocketed past, making barely a sound beside the ground moving.

'Electric lorry,' Danny said. 'Maybe they enter round the back?'

'Maybe,' she said. 'That thing's scary.'

'Don't worry,' Danny said. He grasped her hand and got a firm grip in response. It felt warm, slightly clammy, but human. 'Nothing to be scared of. Let's follow the truck.'

Hailey nodded. They proceeded to go in the shadow of the tail lights that meandered down the street, turning right. It was a good start. Danny followed, pulling Hailey with him. He smiled. He was finally getting a break. Finally the odds were swinging, he just knew it-

'Shit,' he cursed. Hailey nearly tripped up behind him. 'Stay there!' he warned.

'What?' she said.

'Look,' he pointed. 'A guard shack. He's checking the lorries in.'

Beyond the curve of the road, the lorry had stopped. A couple of Yellowstone employees peeked around the front. The cab was illuminated as the driver got down. Beyond, a dozen other lorries were parked, their running lights dormant over the angular bodywork.

A dozen sleeping dragons waiting to be woken up.

'Okay,' Hailey said. 'So we can't just walk in. They're checking.'

'Right,' Danny said. He looked at the fence. 'Still don't fancy climbing that...' he ducked. Another lorry whooshed past at speed.

'We need to get on one of those lorries,' Hailey said. 'We need to stop one.' She walked off a few paces in front of Danny, and reached for her phone.

'Are you mad?' he said. She smiled at him, lowering her brow as she mumbled a few words. 'Because if you are, I'm so into that!'

Replacing her phone in her pocket, now it was Hailey's turn to grasp Danny's hand. He gladly took it.

'Come on, lover,' she whispered in his ear. 'Let's go hitch a ride.'

Danny followed as Hailey doubled back.

'Where'd you think you're going?'

'We'll go to the end of the road, by the roundabout. See if we can sneak on one of these things and get in that way.'

The bush by the roundabout rustled. Danny froze.

'Someone's there. Hey, you!' Danny called. 'Yeah, I know you're there!' The bush trembled. 'Come out, now, no more silly bollocks!'

'Ah, fuck,' the bush said. Danny's head rotated with curiosity. He reached into his pocket, pulling out his phone and thrusting the torchlight from the back just as a figure wriggled out, scraping on the cracked and undulating pavement.

'Sparky? What the hell are you doing here?' Danny called.

Sparky dusted himself off. 'We're here to help.'

'But… how?'

'Ask her,' Sparky said, pointing to Hailey. 'She called us.'

'We need to get in,' Danny said. 'Just us, though. Don't risk breaking your neck.'

'No chance,' Sparky said. 'Come on, I've got an idea.'

He led them down the side road a little to a car parked underneath a street light that didn't work.

'What's your plan, Danny?' Sparky asked. Danny explained. 'Okay, easy. Got my toolbox here,' he said, opening the back door. 'Take a set of cutters.'

Danny reached in and pulled the heavy metal bolt cutters. 'You carry this all the time?'

'Special occasions such as this. I didn't expect they'd let you in the front door. Now, I'll take this old rust bucket and join the queue of traffic. Then,' he smiled wickedly. 'Easy enough to, er, grind out the clutch.'

'Isn't that a bit obvious?'

'It'll buy you enough time to snip the lock and get in.'

'Okay,' Danny said. 'Guess it's worth a shot.'

'Attaboy!' Sparky said, opening the driver's door. 'Be ready. I'll drive up the road a mile or so, make it seem like I was always there.'

'Okay,' Danny said. 'And thanks.'

'Thank me later with a brew!' Sparky said. He closed the door and the engine of the car rumbled into life. Grey smoke plumed from the rear. The car bounced off, faded brake lights peering out into the gloom before turning off.

Turning, they scampered for a few feet along the pavement until Hailey stopped dead. A trill sound came from her pocket. Danny sidled up as she pulled out her phone. She waved the screen at her.

Henry.

Danny felt the blood in his face empty.

'Answer it. Speaker,' he said. She did so.

'Hailey? Hailey?! Where the hell are you?'

'Dear brother,' she said into the handset, which she held flat in front of her. 'How lovely to hear from you.'

'You're not at home and dad's car is missing. He's going to bloody kill you.'

'Thank you for your… concern.'

A moment of silence, interrupted just by the wind reverberating on the microphone. 'Who else is there? Where exactly are you? Tell me Hailey. Oh, it doesn't matter if you tell me or not. I'm coming to pick you up.'

'What do you mean?' she hissed into the handset.

'I know where dad's car is after all. Now, tell me what you're doing.'

'No need,' she said quickly. She glanced at Danny. His face was set like iron. 'I'm out with a… friend, yes,' she added. Danny grasped her hand. The warmth of her palm was good. 'A friend. We're doing a video. Best one yet.'

'Don't be stupid, dear sister,' he said. 'Don't think you can change anything—'

'Dear brother,' she said, a coldness invading her voice. 'You're not the boss of me. You don't care. I'll come home in daddy's car when I'm good and ready.'

'The friend, Hailey. Who is it?! Is it?'

'Never you mind,' she said, grasping Danny's hand and terminating the call with her other. 'Come on. He'll be onto us.'

'He said it doesn't matter if you told him where you were?'

'Yeah,' she said, throwing her phone into a nearby bin. 'He's tracked Dad's car. Well, there goes the element of surprise.'

'No,' Danny smiled. 'Big place. Plenty of surprise left. He's going to be obsessed now.' Beyond, a rattling came down the road. He glanced, seeing the grey smoke in the distance. 'Here's Sparky.'

Danny knelt down, watching for the car to come alongside. It was hemmed in by lines of the trucks, some waiting to go in, some waiting to turn out onto the street with military precision.

Sparky's car was level with the dip in the kerb. Then…. *Crack*! The engine misfired with a roar of combustion and a splutter of exhaust. The car stopped with a screech, turning to block the whole road.

Lorry horns blared, and from both ends, the car was bathed in headlights.

'Now!' Danny called, running out. He ducked behind one of the lorries going in. A cab door opened. Danny swooped around, falling with his back against the tailgate. Hailey followed.

'You ready?' he said.

'Yeah!' she panted. 'I'm ready.'

Danny glanced at the cab of the lorry behind them. The door was open. Nobody home. He spun around and hefted the cold metal bolt cutters up onto his shoulder. The lock at the back of the tailgate fell between the pincers.

He heaved. Nothing.

'Shit!' he hissed.

Hailey poked her head around, following the sound of remonstrating voices. She turned back. 'They're losing patience with Sparky.'

Danny heaved once more. His knuckles pushed on the handles, going white-raw. He roared. Then the bolt cutters clicked, and he fell forward with a thud. 'Fuck!'

'Quick,' Hailey hissed, as footsteps approached from up front. 'I think someone's coming.'

Danny heard the mumbles, too. Clenching his teeth, he pulled hard on the handle. It squeaked, and the door popped open with a hiss of gas struts. 'In!'

'Shit!' she cursed. The inside of the truck was cordoned off with synthetic mesh.

Danny reached into his waistband and pulled out a knife.

'Danny!' she hissed. 'What are you?'

'Insurance,' he said. The mesh tore as he sawed across it with the serrated blade. 'I hope this is all I need it for.'

'Okay.'

'Quick.'

A door opened at the front of the truck, and the whole chassis vibrated with a girthy rattle. They clambered in, the door wheezing closed.

'Bloody stinks in here,' Danny said to the darkness inside the truck. The bed rattled. 'Jesus, we're on the move!'

'Danny!' Hailey called. He held her close. Her scent dispelled

313

the stink of the rest of the truck. A sour, false and chemical smell. The truck rattled again and moved forward, slowly. Outside, chains rattled, doors clicked and voices called.

'Danny,' Hailey asked as the truck moved beneath them. 'How are we going to get out without being seen?'

He looked to catch her glistening eyeballs. 'Good point.' The truck whinnied to a stop. 'Let's find out!' He pushed toward the back of the truck, where the door was. The door rattled, still loose from their entry.

'Steve,' a voice called from outside.

'Yeah?' Another added.

'Park this one up in bay six while we load the others.'

'Alright,' the second voice said. From the front of the truck, a door opened and closed. The truck moved, this time backwards. White-noise wheeshes indicated the reversal. The tyres slipped with a squeal on the ground, before the truck finally stopped. The driver got out and stepped away, their footsteps echoing into nothingness as they left.

'Now,' Danny said, pushing at the door. It opened, but not far. The truck was backed right up against a metal barrier that was just at door level. 'Shit,' he said. 'Bit of a squeeze.'

'I'll be fine,' Hailey said, laying down and sliding out feet first. She stopped as her midriff hit the threshold. She was free with a wiggle. 'Come on, Danny,' she said.

Danny followed her lead. 'Christ,' he said, the squeeze uncomfortable on his chest. He felt a lug digging into his front. With a wince, he pushed past his arms over his head and scrabbling on the truck bed. Filth and rubbish moved, sticking to his hands. Fabric tore, and with a gasp, Danny emerged into the apron of the warehouse.

Hailey smiled. 'Nice.'

'What?' Danny asked. She nodded. He looked down to see his T-shirt ripped open and black grease marking his skin. 'Oh.'

Hailey went forward. Danny followed, edging toward the front of the truck.

'There's a load of them,' he said. Yellowstone associates were buzzing around the vast space beyond. It was a hive of activity.

'You're going to need to change,' she said.

'Yeah,' Danny agreed. 'We need to blend in.'

'Okay,' she said. 'Where to?'

'Crew room maybe?'

Hailey nodded. Danny peeked around before edging out.

'I think over there,' he said, pointing toward a door. 'Reckon you can make it?'

'Sure,' she said.

'On three. One, two…' Danny counted down, then scarpered. He pushed against the door, which resisted at first before opening. He turned in the doorway. 'Come on!'

Hailey followed, and the door closed. They were in a corridor of bare breeze blocks that led onward. Danny started opening doors, closing them in quick succession with a look of disappointment on his face.

'Nothing.'

Voices came from outside.

'Quick,' Hailey said. 'Someone's coming.'

Danny wrenched the closet door open and pressed himself in. Hailey squeezed in too, and the door clicked closed. They pressed together in the cramped space, staring through the gloom at each other.

'Any sign of that special shipment?' a voice asked from outside. A man. Young-ish.

'I thought that went up to the fourth floor,' another voice

answered. A woman. Older, but not by much.

'What did they want it up there for?'

'Beats me, but I ain't going up there again. Security has a right broom up their arse about it,' she said.

Outside, a door opened. 'You two,' a brisk, bellowing voice hollered. 'Back to work. You're paid to work not to chat. I told you this before, and you don't bloody listen. Do I have to report you *again*? Pisstakers.'

Feet shuffled, and the door closed again.

Danny finally exhaled. He pushed the cupboard door open and left. Some of the packets of tape and supplies fell out from the cupboard onto the floor.

'We need to find some uniforms,' he said to Hailey.

'That was my idea!' she said, but followed. They went through the door at the end of the corridor and emerged at a junction. They looked lost, left and right.

'You two!' a voice called from the left. 'What are you doing here?'

Danny pivoted to see a Yellowstone employee approaching. The voice was familiar. The balding head, greying hair and weathered features. It was a definite match.

'New recruits,' Danny said. He glanced at Hailey. Her face was horrified. 'Isn't that right?'

'Y-yeah!' she said, turning her head back to the Yellowstone man. He hummed.

'Is that so? And how, pray tell, did you get here? I wasn't expecting any new hires today.'

'Security let us in,' Hailey said. 'Told us to come right in and find you.'

'That's not the process.'

'Yet here we are,' Danny said. 'Got any better explanation?'

The man shook his head, suppressing a laugh. 'Am I meant to believe any of this?'

'Like she said,' Danny said, 'we're new recruits, and you're *just* the man we've been told to see. Unless…'

'Unless?'

Hailey picked up the stream. 'Unless you want to have to actually tell *them* your incredible story about finding two trespassers this far in… on your watch.'

The cogs in the man's head whirred. Then they clicked. His face fell just enough. 'You'll come with me, then, and we'll get you checked in. Upstairs. I'll lead the way.'

'Oh,' Danny said, following belatedly. 'Is that… necessary?'

The man stopped to turn. 'Are you…?'

Danny grinned. 'I just want to work. We both do. We're just so glad to be part of this,' he gestured to the surrounding building, 'thing we're in.'

The man looked them up and down. 'Right, if you're that keen, I'll put you to work. But you can't go out into the floor dressed like… well,' he pointed at Danny's ruined T-shirt, 'however the hell you're dressed. This company is proud of its employees and you should look like you're here with pride. Follow me to the admin office upstairs and we'll get you the basics, uniforms, then get you checked in. Though,' he added, 'who sent you here?'

'Er,' Danny faltered. 'What do you mean?'

'Who sent you? Simple question.'

'Oh, of course,' Danny clicked his fingers. He needed a name. 'Henry Archer. He works here, right?'

The man beamed. 'Archer? Assistant to the Chief Executive?!'

'The very same.'

'Why didn't you say? Let's get you kitted out, then you can be off to see what he has planned for you.'

'Henry has… plans?'

'Of course. Surely he told you?'

Danny mumbled, composing a response. 'Yeah! Can't wait to chat to him about it.'

'Follow me,' the man said.

They did, trooping up a set of concrete stairs.

'What's up there?' Danny asked as they paused on the first floor landing.

'Never you mind,' the man said. 'This way.'

Danny and Hailey followed through a door. The man promptly disappeared into a room.

'Are you not coming in?' he called. Danny and Hailey looked at each other before following into a room with tables.

Danny suddenly felt nostalgic for the training room at Kier Wood. The square ring of tables, plastic chairs, and posters full of positivity completely divorced from a reality outside of work… it was the same, but with none of the heart. The posters were immaculate, the floor clean, the room full of that plastic smell of newness.

'Sorry, son,' the man said. 'I'm over here.'

'Sorry,' Danny said, shaking his head. 'Just reminded me, this place.'

'Well, get back to work, now, as you've work to do. Now, what's your shirt size?'

'Medium,' Danny answered.

'Good.' The man shoved a plastic-wrapped shirt and trousers at Danny. 'Get changed.' He nodded toward Hailey. 'You too.'

***

Danny emerged from the locker room a few minutes later. Hailey appeared at the same time.

'Good timing,' he said.

'You too,' she added.

'What did you do with your old clothes?'

'Stuffed them down the toilet,' she said. 'Filmed it too. For the intro.'

Danny laughed. 'Wish I'd been that creative.'

'Well,' she said, moving down the corridor, 'I don't plan on staying. Where's that bloody prat gone?'

'Upstairs, they said fourth floor, yeah?'

'Yeah.'

They retraced their steps toward the stairwell.

'Never you mind,' Danny said mockingly. Hailey laughed.

'You're going to get us in so much trouble.'

'Aren't we already? We're going to get found out.'

'Danny,' Hailey said. 'Whatever happens… we're here for the right reasons. Family. Your nan. Whatever… secrets she knows.'

He reached for her hand. 'I know. It's just… the here and now. I'm so close, but it could all go to pot at any one minute.'

'I won't let that happen, Danny. Whatever happens.'

'Thank you,' he said. 'No-one else I'd rather be in trouble with.' Then he pulled as they rushed up the stairs. Another landing passed, then another. Finally, the top was visible and a dark set of double doors against the artificial lighting that bathed the metal stairs in cool luminance.

'You ready?' he asked.

'What's beyond those doors?'

'Hopefully my nan,' Danny said. He pushed on the door. It didn't open. 'Need a way in.' He fumbled around the frame, coming to a small black panel with three little lights. 'Bloody key card, just what we need!' Hailey smiled wickedly. 'What?' he asked.

'What did you do?'

As if performing a magic trick, Hailey pulled her hand from behind her and waved a piece of credit card-sized plastic in front of her. The white plastic carried the Yellowstone logo on one side, with a picture of the man on the other.

'Swiped this, might help,' she said, passing it to Danny. 'I also made a call.'

'Walton Mitchell,' Danny read the man's name. 'Arsehole. Good work,' he said. 'Who'd you call?'

'My friends. They'll meet us outside at midnight.'

'They coming in?'

'No,' she said.

He checked his watch. It was just coming toward eleven. 'Let's hope we're out of here by then. You ready?'

'Do it already,' Hailey said.

Danny nodded and pressed Walton's card to the keypad. It bleeped, and the doors swung open inward.

'Wow,' Danny said, stepping forward into a sphere of golden light. The whole space was illuminated from the ceiling by panels of LED lights that pulsated and glimmered. Glass partitions laid out offices, the walls frosted for privacy. Above, air conditioning whirled and a gentle, cool breeze hit the nape of Danny's neck.

Pressing forward, one of the glass doors of the office opened. A man in a svelte suit emerged, regarded Danny for a passing moment, then walked off.

'It's like we're invisible,' Hailey said. 'They hardly notice us.'

'Obviously far too important for us drones. Let's be quick,' Danny said, swooping down one of the passageways past the offices. 'The longer we're here, the faster until we're figured out as not meant to be here.'

'Where're they holding your nan then?'

'That,' Danny said, 'is the question, isn't it?'

They passed the glass-fronted offices to a corridor of more standard construction. Beige doors set into beige walls.

'Worth looking in these?' Hailey asked.

'Could do,' Danny said. Then he stopped, backing up against the wall.

'What?' Hailey said, puzzled.

Danny put a finger to his mouth, as if to say *be quiet.* He listened to one of the doors. Below the sound of the air conditioning, he heard shuffling.

A door down the hall opened.

'What do you mean you've lost your card, Walton?' a voice said to thin air.

Danny looked right at Hailey. They both recognised the voice. Henry, Hailey's brother.

'The hell is he doing here?' she gasped.

'Wasn't he at home? Your house?' Danny asked.

'Well, no…'

Danny crossed his eyebrows and pointed a vertical finger at his lips. He stretched toward the corner.

'Well that's bad news. Two new recruits, you say? Where were they… okay, calm down,' Henry said into a phone propped to his ear. 'They couldn't have got far. We'll get security to check 'em out. You need to be more careful, for Christ's sake,' Henry said, hanging up. 'Idiot.'

Danny pivoted, leaping to open the beige door next to him. The room was full of files and archives. The door opened, letting the light from the corridor in. 'Oh, thank god,' he said as Hailey emerged into the room. 'I'm glad it was you.'

'Stay here,' she said, 'and don't be seen.'

'No way. Let's go find who we're looking for.'

'My brother?'

'Afraid so,' Danny said with a menacing shadow across his face, 'Let's just hope we don't have to deal with him.'

CHAPTER 27

Hailey and Danny emerged from the storage room, right into Walton Mitchell.

'Hey, you two!' he said, then looked past her at Danny. 'You! Give me the card back, now!'

'Don't know what you're talking about, mate!' Danny said, erupting into a run. His shoes squeaked on the shiny lino floor.

'Wait!' Walton said, pounding after.

'Find her!' Danny yelled, his voice becoming an echo against the retreating footsteps.

Hailey faced the corridor alone. 'Great!' Around her, more serene footsteps echoed, like that of a normal business day. She walked in whatever direction she faced.

Turning a corner, she caught the eye of a group of three Yellowstone workers, who gave her a single look before continuing with their conversation.

Hailey approached. They still paid her no heed.

'Say, guys,' she said, making her cadence as saccharine as she could. 'Can you help me?'

One guy, his hair blonde and spiky, turned first. 'What?'

'I'm looking for…' she started, but not knowing how to finish.

'For?' the employee said, waving for her to continue.

'I don't know. Someone?'

'Do you not know what you're even looking for?' the blonde man said. His two colleagues snickered, but he remained impassive and stony. 'We're busy people here. You should know that.'

'Thanks, well,' Hailey said, her face falling. She backed away.

'You must be on Walton's team,' he said. 'Though if you don't know where you are, you shouldn't be here.'

The other two employees laughed again, this time audibly.

'Well,' Hailey said, turning, 'you've been a great help.'

'Hey,' the man said as Hailey was about to turn around a corner. She stopped. 'Tea room's downstairs. Make it quick.'

They laughed again. She didn't. Instead, she stomped away, letting their cackles fade.

With a face like thunder, Hailey avoided a few more Yellowstone drones. But one didn't avoid her.

'Can I help?' another woman said, touching her on the shoulder. Hailey whipped round.

'What? I don't need any help finding the sodding tea room.'

'No,' the woman said. Hailey glanced. She was barely older than Hailey, and her eyes were filled with fatigue – black bags fell under them, nearly to the ground. 'Ignore those guys.'

'I planned to. What are you doing, anyway?'

'Big board meeting,' the woman said. 'Look, come with me and help, please. They want me to take in some… refreshments.'

'Refreshments?' Hailey said. 'I hope you mean drinks and nibbles, and not—'

'It's not like that,' she said. Her eyes darted. 'Not all the time, anyway.'

'I'm sorry.'

'Please,' she said. 'Let's just go.'

'Okay.'

Hailey followed the woman around the corridors until she reached a small, boxy kitchen. Hailey closed the door behind.

'What's your name?' she asked.

'Melissa,' the woman said.

'Hailey. Tell me.'

'Tell you what?'

'What did they do to you?'

'I couldn't pay for Prime. Next thing I know, I end up here.'

'As a sl—'

'No!' Melissa said. 'Indentured servitude. Until my debt is paid.'

'Gross,' Hailey said. 'How is that legal?'

'Does it matter? They do it. Now, please, they'll be watching how long this takes. I think they did it on purpose. I can't keep up with this.'

'Where do they hold you?'

'Downstairs. With the others. Though we all got moved out yesterday, they cleared the whole floor.'

'What floor?'

Melissa didn't say. 'Someone important.'

Hailey watched Melissa hurriedly load a trolley full of Yellowstone branded sundries before reaching for the door.

'I'm surprised they don't use robots,' Hailey said.

'Oh, they did,' Melissa said, pushing the trolley out. 'It's just this makes a bigger statement, doesn't it?'

Hailey nodded, and reached for her bag around her shoulder, wishing she'd got that on film.

Hailey and Melissa walked along the corridor toward a lift. From a room off the corridor, a door opened and a man in a suit emerged.

'The hell's taking you so long?'

'Sorry, sir,' Melissa said. The man blanked at Hailey.

'Do better, you, or I'll add this to your debt.'

'Yes, sir,' Melissa said.

Hailey reached down and squeezed her hand, feeling the coldness. She got a squeeze back.

The man walked a couple of paces away. Melissa yanked on the trolley and it shrieked, shedding a stack of plates onto the floor.

'Oh, this is ridiculous!' the man said. Melissa nudged the man as she ran to pick up the pieces of broken porcelain. 'Get on with it!'

He walked away, leaving Melissa to pick up the pieces. As soon as he turned the corner, she abandoned the mess and walked quickly with the trolley to the lift.

'Go to the basement,' she said as the lift doors approached. 'Go, Hailey. I know who you're after.'

'You do?'

'I'm one of them,' Melissa winked. 'Bring it all down.' She pushed something into Hailey's hands. Hailey looked down. The keycard was black with gold lettering.

'Executive access. Big sheet of paper. Remember that.'

'What do you mean?'

'When you get down there. Think of a big sheet of paper.'

Hailey stood there for a moment, then the lift door opened. 'Thank you. I'll get you out of here,' she said.

'You do your job,' Melissa said, 'and I'll do mine.' She pushed the trolley into the lift, which arrived with a subtle chime.

'If you see Wendy Tunt,' Hailey said. 'Stick her head in that tea urn, right?'

'I'll say it's from you,' Melissa said as the doors closed, nodding to the left.

Hailey saw the stairwell door. She took a step, then stopped.

Someone was coming.

Hailey ducked into an alcove as the woman swept around the corner, not even noticing her.

'You damn well should be,' the businesswoman said. Hailey pivoted. The woman stopped, her back to Hailey. Hailey slid along the floor toward the stairwell door. She recognised the outline. The shoulder pads. The bob of hair. The heels.

Wendy Tunt. And all she needs to do is turn around.

Tunt put a finger to hear ear. 'Archer,' she said. 'Meet me in the conference room. We've a few legal things to go through. And if that bitch fucks up the tea—'

Hailey didn't wait, instead stealing into the stairwell as the door slid closed. She pounded downstairs, but stopped once she was a couple of floors down. A great glass panel gave a fantastic vantage of the Grid. Robots zipped around plastic bins, with a few Yellowstone employees meandering on catwalks. The robots seemed to hover over the bins before zipping away in an intricate, electronically-choreographed dance.

Hailey was almost drawn into a trance, but continued downward.

If I can see in, they can see out.

She emerged at the bottom of the stairwell to a maze of metal-walled cells. She tried the card on a couple. Red lights, no entry.

'Shit,' she said. 'She could be anywhere.'

What did Melissa say? A big sheet of paper?

She glanced at the door numbers. B-16. D-84.

No, this sequence isn't right.

She turned one more corner.

A-4.

That was a fairly small piece of paper, she thought. Then she smiled.

'Is it that obvious?' she laughed, then started counting down the rooms: A-3, A-2 and A-1.

Then A-0. She pressed the card on the reader. Green. Hailey held the handle and pushed the polished metal down. The door clicked. Gloom waited on the other side. Then shuffling.

A chair creaked. Hailey slipped in, the door clicking closed.

'Whatever it is you want,' a voice trembled, 'I've told you. You can do what you want to me. I'll never tell you what you need.'

'And what's that?' Hailey asked. Her hand scrabbled to the side, looking for a light switch.

'Oh, pull the… wait?' the voice said. The light clicked. The reduced form of the woman tied to the chair seemed to shrink.

'Oh my god,' Hailey said.

'You… you're the Archer girl. Get away, vile bitch!' the woman in the chair flinched. 'Away with you!'

'No, I mean, yes!' Hailey said. 'I'm here to get you out. Ms Jane Greene, am I right?'

'Don't act like you don't know,' Jane spat. 'Got some nerve. You all in on it, eh?'

'In on what?'

'Please,' Jane screwed up her face. 'I welcomed you in and trusted you. Danny trusted you. Can barely leave this room to eat and shit. What you lot have done is… it's unimaginable.'

'Tell me,' Hailey said, approaching. 'He's here. Danny, he's here.'

'Liar. I said don't come anywhere near me.'

'I'm trying to… look,' Hailey said, holding her hands up. She walked around the chair and adjusted the nylon cable. Jane's shoulders relaxed. 'Is that better?'

Jane sighed a long, deep sigh. 'It is. Thanks. But it's hardly consolation for where I find myself. What do you want, anyway?'

'I'm with Danny. We're here to get you out.'

'Bullshit,' Jane said. 'You think I'd trust another Archer? Robert's son turned out to be a right shit. Who's to say what you're not just as rotten to the core?'

'You lot, you said? My brother?'

'Your greedy shit of a brother. Henry. So far up that woman's arse he'll be seeing out her mouth. I was stupid to let them get me. But it was bound to happen, eventually.'

'Wendy Tunt?'

'The very same. You familiar with her?'

'I've heard about her,' Hailey said. 'I met her once.'

'One time too many, right?'

'Tell me,' Hailey said. 'What has my brother done? He's not one for sharing.'

Jane sighed. 'Why does that not surprise me?'

'We've never been close. Now, I think, we'd kill each other if we met again.'

Jane now shook her head. 'So he didn't tell you how he sold you, me, and Danny out? God,' she sighed. 'He's had us all, hasn't he?' She reached out for Hailey's hand.

Hailey took it. 'That's my dear brother,' she gulped. 'I just hope Danny doesn't run into him.'

'Danny's here?!'

'I told you. You going to believe me now?'

'Danny's here?! Shit, where? He needs to get out of here! You too, it's too dangerous, they're going to come back any time soon.'

'Who are? And why?'

'Danny needs to do his duty, and if he gets caught, we're finished. I presume he knows.'

'Mertons? Yeah. Happy birthday to him, I guess.' She adjusted and fished her camera out of the bag. 'Mind saying anything to…'

she gestured. A little red light shone from the camera onto Jane's face.

She looked at it, puzzled. 'It's vital he protects everything the family's worked for. It's all for him. For what his mum and… Jesus,' Jane said, her eyes glossing over. 'Poor Lewis…'

'It's alright,' Hailey knelt down to be on level with the older woman as she trembled in sadness. 'He's here for you.'

'Get him out. Get him to Mertons, wherever, they'll… I told them to make plans. Just for this. I only hope they bloody listened.'

'The head office?'

'No,' she said. 'There's one specific depot. Run by a man called Claggett,' she said, reciting an address. Hailey swallowed, recognising the address. *He's been there before.* 'He'll be protected there. Our boys will look after him, get him ready for the… you have to go!' Jane hissed. Hailey heard footsteps nearby. 'Get out and get Danny!'

'He won't go without you!'

'Foolish boy! It's probably that Tunt bitch.' The footsteps passed by the door, leaving it unmolested. 'Please, Hailey. Look after Danny for me.'

'I will,' she said. 'Danny means a lot to me.'

Jane managed a smile. 'I'm sure you mean a lot to him too.'

Hailey placed her hand on the top of Jane's. 'I'll go get help.'

'That's sound. Get proof though. Before you leave, get proof.'

'Of what?'

'What they're doing. It's more than just Mertons. It's the whole damn country! Just go! You'll figure it out. Just avoid your treacherous brother.'

'Christ, what we've all thought wasn't possible…'

'Go, love! Go!'

Hailey paced the room a couple of times, waving the camera around. She captured the abject despair of the room as frames on solid-state memory. She smiled, thinking this footage would be excellent, then glanced at Jane. Helpless. Trapped. Alone. It extinguished her smile.

'Thank you, Hailey,' she said, her lip quivering. 'Thank you for being there for Danny.'

She then honed in on the door. Opening it, she slipped out. Every second here was seconds wasted, and seconds closer to detection. 'Don't worry,' she said. 'His comeuppance will come. And I will do my best to make it soon.'

Hailey rushed out of the room and the door swept closed behind her. She looked left and right. The corridor was empty, but a shadow appeared opposite. She ducked into an alcove as the footsteps followed the shadows round the corner.

'They've got to be stopped,' Henry said.

'What's the problem?' a second voice asked. The same severe-sounding woman that Hailey had bumped into.

'I'll explain soon,' Henry said, opening the door to the room that Hailey had just ducked out of. 'And how are we this evening?'

The door closed. Hailey fled, but nearly ran into the door of room A-5 as it opened.

'What are you doing here?' a man asked, straightening his tie. 'Shouldn't you be downstairs?'

'Er,' she stuttered, looking over his shoulder. A monitor showed flickering pictures within the room.

'Say, Jim,' another Yellowstone man said, pivoting on an armless chair. 'I think someone's been in with the, er... special package next door. I checked the logs on the door,' He looked to Hailey. 'I think we know who the someone is.'

331

'Oh really?' the first man said, his head flicking back like a whip. 'Maybe you know something about this?'

'Why would I know this?'

'You're not meant to be here, are you? You don't even work for this company. Do you?'

'Now what makes you say that?'

'The credo. The thing they taught you at the very start. It's on the application form.'

Hailey's mind turned to static. 'Er, the credo, yes…'

'Come here,' the man said, yanking on Hailey's arm.

'Hey!' she protested. The man ripped her sleeve up.

'You're a fake,' he said. 'The credo is tattooed here. Shows your loyalty. Of which you have none.'

'Get off,' Hailey shuddered backward. 'Ask that Walton who I am. He knows me. He knows I'm a new girl.'

'You're talking bollocks. Walton's a moron. There aren't any *new girls* today.' The man lunged forward. 'You're one of those intruders, aren't you?' He turned to his colleague. 'The alarm! She can't leave! She's seen too much!'

The other colleague reached for the keyboard. Hailey jumped as the first man reached with splayed arms. She ripped from the man's arms and sprinted out into the corridor. A few moments later, a siren blared. The lights in the ceiling turned from a calming gold to a pulsing, serious red. She ran, pushing past a couple of executives who were caught unawares. A tablet computer thudded to the ground. Hailey didn't even look, skidding around the corner.

Eventually she came to the door set into the back of the wall, thrusting it open.

'What's all that bloody noise?' Danny asked, standing up.

'Yeah, about that…' Hailey started, panting. 'May have bitten off a bit more than I can chew… I found your nan, though. We have to go.'

'You found her? Where the hell is she?'

'Like I said,' Hailey gestured for Danny to come toward her. He took a few steps. 'We have to go. Now.'

Danny paced over. 'What aren't you telling me…'

'Danny!' she shouted. 'Will you bloody listen to me already!'

Danny took a couple more steps. 'Hailey, tell me. Where is my nan?'

'She's bloody here,' Hailey said, grasping Danny's hand and pulling him toward the door. 'We have to go, right now!' Hailey nearly tripped over the helper robot as she pulled Danny out of the room. 'Where's the stairway again?'

'This way,' Danny said, now pulling her. He looked over his shoulder at Hailey. 'What's happened?'

'She's… it was awful.'

'Hailey,' Danny slowed down. They approached a door at the end of the corridor. It beckoned, bathed in shadow. He stopped. 'What's happened?'

'It's… better you don't know. Now come on, you heard the alarm!'

'I'm not going anywhere, not without her! She's here, and I can't—'

'Danny!' Hailey barked. 'Listen to me. The best thing you can do if you don't want to get caught and thrown in a windowless room until you're your nan's age is to come with me. Please.'

'Hailey, don't make me choose…' he whacked the side of the building, his fist thudding into the brick. He winced, and his unclenched fist turned red. That must've hurt.

'She told me to get you out. You believe me? I don't care. I haven't come all this way, put my own neck on the line, for you to act like a stupid twat now.'

'Hey! That's—'

'Do I need to repeat myself, Danny Price? Will you just bloody trust me for once.' She watched his lip quiver. She moved over, holding Danny's hand.

'She's all I've got left, Hailey. After my mum, my brother… I can't let that go. I'll have nobody left.'

'You won't.' She squeezed his hand. 'You've got me. But we need to go, I know how much it hurts, I really do. But if we want to get her out soon, we have to go now.'

Danny breathed a few times, then swallowed.

'Okay.'

Hailey pushed through the door into the stairwell. Instantly the air-conditioned ambiance of Level Four was blown away by an industrial draft. The stairs rung with metallic groans underfoot.

'Did she say anything to you?'

'She told me how important you are. How you're the only thing left.'

'She… said that?'

'Yeah,' Hailey said, flicking her hair out of her face. 'Look, let's get out of here and we'll—'

'There you are,' a sneer came from the door behind. 'You've made me look quite a fool.'

Hailey pivoted. Her skin shrunk. 'Walton Mitchell.'

'I'm glad, miss, that you've finally learned the name of your superior.' Walton's eyes drooped. His lips glistened.

'Eyes up here, creep,' she said. Walton's gaze rose. 'What do you want?'

'You've caused us a great deal of trouble,' he said. 'You've embarrassed me, and worse for you…'

'You keep your filthy hands off her,' Danny said, sweeping in front of Hailey. 'Touch her and your block's coming off.'

Walton laughed. 'Add assault to the trespassing charge, not that the police will be any good to you. But you,' he looked past Danny to Hailey, 'we'll see what work we can put you to. Filthy, dirty work.'

'That's it,' Danny said, roaring as he thrust a fist into Walton's chest. It landed with a crunch and a thud.

Walton wheezed, bending double before falling to the ground, clutching at his front.

'Let's go,' Danny said. He took the first step down. 'You know what I'd have done if he's so much as laid a finger on you?'

Hailey watched Danny's body rise and fall with the excitement. Seeing him so tense, she almost knew the answer, but asked anyway. 'What's that?'

'I'd have killed him,' Danny said.

They emerged at the bottom of the stairwell and opened the door, expecting to see the low-ceilinged corridor from before.

'Shit,' Danny said. 'We've come down on the wrong side!'

'And the exit is all the way over there,' Hailey pointed. Beyond was the grid, a huge chamber full of the whizzing and dancing Yellowstone robots. 'How are we going to get out?'

Danny walked out from the stairwell. Hailey followed.

'Wait, Danny!' she hissed. A slight but noticeable electrical whizzing sound had briefly filled her ears. She looked up. 'Oh, great.'

'What?'

Hailey pointed up at the glass dome in the ceiling's corner with a little green LED light. It winked.

'If they ain't seen us yet, they have now.'

They took a step toward the Grid. The construction was

massive, with catwalks around the edges of the space. The platforms were ten feet off the concrete floor, with the tops of the plastic bins just visible from their vantage point. The noise of the robotic pickers whizzing around on top dominated the space. The cacophony of the Grid, the alarms and the droning noise of air conditioners made it hard for Hailey to hear herself think.

She felt a nudge in her side.

'Look,' Danny shouted to Hailey. 'On the other side. Emergency exit. We have to cross.'

'Okay!' she shouted back. Danny moved forward toward the stairs. A gate across them rattled.

'It's locked!'

'Swipe card!' she said, pointing now to the touch-pad next to the gate that had flashing red lights. 'Do you still have it?'

Danny fumbled in his pocket. He pulled out Walton Mitchell's swipe card. 'Yeah.'

'Do it, then,' she said. He pressed the plastic to the pad. The lights stayed red.

'It's not working!' he said. Hailey could see this.

'How do we get across?' Danny glanced up at the metal frame of the Grid. He splayed his fingers in anticipation. 'Danny, no,' she said, seeing him move. 'It's too dangerous!'

'There's no other way,' he said, gripping the first aluminium cross member. He pulled on it. It trembled but held. He climbed. 'Come after me!'

Hailey looked around. The space outside the Grid was empty. Too empty. That camera was surely watching them. But would anyone follow? 'Okay!' she called. She ran toward the Grid and leapt, grabbing part of the metal framework a couple of feet above her and just below Danny.

'Great!' he said, exerting. 'Whoa!' he yelped as the framework jittered.

She glanced up. The body of one of the picker robots was above them. 'It's one of the robots! It's getting something from the bin just on the other side!'

'Right,' Danny said pausing until they felt the robot scuttle off, the reverberations dying away. 'We're nearly there,' he said, pulling himself up.

Hailey followed as Danny pulled himself up over the ledge. She jittered. 'Whoa! What the hell?'

Danny caught her as she teetered. 'Careful!'

Beyond seemed like an epic field of dark square holes. Dozens of cube-shaped robots were zipping around in what seemed like a random pattern.

'Get your foot in here,' Danny said. Hailey looked down to see a slither of silver metal between the plastic bins about a foot wide. Her feet slid into the gap. 'Now we have to get over there!'

Hailey followed Danny, but the footway was slippery and jittered as they stepped on it. Below the perforated metal was a mass of cables and support structures.

Worse were the robots that zipped around at a tremendous pace, coming to a halt almost instantly. There was no predicting where they were going, the robots coming out of all corners. Doors underneath the robots clattered, a hook extending into the bin to retrieve an item.

'Try not to look down,' Danny said. 'This must be the biggest Grid in the country...'

'You've been here before, remember! At the interview? I was there too!'

'Shit...' Danny said, remembering now. He recalled the ruckus, but never saw the responsible parties. 'That was you?!'

'It was.' She tapped the camera. 'All on film, too. Told you, working on something big.'

'Holy shit!' He couldn't help beam a smile at her.

Hailey's eyes danced. 'Shit,' she said. 'They're watching!'

'Who are?' Danny said, his glance swaying to match Hailey's. 'Oh.'

'Oh,' Hailey repeated. She saw a handful of Yellowstone associates on the other side of the fence that surrounded the Grid.

'Hey, you!' one shouted.

'Get off there, now!' another added.

'It's them!' the first said to his comrade. 'They're the intruders!'

'Danny, quick!' Hailey said, pushing forward.

'Halt the bots!' one associate said. 'Stop 'em!'

The other hesitated. 'Jeez, are you sure, we'll get in so much—'

'Do it!' the first said.

The second nodded and reached for the mesh gate. It squealed open and the associate reached out.

'You there! Get outta there!'

'Quick!' Danny hissed to Hailey, pushing her. 'Out!'

Hailey followed the momentum of Danny's push, her legs automatically splaying to take big, awkward strides along the walkway. She ducked, nearly clipping a robot as it sped past.

Then the robots stopped dead, some halfway between the containers. Hailey didn't expect this and toppled, catching herself on the edge of one container and feeling the ground disappear underneath her. She yelped as her shoulders grazed the smooth plastic bins, her fingers grappling for the sharp edge but not catching it.

She felt, momentarily, weightless, the polyester of her clothing whipping in freefall.

Her fall was broken by the uneven, pointy surface of packaging. She looked up, seeing nothing but the ceiling. Grey metal and bright, fluorescent lights filled the square-shaped vantage.

Then Danny's head appeared, his hair loose and messy against the harsh angles of the rest of the artificial shapes.

'Quick,' he gasped, putting an arm down to catch Hailey's. He grunted, pulling Hailey out and onto the walkway. 'Careful,' he said as she teetered, 'don't want you falling in again.'

'Cheers,' she said. 'Shit!'

Four of the Yellowstone employees had entered the Grid and converged on their position.

Scrabbling, Hailey followed Danny as they danced around the dormant robots, avoiding further pitfalls. The bare, grey concrete wall beckoned, and the yellow-painted door grew.

Jumping down, Danny pushed on the horizontal bar on the door. It clicked, teasing him. He pushed.

'No!' He yelped. The door didn't open.

'Danny!' Hailey yelped, pulling him to the side, where one of the mesh gates stood open. 'This way!'

He followed as Hailey bounded down the little flight of metal steps on the other side of the gate. He pulled the gate closed but it hung impotently on its hinges.

Hailey made for another door along the same wall as the first. It clicked open. Beyond this was a small room. A stairway led upwards to the left; another shorter flight of stairs led to the right, to the other exit. Directly in front was a door to the outside.

Hailey pressed her weight on it as Danny followed.

The door didn't open.

'Hello, dear sister,' a voice said from above. Hailey pivoted. The Yellowstone workers blocked the path back out to the Grid.

The voice rose from the tall metal staircase next to her. 'And Danny Price, my dear friend. Lovely to see you both.'

'Friend? Pah!' Danny spat. 'Some friend. You're a bastard. Turncoat. Traitor!'

'Henry,' Hailey said, as her brother emerged on the landing, between them and the one open exit they could see and stepped toward her.

CHAPTER 28

'They're not going to get anywhere,' Henry said as the air-conditioning massaged the nape of his neck. 'I don't know what you're worried about.'

'They got in, which was bad enough. There's things here I don't want them to see.'

'Wendy, please,' Henry said. 'They can't achieve anything.'

Tunt swung around the room. 'You. Mitchell. How did they get this far?'

'I'm sorry,' Walton said, hardly able to meet Tunt's gaze. 'It was her, the one with the hair,' he pointed at Hailey on the monitor. 'She got my card. They scarpered.'

'That's really not good enough,' Tunt said. 'You know how important this time is for the company, right?'

'I do, look, Wendy—'

'That's *Ms Tunt* to the likes of you!' Henry spat.

'Alright, take it easy,' Tunt said, not breaking her gaze with Walton Mitchell. 'Maybe you can make it all better.'

'I can, yes Ms Tunt…'

'They're heading downstairs. Hold them up. They can't leave the facility al…' Henry caught himself. He chuckled nervously.

Walton nodded.

'Well, get on with it!' Tunt said. Walton scarpered out of the room. 'Come on, you,' she said to Henry. 'Let's see what our precious visitor has to say.'

Henry nodded as Tunt left the room, catching the door before it swiped closed. She swiped her pass card against the adjacent door and went in. Henry caught the door again.

The room was in darkness.

'Want us to turn on the lights?' she asked.

'Do what you bloody like,' the voice in the room murmured.

'Well,' Tunt said, 'I can afford the bill…' The switch clicked. 'That's better now, Ms Greene, isn't it?'

'You again,' Jane Greene said. Her face was ashen, dirty and her hair asunder. 'See you brought your pet.'

'Did my sister have anything to say to you?'

'She knows you're a little snake,' Jane said. 'Is that good enough?'

Henry laughed. 'Dear old Hailey. She'll never know the joy that'll fill my dad's eyes when all this comes to pass. She'll be out in the cold. About time, damnit.'

'Enough,' Tunt said. Henry stopped laughing. 'Are you still declining our generous offer?'

'Generous? Pah!'

'Maybe you'll reconsider,' Henry added, 'once Danny is sitting on that chair next to you.' He nodded to an identical seat to the one Jane was sitting on. It was empty by the wall, but a bundle of the same nylon rope sat on it. 'He'll be here soon.'

'Bastard!' Jane said. 'Fiend! He'll get out and tell the whole world what you're up to.'

'Then what are they going to do?' Henry said. 'Leave us a load of bad reviews? I think not.'

'It doesn't matter where you have the stuff,' Tunt said. 'I've bought the votes. You were determined to make it as hard as possible, weren't you?'

'Cry me a river,' Jane said. 'I'm sure Grayson Laurie can afford the tab.'

'You didn't *have* to make it hard. You could've been farmed off to a nice retirement home on the coast. I hear Eastbourne is lovely at this time of year,' Henry said.

'Enough. Come on,' Tunt said. 'We've work to do.'

'See you soon,' Henry said, turning the light off on his way out.

He walked down the corridor and over the walkway. Below was the Grid, a massive space of plastic bins holding products with the latest robot technology gliding on rails over the top to pick them for dispatch. It was the biggest one he'd seen. A handful of Yellowstone employees stood on gangways to the side of the Grid with tablets in hand. On the other side, more were depositing goods from pallets into the chutes underneath. A complicated series of belts and arms placed these items into the plastic bins for the main robot workforce to pick later.

One of the Yellowstone employees glanced up, catching Henry's gaze. Henry broke the gaze quickly and continued across the walkway. He entered one of the rooms framed with opaque plexi walls.

'Archer,' Grady nodded. 'I trust there's no problems?'

'Are the Commission here?'

'They are en route. Not too happy about being wrenched away from home at this hour. But now they play by our timescale, not theirs.' He couldn't help but express a chuckle. 'Six weeks, really?!'

'It won't matter by the time morning comes,' Henry said. 'We have the votes and nothing they can do or say can stop it. They're about to be made redundant.' A chime came from Henry's pocket. 'Excuse me,' he said, stepping back out.

Pulling out his phone he saw an alert.

'Yes?' He said into the phone. 'Put me through.' The call terminated. A video blared onto the screen - a feed from the security cameras outside The Grid.

Danny and Hailey, thick as thieves, trying to get out. Hailey glancing right at the camera, then whipping her head away. *Too late.* Henry swiped a finger on the screen. It tracked them as they ran toward the structure of The Grid. They had started grappling on the outside.

Jams had seen enough. He pivoted on the carpeted floor and slid along toward the stairs. He opened the stairwell door, feeling the harsh, industrial fans blasting the coldness right onto him from below. He started the descent.

He emerged on the first floor landing. Below him, a struggle. Doors opening. Gasps of frustration. The scrabbling of feet on the rough cement floor. He smiled, feeling the stairs surge. Rounding the last landing he saw the legs of two people he thought he might never see.

'Hello, dear sister,' he said, his voice filling the stairwell with a harsh echo. The first fugitive spun, her mouth wide open. His description hadn't been wrong at all. And beside her, her new beau. 'And Danny Price, my dear friend. How lovely to see you both.'

Danny's face curdled. 'Friend? Pah!' he spat. 'Turncoat! Traitor!'

Hailey was more resigned. 'Henry,' she said, as he took a step off the stairs and onto the floor.

'And so we meet,' Henry said. 'Dear sister, you'll tell me where you parked Dad's car. As for you,' Henry turned to face Danny. The friends exchanged a look. Danny's brow furrowed with contempt. But Henry laughed. 'You've come to apologise, right?'

'Are you having a laugh?' Danny asked. 'What on earth am I apologising for?'

'Making a fool out of me,' Henry said. 'That day some months ago. Yellowstone campus. You made a fool of me.'

'Oh. Oh,' Danny said, the penny dropping. 'You thought I embarrassed you when I walked out of that office with my soul intact? Because I wouldn't become what you have - a pathetic lackey. How many of us have you sold out, Henry? How many?!'

Henry shook his head. 'You got it all wrong, Danny, don't you see? This,' he indicated to the surrounding structure, 'this is the future, man. You turned down a big chance to carve your name on the future.'

'And you wanted to carve yours right on top, right?' Danny retorted.

'Hailey,' Henry glanced the other way. 'As Danny brings up the subject of family, you've been most disloyal. You don't know what I'd do for this family.' Hailey couldn't suppress a guffaw. 'Don't you laugh at me!'

'You think Daddy's going to be proud of you? You didn't want to put the family name on this,' she said. 'You just wanted to put *your name* on it.'

'Oh, I know exactly what *you*'d do to this family. Break it. That's all you've ever wanted to do. Never wanted to comply.'

'Why would I want to comply in a family of cheats and frauds? Maybe I wanted Daddy to push you away. Maybe it was some way of saving you. Though you'd only ever save yourself if you could.'

'Well, it's *your* fault!' Henry said. 'Anyway, Dad was what pushed me this way. He loves how I'm going to turn the Archer family name into the stuff of commercial legend now. All through partnering with Yellowstone. They had the vision you both lack!' He gasped after expelling the syllables from his mouth.

Danny nodded for a second before speaking. 'Mate, tell me one thing. You actually *believe* any of that shit you just came out with?'

'Every damn word,' Henry said. 'I'll show you. Guys,' he indicated to the Yellowstone figures in the door. Henry strode forward, past Danny and Hailey, toward the short flight of steps opposite the doorway. 'Bring them with me.' Henry bounced up the stairs and pushed the door open. 'Start the Grid up.'

'Sir, Mr Archer…' one of the Yellowstone associates peeped.

'What? Do it!' Henry barked. The man blinked and threw his hands up in defeat.

'Whatever you say.'

The sound of the robots clattering back to life filled the air above the Grid. Danny and Hailey were muscled up the step onto the catwalk.

'You see, it all started here,' Henry said, not looking away from the technical marvel. 'And we're going to make this country a better place. We're going to sweep the old away and replace it with the new. Just you wait.'

'And what about those who can't pay? Or want a choice? What then, dear brother?' Hailey said. 'Get your damn hands off me,' she added to the associate who held her.

'They'll learn to better themselves,' Henry said. 'The rewards for those that embrace the future are impressive. The punishment for those who fail to seize the opportunity,' he finished, stealing a look at Danny, 'is considerable for their folly.'

Henry reached into his pocket and pulled out a key. It glimmered in the fluorescent light. 'Don't you want to see this, Danny? Let him go,' Henry said to the people holding Danny back. 'Leave us.'

'Are you sure?' the Yellowstone guard asked.

'You do what I say without question!' Henry barked. His head swivelled. 'You want to know? I'll tell you, Danny.'

They shrugged and let go, trudging down the stairs. Danny grunted, then took a single step forward. He peered at the key.

'What is it?'

'The key to my office,' Henry said. 'Old fashioned, but sometimes you need a bit of pizzazz. You want to see your nan again?' Henry saw Danny's eyes widen. The intended reaction.

'Don't listen, Danny! I saw her, remember? She's not there. It's a lie!'

'Quiet,' Henry said. 'Do you think we'd keep her there now? That place is too nice for you.' Now he turned back to Danny. 'Do what I say. Come with me. I'll show you to her. She'll explain everything. Then you turn it to my superiors.

'Danny, don't!' Hailey said, pushing toward him in a futile effort.

'What do you say, friend?' Henry smiled. 'Just like the old days? There's still a place here, a place for you.' He looked as Danny regarded the glinting piece of brass he held vertically between two fingers.

'Danny, you take that key and you'll never leave this place alive!'

Danny smiled. 'You know what, Henry?'

'Yes?' Henry answered. 'Are you going to join me?' Danny laughed. 'What's so funny?'

'I would rather,' Danny started, not taking his eyes off the key. 'I'd rather stick that key up your massive, egotistical arse. Then I'd twist.'

Henry's face fell, but Danny's hardened into a glare. Then the room started spinning. Danny's hands turned into fists that moved in a blur into Henry's chest.

'Oof!' Henry said, winded.

'Don't you see,' Danny snarled, grabbing Henry's head and pulling it into view. 'You stupid, *stupid* idiot,' he continued between laboured breaths.

'One move, Danny,' Henry hissed, 'and I call the guards.'

'Do what you fucking like, but you will *listen* first. You're being used and you're too fucking dense to know what's happening.' Henry cried, feeling another couple of punches. 'And then,' Danny started again, 'you sold out me, your sister… your own family. To be a fucking puppet. You're pathetic. And you know the worst thing? You don't even fucking realise that once they have me, you're toast!'

Henry's eyes twitched, and he countered, pushing back against Danny's onslaught. He teetered but didn't fall, and the next punch missed. This was a chance. He clenched his own fist and slammed it toward Danny. Danny heaved, the impact crunching Henry's fist and radiating through his friend's chest.

'Me? Pathetic? Look at what I control,' he said to Danny, pushing him. Danny overbalanced and fell onto his back. 'Get up.' Henry dragged Danny back to his feet. 'Pay for your insult.' Henry racked a fist back up, one hand holding Danny, and thudded the punch toward Danny's face. Danny wriggled, the fist hitting his shoulder. 'Fuck!' Henry yelped.

Now Danny had a chance and, bent over, bowled into Henry. Now it was Henry's turn to fall backward, crashing onto the metal walkway with a big crash.

'Whatever you've done, whatever this scheme is,' Danny said, 'call it off! Stop it! Now!'

Henry smiled. 'Oh Danny. Dear friend…'

Danny's eyes bulged. 'Don't call me that! You lost that right the minute you did all this!' He thrust a hand around Henry's neck. 'I'll fucking *kill* you, you bastard!'

'You'll never see her again,' Henry gargled. The vice-like grip around his throat disappeared.

'What did you say?'

Henry coughed hard. Phlegm felt lodged in his throat. It disappeared. 'I said, you stupid fool, that if you kill me you'll never see your precious nan again. She'll go the way of your parents. *Your brother.*' Danny's pupils twitched, his eyes bulging and bloodshot. 'That's not a threat, that's a promise.'

Danny shook his head lazily, then went for Henry again, grabbing his neck.

'Fucker!' Danny raged, spittle flying into Henry's face. Henry felt the bar of the walkway rail in his back, putting pressure on his spine and kidneys. 'Go to fucking hell for what you've done!'

Henry laughed, but what Danny did was unexpected. The lighting rig on the ceiling seemed to pivot, and he felt weightless. Then a pinching in his thighs and under his arms as he was lifted. 'The hell are you doing?! Danny?! Hailey,' Henry gasped. 'Stop him! He's going to throw me into the Grid!'

'Damn right I am,' Danny heaved.

'Hailey!' Henry started, seeing his sister standing behind Danny.

'No, you deserve it,' she said. 'You say I always win, *dear brother*? Well, maybe I do, and I get to walk out of here.'

Henry looked at Danny. 'Please, Danny. I… I'll do anything!' Henry's lips trembled and his eyes glassed over, making the view of his former friend misty and indistinct.

'Give it to me,' Danny said, his arms trembling. 'The key. Give it to me.'

'You… you'll never make up there,' Henry said. 'Too much security. I made sure of that. Too much at stake right now.' He felt Danny's grip waver. He dropped an inch.

'I'm serious, Henry!'

'I'll tell you everything! Please, I don't want to get hurt!'

'Too late. For me, Hailey, my family… for thousands of people

349

who will suffer because of what you've done. This isn't just fun and games, numbers on a spreadsheet. What you've done will make thousands suffer.'

'Alright,' Henry fished into his pocket. 'Please, enough! Take it!'

'Hailey,' Danny mumbled. She slid the key from Henry's grasp into her hand.

'Now,' Henry smiled. 'How about helping me back from this ledge, I don't want to get hurt by all these robots...'

'Oh,' Danny said, pushing Henry further over the edge. 'You've gotta pay the price for your betrayal, Henry. No free lunch.'

Henry screamed, feeling Danny's grip disappear. He tumbled, whacking his side on one of the metal rails that the robots ran on with a thud. He struggled to move, dragging himself away. He screamed again, looking up. One of the robots careered toward him.

'Stop!' he screamed, but the robot didn't. Henry ducked but didn't balance. He watched as Danny and Hailey's heads disappeared from the parapet. Then his body was thrust asunder, the robot teetering on the track. The pain exploded from his leg, and he slipped on some white plastic. He scrambled for grip, but found none until he tumbled into the darkness of the bin which clattered closed above his battered frame.

CHAPTER 29

A blood-curdling scream erupted as Danny let Henry drop into the Grid. Peering over, he saw a smear of red against the clinical white plastic.

'Come on,' he said to Hailey, and they pivoted out of the door that led to the stairway.

'What did you do to Mr Archer?' the Yellowstone associate outside said. 'I heard shouting!'

'Go and see for yourself,' Danny said. The man pushed past. 'Quick,' he said to Hailey. 'Before he realises.'

'Okay,' she said, and followed Danny to the stairs leading up. Shouts came from the Grid.

Danny looked over his shoulder to see the man emerge onto the now-empty landing, scrabbling to find help.

'Danny, stop,' Hailey said as they reached the first landing.

'Stop? Why?' he said, panting, his shoulders rising and falling. 'I can't stop!'

'You can,' Hailey said. Danny saw her arm touch his. The warmth helped. 'You have to. We have to get out, remember?'

They both ducked. An alarm blared through the concrete and steel structure, the decibels flooding the stairwell.

'You've got the key, we could—'

Hailey shushed. 'No, we need to come back in a better place.' She took his hand. 'Before we get caught again. We have to get out. Now.'

Danny nodded, taking her hand. 'You're right.'

'You didn't actually kill him, did you?'

'I don't think so,' Danny said, 'but that big robot probably didn't do him much good. Sorry.'

'He's my brother, Danny,' she said, gasping for one big lungful of breath. 'Holy crap.'

'Are you ready?'

'I think so,' she said after a moment. 'Let's get outta here.'

Danny emerged with Hailey onto the ground floor landing. They didn't emerge right into the portal of the doorway to the Grid. Outside, footsteps and shouting.

'Good time to slip out,' she said.

Turning and walking past the stairs, Danny followed Hailey.

'Do you know where you're even going?'

'Nah,' she said. 'But best keep out of sight.'

Danny nodded. 'Look, there's another door.'

'Let's try it,' she said.

Danny gave the door a shove. It clicked open. The night air rushed in, swirling around the hair on Danny's arms. He slipped out, hugging the corrugated exterior of the building.

'This isn't where we came in,' he said. Beyond the door was a yard teeming with Yellowstone activity.

'Blend in,' Hailey said. 'We're still in Yellowstone threads.'

'Exit's over there.' Danny pointed past a line of trucks that were bustling in and out of the giant maw of an opening. He stepped forward.

'Careful Danny,' Hailey warned. 'Probably got cameras everywhere.'

'I know,' he said. 'Did you say you had help coming?'

'Yeah,' she said. 'Got the time?'

'Just past eleven forty-five.'

'They'll be here soon. We've just got to meet them by the west gate.'

'Which one's that?'

'The one we came in from.'

'Okay,' Danny said. He stopped. 'Back that way. Away from the crowds.' He walked carefully between a series of bins that led through a gravel-lined pathway. Beyond was a gate that was illuminated just by the moon above. No lights. No glistening glass camera domes that he could see. The sound of the alarm outside was muffled by the darkness and the ambient air. He pushed on the gate and it opened, resisting. He held it open as Hailey sneaked in, then held it as it closed again. 'Spring loaded,' he explained. 'No noise.'

The alleyway beyond was totally black, with a wall on either side. They walked single-file through before Danny stopped again.

'Look,' he whispered. In front, where the path turned at a right angle, a disc of torchlight. 'I'll sort it.'

'Be careful,' she whispered back.

Danny took a step toward the corner of the building. He peeked around the corner. Just one guy, the torch lazily hanging from one wrist, a smartphone less inattentively held from the other.

'One guy.'

'Security?' she said.

'Nah, just a guy,' Danny said, putting a finger to his lips. He pressed his foot into the tarmac. It was just slightly pliable. No noise. He put one foot first, holding his breath.

He'd better not turn around until I'm ready…

In eight paces, Danny was behind the Yellowstone employee. He breathed, hard, on the back of his neck. That was enough. The man turned.

'Hey, what are you—'

Danny pulled on the torch, wrenching the man's arm toward him with a single yelp. He grabbed the man's wrist with his free hand and twisted. A bone cracked. The man yelped again. Danny pushed him to the floor. The smartphone dropped to the gravel and smashed with a minute tinkle. Danny looked down as the man scrabbled to hold his ruined wrist. He stamped on the phone, finishing the job.

The man screamed, the note piercing the gloom. Danny kicked him, and he stopped.

'Come on,' he said to the darkness behind him. Hailey emerged and ran past the incapacitated guard.

'What did you do to him?'

'Enough,' Danny said. 'I did enough. Look, there's the gate,' he said. 'And no-one's there.'

'Let's go then!' she said. 'Nearly time.'

They ran. The gate approached. They rounded the corner, their shoes scuffing on the concrete kerb.

'Look out!' a voice called. A horn blared. A huge bar of light filled the gate where the space had been.

'Hailey!' Danny called, pulling her out of the way as the massive truck screeched to a halt. It reared up, the load in the back crashing and heaving.

'What the hell are you two playing at?' the driver yelled. 'Get the hell off the road!'

'Gladly!' Danny yelled back, pulling Hailey with him. 'There's the gate!'

'Come on!'

They ran past the truck, seeing the tarmac of the road outside beckon.

And beyond, parked on the opposite corner, a Mertons van.

'Told you!' Hailey said. 'Run!'

'Close the gate!' a voice called. It came from the other side of the truck that was wheezing back into motion. 'There's intruders! Do not let them out!'

'Don't stop,' Danny yelled to Hailey between deep breaths of air. 'Whatever you do, don't stop!'

'Hey, you!' another voice called from across the way. Danny glanced. A man in the gatehouse. 'You're not meant to…' then the realisation. 'You're them!' the guard reached for a handset on the little plastic table next to him.

Danny growled, then gasped as the gate squealed. It was moving. Beyond, a dark little van roared into the road, spewing blue smoke from its backend. With one last gasp and duck of effort, Danny sailed between the gates as they swept closed.

He smiled, getting up. 'Hailey?'

'I'm here,' she said, her voice severe. Danny looked at his side. No sign of her. The blood drained from his face with an uncomfortable pall through his skin. He pivoted.

'Hailey, no!' he said. Hailey stood there, ashen faced on the other side of the closed gate. Yellowstone employees buzzed around, grabbing her with a scream. 'Don't you fucking touch her!'

Headlights flashed. Danny turned around, squinting. It was the mysterious van.

'Get in, now!' a voice called from behind the lights. Danny couldn't see, but stumbled forward. The van's diesel engine roared as he approached before he was dragged into the van. A sliding door rattled closed, and the van took off.

Danny opened his eyes. The interior of the van was empty, gutted of all shelves and parcel areas. 'Who the hell are you lot?'

'Nice to see you too, Danny.'

'Brian?! What are—'

'Be quiet and listen to what your dad has to say!' another voice called from beside Brian.

'What are you going to do? Hailey's still there and…' Danny trailed off. 'What did you just say? My *dad*?! Brian, what's going on?'

'We'll explain everything,' he said, knocking on the partition behind him, 'once we, and you, are in a safe place.'

'Where are we going, then? You can't leave Hailey, you just can't!'

'The depot on the river. It's our strongest position. Time check,' he said to the woman next to him, about his age.

'Eleven fifty-six. We won't be back by the time the situation changes.'

'Situation? What?'

'She's making an announcement,' the woman next to Brian said, passing her phone to him. They all squinted as an image came up of the screen.

'That's Downing Street!' Danny said. 'And that's the bloody Prime Minister!'

On the screen, a taut, blonde woman wobbled toward a podium. Her hands quivered as she opened a leather binder, no doubt containing her speech. 'Thank you, everyone, for coming out on this historic night. It's doubtless that the United Kingdom has faced challenges over the last few years. Nothing has been further from this government's attention,' she started.

'Bloody hell,' Brian hissed. 'Get to the damn point.'

'This is a government of talents, and it is with that aim that I announce, as of this moment, that we turn from our inefficient public sector to the future: a government energised by Yellowstone,' the Prime Minister continued, her nasal voice reverberating from the tinny speaker. The van continued to buffet as she continued: 'All government functions, as laid out in the Act which has now received his Majesty's Royal Assent, will be transferred to the control of Yellowstone. You have nothing to fear from this change, and will reap the benefits of this partnership for years to come. They will deliver for you, the British people, as this government has delivered in these unprecedented times. Thank you.'

The phone fell silent.

Brian turned to Danny. 'Danny, just sit tight and once we're safe, I'll let you in on everything, I promise. In the meantime, tell me what the hell is going on in there.'

'It was awful,' Danny said. 'A real fortress. It's where they're holding my nan. And now Hailey. Not just distribution, but they're centralising some kind of power base there.'

'Makes sense,' Brian said. 'In about thirteen minutes, Yellowstone will assume control over all Blue Zones. Then it's open season.'

'You're kidding.'

'They were on a tight deadline for a reason. They've got the votes in Parliament. The law takes effect at midnight.'

'The turkeys voted for Christmas,' Danny said. 'How could they?!'

'Stuffed with money. Yellowstone probably knows their secrets, too. Aren't all politicians weak?'

'What happens to us?'

'The company will exist, but they'll assume control of the relevant assets.'

'So why are we going to a depot that's going to be controlled by Yellowstone in the next fifteen minutes, you say?'

'They're good people,' Brian said. 'Whatever happens, Danny, we have them on our side. You have my word.'

Danny hummed. 'Yellowstone were outfitting the Deliverangels,' he explained. 'My poxy mate Henry Archer was running the whole thing. Damn,' Danny cursed. 'He'd been to my house. He gave the order, the bastard. To trash it. That's how they knew they were there. Bloody bastard.'

'It's alright,' Brian started.

'No, it isn't!' Danny cursed again. 'I was stupid. Now they've taken the only family I've got left. And they've got Hailey.'

'Hailey…' Brian mused. 'Are you sure, Danny, we can trust her? She's an Archer, after all. We know about her brother. And her dad. You know all about apples falling from trees?'

Danny swallowed. 'You're joking, right? You're the friends she had coming to pick us up?'

Brian glanced at his companion, who shrugged.

'Danny, it's safer if you stay with people you know.'

'She knows, yeah? About your… connection to the company?' Brian added.

'I told her, yeah. Because I trust her. She's put a lot on the line. She's cast her brother and dad aside, Brian. No way back for that. Plus, you know, I think I…'

'What, Danny? What do you know? Is this information we can use?' the person next to Brian bent forward on the bench seat. 'Tell us, then we can use it.'

'Well,' Danny began. 'It's not really information as such, but it's just, Hailey…'

'Go on, Danny,' Brian said as the van rocked around them.

'I love her,' he said. 'That's the rub. Pure and simple.' He watched Brian's gaze turn to the person next to him. 'I hope that doesn't disappoint you.'

'Danny,' Brian said, taking a big breath. 'That's great. That'll help us, it really will.'

'Channel that passion, Danny, into the days and weeks to come,' the other person said. 'You'll need it. Anyway,' they said. 'We're here.'

The engine of the van rumbled to a stop. The torch fizzled out, plunging the back into darkness.

'We are?'

'Come on, Danny,' Brian said. 'It's going to be a long night.'

The doors to the rear of the van clicked and scraped open.

'Hi, boss,' a pair of eyes said from the gloom. 'Who've you got in here, then?'

'Danny,' Brian said, emerging onto the ground outside. 'I believe you and Claggett have met, yeah?'

Danny emerged and recognised the grizzled face under the cap and beard. 'Nice to see you again.'

'And you, young man,' Claggett said. 'This way, please.'

'What's the time?'

'Eight past midnight,' Claggett said up front. Danny followed.

'So, you stopped working for me eight minutes ago,' Brian said. 'Sure you don't want to…'

Claggett laughed. 'Brian, I've worked for this company for thirty years. Those Yankee clickers don't mean squat to me. Plus, I don't see them getting in, do you?'

Brian didn't answer. They walked through a great shuttered door that was lifted open. Burly lads stood, arms crossed, their eyes glimmering in the moonlight. Some held bits of pallet, metal bars, all implements that would cause a pain in the ear of any errant intruder.

'What was that?' Danny spun around, hearing a racket in the distance that prickled through the quiet night sky.

'Trouble,' Claggett said. 'Come on, lad. I'll show you to the office.'

Danny turned, entering the dark maw of the warehouse doors. The cavernous space was largely empty of stock but filled with vans and vehicles. Most were tired and their paintwork worn, but a driver stood by each.

'This all that's left?' Brian said, following Claggett to a door in a wall.

'These are our best,' he said, opening the door. 'It's been a tough night. More will come, though, don't be afraid.'

Brian nodded. 'Danny, come with me. I'll brief you on what happens next.'

Danny nodded, jostling past Claggett. The older man slapped a hand on Danny's shoulder as he crossed the threshold.

'These men are at your service, lad,' he muttered. 'We stand ready for you, the firm and the family. Aren't we, lads?'

The men gave a roar of assent.

'Thanks,' Danny said, his mind tumbling. 'Thanks a lot.'

He followed Brian through the door which closed behind him with a snap. He didn't know then, but was about to find out, that his old life was left on the other side of that greasy door.

Danny followed Brian and his companion up a set of dirty stairs.

'Right,' Brian said as they emerged onto the landing at the top of the stairs. He opened a door and clicked a light on. 'In here, you.'

Danny followed.

'Would anyone like to explain to me what's going on?'

'Sit down,' the companion said. They shoved papers in front of Danny. 'Welcome, sir.'

'Sir?'

'Yes,' the companion said. 'I'm the legal representative to make sure we honour John Merton's wishes to the letter.'

'Wishes?' Danny turned to Brian. 'What's happening?'

'Ms Greene is unobtainable at present, as you well know. So, we move down the chain. In lieu of your parents,' the companion stole a glance at Brian. Danny focussed on them, though. 'We move to you as the next generation.'

'The company is yours, Danny,' Brian said. 'You're the leader not just for an esteemed British institution but, we think, given the developments, you'll be the one to lead Britain itself out of the clutches of Yellowstone.'

'Whoa, whoa,' Danny said, pushing against the table. His chair squealed against the floor. 'This is all a bit much, isn't it? You don't have anyone else?'

'Danny,' Brian said. 'You've got what it takes, right? And the firm… part of the whole appeal, our reason d'etre, the family connection. The founders wanted it this way. The firm stays in the family. Come what may.'

'I see,' Danny said. 'I… I suppose it's my duty, right?'

'The company is loyal to the family, first and foremost,' Brian said. 'Yellowstone won't just be able to walk in.'

'They did for Kier Wood. And they nearly creamed Lower Crayford.'

'That's… true,' Brian faltered. 'We prepared since then. In the last three days…' He looked one of the uniformed men. 'Any news yet?'

'Nothing. Maybe no news is…'

'Let's hope so,' Brian finished.

'You make it sound like we're resisting an invasion.'

'In a manner of speaking, we are. There was precious little time to prepare. Now Yellowstone has judicial powers it'll seek to crunch down on dissent. We're the dissent, you see.'

'It's not just about business,' the companion said. 'It's a way of life. Life in the Yellow zones is good on face value but you pay a high price. And now Yellowstone has privatised the government.'

'What about the Commission?' Danny asked. 'You can't say they'd just go along with it.'

'The Commission have been removed from proceedings,' the companion said. 'It's us versus them.'

'Christ,' Danny said. 'Things moved quickly.'

'Sign the papers, Danny. We have to keep it official.'

'You said,' Danny continued as he took a pen from the companion, 'Yellowstone was the law.'

'The Act they've forced through certainly delegates many functions to them but remember, the courts are the King's justice, not theirs. That won't be an easy nut to crack. But yes, in essence they've purloined enough levers of power to make do. To make their corrupt society a reality at least.'

Danny didn't say anything. He palmed through the papers, signing at stickied sections.

'There. You happy?'

'Thank you,' the companion said, taking the forms away. 'You're now the Managing Director of Mertons.'

'That's the first step,' Brian said. 'Come with me, there's someone you need to meet.'

'Brian…' Danny asked with a growl. 'We need to—'

'Not now. But soon, I promise.' Brian left the room. Danny followed.

'First order of business,' Brian explained, 'will be to consolidate our holdings. Look, just a minute, let me show you.' He led Danny into another room. A screen lit up on the opposite wall.

'These are our holdings,' Brian said, muscling around the

table. The map lit up with a series of dots peppered across the United Kingdom.

'Were you preparing? For this? Because it came out of the goddamn blue for Kier Wood.'

'The cogs have been whirring. We were stretched, we wanted to maintain normality. Now...'

'No such thing exists, Brian. Not any more.'

A door clicked behind Danny. It was the companion.

'You giving him the walkthrough?'

Brian nodded past Danny at the companion. 'Our concentration is here, in the South East.' He tapped the screen. Some of the dots turned into stars. 'That's the latest data on, er, how would we call it?'

'Possession attempts?'

'Sounds good.'

'How long can we possibly hope to hold out if we try to form some kind of, what, underground anti-culture?'

'That's where our special guest comes in, Danny,' Brian said. 'Come and meet him now.'

Danny turned as Brian led past him back into the corridor. He stopped.

'Just a minute, Danny,' Brian said, gesturing for the companion to join him. For a couple of minutes, they huddled. The companion stole a few glances at Danny.

'Okay, now,' they said. 'Come on, you.'

They paced down the corridor.

'You said you had someone to meet me?' Danny said, walking alongside Brian down the corridor in the depot.

'Yes, I do, Danny,' Brian said. He opened a door. Muffled voices could be heard from a room not too far away. Brian approached a door off the corridor right at the end. 'Now, Danny, given everything that's happened…'

'Get on with it, Brian,' Danny said. 'Who is this guy? We'd need the King of England to get us out of this mess.'

Brian opened the door and pushed it open. He gestured for Danny to enter.

Danny did so. He stopped, taking one look at the occupant of a chair behind a table. A cup of canteen coffee stood amongst a load of papers.

'Danny! Good to see you!' a chipper American voice rang out. 'I was just talking with you people,' the voice continued. A man got up from behind the table.

'Wh… what can I do for you?' Danny said as the man approached. He wore a hoodie and jeans, but looked a lot more dishevelled and weathered than from when they'd last met all those months ago.

'Danny, our mission is simple,' Grayson Laurie said, beaming a weary smile to Danny. Grayson's weathered, dirty face wrinkled, the smile shrouding a world's worth of stress. 'I need your help.'

The story continues in…

PRICE TAG

coming soon!

ACKNOWLEDGEMENTS

Getting *Price War* written has been a journey.

I spent ten years in my youth working in retail, and the experiences and settings of that time were no doubt infused into the DNA of this book. The prologue, or a form of it - *Mad Max* style battles between heavily-armed delivery vans in a suburban post-apoc hellscape - has been a scene in my minds eyes from years of 5AM starts. So, writing this book *should've* been a doddle, right?

The journey this book has taken from that initial scene in my mind to the thriller you have read and (hopefully) enjoyed throughout the writing process in 2022 has been a learning experience and something I will look back on fondly. I have learned many good things about myself that I will certainly apply in future – if you don't learn something from each project, what's the point?

I am extremely proud of *Price War* as it has shaped through the development process to the book you hold today. It's not always been easy and there's been many emotions and self-doubt but now it's finished and done I can look back with some pride, while looking forward to what's to come – the sequel, at the very least.

Thanks to my wonderful friend and editor **Dan Hook**, on which this project has been a pleasure to collaborate. Thanks for your many suggestions, encouragements, and support throughout. I'm grateful to have you around!

Thanks to my feedback group – **Victoria Wren**, **Ben Pick** and **Martin Lejeune** – all talented and brilliant authors, who offered sage counsel and worthy feedback to help me make *Price War* the best book that it can be. I'm lucky to know you all from the **Author Pals** Discord server which, over the past two years, has been a wonderful community to be a part of.

Thanks, as ever, to my brilliant friend **Chris Kenny** who remains a constant source of inspiration and pushes me to be the best author I can be. Thanks for your support and, occasional, tough love to help me get this over the line. Thanks for believing in me and for always being there.

Thanks, finally, to you the reader for both taking a chance on my book, and hopefully enjoying it. I appreciate you immensely, and if my work has even remotely entertained you, I have succeeded. I do hope I'll see you for more, as my head is full of cool ideas!

Richard Holliday
January 27th 2023

ABOUT THE AUTHOR

Richard Holliday is an author from London. He graduated in 2018 with a degree in Creative Writing with English Literature from Kingston University. He has been writing since a young age. In his writing, he aims to make the macabre out of the mundane we all know from our everyday lives. He lives with two cats.

Discover more of Richard's work and sign up to his newsletter at
richardholliday.co.uk

ENJOYED PRICE WAR?

Enjoyed *Price War*? Sign up to Richard's newsletter for monthly updates on his writing process, project updates, personal anecdotes and be the first to see exclusive content before anyone else!

Sign up on Richard's website by scanning the QR code on this page and be one of the first to hear about the exciting followup to *Price War* - coming soon!

richardholliday.co.uk

Printed in Great Britain
by Amazon